Even so, when he laid her on the bed, vulnerability swamped her.

He straightened and tugged the shirt over his head, revealing a tattooed and battle-scarred chest. Some scars were old and faded to white, some new and still jagged; knife and bullet wounds cut into hard muscle and firm ridges. "Nothing happens you don't want," he said, his hands going to his belt buckle as he read her with impressive accuracy.

The sound of the streets echoed in his tone, the tenor somehow intriguing and full of warning.

Masculinity could be both beautiful and devastating in its brutality. She hadn't realized that before. Even after months of fighting and months of hiding, she hadn't seen the elemental nature of man at such a level. "I want you," she whispered.

MERCURY STRIKING

REBECCA ZANETTI

ZEBRA BOOKS
KENSINGTON PUBLISHING CORP.
http://www.kensingtonbooks.com

ZEBRA BOOKS are published by

Kensington Publishing Corp.
119 West 40th Street
New York, NY 10018

All Kensington titles, imprints, and distributed lines are available at special quantity discounts for bulk purchases for sales promotion, premiums, fund-raising, educational, or institutional use.

Special book excerpts or customized printings can also be created to fit specific needs. For details, write or phone the office of the Kensington Sales Manager: Attn.: Sales Department. Kensington Publishing Corp., 119 West 40th Street, New York, NY 10018. Phone: 1-800-221-2647.

Zebra and the Z logo Reg. U.S. Pat. & TM Off.

First Printing: February 2016
ISBN-13: 978-1-4201-3794-1
ISBN-10: 1-4201-3794-8

eISBN-13: 978-1-4201-3795-8
eISBN-10: 1-4201-3795-6

10 9 8 7 6 5 4 3 2 1

Printed in the United States of America

This book is dedicated to my Kensington editor,
Alicia Condon,
who is brilliant, unflappable, kind . . .
and who jumped off a cliff with me
by saying the words,
"I like the Blue Heart story."
Thank you.

ACKNOWLEDGMENTS

I am so excited about this new series, and I have many people to thank for help in getting this first book to readers. I sincerely apologize to anyone I've forgotten;

Thank you to Big Tone for taking the kids snowmobiling for weekends while I wrote this book, for cooking interesting concoctions of noodles and, well, noodles for dinner, and for being a better hero than I could ever create. Thanks to Gabe for the entertainment and support, and thank you to Karlina for the fun and love.

Thank you to my talented agents, Caitlin Blasdell and Liza Dawson, who have been with me from the first book and who have supported, guided, and protected me in this wild industry;

Thank you to the Kensington gang: Alicia Condon, Alexandra Nicolajsen, Vida Engstrand, Michelle Forde, Jane Nutter, Justine Willis, Lauren Jernigan, Ross Plotkin, Stacia Seaman, Steven Zacharius, and Adam Zacharius;

And thanks also to my constant support system: Gail and Jim English, Debbie and Travis Smith, Stephanie and Don West, Brandie and Mike Chapman, Jessica and Jonah Namson, and Kathy and Herb Zanetti.

In the end, there is no doubt that Mother Nature will win.

—Dr. Franklin Xavier Harmony, *Philosophies*

Chapter One

Despair hungered in the darkness, not lingering, not languishing . . . but waiting to bite. No longer the little brother of rage, despair had taken over the night, ever present, an actor instead of an afterthought.

Lynne picked her way along the deserted twelve-lane interstate, allowing the weak light from the moon to guide her. An unnatural silence hung heavy over the barren land. Rusting carcasses of vehicles lined the sides; otherwise, the once-vibrant 405 was dead.

Her months of hiding had taught her stealth. Prey needed stealth, as did the hunter.

She was both.

The tennis shoes she'd stolen from an abandoned thrift store protected her feet from the cracked asphalt, while a breeze scented with death and decomposing vegetation lifted her hair. The smell had saturated the wind as she'd trekked across the country.

The world was littered with dead bodies and devoid of souls.

A click echoed in the darkness. About time. Predators, both human and animal, crouched in every shadow, but she'd made it closer to what used to be Los Angeles than she'd hoped.

A strobe light hit her full on, rendering sight impossible. The miracle of functioning batteries brought pain. She closed her eyes. They'd either kill her or not. Either way, no need to go blind. "I want to see Mercury." Since she'd aimed for the center of Mercury's known territory, hopefully she'd find him and not some rogue gang.

Silence. Then several more clicks. Guns of some type. They'd closed in silently, just as well trained as she'd heard. As she'd hoped.

She forced strength into her voice. "You don't want to kill me without taking me to Mercury first." Jax Mercury, to be exact. If he still lived. If not, she was screwed anyway.

"Why would we do that?" A voice from the darkness, angry and near.

She squinted, blinking until her pupils narrowed. The bright light exposed her and concealed them, weakening her knees, but she gently set her small backpack on the ground. She had to clear her throat to force out sound. "I'm Lynne Harmony."

Gasps, low and male, filled the abyss around her. "Bullshit," a voice hissed from her left.

She tilted her head toward the voice, and then slowly, so slowly they wouldn't be spooked, she unbuttoned her shirt. No catcalls, no suggestive responses followed. Shrugging her shoulders, she dropped the cotton to the ground, facing the light.

She hadn't worn a bra, but she doubted the echoing exhales of shock were from her size Bs. More likely the shimmering blue outline of her heart caught their attention. Yeah, she was a freak. Typhoid Mary in the body of a woman who'd failed. Big time. But she might be able to save the men surrounding her. "So. Jax Mercury. Now."

One man stepped closer. Gang tattoos lined his face, inked tears showing his kills. He might have been thirty, he might have been sixty. Regardless, he was dangerous, and he smelled like dust combined with body odor. A common smell in the plague-riddled world. Eyeing her chest, he quickly crossed himself. "Holy Mary, Mother of God."

"Not even close." A silent overpass loomed a few yards to the north, and her voice echoed off the concrete. The piercing light assaulted her, spinning the background thick and dark. Her temples pounded, and her hollow stomach ached. Wearily, she reached down and grabbed her shirt, shrugging it back on. She figured the "take me to your leader" line would get her shot. "Do you want to live or not?"

He met her gaze, his scarred upper lip twisting. "Yes."

It was the most sincere sound she'd heard in months. "We're running out of time." Time had deserted them long ago, but she needed to get a move on. "Please." The sound shocked her, the civility of it, a word she'd forgotten how to use. The slightest of hopes warmed that blue organ in her chest, reminding her of who she used to be. Who she'd lost.

Another figure stepped forward, this one big and silent. Deadly power vibrated in the shift of muscle as light illuminated him from behind, shrouding his features. "I didn't tell you to put your shirt back on." No emotion, no hint of humanity echoed in the deep rumble.

His lack of emotion twittered anxiety through her empty abdomen. Without missing a beat, she secured each button, keeping the movements slow and sure. "I take it you're Mercury." Regardless of his name, there was no doubt the guy was in charge.

"If I am?" Soft, his voice promised death.

A promise she'd make him keep. Someday. The breeze

picked up, tumbling weeds across the lonely 405 to halt against a Buick stripped to its rims. She quelled a shiver. Any weakness shown might get her killed. "You know who I am," she whispered.

"I know who you say you are." His overwhelming form blocked out the light, reminding her of her smaller size. "Take off your shirt."

Something about his command gave her pause. Before, she hadn't cared. But with him so close she could smell *male*, an awareness of her femininity brought fresh fear. Nevertheless, she again unbuttoned her shirt.

This time, her hands trembled.

Straightening her spine, she squared her shoulders and left the shirt on, the worn material gaping in front.

He waited.

She lifted her chin, trying to meet his eyes although she couldn't see them. The men around them remained silent, yet alertness carried on the oxygen. How many guns were trained on her? She wanted to tell them it would only take one. Though she'd been through hell, she'd never really learned to fight.

The wind whipped into action, lifting her long hair away from her face. Her arms tightened against her rib cage. Goose bumps rose over her skin. She was accustomed to being vulnerable, and she was used to feeling alone. But she'd learned to skirt danger.

There was no doubt the man in front of her was *all* danger.

She shivered again.

Swearing quietly, he stepped in, long, tapered fingers drawing her shirt apart. He shifted to the side, allowing light to blast her front. Neon blue glowed along her flesh.

"Jesus." He pressed his palm against her breastbone— directly above her heart.

Shock tightened her muscles, and that heart ripped into

a gallop. Her nipples pebbled from the breeze. Warmth cascaded from his hand when he spread his fingers over the odd blue of her skin, easily spanning her upper chest. When was the last time someone had touched her gently?

And gentle, he was.

The contact had her looking down at his damaged hand. Faded white scars slashed across his knuckles, above the veins, past his wrist. The bizarre glow from her heart filtered through his fingers. Her entire chest was aqua from within, those veins closest to her heart, which glowed neon blue, shining strong enough to be seen through her ribs and sternum.

He exhaled softly, removing his touch.

An odd sense of loss filtered down her spine. Then surprise came as he quickly buttoned her shirt to the top.

He clasped her by the elbow. "Cut the light." His voice didn't rise, but instantly, the light was extinguished. "I'm Mercury. What do you want?"

What a question. What she wanted, nobody could provide. Yet she struggled to find the right words. Night after night, fleeing under darkness to reach him, she'd planned for this moment. But the words wouldn't come. She wanted to breathe. To rest. To hide. "Help. I need your help." The truth tumbled out too fast to stop.

He stiffened and tightened his hold. "That, darlin', you're gonna have to earn."

Jax eyed the brunette sitting in the backseat of the battered Subaru after rifling through her backpack. Water, leather bound journal, and granola bars. No weapons, and he'd frisked her, finding one little knife by her calf, which he'd let her keep. She was at the wrong angle to harm him, and if she struck with the blade, he could easily take it.

He forced his body to release necessary tension and tried

to relax into the worn seat. He'd stolen the vehicle from a home in Beverly Hills during the riots for food and supplies. The gardener who'd owned it no longer needed it, considering his dead body had joined the neighborhood burn pile after he lost his battle with the Scorpius bacterium.

The luxury SUV sitting so close to the Subaru had tempted Jax, but the older car would last longer and use less gas, which was almost depleted, anyway. Everything they had was almost depleted. From medical supplies to fuel to books to hope. How the hell did he refill everybody with hope when he could barely remember the sensation and needed his energy focused on shoring up his defenses?

Tonight's raid had been a desperate hunt for gasoline from abandoned vehicles, not a search party for survivors. Based on early reports, when the news had still been broadcast, Lynne Harmony had completely disappeared with no explanation. Most people thought she was dead; others believed she had gone on the run, hiding from vigilantes who blamed her for the epidemic. The government, such as it was, had immediately put a reward out for her safe return. He'd never thought to find her in Vanguard territory.

How fortunate his vehicles were always stocked with restraints and hoods, just in case.

The woman had closed her eyes, her head resting against the faded leather. Soft moonlight wandered through the windows to caress the sharp angles of her face. With deep green eyes and pale skin, she was much prettier than he'd expected . . . much softer. Too soft.

Though, searching him out . . . well now. The woman had guts.

Manny kept looking at her in the rearview mirror, and for some reason, that irritated Jax. "Watch the road."

Manny cut a glance his way. At fifty years old, beaten and weathered, he'd tossed the cap and monkey suit needed as a Bellagio chauffeur and now drove in threadbare clothing wearing unruly scruff on his chin. But he took orders easily, which was a necessary requirement in Jax's camp. "There's no one out here tonight but us."

"We hope." Jax's gut had never lied to him. Something was coming. If the woman had brought danger to his little place in the world, she'd pay. "Dawn will arrive in less than an hour. Speed up."

Manny pressed his foot to the pedal and swerved around what looked like an overturned hot dog stand near a park being molested by spreading bushes and trees. He frowned and leaned forward to peer up at the sky. "Shit. Less than an hour."

The faintest scent of fear cascaded off him.

Jax took inventory of the weapons within reach and allowed just enough adrenaline to flood his system to be effective. The presence of survivors marked shop alleys as they left the commercial area and entered slums lined with dilapidated former crack houses. His territory. The desolate smell of decomposing tissue followed them. It was time for another scouting to burn deceased bodies.

He glanced back at Lynne.

Her eyes flashed open, directly meeting his gaze. The pupils contracted while her chin lifted. Devoid of expression, she just stared.

He stared back.

A light pink wandered from her chest up her face to color her high cheekbones. Fascinated, he watched the blush deepen. When was the last time he'd seen a woman blush? He certainly hadn't expected it from the woman who some thought had taken out most of the human race.

Around them, off-road vehicles kept pace. Some dirt bikes, a four-wheeler, even a fancy Razor confiscated from another mansion.

They drove into the inner bowels of Los Angeles, skirting abandoned vehicles and weakened buildings. Climbing vines attacked brick, while many places had been burned in the riots. Most storefronts gaped open from broken windows or trashed doorways. The first survivors had looted quickly, not knowing that the bacteria hadn't finished spreading.

Most of the looters were dead . . . or worse.

Tension rode the air, and some of it came from Manny.

"Say it," Jax murmured, acutely, maybe too much so, aware of the woman in the backseat.

"This is a mistake," Manny said, his hands tightening on the steering wheel. "You know who she is. What she is."

"I doubt that." He turned to glance again at the woman, his sidearm sweeping against the door. She'd turned to stare out at the night again, her shoulders hunched, her shirt hiding that odd blue glow. "Are you going to hurt me or mine?" he asked.

Slowly, she turned to meet his gaze again. "I don't know." Frowning, she leaned forward just enough to make his muscles tense in response. "How many people are yours?"

He paused, his head lifting. "All of them."

She worried her lower lip between two teeth. "I'd heard that about you." Turning back to the window, she fingered the glass as if wanting to touch what was out of reach.

"Heard what?" he asked.

"Your sense of responsibility. Leadership. Absolute willingness to kill." Her tone lacked inflection, as if she just stated facts. "You are, am I correct? Willing to kill?"

He stilled, his eyes cutting to Manny and back to the woman. "You want me to kill somebody?"

"Yes."

He kept from outwardly reacting. Not much surprised him any longer, but he hadn't been expecting a contract killing request from Lynne Harmony. "We've lost 99 percent of the world's population, darlin'. Half of the survivors are useless, and the other half are just trying to survive. You'd better have a good reason for wanting someone dead."

"*Useless* isn't an accurate description," she said quietly.

"If they can't help me, if they're a hindrance, they're fucking useless." Months ago, he'd turned off the switch deep down that could see a gray area between the enemy and his people, and there was no changing that. He'd become what was needed to survive and to live through desperate times. "You might want to remember that fact."

Her shoulders went back, and she rested her head, staring up at the roof. "I'd love to be useless."

He turned to the front. Her words had been soft, her tone sad, and her meaning heartbreaking. So the woman wanted to die, did she? No fucking way. The blood in her veins was more than a luxury, it might be a necessity. She didn't get to die. "Tell me you're not the one I'm supposed to kill," he said, his body on alert.

Silence ticked around the dented car for a moment. "Not yet, no."

Great. All he needed was a depressed biological weapon in the form of a sexy brunette to mess with his already fucking fantastic daily schedule. "Lady, if you wanna eat a bullet, you should've done it before coming into my territory." Since she was there, he was making use of her, and if that meant suicide watch around the clock, he'd provide the guards to keep her breathing and helpful.

"I know." Fabric rustled, and she poked him in the neck. "When was your last injection?"

His head jerked as his neurons flared to life. He grabbed her finger before turning. "Almost a month ago."

She tried to free herself and then frowned when she failed. "You're about due, then. How many vials of B do you have left?"

He tugged her closer until she was leaning over the front seat, his gaze near to hers. "Doesn't matter. Now I have you, don't I? If we find the cure, we won't need vitamin B." This close, under the dirt and fear, he could smell woman. Fresh and with a hint of—what was that—vanilla? No. Gardenias. Spicy and wild.

She shook her head and again tried to free herself. "You can have all my blood you want. It won't help."

They drove past structures, and for the briefest of moments, empty lots full of decomposing fast food wrappers and broken beer bottles bracketed them on both sides. "Stop the car," he said to Manny.

Manny pulled over as if he'd been waiting for the order. Jax released Lynne, stepped out of the vehicle, and pressed into the backseat next to her.

Her eyes widened, and she huddled back against the other door.

He drew a hood from his pocket. "Come here, darlin'."

"No." She scrambled away, her hands out.

With a sigh, he reached for a zip tie in his vest and way too easily secured her hands together. A second later, he pulled the hood over her head. He didn't like binding a woman, but he didn't have a choice, since she just might be working for an enemy. While the location of his territory was generally known, the weaknesses of entry and exit were not. "In the past year, as the world has gone to hell, hasn't anybody taught you to fight?" he asked.

She kicked out, her bound hands striking for his worn bulletproof vest.

He lifted her onto his lap, wrapped an arm over hers and around her waist, manacling her legs with one of his. "Relax. I'm not going to hurt you, but you can't know our route or see our defenses."

"Right." She shoved back an elbow, her warm little body struggling hard.

Desire flushed through him, pounding instantly into his cock. God, she was a handful.

She paused. "Ah—"

"You're safe. Just stop wiggling." His voice lowered and was hoarse. Jesus. When was the last time he'd gotten laid? He actually couldn't remember. She was a tight handful of energy and womanly curves, and his body reacted instantly. The more she gyrated against him, trying to fight, the more blood rushed south of his brain. He had to get her under control before he began panting like a teenager.

"No." Her voice rose, and she tried to flail around again. "You can't manhandle me like this."

If she had any clue how he'd like to handle her, she'd be screaming. He took several deep breaths and forced desire into the void, where it belonged. He wanted her hooded, not afraid. "If you were mine, you'd know how to fight." Where that thought came from, he'd never know.

She squirmed on his lap, fully contained. "Good thing I'm not yours, now isn't it?"

He exhaled and held her tighter until she gave up the fight and submitted against him. The light whimper of frustration echoing behind the hood sounded almost like a sigh of pleasure. When she softened, he hardened. Again.

Then he released his hold and whispered right through the hood to her ear. "That's where you're wrong, Lynne Harmony. The second you crossed into Vanguard territory, the very moment you asked for my help, that's exactly what you became."

"What?" she asked, sounding breathless now.

"Mine."

Chapter Two

—◆—

Fairy tales do not tell children that dragons exist.
Children already know that dragons exist.
Fairy tales tell children that dragons can be killed.

—G. K. Chesterton

Lynne tried to hold still and ignore the very solid body surrounding her. Heat emanated from him, and for so long, way too long, she'd felt nothing but a constant chill. As hard as she tried, she couldn't help but relax a little into his warmth.

"There you go," he murmured, his mouth near her ear. "Sorry about the hood. If you're claustrophobic, it'll pass."

As long as she wasn't submerged in water, her one phobia, she was fine. But she sure as hell wasn't going to reassure him of that fact. So she stayed silent.

He sighed and seemed to stretch out a little, taut muscles relaxing. "I have six soldiers around us, and we'll make it back to the base before dawn arrives. Even though we have a partially cleared route through debris, we have to keep to alleys and side roads to avoid attack."

"So?" Her voice emerged muffled from the damn hood.

"So take advantage of the moment and get a quick nap. You're not going anywhere, and I promise nobody will hurt you on my watch. Take the moment, Lynne Harmony." He moved enough to jostle her, resettling her in place, and she would've bet her only pair of socks that he'd lain back his head and shut his eyes.

She considered her options.

"If you even think about going for the knife strapped to your calf, you won't like my response," he whispered. One hand banded around her neck and drew her face against his upper chest.

"I hadn't," she protested without thinking, her cheek against his shoulder. "I have an IQ well into the triple digits, Mercury. Killing you right now surrounded by your people would be incredibly stupid. I'm not stupid." Plus, she needed him. Needed not only his protection but his resources. So he'd noticed her knife. It was a little insulting that he'd let her keep it, obviously not fearing her ability to use it on him.

His breathing evened out.

On all that was holy. She carried a blade, was feared by half of the remaining world and hated by the rest. Against all logic, Jax Mercury had just fallen asleep holding her.

Of course, she'd known he was well trained. Didn't soldiers learn to catnap whenever there was a brief break in the fighting? But she wasn't a soldier and never would be, so sleep was out of the question.

The car jumped and hit several potholes before leveling out. Her nails dug into his chest to keep her upright. She could push back up and sit like a stiff board, or she could keep her face against his broad chest, where he'd put her. Where for the briefest of moments, it felt safe.

While she couldn't relax enough to sleep, considering she had no clue what he was going to do to her once they arrived at his headquarters, she could at least concentrate on loosening her neck muscles and diminishing her constant headache.

The unthinkable idea that she was snuggled up to Jax Mercury, rebel leader of Los Angeles, showed just how bizarre reality had become.

* * *

Jax held the woman close as Manny barreled through a devastated area of Los Angeles. A surprising amount of greenery had started poking through concrete and climbing crumbling slum buildings. Some of the greenery was edible, so the homeless and crazy were probably close by. The number of Rippers in the area concerned him, and the really insane ones wouldn't hesitate to attack a moving vehicle.

Manny swore and skidded around a tangled mess of what appeared to be a massive motorcycle accident. "Need lights."

"No," Jax whispered, stretching his damaged arm. When the atmosphere changed, right before a storm arrived, his scarred flesh ached. "The sky is bright enough even though the sun hasn't risen." Thank God. Thunder clamored in the west as clouds over the ocean gathered force. They had to hurry, damn it.

Lynne Harmony didn't move. Finally, she'd fallen asleep—a testament to how exhausted she must be to finally lose consciousness on his lap while hooded. Jax removed the hood from her face so she could breathe, and she snuggled her nose into his neck, igniting a wave of protectiveness that pissed him right off.

Manny glanced in the rearview mirror. "Do you think she'll tell us about the outside world? What she knows?"

Jax nodded. "She'll tell us. Although it's doubtful she knows about specific people."

"I understand." Manny turned back toward the road.

Jax sighed. The man had family in Florida, and he hadn't heard from them in months. Chances of their survival sucked. "I'll ask her after she gets some sleep."

"She's prettier than I thought," Manny said quietly.

Yeah. She was. "The cameras didn't do her justice." Jax shifted his shoulder to rest against the door. "She's also

younger than I expected, considering her job at the CDC."
She had been the head of infectious diseases, and when she'd
gotten infected, she'd been up front with the news as soon as
she'd come out of the coma. Until somebody in the government had stopped allowing news out.

"Do you think she knows a cure?" Manny asked.

"I don't know." Jax forced his eyelids to remain open. With
a warm, snuggly woman in his arms, his body wanted to rest
and enjoy the moment. "I think she has information we need
about the current status of the government and hopefully a
possible cure for the plague. Or maybe a way to find a cure."
Almost absently, he rubbed his chin against the top of her
soft hair. "Though I'm struggling to figure out her agenda."

"Agenda? You mean why she just walked into Vanguard
territory?" Manny jerked the wheel to the left to avoid a
downed bread truck.

Jax tightened his hold so Lynne wouldn't awaken. "Yeah."

"For protection. The world either wants her dead because
they blame her for not stopping the illness, or they think
somehow there's a cure in her blood since she's the only one
with a blue heart. She came to us for protection," Manny said.

"No." Jax leaned back his head again. "When we decided
to take L.A., we sent out news and rumors, warning the world
to stay the fuck away. This is not where a woman would come
for protection, especially this woman."

"You've heard the other rumors about her, right?"

"Yes." Refugees from different camps had whispered of
tales that Lynne Harmony carried a more dangerous form of
the Scorpius bacterium and wanted to infect the entire world.
The Mercenaries, a deadly group from the north, were known
to be ferociously hunting her because of a reward posted by
the government for her return. "I don't listen to scary stories
told around campfires," Jack said evenly.

"What if they're true? Maybe she's a Ripper and she's

crazy," Manny whispered, his shoulders stiffening. "I mean, not one of them disorganized Rippers, but one of them super-smart genius ones. There's two main types, right?"

"Yeah." Jax inhaled the scent of woman. "If she's a genius serial killer, I still don't see why she'd walk into my territory." He could break her neck with minimal effort if she tried to infect anybody with a new contagion. "She definitely has an agenda, and it has something to do with either me or our land. My guess is that it's the territory, but I could be wrong." The woman had asked for him by name, and the desperation in her initial plea had rung true.

"I think we should've left her on the side of the road." Manny shuddered.

Thunder bellowed louder, obviously creeping closer.

Jax glanced down as very weak light slid over the delicate features of Lynne Harmony's face. They had a distance to go before he needed to hood her again. Hopefully he hadn't made a colossal mistake in letting her live.

He'd find out soon enough.

Chapter Three

A friend is one who has the same enemies as you have.

—Abraham Lincoln

What had she done? Lynne had actually fallen asleep on Jax Mercury. She awoke, blinking inside the stifling hood, just as he lifted her into the cool morning air and easily strode over uneven ground. A slight change of temperature hit her, and his steps leveled out.

Inside. They were inside somewhere. The smell of dust and burned tomato soup tickled her nose, but no sound provided a clue as to their whereabouts. All but blinded, she tried to tune in to her other senses. Jax's boots clomped heavily across a hard surface, and his heart beat steadily against her shoulder.

His stride didn't hitch as he climbed stairs, turned, walked in a too-quiet area, and opened a door. The world tilted, and he placed her, gently actually, on what felt like a fake leather sofa.

He yanked the hood off.

Light from halogen lamps assaulted her wide pupils, and she winced, her eyes tearing. "You're an ass."

Silver flashed, and he cut the zip ties. "So it has been said."

Heat climbed into her face. The man had carried her easily and didn't seem winded a bit. Even so, the legends whispered around campfires and refugee camps across the country had to be exaggerated. Nobody was that tough. "We need to talk," she gritted out.

He yanked a kitchen chair toward her, turned it, and straddled it. Now, in the light, she was struck by how young he really was. Maybe midthirties, black hair, dark brown eyes, and rugged facial features. Handsome in a pissed-off kind of way. A scar cut under the left side of his jaw, white and deadly. "So, talk."

She swallowed and tugged her backpack to her chest, glancing around what appeared to be a small apartment. A kitchenette took up one wall, an unmade bed the other, with dented furniture in between. Sofa, metal coffee table, wood-laminate kitchen table, paint peeling pink kids' dresser, and mismatched kitchen chairs. Maps covered the table, spread out haphazardly. "Where am I?"

"You don't get to know that." He rested his arms on the top of the chair, muscles flexing.

She bit her lip. Men's clothing littered the unmade bed, and the smell of musk and male filled the atmosphere. "Whose place am I in?"

"Mine." He lifted a shoulder, his gaze unwavering. "And yours now, I guess."

She pushed back into the torn leather. "I'm not, I mean, I—"

One dark eyebrow rose. "You're here because I'm keeping an eye on you and making sure you don't infect anybody else."

"I won't infect anybody else," she said slowly, her nails digging into the couch until the pads of her fingertips protested.

"We don't really know the truth about that statement, now

do we? You're the ultimate carrier of the most dangerous plague to ever attack mankind." He lowered his chin, the movement somehow menacing. "You're also here so I can make sure you're not ready to check out."

She rolled her eyes. "If I'd wanted to kill myself, I wouldn't have traveled this far to do it."

"Fair enough."

She glanced at the unmade bed. Too many women had become victims as the world had disintegrated; the strong overcame the weak. She wasn't weak, and she was no man's plaything. "I'm not here for your amusement."

"I'm not amused." He leaned toward her, and her breath caught in her throat. "Let me be perfectly clear. I don't force myself on women, and neither do any of my men. Any people here, and anyone we come across, remain safe from personal attack. Rape is a crime dealt with by death, so you have no need to fear."

She'd heard that in the rumors and tales, but she hadn't known it to be true. "Women don't earn their keep, earn their protection, with sex here?" Wherever *here* was.

"No."

"You were in an inner-city L.A. gang. Years ago." She lifted an eyebrow. "Rape was against the rules?"

His face blanked. "No, but I've never forced a woman." Those dark eyes narrowed. "My past is my own. You sure know a lot about me."

Not really. He'd become a folk legend fighting in L.A. before the news had shut down. Since then she'd been trying to gather facts, but there were still blanks. "Why did you leave the gang? I've never heard why you entered the army."

He rubbed his chin. "Judge gave me a choice. Prison or military. I guess he saw something in me."

She let her shoulders relax. "I wondered."

"Yeah." Jax eyed her shirt just at her neck. "Can I see again?"

Well, she couldn't really blame him. She set aside the pack holding her father's precious journal. Her fingers remained steady this time as she unbuttoned the blouse and drew open the sides.

Jax's nostrils flared, while a tension, one she barely remembered as sexual, overtook the atmosphere. "Does it hurt?"

"The blueness?" She glanced down, her lungs suddenly too tight. "No. I don't feel anything."

He reached out and gently took her wrist, shoving the sleeve up to reveal the track marks on her elbow. "This must hurt."

His touch stirred awareness deep in her abdomen, and surprise paused her at the feeling. When was the last time she'd felt desire? Or even warmth from another's touch? She glanced down at the scars caused by drawing so much blood. So many times, and outside of normal medical procedures after a while. "Yes. That hurts."

"I knew a junkie once with an arm like this." Jax shook his head and unrolled her sleeve. "The irrationality of a thing is not an argument against its existence, rather, a condition of it," he murmured, securing the buttons at her wrist.

She frowned as the familiar words rolled around her head. "Einstein?"

"Nietzsche." Jax lifted an eyebrow. "Rumor has it you're carrying an advanced form of Scorpius. True or false?"

"False rumor to isolate me." She tried to keep her tired eyes open.

Jax gestured toward her pack. "I get the food and water you have, but what's in the journal?"

She sighed. "Sorry, but there's nothing about Scorpius. My dad was a physicist and a philosopher. He wrote a lot down."

Jax blinked. "That's quite the combination."

"Yes." The words on paper were all she had left of her parents.

Jax studied her and then looked toward the gas lamp on the counter. "We have lanterns left, but not for long unless we get more fuel. So keep an eye on the lamp but extinguish it if you go to sleep."

"I understand." The guy was quoting Nietzsche? What kind of an ex-gang member turned army special ops turned leader of a vigilante group knew philosophy? She shook her head. Time to negotiate. "I'm here for a reason."

"I'm sure." He eyed her blue heart again. "You can cover up."

She fumbled in refastening her shirt. "I'll teach you everything I know about the illness, and you provide temporary protection and one kill." The mere idea she was contracting a murder banished the desire humming inside her and replaced the heat with a lump of cold rock.

A veil fell over Jax's eyes. "What makes you think we don't know everything you do about the illness?"

She shrugged, wondering if he knew what kind of information he might have stored away just from his ransacking labs. "The Internet went down fast, much faster than anyone would've thought, and the news and television thereafter. No way do you know what I know."

He watched her patiently, as if waiting to strike. "The Internet went down because of a guy named Spiral."

She blinked. Wow. So Jax Mercury had some seriously good intel. "True. He was infected with the illness and then reacted by creating a world-class computer virus. Figured if bodies died, so should technology, since it got us in this fix in the first place." Her instincts hummed. Underestimating Mercury would be a colossal mistake. Suddenly, and for the first time in way too long, hope struggled to unfurl within her. "I still know more about the illness than you do."

"Probably." He studied her for a few moments longer before cocking his head to the side. "What else?"

She cleared her throat. "I assume you've scavenged the area you control?"

His chin lifted. "So?"

She swallowed, her body stilling. "Did you scavenge the emergency CDC outpost on the southeast side of L.A.?" Her blood pumped so fast she could feel a vein in her neck bulging.

"Yes. Why?" he asked softly.

The softness contained a deadly intent that rippled a shiver down her spine. Her fingers fidgeted. "They had the most recent research, and combined with mine, we might have hope." They also had intel on where Myriad, the ultra-secret lab, might be located.

He studied her. "We raided the CDC outpost and took all the medical supplies and paper records. Our limited medical personnel went through the files looking for cures, but I have to be honest, none of them are researchers with your background."

Lynne leaned forward. "I'd be happy to go through all the information and decipher it for you." Oh God. Maybe the risk of heading into Mercury's territory would actually pay off . . . if she could find Myriad. "Could I look through the data?"

He leaned back and studied her. "Sure. Are you telling me there may be a cure?"

"We haven't found a cure yet, and I think it's unlikely. But maybe possible?" How many times in her life would she have to say those words? "There was some cutting-edge research into vitamin B and protocols for making it permanent in the body." The vitamin helped infected survivors retain their sanity, somehow halting the stripping of the brain that the Scorpius bacteria caused. It worked even better if built up in the human system before infection, hence the inoculations. She could tell him that much, which was all true. And if the location of the lab that had done that research was in those documents, she'd finally find Myriad.

Jax stiffened. "Permanent? Meaning no more inoculations?"

"Yes. *If* we can get the human body to create its own B to slow down the fever and the damage to the center in the brain that controls empathy."

His eyebrows lifted. "Looks like you're going through boxes of paper starting tomorrow. For now, who do you want me to kill?" At the question, a new hardness entered his eyes. A look that judged her.

Her eyes stung, but she refused to look away or lower her gaze. "I'll tell you when I'm ready." For now, she didn't know if she could trust him. "Do we have a deal?"

He frowned and rubbed his whiskers. "You know I have your knowledge to demand if I want, right?"

Her chin lifted. "You said you don't force women."

"I don't force women to have sex." He reached out and tapped her chest above her heart. "I have no problem refusing you food and sleep until you give up everything you know or even suspect about this illness. You should probably have thought of that before coming here."

She had considered all the consequences, and the risk had seemed worth it. "You won't torture me."

"I will." The softness of his tone was all the more deadly than if he'd yelled, proving his control and absolute conviction. "I don't want to hurt you, but I will."

Would he? No wavering, no conflict showed on his hard face. But everything she'd studied, and everything she'd found, indicated he wouldn't torture a woman. Of course, desperate times and all of that. "This will go easier if we work together," she said levelly.

His gaze delved deep. "You're right." He clasped her hand in his warm one and shook. "You give me what I want, and I'll protect and even kill for you." Releasing her, he stood, reached into the dented dresser, and tossed a faded Los Angeles Dodgers T-shirt her way. "Besides the car ride here, when was the last time you slept?"

She caught the worn cotton as well as the scent of soap. Something clean? It was almost too much to hope for. "I, ah, don't know."

He lifted his head. "Right. Bathrooms are outside, and they're not bad. We confiscated new honey buckets from a warehouse, and if you need to go, there's a guard waiting to escort you. No hot water anywhere here. Do what you need to do, change into the shirt, and the bed is yours for a few hours."

Her eyes ached they were so tired. "I don't need to sleep."

"You're no use to me if you pass out from exhaustion." He lifted her to her feet as if she weighed absolutely nothing. "Take a nap—just change your clothing first."

Her instincts hummed, and she eyed his amazing physique. He obviously trained often. "What kind of fighting forces do you have here, anyway?"

He brushed a strand of hair from her face and then grasped her chin, tilting it up. The switch from gentle to firm was undoubtedly on purpose, and the tactic stopped her short. "Let me be clear on how this will work after your nap. I ask questions. You answer questions. That's it. No more. Do you understand?"

Heaviness weighed down her limbs, and grit scratched her eyes. Every ounce of spirit she still owned wanted to defy him. To take him on, just for pride. But her intellect and her body won. This time. "I understand."

"Good." He released her and stepped back. "Do I have to stay and put you in that bed?"

An image of his hard body in bed shot through her head, weakening her knees. What in the hell was wrong with her? She'd seen good-looking men before. This one took handsomeness to deadly in a way that stirred her blood too much. Although it was nice to feel something other than fear and desperation. Plus, she could certainly rationalize her physical reaction to him.

When death loomed near and survival became everything, biology made a fighter, a soldier, like him desirable. Need easily created lust.

He grasped her arm, yanking her from her thoughts. "Lynne?"

"You can leave." She sidled out from his hold, and he allowed it. "I could use a couple hours of sleep."

"Good." He pivoted and headed toward the door, his broad back remaining to her. "I'll have guards right outside, just so you know."

She clutched the shirt to her chest. Her freedom had been bartered the second she'd made the deal. "I know."

He left, and she quickly changed, her mind too tired to process much beyond the softness of clean clothes. Drawing out her father's journal, she ran a finger over the imprint of his name. DR. FRANKLIN XAVIER HARMONY, PHILOSOPHIES. God, she missed him. Gently, she tucked the precious journal into the pack and moved toward the mattress.

Pressing one knee on the bed, she peered between rough boards on the window to the dark world outside. Dawn had been covered by a thick mass of black clouds. Just her luck to arrive in Los Angeles during the short but brutal rainy season. She couldn't see a thing.

Sleep. As a scientist, she understood the value of regenerating during a sleep cycle. Sliding beneath the covers, she inhaled the masculine scent of Jax Mercury.

As she lay in his bed, having met him in person, there was no doubt in her mind that she'd underestimated him. He was much more intelligent, much sharper, than she'd thought. While she'd known of his absolute dedication to Vanguard, she'd figured she'd be able to maneuver around him.

Something told her she'd been wrong.

Chapter Four

*It is a miracle the earth survived the violence of space,
and it's a bigger miracle that humans
have survived the earth.
At the end, we will pass the way of the dinosaur.*

—Dr. Franklin Xavier Harmony

Jax rubbed his gritty eyes and left Lynne in his room, already planning how to best use her. He strode down the worn concrete stairs to what had always been a crappy alcove that served as the entrance to the upper two floors of the rent-controlled brick building. The first floor had consisted of a free medical clinic, soup kitchen, and offices for attorneys down on their luck. When he'd created the Vanguard head-quarters, he'd changed the clinic into a triage infirmary, the soup kitchen into a soldier cafeteria, and the offices into his war rooms. He'd tossed legal books out in favor of weapons.

Well, he'd actually burned them for fuel. The old laws no longer mattered.

Then he'd promptly punched doorways between the three areas for better access.

He hit the alcove, turned to go through the new doorway to the soup kitchen, which was dead empty at the hour of dawn. The smell of burned tomatoes followed him as he skirted tables and rickety lawn chairs for another new doorway, this one to the former waiting room of the clinic.

Banging echoed from the back of the suite, so he crossed behind the dented reception desk. He found his man in a room that used to be the lunch room of the clinic. A blue halogen lantern gave off an otherworldly glow in the small space. "How much B do we have now?" he asked.

Tace Justice, dressed in full combat gear, glanced up from a microscope they'd found at a junior high several months ago. It rested on a surprisingly smooth wooden table in the center of the room, across from a counter lined with other medical supplies. "Finished the inoculations for this month, except for yours, and this is it. We're out, kaput, done." He stood and grabbed a syringe. "Since you're here, let's wrap this up."

Jax grimaced and tilted his head to the side.

The needle slid in, and fire flamed through his neck. "You have the finesse of a fucking elephant," he muttered.

Tace shrugged. "I was a field medic, not a doctor or a nurse. Take it and shut up, or go to the main infirmary for civilians in the center of Vanguard territory."

Jax scrubbed both hands down his face and glanced at a child's drawing of a distorted blond guy with his head open taped to the wall. "Is that supposed to be you?"

"Yep." The Texas twang deepened. "Not sure what it means, and the open head is a little creepy, but it's nice the kids found some crayons."

"Lena?" Jax asked with a sigh.

"Of course."

The little girl often found a way to wander into military headquarters to give presents, and Jax had a drawer in his quarters of oddly shaped and painted rocks she'd showered on him. "They need to do a better job of keeping the kids inner territory."

"Then you should go inner territory more so folks can see you," Tace said.

Jax avoided going beyond his command unless absolutely necessary and stuck to the perimeter of the seven square blocks, making sure their defenses stayed shored up. Barbed wire fencing protected the entire territory, which was a trick he'd learned from serving at several military bases, and he didn't want to discuss going inner territory. "We've been getting shot up with B for months. Is there any chance our own bodies will take over production of the vitamin so we don't need the shots?"

"Hell if I know, and so far, the new data hasn't helped. Nobody knows about Scorpius." Tace winced. "I can just affirm from my own review of the public documents initially sent out by the CDC that vitamin B, in this concentrated form, provides a protection so that if somebody contracts Scorpius, they might live through it. The B seems to keep the bacteria from spreading in the body. By testing those who have confessed to being survivors, the CDC discovered the Scorpius bacteria localizes just in saliva and blood." Tension rode his words. "Of course, most survivors don't tell me the truth about it in our community, so I don't know who has been infected."

In his past life, Tace had been an army medic after having grown up on a Texas ranch with several siblings, all of whom had succumbed to Scorpius. Now he gave off a vibe of being one with the universe and at peace. But he was a damn good medic who at least somewhat understood Scorpius and vitamin B.

Jax grimaced as thunder rolled again. Shit, they needed rain but not bad wind. "It's a vitamin," he muttered. "Vitamin fuckin' B."

Tace blew out air. "The B vitamins deal with dopamine and serotonin in the brain, which has something to do with hormones and empathy. That's all I know."

Jax scratched his stinging neck. "Have you had much of a chance to go through the data we took from the CDC outpost and contracted labs in the area?"

"We went through it for medical data, but some of it was pretty confusing." Tace stretched his shoulders. "Why?"

Jax rubbed his chin. "Lynne Harmony thinks she might be able to find a concoction that creates B in the blood so we won't need constant injections. She's not telling me everything, but I think she was truthful about that."

Tace stilled. "Interesting. The research I read did talk about B quite a bit, but some of it might as well have been in Sanskrit."

"You don't know much."

"Probably not nearly as much as Lynne Harmony does." Tace turned and leaned back against the counter, scattering papers. "Is it true? Do you have her?"

"Yeah." Jax looked at the collections of drugs, chemicals, and test tubes, which had already been in place in the building. They'd made good use of the facilities, mainly because the compound was situated perfectly to protect and defend. A row of warehouses lined the rear of his territory, backed by an old street and several worn railroad tracks. Then many apartment buildings congregated around an old elementary school that now served as the main hospital for his people. Several businesses took up space with a church in the center.

The seven square blocks also had held a food distribution center by the warehouses, which was now well guarded. He'd immediately run barbed wire around the entire territory inside the public roads while barricading it with semitrucks, vans, cars, and piles of tires on the roads outside.

Yet an attack was coming. He could *feel* it. "Do you have the facilities necessary to study her blood, if she gives it?"

"If?" Tace asked slowly, crossing his arms.

"Answer the question," Jax ordered his chief medic. Now there were three doctors inner territory, but he trusted

Tace the most. They'd known each other for almost six months and had fought, killed, and nearly died next to each other during rounds of attacks. The six-foot blond had been on leave from the army when the shit had hit the fan. "Please answer."

"No." Tace rubbed his square jaw. "We don't even remotely have the resources to study her blood, so there's no reason to take any of it. Did you see her heart? Is it really neon blue like in the pictures?"

"Yes." The CDC and newspapers had shown pictures of Lynne's heart before the epidemic had spread. "If I can somehow find you the right equipment to take her blood, maybe you can create a cure?" Jax asked.

Tace snorted. "Sure. I mean, the CDC and some of the smartest doctors on the planet were unable to do so, but why the hell not?" He gestured around the makeshift lab. "Without electricity and millions of dollars of high-tech equipment, the most I can do here is look under an old microscope. There's no way for us to find any sort of cure in her blood, even if there is somehow a cure that the real CDC missed."

Jax exhaled slowly. "No need to be an asshole. Just think about it." The second they lost hope of survival, they lost everything. "Hope is the dream of a waking man."

Tace snorted. "I like that quote better than the 'we're all gonna die' quotes you spouted yesterday."

Jax rubbed his aching temple. "I was moody, and now you seem concerned." Tace was as good-natured as they came, and Jax relied on him to cheer up the troops when necessary, which was more often than not.

"Concerned?" Tace slowly nodded. "Based on the rumors we've heard, you've brought a woman rumored to be carrying something more dangerous than the Ebola, AIDS, and smallpox viruses combined with the plague, meningitis, and flesh-eating bacteria into our barely secured home base, and you're keeping her at command headquarters."

"Her knowledge is our hope. Our only hope." Jax rolled his shoulders. "You know as well as I do that there are a million unfounded rumors out there. Yeah, they say she's carrying a new, even more deadly mutation of the contagion, but you know that's probably not true. We know for sure she's the one person still alive with the best chance of finding a cure." Though he'd expected resistance from his men, he hadn't thought Tace would be reluctant. "This could turn the tide."

"If you say so." Tace shook his head. "A betting man would argue that the tide is over, brother."

Jax tried to keep his patience, but his teeth still ground together. "Knock it off."

Tace, as usual, switched moods quicker than a fox on a hunt. "Is she pretty? In the pictures, she looked hot."

Jax slowly shook his head. "You go from calling her a dangerous carrier to asking if she's good to look at?"

"Yeah," Tace drawled. "There's something sexy about a woman so dangerous she can kill you by biting your finger. Is our great hope pleasing to the eye?"

Yes. Lynne Harmony was stunning as well as desperately wounded. Delicate and fierce. One hour with her, and she'd brought out something in Jax he neither wanted nor needed—the urge to save her. He couldn't appreciate what made her pretty, and he couldn't compromise on the mission. Neither could his men. "She's a woman who's been through hell, and she's a prisoner here to share any information she has learned. Don't confuse things."

"Yes, sir," Tace drawled. "I think you found her appealing."

Way beyond that, actually. The woman had a brain, and he'd always been fascinated by smart girls. Always. "Please concentrate."

Tace reached for a drawer and drew out several foil packets to throw at Jax. "Just in case."

Jax caught the condoms and leveled him with a hard look. "Are you kidding me? I don't have time for sex."

"There is always time for sex." Tace flung out his massive arms. "Don't you get that? If you have a good moment, take it. For now, our best hope is to forget a cure and somehow put off death and craziness with vitamin B."

The door pushed open, and Wyatt Quaid stomped inside. "There's craziness? We have a Ripper?"

"No." Jax shook his head, sliding the condoms in his pocket, not because he needed them but to get them out of sight. The room was suddenly too small with all three of them in there. "Don't eavesdrop. You get things wrong."

Wyatt shrugged. "My bad. We have a newly trained squad of scavengers who go out on their first mission tonight. I need you to come give them a talk."

Jax stilled. "Where?"

"Main training facility."

Well, at least it was close by. If he went out the rear door of his headquarters, passed the outside showers, crossed a now-defunct street, he'd be at the training facility that used to hold six businesses, including a pawnshop and nail salon. When he'd taken over, he'd gutted the shell, torn down all the walls, and created a training and meeting area. For other people. "I don't deal with civilians," Jax muttered.

Wyatt breathed out, moving his massive chest. "They're not civilians, they're scavengers, and they provide a service. A good one. And a test and a question-and-answer session by our leader would go a long way. Consider it a favor."

Fuck, fuck, and double fuck. "Fine."

"Good. They're waiting." Wyatt grinned, his teeth unbelievably white against his midnight dark skin. He was Jax's main liaison with their territory of about five hundred people, and he rarely asked for favors.

"Tace, get anybody who understands scientific research ready to work. Wake everyone up if you have to." The damn clouds were keeping it abnormally dark; otherwise people would be out of bed and ready to work by now. Jax jerked his head toward Wyatt. "You talk to the new guy?"

Wyatt shook his head. "The guy won't really talk, but he sure moves like you do."

Jax frowned. "Moves like me? What do you mean?"

"You don't make a sound. Serious training," Wyatt returned.

Yeah, Jax had noticed the guy who'd calmly walked into camp the week before, saying he wanted to help fight outlying gangs and take out the main one, Twenty. He'd been armed with knives and guns, yet had kept his hands free. "What kind of a name is Raze, anyway?"

Tace whistled. "Not so different from Jax."

Whatever. Jax needed to sit down and figure out if Raze was a threat or a godsend. For now, Jax gave Wyatt a look. "Let's get this over with. Your scavengers had better be ready to do some work and find me fuel and food."

Wyatt nodded. "There's our happy leader."

Whatever. Jax shoved out of the room, strode past three partitioned examination rooms and out the back door. Crisp air pummeled him right before droplets plopped onto his head. "We're in L.A., damn it. Where's the sun?"

"Rainy season," Wyatt mumbled, following him onto the cracked concrete of what used to be a busy roadway and now just led to the main training facility. Barrels lined both sides of the street, already capturing crucial rain water, while a row of makeshift showers took up the far side of headquarters.

The world was too dangerous to worry about modesty.

Jax clomped across the road and empty parking lot and pushed open the main door to what used to be a pawnshop. "I'm glad they're coming here," he muttered, crossing into the main area, which was littered with metal tables from a former smokehouse.

"Of course—they're on the way. God forbid you go inner territory and actually meet some of the people you're willing to die for." Wyatt pulled out a chair and dropped into it, winced, and tugged a knife from his back pocket.

Jax sat and leaned his elbows on the metal table. Dawn had finally arrived, and even with the storm, a barely there soft light flickered into the room, making lanterns unnecessary. He'd worked with Wyatt for six months, and he trusted the man with his life. For now, they could get back to business. "Any indication the woman was followed here last night?"

"No. The area surrounding us is secure." Wyatt grabbed a pencil and twirled it on his dark fingers, one of which held a Super Bowl ring. "Where is the woman, anyway?"

"My quarters, under guard." Jax leaned back. "She was barely standing up, she was so tired. Probably has been traveling hard, hiding out, trying to keep from being seen." He'd get her entire story later, when he had time. Right now, he had fires to put out. "I've ordered the soldiers who saw her blue heart to stay quiet for now and not share with the rest of the group. Are you with me on this one or not?"

"I'm with you." Wyatt focused intently, a six-and-a-half-foot ex-linebacker for the San Francisco 49ers who now shot a rifle as well as he used to hit quarterbacks. "If the Twenty gang finds out we have her, they'll attack."

Jax had been expecting an attack any day. "They want our medical supplies anyway. Keep the patrols up and keep everyone prepared. They're gonna hit us soon."

"I know, and I'm worried about the Mercenaries." Wyatt grimaced, stood, and held his stomach. "Ah, I'll be right back."

Jax snorted. "Did you eat the burned soup?"

"Shut up." Wyatt turned and ran for the door.

Poor guy. Human digestive tracts had gotten lazy with civilization. Jax leaned back his head and shut his eyes, allowing the quiet to center him. He'd created family in the military, as close to family as the gang of his youth and the survivors he now led. Wyatt had been his first trusted soldier in the new world.

Jax had caught the illness in Afghanistan and had watched the bacteria kill most of his unit in dust-filled tents with medical personnel who had died right along with them. The second he'd regained his health, he'd hopped on a transport home, where hell had already descended.

He'd learned his brother had been killed months before by a bullet, and since he had no family left after Scorpius, nobody had told him.

He drifted deeper into the past as he waited for Wyatt to return.

Buildings crumbled like they always had in the rough area of L.A., and shadows lingered, like before, waiting to harm. But these were different. Jax wandered down the street, looking for survivors, when the patter of gunfire stopped him cold.

The small distribution center. Shit.

Dodging into a run, he hurried around rusting cars to the warehouse, finding a group of Twenty gang members firing on a huge black guy wearing a bloody football jersey. The man looked familiar and seemed to be protecting the warehouse.

Keeping out of sight, Jax had angled around to the back, only to find a bunch of elderly people and kids hiding in the warehouse near a barrel of what looked like toasted oats.

The gang would kill them without a thought.

Jax hustled by them, gun out, and inched up behind the football player's side. "I'm with you."

The guy half turned, a wild glint in his dark eyes. "You sure?"

"Yep. Jax Mercury." He angled farther and fired, clipping a Twenty member in the side, having given up his allegiance

the second he'd taken his oath in the military. "You have any combat experience?"

"Wyatt Quaid. No."

"From the Niners?" Jax took aim and fired again. A yelp of pain filled the afternoon.

Wyatt fired and hit the dirt. "I used to be."

"Go left, and I'll go right," Jax said, shifting into command mode. For now, he had a mission, and he'd win it.

"Jax?" Wyatt asked, yanking him back into the present.

"Is your stomach okay?"

"No." Wyatt grimaced. "You ready?"

"Yep."

The back door to the cavernous space opened, and a group of fifteen people filed in. They wore torn clothing but had jackets and hand-stitched patches on their arms showing they'd completed the training for scavenging. Jax breathed out. "Fuck, they're young."

Wyatt winced. "No shit."

"They're supposed to at least be sixteen years old," Jax muttered.

"They are." Wyatt stood. "Line up."

The kids, and there was no doubt they were kids, formed two lines of ten. Jax shoved to his feet, eyeing them. A couple kept his gaze, while several more dropped theirs to the floor. "How many sections are there inside our grid?" he asked.

"Seven," a blond girl in the back said.

The girl should've been planning for college and going to dances, not memorizing the layout of their territory. "Good. How many sections outside to the west?"

"Fifty sections straight west," a kid barely sporting a goatee said from the left.

"Good." Jax walked back and forth in front of the line. The

kids were smart so far. "Do you ever go out of your ordered area?" he asked.

"Only in extreme situations to avoid Rippers." The blonde spoke up again.

"What's a Ripper?" Jax asked.

A couple of the kids chuckled. "Zombies," one muttered.

Jax cut a hard look at Wyatt.

Wyatt shook his head. "Zombies don't exist, dumbass."

The kid with the goatee shot an elbow into his buddy's gut. "We know that. First of all, zombies aren't real." He stood at attention. "Second of all, if zombies did exist, then they'd be what was left over after a human died. The person dies, and then the zombie bug takes over. Everyone who ever watched *The Walking Dead* knows that." He sighed and looked down at his feet. "And third, zombies don't exist in real life."

"That was number one," his buddy drawled.

"No shit." The kid rubbed his eyes. "But if they're still human, it seems like we could reason with them."

Jax rolled a shoulder. So long as the kids knew how to scavenge and how to defend themselves, he had to send them out. "You have to understand that the bacteria does not always kill human beings; sometimes the patient survives, but the Scorpius bacteria still remains within the body, stripping a small part of the brain. The contagion alters brain activity in everybody who is infected, but only turns half of the folks into killers. We don't know why. It might have something to do with oxytocin, which is a chemical we think relates to empathy. Some folks lose it all, and some only part or none."

The kid nodded. "So there's no hope for Rippers."

"No." Jax kept the kid's gaze. "Don't try to reason with them. There are two main types of Rippers. The first is organized and intelligent like a serial killer. If one of these attacks you, it's planned, and they have bad things in mind for you. The second is disorganized and just plain crazy, and they're more likely to rip you apart like an animal. Run from either."

The kids started to shuffle their feet.

Jax put a bite into his voice. "When you're out on a mission, your goal is to be as quiet as possible. Don't be seen, and definitely don't be heard. What's your motto?"

"Shoot first, question later," the kids said in unison.

"Good." Jax clasped his hands at his back and walked toward a small girl, another blonde, this one with bright blue eyes. What was her name? Haylee. Yeah, that was it. Her mother, April, worked as a cook at the soldier headquarters. "Who's the enemy?" he asked softly.

Haylee kept his gaze. "Everybody not in Vanguard." Sadness and determination lifted her chin.

"Yes. Out there you'll find Rippers, rival gangs, and just ordinary people willing to kill you over a bottle of water. You wouldn't be wearing that patch if you weren't fit and prepared to fight." He'd set the training requirements himself, and they included learning how to fight hand-to-hand, with a knife, and with guns. The kids were as much soldiers as scavengers, but he needed supplies more than protection right now. "We require medical supplies, food, water, and gas. Go out and find some."

Haylee drew in air. Her eyes held both an old wisdom and a desolate acceptance. "To what end?"

Jax paused. "That's a good question. Right now, it's to survive. The bacteria is still running its course, Rippers are either getting reckless or planning big, and rival gangs want our supplies. For now, we fight."

She swallowed. "For now."

Smart kid. "Then hopefully we find a cure or at least a way to live with the infection, and we build anew." Including some sort of civilization.

"But now we fight," she whispered, her face too pale.

He tried to infuse confidence and arrogance into his voice. "And we win."

The kids stood at attention and then slowly filed out.

Jax eyed Wyatt.

"I know. They're young and have no clue what a Ripper will do."

Yeah, but who did? Jax loped toward papers taped to the west wall where the entire seven square blocks of his territory had been painstakingly drawn. The outside buildings had all been fortified with turned-over trucks, vans, and other vehicles. Kids and the elderly were in the dead center near the hospital, which used to be an elementary school, and the current food depot, which had once been a small grocery store.

He'd planned every single inch of Vanguard territory with protection and survival in mind for his force of five hundred people, but it was getting more difficult to keep the enemy outside. "We need to shore up the eastern edge," he said, pointing to a series of old apartment buildings.

Wyatt nodded. "We have a new force of soldiers ready to defend, but none have seen combat."

"They will soon enough." Jax rubbed his left eye to get rid of the pain behind it.

"When's the last time you slept?" Wyatt asked.

Jax shrugged. "Day before yesterday? Maybe?"

Wyatt shook his head. "How do you do that?"

"Military training." Jax turned to recheck the security for headquarters. Training wasn't all, though, was it? He swallowed and kept going, not looking back. Now wasn't the time to share his secrets, not even with Wyatt.

Chapter Five

Trust your instinct to the end
though you can render no reason.

—Ralph Waldo Emerson

Lynne awoke cocooned in warmth, her body luxuriating in the feel of fresh clothes, her mind clearing after sleep. Real sleep. She stretched and instantly stilled, her eyelids crashing open. A hard body spooned her from behind.

Panic ripped into her and shot adrenaline through her veins. Sunlight slid in from the boarded-up window, making it maybe late afternoon?

"Relax," a deep voice rumbled.

Slowly, like prey, she rolled over to face Jax Mercury, bare chested, cascading heat. A jagged tattoo made up of complicated lines and sharp edges wound over his left shoulder. She could make out a 20 in the center, covered and crossed over by lines. A special ops tat with a 44 in it shifted in the muscle on his left arm. A military designation of some type? "You promised," she whispered.

He opened one brown eye. "I'm not attacking you, am I?"

"Well, no." She inhaled, trying to slow her heart rate before a panic attack swamped her. She eyed him, tousled and relaxed. His right bicep held a tattoo with sharp lines, a shield, and the word VANGUARD written through a heart. A dark lock of hair had fallen over his forehead, and a bristly shadow covered his square jaw, giving him the look of a lazy panther.

Panthers didn't really get lazy, now did they?

He sighed and reached for the comforter, frowning when she flinched. Sighing, he pulled up the threadbare fabric to her neck, covering her completely.

"I need to know what I'm dealin' with here, darlin'," he rumbled, opening both eyes and focusing on her.

She curled her knees up toward her chest, hitting his hip bone on the way. "What do you mean?"

His gaze roamed her face, lingered on her lips, and returned to her eyes. "The world has turned shitty-times-ten for women without the ability to fight."

She blinked. "I know." Predators always found the weak.

"What really happened when you disappeared from the CDC? Kidnapping or escape?" he asked.

Apparently the questioning would begin in bed. She tried to move back, but the wall stopped her. "I'd rather discuss this later while clothed."

"That's unfortunate, because we're discussing it now." His tone remained gentle.

She'd have to crawl over him to get to the floor, and no way was she getting in a tussle in bed with him. "I escaped."

"Three months ago."

"Yes." She plucked at a string on the comforter. "The contagion spread, and soon the people in control weren't the people who should be in control. I ran."

He nodded. "Right about that time, the news stopped."

So many people had succumbed to the illness, the world had seemed to stop. "I know."

"Where have you been for three months?"

She tightened her jaw to keep her lips from trembling. "Before the Internet crashed, the battles in L.A. were broadcast continually. I saw you fight, and I later read about the group you've formed here. Even the worst of the worst know not to come within five miles of inner Los Angeles, or they face the wrath of Jax Mercury."

He lifted one dark eyebrow. "Those reports were exaggerated."

"Of course." She rubbed sleep from her eyes, her heart rate finally slowing. "The remaining doctors at the CDC tried to contain me, but I got loose. I knew I needed to get here, that with your vitamin B stores and fighting troops, maybe I could be safe and help find a cure." That wasn't the whole story. But she couldn't trust him with it yet.

"Did you meet trouble on the way?"

"Of course." There was always trouble, and she'd seen too much. "But I made it here."

He touched her cheek. "Did anybody hurt you?"

She frowned. Oh. "No. I traveled with my uncle Bruce, who was a hell of a cop in his day. He helped me to break out of the CDC—the center we created in the nation's capital the second Scorpius got out of hand."

"Wasn't the CDC branch in D.C. just policy oriented?"

"Yes, but we took over a hospital and started researching there, and once I was better, I worked there. It was supposed to be temporary, but as you know, everything happened so quickly, so we never returned to the main CDC hospital in Atlanta."

Her uncle Bruce had visited her many times in the hospital, and when it became evident that several of the CDC doctors had been infected and were considering making Lynne a prisoner, he'd come up with a plan to get her out. "He posed as a lab technician to get me out of the facility, and then he had an elaborate scheme that included three stairwells, one secured lab, and finally a row of windows." She smiled and then faltered. "We'd been on the run for months, and he'd taken great pains to protect me. He died a month ago." The pain was fresh and almost doubled her over. She'd lost so many family members and friends, as had any survivor. God, it hurt.

"I'm sorry." Jax ran a knuckle across her chin. "Scorpius?"

It'd be easy to just nod and lie. "No. Bruce was killed by one of the groups seeking me. Many people are hunting me, believing I either started the apocalypse on purpose or I have knowledge about a cure."

She had knowledge about Myriad but no cure. "After my uncle's death, I continued my search for you and safety, meeting stragglers on the way and staying away from most encampments. Foraged for food when I could." Of course they were hunting her now. It was amazing she'd survived, considering she could trip over a smooth floor, she was such a klutz.

Her former lack of grace was the least of her worries. At some point, she'd need to tell Mercury everything, especially if he wouldn't let her out of the room. But not now, and definitely not while in such a vulnerable position. "I haven't been attacked, Jax."

"Good." His smile seemed almost sinful. "Then you can relax here in our bed and not flinch when I pull up the covers."

Heat flared through her. *Our bed?* "Oh, hell no. I'm not sharing a bed with you."

He glanced at her, at the bed, down at his chest, and then back at her. "I believe you are."

She shoved him. "Absolutely not." When he didn't move or respond, she coughed out air. "Why? Why would you want to share a bed?"

He sighed. "It's not personal. You're a danger to people, and some of them might be a danger to you. So you stay with me, under guard, where I can protect everybody." He pointed to the stacked locks on the door, which she'd failed to study the day before. The door was metal, huge, and obviously not native to the building. "There are locks on both sides, and I have all the keys. One of us could take the couch, but frankly, it sucks."

What should've been the worst come-on she'd ever heard actually sounded like the truth. It was a pretty cage, but a cage nonetheless. She needed freedom. "I want my own place."

"You're not safe, and I can't have guards on you 24/7. Sometimes it's just me, and I need sleep. So you sleep when I sleep, and everybody stays safe. Period." He stretched an arm above his head, showing that amazingly cut chest. "Like I said, I won't force you. You want the couch? It's yours."

She eyed the cold-looking, rather worn leather. It was a freakin' luxury compared to sleeping on the hard ground, but even so, now she'd had a taste of a real bed again . . . "A gentleman would give me the bed."

He scratched the stubble next to his scar. "All the gentlemen are dead, baby. Soldiers and survivors are what we have now."

She pushed up to one elbow, discreetly eyeing the locks on the door before studying him. "How dangerous is it here for me?"

"Very." His eyes darkened from bourbon to Guinness. "We have many who haven't been infected, and you are a carrier."

"Anybody who survived the fever is a carrier."

"As you know, there are rumors that you carry a new strain of the disease."

More lies meant to force her away from other people. "We already discussed that. Either you believe me or you don't," she whispered.

His expression didn't gentle. "There are so many rumors and ghost stories out there; I don't pay attention to them."

She swallowed, her throat clogging. "Good. There is no

new strain of the bacterial infection. I'm no different from anybody else who's survived Scorpius."

"You're the only one with a blue heart."

"I know. I was infected with the main strain, and then we used one of the many experiments to save my life, turning my heart blue. We were never able to duplicate the exact concoction again, although since it didn't cure me, I'm not sure it matters."

"You're different. How can it not matter?"

She sighed. "My heart is blue, as are a few veins around it. I have both photosphores and chromatophores in my heart, which without the initial bacterial infection would be impossible. Squids and octopi have the same materials, essentially, and they can turn different colors—usually blue."

"So you have squid genes?" His brows furrowed, and his gaze pierced her.

She snorted. "Not exactly, but close enough."

"Wait a minute. Aren't squid and octopuses high in vitamin B?"

Wow. Smart guy, wasn't he? "Yes."

"How does that relate to your heart?"

"I don't know, except when we were experimenting for a cure, we used a lot of B. Obviously."

For a moment that ticked into tension, he just studied her with those dark eyes.

She had to look away from such intensity, so she glanced at the boarded-up window. "How secure is your facility?"

"Very, but we're known, and the battles in L.A. aren't finished. We're all regrouping."

Her stomach rolled over. "The battles aren't over? But the news reported—"

"The news was wrong. We still have groups vying for position and for food sources. In fact, once we're stronger, we might have to move north to more fertile land. The food here won't last much longer." He sighed. "Can you give me any statistics on what's out there right now?"

She bit her lip. "Lots of smaller groups trying to organize, from what I saw. We stayed away from cities, so I don't know the stats of how many people are still untouched and how many are Rippers."

"What about the status of the U.S. military? Or, shit, the entire world?" he asked.

"I don't know." She rubbed her eyes. "Even before I escaped, I wasn't in the loop, not really. We were contained in the CDC, doing our research. I wasn't allowed out very often."

"Billions are dead."

"Yes." Her chest grew heavy. "Billions are definitely dead. I hoped I'd be safe here."

Jax shook his head. "We need to move soon, and I need data about the threats out there. The north of L.A. is controlled by a group called the Mercenaries, and they're worse than Rippers."

She internalized a truth she hadn't fully realized. There was no safe place. Studying him, she frowned. "Most people would be afraid to be in a bed with a Scorpius survivor. Scared they'd catch the contagion."

"Not much scares me." He rolled his neck on the pillow. "Plus, that knowledge in your head? It's pretty much our only hope. On the off chance that you're carrying a more dangerous disease, I'd rather be a guinea pig than do nothing."

"I'm not carrying a new strain."

"I believe you." He leaned up on one muscled arm, mimicking her pose. "Like I said, I don't listen to rumors."

"Good. But you have to know there's a bounty on my head." After she'd escaped, the Elite Force had been created to hunt her down, and they'd offered money for help.

He frowned. "Well, I know there's a reward for your safe return. How is that a bounty?"

"How is it not?"

"Did you know the latest reward is not only money but stores of vitamin B for anybody who brings you back to the CDC?"

Her lungs compressed. Vitamin B was more valuable than money these days. "That would help a lot with infected persons."

"Maybe. It seems to me that anybody infected with the bacteria is screwed."

She shook her head. "Not everybody continues changing, especially if they keep up regular injections of vitamin B."

"Uh-huh. If you say so."

"Even if some folks who initially survived the plague turned into killers, that doesn't mean they all will. There's still a chance." She knew more about the survivors than he did.

"I don't think so. Anybody who caught the fever, even if they seemed to survive it, will eventually succumb and become a Ripper," he said.

"I hate that name." She flopped back down. "Jack the Ripper shouldn't be immortalized, even if half of the survivors basically turn into serial killers with no empathy."

Jax shrugged. "What else would we call them?"

She shook her head, not having a better answer. Silence ticked around them, and a new tension filtered through the room.

Vulnerability and an unwelcome sense of curiosity swamped her. She was in bed, practically nude, with Jax Mercury. What now?

Chapter Six

The whole course of human history may depend on a
change of heart in one solitary and even humble
individual—for it is in the solitary mind and soul
of the individual that the battle between
good and evil is waged and ultimately won or lost.

—M. Scott Peck

Jax kept still and tried to banish the hard-on partially hidden under the bedspread. The last thing he wanted was to spook the woman, and truth be told, he'd just had his best sleep in months. Something about wrapping his body around the tiny brunette, holding her close, and smelling her gardenia scent had relaxed him on a subconscious level. Yeah, she was dangerous as hell, but there was a delicacy within her that called to him. On too many damn levels.

Unfortunately, he needed to get his ass out of bed and get to work. Medical supplies were dangerously low, and he'd already planned three raids for the day at clinics in the Malibu area. Chances were the places had been raided already, but he had to find some penicillin. There were several pet shops between Vanguard territory and Malibu, so he'd scavenge there, too. Fish food held plenty of antibiotics, and most survivors didn't know that fact.

First he had to get Lynne Harmony to Tace's lab to go through documents. She obviously had a plan and needed his documents to make it happen. "What do you hope to find in the research we raided?" he asked.

She bit her lip. "I need the actual research results because ours were destroyed in the explosions at the CDC facilities. So much goes into synthesizing vitamin B that I can't remember the formulas. Not all of them, anyway."

His instincts started to hum. The woman kept a straight face, and her eyes remained focused, but he could almost smell the lie on her. "What else?" he whispered.

She shivered.

Damn, but he didn't want to threaten her again. "Tell me, Lynne. You have no choice."

Her pretty green eyes searched his face. Finally, whatever internal debate she was waging seemed to end. "There's a top-secret lab called Myriad located somewhere in Los Angeles." She held up her hand as he started to speak. "I don't know where it is, but I'm hoping the location is buried somewhere in the data you stole from the other labs. It has to be."

Heat flushed through him. "What's at Myriad?"

She pushed away from him, setting her back against the wall again. "At a minimum? The formula for stabilizing vitamin B in the body."

"At the maximum?"

"Maybe a cure?" She shook her head. "Or at least the beginning of the research for a cure to Scorpius." Suddenly, she grabbed his arm with surprising strength. "But I'm not the only one looking for that cure. There are people coming who want to destroy any possible cure and let nature run its course."

An alarm blared through the day before he could ask another question.

"Shit." He jumped from the bed and reached for a walkie-talkie. "Status?"

"Attack from the south and straight at headquarters," came the garbled response. An explosion rippled up, and the building shook.

"Damn it." He yanked on jeans, T-shirt, and a refurbished LAPD bulletproof vest, donning his shoulder holster and shoving various knives into place. Two steps took him to the cupboard under the sink, where he yanked out pistols and an AK-47. Striding toward the door, he turned back to the bed.

Lynne sat up, her hair mussed, her green eyes wide. Defenseless and so damn feminine his gut ached. The woman had sought him out, and she had no reason to harm his people. Knowing it was a fucking mistake, he tossed her a pistol. "Get dressed and get ready to run. Stay in the room unless I come and get you—stay out of the way. Don't let anybody, and I mean *anybody*, see you." He paused. "Shoot anybody who tries to hurt you."

Jumping into his boots and lacing them up, he elbowed out the door and quickly locked it from the outside. Lynne would have to lock the one inside, and he was the only person with the key to release that one.

He ran toward the stairwell as gunfire echoed outside the building. A large crash shook the ceiling tiles, and the smell of smoke assaulted him. He took the stairs down three at a time, his gun out, his senses on full alert.

Leaping through the outside door, he ran across the abandoned parking lot and dodged through the slightly open fence that surrounded the entire property. If it was open, soldiers had already hurried outside.

Keeping low, he quickly ducked behind a barrier made of three dented soccer mom vans and slid in next to Wyatt. The barrier of downed vehicles took up the entire road across from a vacant lot and a damaged three-story brick building he hadn't been able to demolish yet. God, he needed some C-4 or good explosives.

A burning truck at the edge of the vacant lot set the surrounding weeds on fire, and the smell of charring metal corrupted the air. Several other vehicles flanked the burning one, with men firing from the other sides. The empty apartment building rose behind them, silent and dark. "What the fuck?" he muttered.

Automatic weapon fire pinged against the nearest van. Wyatt ducked, his weapon out. "They sent in a truck to explode."

Jax jerked his head, his gaze focusing on Wyatt. "They wasted fuel like that? How much?"

"Too much." Wyatt coughed. "Your boy isn't thinking."

"We don't know it's Cruz." If it was Cruz, and he'd wasted so much fuel, he was using meth again. Without question.

"Yeah. We do." Wyatt shifted over and pointed. "Check out the carcass."

Dread dropping like lead into his gut, Jax peered through a broken window at the Twenty symbol painted and burning on the side of the Mazda. His old gang. "Fuck." He checked his clip and yelled out, "Cruz? What the hell?"

The weapon discharge ended. "Mercury? That you, buddy?"

"Who the fuck else would it be?" Jax loosened his hold on his weapon and took a deep breath. If he had to end Cruz in front of everyone, he'd do it. "What do you want?"

"The medical supplies and guns. All of them." Cruz sounded closer, as if he'd stood up. "Take a look at what I can give to you, *hermano*."

"You and I have never been brothers." The words felt false, cut like a knife. At one point, Jax would've died for Cruz without hesitation. Things had changed. Jax stood, and his gut froze. "Shit."

Cruz smiled, angled to the side of a truck, his arm wrapped

around a teenage girl's chest, his Ruger 23 pointed at her temple. Tears streaked down the girl's pale face, mingling with dirt. Terror filled her blue eyes. "I have something of yours."

Snyder's kid. Haylee had gone scavenging earlier that day. "He's got Snyder's kid," he said to Wyatt.

Wyatt groaned and stood, his gun pointed toward Cruz. "Remember? She was part of the group scouting earlier in local businesses. Didn't even know she didn't make it back."

"I remember." Jax kept his gaze on his old friend and not the girl. "We need better procedures in place."

"No shit. We need more people in general." Tace crab-crawled to his other side, still wearing his combat gear. As usual, he'd probably spent all day in the lab and hadn't bothered to sleep or change. "What's the play here? That prick won't really kill a kid, will he?" He stood, set his elbows on the van, and pointed his weapon toward Cruz, who stood at the edge of the vacant lot with the girl.

The attackers hid behind cars they'd driven into the abandoned lot. Maybe the cars still had gas.

Jax studied Cruz across the distance. Olive skin, gang and kill tats along his neck, lines of experience too hard for the face of a thirty-four-year-old. His former buddy had had a rough life on the streets and behind bars. "Yeah. He'll kill her." Hopefully he hadn't done anything else to her yet, but it wouldn't surprise Jax. "Stop hiding behind a little girl," he yelled.

Cruz smiled and nuzzled his nose into the kid's hair, his mouth moving as he whispered something.

She answered him, fear all but shooting from her eyes, but the crackle of fire covered her voice.

Cruz nodded. "She's not so little. Sixteen, apparently. There was a time, brother, when we fucked our way through sixteen-year-old girls."

Jax settled into kill mode. "We were in the tenth grade, asshole. Now you're just a pervert with a gun."

"And you're a coward who ran." Cruz must've tightened his hold, because the girl cried out, tried to struggle, and then quickly stopped. "Away from home, away from us, and decided to act like a soldier boy. While I did time."

"You deserved time." A snap of a board springing loose caught Jax's attention, but he didn't turn. If he had to guess, he'd say Lynne had just uncovered his window to watch the action. If anybody saw her, he'd kick her ass. "It was your third offense, and you fucking deserved to go away." The prick had shot at a defenseless shopkeeper.

Cruz grinned, and a gold front tooth glittered in the sun. "You half-breed piece of shit. I should've never allowed you in Twenty. Jax Mercury. A boy with a white daddy who probably paid for your mama's cunt. You have a made-up name."

Yeah, and he'd earned it. The second he'd been born, his mama had changed her last name to Mercury, giving them a family name that sounded strong. "You're boring me. Let the girl go, and I won't blow off your head."

Forces of three, guns drawn, spread out alongside Cruz. Some former Twenty members, others from rival gangs. Jax's chin lowered. Apparently Cruz had discovered how to bridge the gap and combine forces. With everybody but him. "I don't like you, and you don't like me, but we have the numbers to work together against Rippers and whatever else is coming." He didn't like it, but he'd do it, and then he'd probably kill Cruz. The bastard deserved to die.

"Work with a traitor?" Cruz tangled his fingers in the blonde's hair and jerked back, exposing her jugular. She cried out and went up on her tiptoes.

"I don't have the shot," Tace muttered.

"I'm not sure of the shot," Wyatt whispered. "Might hit the girl."

Jax could make the shot, but Haylee had to move to the

left. And even if he took out Cruz, there were six guns ready to plug the kid before she got to safety. "Work with me, or I'm going to make sure you die, and it ain't gonna be slow. You know how personal this is."

Wyatt stiffened, and Tace breathed out. They'd heard him threaten folks before, but apparently enough truth lived in his words that they believed him.

"You're the one gonna die, mulo, and you're the one who screwed up by leaving your brothers. Any sorrow is on you." Cruz's upper lip curled as hatred filled his eyes. "Give me the supplies, or you're going to burn. You and the rainbow of pricks you're standing with right now."

Wyatt glanced over at Tace. "Rainbow? Fucking rainbow?" He settled his stance and steadied his weapon pointed toward Cruz. "I'm black and he's white, dickhead," he yelled over the fire. "There aren't any colors here. Dumbass son of a bitch."

Jax slowly turned his head. "You okay, now?"

Wyatt harrumphed. "Just hate dumb people. You weren't a racist way back when, were you?"

"No." Jax fought the urge to look up and back, feeling Lynne's eyes on him. "I was all about brotherhood, safety, and survival. Didn't give a shit about skin color then any more than I do now."

"Good, because I tell y'all, it's tough being black," Tace drawled.

Wyatt snorted. "You're the whitest white boy I've ever seen, Texas."

Jax caught movement on the roof of the abandoned apartment building behind Cruz. In the distance, Jax could see Raze's dark hair and odd blue eyes as he unpacked a rifle. "Sniper in position, but a kill shot won't help the girl." At the moment, Jax had no choice but to trust the new guy and hope he didn't shoot him. Frustration heated his throat, and echoes pinged his mind. Gunshots, fire, blood. Remembered pain flared along his damaged arm and wrist. He shook his head, banishing the flashback to a different war, when he'd lost Frankie in a burning pile of metal. He'd failed, and his best friend had died an unbearable death. But now wasn't the time.

"Mercury?" Wyatt muttered. "We need orders here."

Jax nodded. He couldn't fail. Not again.

"Haylee!" a female voice screamed from behind Jax.

He pivoted just in time to grab April Snyder and take her down to the torn asphalt. She fought him, kicking and punching, her elbows hitting the van, trying desperately to get to her kid. He flattened her until she couldn't move.

She gasped for air, her eyes filling. At thirty-two or so, she had pretty blue eyes and wildly curly brown hair, now matted with dirt. "Haylee."

"I know." He kept his voice low. "If you want her back alive, you'll go inside." April's presence did nothing but escalate the situation, and he had to shut her down and now. "That's an order."

Her lip firmed. "I'm not leaving my daughter." She started to kick again.

Damn it. He needed Wyatt and Tace on the guns, and everyone who could fight was in position. If he left to drag the woman back, there was a good chance Cruz would get frustrated and just shoot the kid. "April. Last chance. Go inside so I can save your daughter."

April got an arm free and punched him in the throat, struggling with everything she had.

He went cold as the mission took over. There was no choice. Scrambling off her, he turned her around, wrapping her in a headlock and increasing the pressure. She flopped and fought, but within seconds, she went limp.

He set her against the van and rose back up.

"Was better than knocking her out with a punch," Wyatt said quietly.

Was it? Fuck. He hated this world. "Cruz? I'm done playing. Let the girl go, or I'll blow your head off."

Cruz ducked down behind the girl. "Send out medical supplies, and we can trade. Just a trade. For old time's sake."

The sarcasm hazed Jax's vision. He struggled to think clearly and signaled Raze up on the roof, hoping to hell the guy knew what he was doing in a sniper position. "Tace, sweep left; Wyatt, right on my go." He angled past Wyatt so he could run for the kid. He couldn't crouch and aim, or Cruz would know. So he angled the weapon slightly to the side and appeared to relax his body.

Then he fired.

Chapter Seven

Life begins on the other side of despair.
—Jean-Paul Sartre

Standing on the bed, Lynne gasped, her head spinning, her stomach lurching as she peered down at the fight. Jax and his soldiers were outside the fence yelling at a bunch of guys hiding behind vehicles in a vacant lot across the street. A three-story brick building cast a wide shadow behind them. Most of the enemy wore bright purple.

One second, Mercury was talking, the next he was shooting. His shot, off his hip, hit the guy named Cruz in the arm.

He dropped the girl, and she plunged to the ground.

With bullets spraying from what seemed like every direction, Jax ran toward the girl in a crisscross pattern. Without missing a beat, he picked her up, cradling her, and shielding her with his body.

Cruz scrambled around a dented truck, as did his men who were still standing. Two lay dead in the burning weeds, their eyes open and their blood filling the dirt around them.

Jax ran for the barricade. Blood sprayed from his right arm, but he didn't falter.

He jumped around the van and set the girl down, his hands

doing a cursory check of her arms and legs. Then he grabbed his weapon, jumped up, and started firing.

Cruz and his soldiers backed away, still firing, many of them bleeding. The survivors jumped into two of the trucks and sped away, trash and weeds flying from the spinning tires.

Then, as quickly as it had begun, the gunfire stopped. Only the crackle of fire and echoes in the air remained.

The three Vanguard men behind the van held some sort of meeting, the big black guy picked up the woman Jax had knocked out, the blond guy picked up the girl, and Jax tilted his head until his blazing gaze met Lynne's.

She instantly fumbled away from the window. *Shit, shit, shit.* Her hands shaking, she grabbed the board she'd removed and tried to shove it back into place. Damn her curiosity. Swirling around, she eyed the door. Locks. Although she was locked in, she could lock this side, too.

Instinct ruling, she ran forward and locked the door. Yeah, she knew he had the key to all the locks, even the interior one, but she couldn't help herself.

Silence ticked around her, so odd after the overwhelming firefight. Her shoulders shook, and she shoved away all panic, backing toward the bed. She'd handled bureaucrats, she'd dealt with scavengers, and she'd overcome monsters. But Jax Mercury was all soldier—all man—savvy and dangerous.

She took a deep breath and held it. Okay. Obviously he had a lot to do, especially with the fight and all. Surely he wouldn't come looking for her just because she'd opened a window.

Locks disengaged, and the door flew open to slam against the wall. "What the fuck were you thinking?" he bellowed. He stood in the doorway, stance wide, big and powerful. Dirt marred his cheek, and blood flowed down his left arm.

She swallowed, her entire system going into overdrive.

Without moving her body, she eyed the weapon she'd left on the counter.

"Try it," he said softly. Too softly.

A shudder blitzed down her spine. "I, uh . . ." There wasn't anything to say.

He stepped inside and shut the door.

Any breath she still had whooshed from her lungs. "I . . ."

"If they had seen you, do you have any fucking clue what a shit-storm would've descended on us here? What they'd do to get to you? Half of them want to kill you. The other half think you can save them. Hell. They'd call in anybody they needed, even the Mercenaries." He stalked toward her, menace in every line.

She backed away until the bed at her thighs stopped her. "They didn't see me," she choked out.

"I did." He moved into her space. "What part of 'don't let anybody see you' did you not understand?"

Fear began to dissipate, replaced by anger. Just who the hell did he think he was, trying to intimidate her? She'd survived a hell of a lot worse than Jax Mercury's formidable temper. She lifted her chin to meet his gaze. "I stayed out of the way. I just wanted to see what was happening. Nobody but you saw me."

"You hope." If possible, his face hardened even further. "Do I need to bind you to this bed to keep you from making stupid choices?"

Heat flared through her cheeks, and an inappropriate flare of desire skittered inside her abdomen. At the very thought, anger roared through her veins. Finally. "Not a chance, you lowbrow dick."

His chin lifted, while his eyelids lowered to half-mast. "I don't think you understand the lengths I'll go to here, or what kind of danger you're putting yourself in right this second."

Oh, he did not. "You don't scare me, jackwad." Once her mouth started, she couldn't stop. "You might know how to choke a woman out, but we both understand unconsciousness doesn't last long. And I don't think you'd hit a woman."

"Don't you?" he murmured.

Her heart stuttered. Everything she'd learned about him said he wouldn't. "No."

"You're wrong."

The very fact that his voice had softened somehow bolstered her courage. "I don't think so." She kept his gaze, her jaw setting hard.

Then he moved. So fast she didn't see it coming, he somehow spun her around and planted a hand on her upper back, shoving her head down toward the bed. A boot kicked her legs apart, and the sound of a leather belt yanked through loops swished through the room.

The first hit landed on her ass before she'd put two and two together. The second hit had her crying out, pain flaring her neurons alive. The third hit made her struggle uselessly against the hand holding her too easily in place.

Blows rained down and spread agony across her butt. Finally, he grabbed her arm and hauled her around. "Any questions?"

Her breath panted out, and tears filled her eyes. Both hands went to her seriously smarting ass. That did *not* just happen. "No."

He slowly slid his belt back through his pants, his gaze on hers, until he buckled the leather together. "You're correct that I wouldn't punch you. Ever. But I think we both understand the parameters here now, right?"

Shock fuzzed her brain.

"Lynne?" His hands paused in the buckling.

"Yes." Agreement seemed wise, at least for now. Later she'd figure out how to make him pay.

"Good." He turned and grabbed her pistol off the counter to tuck it in his waistband. "Don't wait up." Without another word, he exited the room, the sound of locks engaging slamming home.

She swallowed and fell onto the bed, wincing as she landed. The bastard had made a smart move by taking her gun. She might've shot him when he returned. Time to calm down and think.

Letting herself be seen by a roving gang was stupid, although she certainly hadn't deserved his reaction. Even though she'd kind of challenged him about hitting women.

One thing was for sure. She wouldn't underestimate Jax Mercury again. Maybe she'd miscalculated in seeking him out, but she'd needed temporary protection. And she'd needed someone who could kill, who'd proved he was the strongest and smartest badass out there.

Now the only question was, could she get free?

Jax strode into the tactical infirmary, his temper still simmering as blood flowed down his arm. He reached Tace just as the medic finished mopping blood from the floor. "How bad?"

"We've had worse." Tace set the mop to the side and jerked his head to the examination table. "Three wounded, all easy to sew up. April Snyder regained consciousness, no permanent damage, and you're forgiven since you saved her daughter."

Jax shrugged out of his vest and sat on the table, his legs extending to the floor. "And the kid? How bad?"

"Scared shitless but not hurt." Tace shoved Jax's shirtsleeve up his arm and hummed at the wound.

Jax cleared his throat, forcing his voice out. "Was she, ah—"

Tace paused, understanding dawning across his broad face. "No. Haylee got separated from the group, so she hid.

Cruz found her and set his plan into action. Nobody touched the girl."

The breath he hadn't realized he'd been holding blew out of Jax. "Good." Cruz must've been on a timetable or he would've taken the time to violate the girl, just to torture Jax. "No more kids on scavenging trips."

Tace leaned in and started stitching up the wound. "Don't have a choice, and you know it. We're limited, and everybody has work to do."

Jax sucked in air and shoved pain away like he'd learned in the army. Failure threatened to crush his skull. If he was doing his fucking job, the kids would be safe.

"Stop." Tace finished stitching and slapped a bandage on the wound. "Don't second-guess yourself." He threw blood-soaked cotton balls into a corner trash can. "Bullet just grazed you and will leave a wimpy scar. Nothing fun."

What was one more scar? "Thanks, Doc."

"I'm not a doctor, and you should probably see one of the real doctors inner territory," Tace said without heat. "That old feud between you and Cruz. It's bad."

"Yeah. It's bad." Jax picked at his bandage. "When I left the service and came home, one of my plans was to kill him."

Tace blinked. "Oh. Um—"

"Don't want to talk about it." Enough of opening old wounds. "Thanks for covering my back out there."

"Of course." Tace, as usual, let the subject drop. "Uh, I heard your window being unboarded during the fight. How bad did you yell at Dr. Harmony?"

"Not bad." Jax unrolled his shirt sleeve. "She doesn't seem to understand her importance. Or the threat she represents."

"Perhaps she knows something we don't." Tace leaned back against the counter, fatigue creasing the side of his mouth. "Did you piss her off so bad she won't help us?"

"She'll help us." Jax needed to get some answers from

her, when they both had clear heads. He probably should've calmed down before storming up to discuss the window with her, but either way, he'd made his point.

"When do I get to meet her?" Tace asked. "I'm ready to figure out this illness, and she knows a helluva lot more than we do. I've had the records from the CDC outpost brought here from the main records building's inner compound."

Now probably wasn't a good time. "Let's give her a couple of hours to calm down from our, ah, discussion, and then I'll bring her to the lab."

Tace exhaled and shook his head. "You yelled at her."

"She deserved it." No need to go into details. For now, he had to figure out a way to allow the teenagers to contribute without putting them in so much danger.

Manny strode inside, a butterfly bandage over his right eye. "Everyone good?"

Jax took in the fifty-year-old badass. "Yes, but I need you to keep a closer eye on the kids and scavengers than we've done so far."

Manny rubbed a hand through thick gray hair. "Shit."

"Thanks." Jax rolled his burning shoulder. "I think April Snyder can help. I'll have you approach her." He turned back toward Tace and paused as a teenager crossed into the room from the soup kitchen, hands full of wires. "Byron?"

The kid glanced up through wire-rimmed glasses. "I'm working on a portable ham radio, just in case we need one on a mission. But I need more wires. If I come up with a list, will you keep an eye out during raids?"

"Sure." Jax studied the skinny seventeen-year-old. "You did a great job rewiring the van the other day. Thanks."

"No problem." The kid glanced at his watch. "Damn. I'm late for target practice. We can't keep using pretend bullets." He knuckled his glasses back up his nose. "I'll try to come up with rubber bullets or something." Muttering to himself, he turned on his torn tennis shoe and disappeared.

Jax looked at the empty doorway. "I like that kid. Just imagine what he could've been before Scorpius."

Tace nodded. "I'd rather imagine what he can do for us now."

Good damn point. "Speaking of fake bullets, we need more real ammo," Jax said.

Tace sighed. "Raid?"

"Yeah. I hate to do it, but I remember some of the stash houses around L.A. Chances are, we'll find some still there. Maybe drugs, too." With so many getting wounded so often, they couldn't be too choosy over painkillers. "I'm thinking of taking the new guy so you can stay here."

Tace's head flipped up. "No."

"Yes. If I don't make it back, you're in command. Plus, you're our only medic with actual combat training. The rest are a couple of nurses and doctors. Young ones. We can't lose you." Jax didn't let any doubt show in his eyes. The Vanguard had to run like the military to survive, so his orders had to be obeyed, and he had to keep his distance from folks.

Suddenly, without a hint of sound, Raze stood in the doorway. He stood shoulder to shoulder with Jax, his body in definite fighting shape. Black hair curled over his collar, and only the odd light blue of his eyes showed his heritage as anything other than Native American. "Is the girl okay?" Raze asked.

"Yes. Nice job on the roof. You've done sniper duty."

"Yes." Raze turned on his heel and disappeared.

Tace wrinkled his brow. "That guy is seriously weird."

Yeah, he was off, but so was the rest of the world right now. "He can fight, and he has experience. Let's hope he stays on our side," Jax said. Jax didn't trust him and didn't know his true agenda, but for now, he could use him. "Anyway, with him on the raid, you can stay busy here as my main combat doctor."

Tace sighed. "Fine. But about Lynne Harmony—she has medical knowledge, right?"

"Yes. Worked for the CDC before everything. Was some brilliant scientist—that comes with medical knowledge, I'm sure." Jax stretched out his wounded arm. "But even if she wanted to help us, most people wouldn't let her touch them. You know that."

"She just has to help decipher the research materials we've confiscated from labs lately." Tace shook his head. "Although I don't want to cover her back all day. How are you going to keep her safe?" He kicked at a roll of garbage that had fallen out of the overflowing bin. "How will I if you don't return from your next raid?"

Jax eyed his second in command and somebody he would've called a friend in the old days. They'd nearly died more than a few times together, and he couldn't lie. "I have no fucking clue."

Chapter Eight

*Passion will hunt us, as we slumber unaware,
and consume us from within.*

—Dr. Franklin Xavier Harmony

So far, Lynne's first full day in Vanguard territory had sucked, and she was still stuck in Jax's room as darkness filtered through the boarded-up window. Damn it. She didn't have time to be a prisoner. She needed to get on with her mission.

She set down her dad's journal after reading some of his more humorous passages and then fingered a worn and faded picture taped to the wall by the door. A much younger Jax with his arm slung around a shorter kid, one with Jax's eyes. A brother? They had the same facial structure and build, so definitely a younger brother.

A timid knock sounded on the door, and Lynne hurriedly unlocked her side, more than tired of talking to herself for the last several hours. She yanked open the door, happy to see whoever ended up on the other side.

Fragrant and steaming, a bowl of soup lay at her feet on the threadbare carpet.

She glanced up and smiled at the woman sidling down the other side of the hall near a soldier guarding the stairwell. "Thank you."

The woman appeared to be about forty with brown hair streaked with gray. She continued inching away. "Someone will be back for the dish later."

"Wait." Lynne leaned down and picked up the bowl. "Would you like to stay? Maybe chat?"

"God, no." Horror widened the woman's eyes. "You're the plague. You shouldn't be here." She crossed herself, her lips pursing. "Only the very devil himself could've infected you with a monstrous blue heart. The rumors about you are true, and now you're going to infect our leader, the one man who can save us all." Turning, she sprinted in worn tennis shoes for the nearest stairwell.

Lynne glanced at the soldier, whose gaze remained focused above her head.

She swallowed and stepped back inside to shut the door. Tears pricked her eyes. How silly. What the hell did she care about some crazy woman who didn't like her? Nobody liked her, and she'd always be alone. She placed the soup on the table, no longer hungry.

Even her bones were exhausted, and sometimes she wondered why she hadn't just died. What had she done that was so terrible to have deserved this? Her heart beat steadily, the small glow showing blue through her shirt.

A tear fell.

Of course, Jax Mercury chose that minute to walk inside.

He paused, an *oh shit* expression crossing his rugged face. She would've laughed, but the struggle to stem the tears was too hard. A frown lowered his eyebrows, and he shut the door, placing several guns on top of the useless refrigerator. "Did I hurt you that badly?"

She paused and waited until his words sank in. "No."

He blinked and glanced around the apartment. "Stop crying."

At the order, a loud sob erupted from her chest.

He stilled. "Ah, what's wrong?"

It was a simple question. A nice question. One a civilized person would ask. The easy words ticked through her, and something exploded deep inside. "Everything." She threw out her hands. "Everybody hates me, the world is dying, and you fucking spanked me earlier." She doubled over as the hurt overcame her.

"Well, shit." A second later, she found herself lifted and cradled in very strong arms. Jax held her against his hard chest, his mouth near her ear. "Nobody hates you."

"Yes, they do," she hiccupped, crying harder, her body shaking.

He sighed and dropped onto the sofa, holding her closer, tucking her face into his neck. "We fear things in direct proportion to our ignorance of them." His breath brushed her ear, and his size provided safety.

"Who said that?" she pushed out between sobs.

"Christian Nestell Bovee." Jax settled his weight and kicked his feet out over the dented coffee table. "He was a writer in the late 1800s."

She tried to keep her balance on his lap as her sobs increased and she let it all out. The fear, the fury, even the future.

Finally, with a couple more hiccups, her tears subsided. When was the last time anybody had held her? Letting herself go, she flattened her hand over his chest, marveling at its solidness. "How do you know so much?"

"Books." He idly played with her hair. "The judge who gave me the choice of military or prison kept in touch, and he loved philosophy and literature. He would send me books all over the world. At first I read just because I owed him. Then I read because I grew. Finally, I read because the words began to make sense."

"I shouldn't have come here," she said dully, her mouth nearly touching his corded neck.

He rubbed a big hand down her back. "Why not?"

"I probably can't help, and now I've added more fear to people already terrified." She'd been only thinking of herself, believing if she gave them knowledge of Scorpius, it'd be a fair exchange for what she needed. It probably didn't come close. "I'm sorry."

"I think you could be very helpful here. If you tell us all you know and don't hold anything back." He caressed small circles up and down her spine.

She bit back a moan of pleasure. "If I tell you everything, will you let me go?"

"No." He stiffened. "Why would you want to leave?"

She lifted back to meet his gaze. "I can't let it happen anymore. Be treated like a bad person, like an infection. People won't even look at me, much less come near me. Touch me." Without gloves and needles.

He cupped her cheek and wiped tears away with his thumb. "I'm touching you."

Tears clung to her lashes and blurred her vision. Her heart hurting, feeling more alone than ever, she tried to pull away. Everything in her wanted to stay in his arms, to touch him, but like any Scorpius survivor, she was a carrier. She might infect him and thus probably kill him.

He held her in place.

"No, Jax. Let me go . . ." To be this close to him, to want him so badly, just heightened her loneliness. She was isolated by her own blood. "This is too dangerous for you. You're risking infection."

His searing gaze held her captive. "You can't infect me."

She blinked. "Wh-why not?"

"I've survived the bacteria."

She stilled. Shock seized her lungs. He was a carrier, too? "The woman before, the one who yelled at me. She said I'd infect you." Oh God. "They don't know?"

"No." His jaw hardened. "Nobody in the Vanguard knows. If they find out, I'll be thrown out or lynched."

Lynne tried to concentrate, to find any sort of thought and grab on to it. But all she could think was that the man holding her so securely on his lap was safe from her. "There have to be many survivors here."

"Maybe, but it's not like we wear a sign."

She nodded, tingles cascading through her. "I can't infect you."

His gaze dropped to her lips. Tension suddenly surrounded them, changing the atmosphere. "No, you can't."

A tingle buzzed through her. Heat uncoiled in her abdomen, and she needed to move away. Instead, she licked her lips and drew in her breath.

He frowned, his gaze lifting to hers. The hand at her spine continued up to tangle in her hair and, almost in slow motion, drew back her head, elongating her neck. Moving at his leisure, definitely in control, he lowered his head, and his lips enclosed her collarbone.

Shock and heat spiraled under her skin. She sighed and pressed back against his hand. He wandered up, licking, to nip her earlobe.

She panted out air, her body revving alive. The most alive she'd felt in so long. Her nipples hardened and her sex softened, with a dull ache setting up in her core. Her fingers curled into his chest, and she shifted closer.

The hand at her nape twisted, exerting control.

She forgot how to breathe.

He traced under her jaw, holding her in place, nipping her chin. Then he hovered, his mouth over hers.

Please, please, please.

She held her breath, not moving, her eyelids fluttering closed.

His tongue licked one corner of her mouth and then the other. She moaned and moved closer into him. He teased her mouth, drawing out the anticipation, keeping her on the edge.

"Jax," she whispered, so much need coursing through her she couldn't think.

That quickly, he unleashed himself on her. Deep and fierce, he took her mouth, driving her head back against his hand. Somehow he shifted them so she straddled his legs, and his free hand grabbed the waist of her jeans and pressed her down on his cock.

Even through their clothing, she could feel his heat.

She moaned into his mouth, both hands threading through his hair, her body gyrating against his. While she should hate him, really hate him for the callous way he'd treated her earlier, for the moment, all she could feel was pleasure. Lust overwhelmed her. She needed him to fill her. All the empty places, all the loneliness . . . he could *fill* her.

The desperation, the earlier fight, the worldly devastation all disappeared in his kiss. In his overtaking her with something beyond mere passion.

He wrenched his mouth free and yanked her shirt over her head.

Neon blue glowed against his olive-colored skin. She paused, her desire banked. For the moment, she'd actually forgotten.

He inhaled, leaned down, and kissed the blue.

Her heart, if that was what still beat there, turned over. For him.

She opened her mouth to say something, anything, when his lips enclosed her nipple.

She gasped, her hands tightening in his hair, her eyelids closing. He sucked. Hard. Nothing could've prevented the low moan that slid up her throat and into his hair. He found the other nipple and pinched.

A mini-orgasm rocked through her.

More. She wanted more. Her body moved of its own volition, her thighs clamping his, rubbing against him.

He manacled her hips and stilled her, leaning back. "Decide now. You want this?"

God, she did. It felt good. After so long, something felt *good*. She didn't care about repercussions, and she had stopped thinking about tomorrows months ago. "Yes." She tried to move again, but he kept her immobilized.

He grabbed her hair and wrenched her head to the side, his gaze capturing hers. "This is *fucking*. Full bore, I'll take you and make you come so hard you'll forget the world for a few minutes. But that's all it is. Not love, not forever, and not a way to manipulate me." Dark red spun beneath his skin, highlighting the angles and deep hollows. His arms vibrated as if fighting his determination to hold back.

She gulped down air, only partially listening, needing to move. So she nodded.

"Say it."

"Fucking," she breathed out. "Just that."

With the words, he changed. Not in an obvious way, but his tension exploded out, and his eyes darkened. With promise and something darkly male.

Standing, he kept her straddling him, his hands cupping her butt. He squeezed fresh bruises.

Pain and then fierce need cascaded through her, throwing her headfirst into a desire hot enough to incinerate. His responding grin held so much sin she blinked, captivated by the raw handsomeness that was Jax Mercury.

For the moment, however brief, he was hers.

"You shouldn't have done that. Earlier," she breathed, gyrating against him, her butt still smarting.

"Point to make." No apology, no regret glimmered in his hard eyes. Only desire, rimmed with lust he did nothing to hide.

The rational part of her, the woman who'd lived before the world had changed, knew she should court caution. Understood she should ask questions.

But questions and caution were things for the past. Only here and now existed, and her body ruled. So alive, for the first time in too long, she took the chance to embrace danger in order to feel again. To be a woman, with flaws and fears, strengths and soul, for one night in time.

With a stranger more deadly than the bacteria that had killed billions.

The rational part of her brain, the scientist that understood human behavior, comprehended the advantage of being tied to Jax Mercury. Safety lay in his savagery, in being protected by a man who had what it took to survive.

But he was more than that. She knew, from the gentle way he'd treated her earlier, the man had depths.

Even as her mind tried to claim the decision, her body and a deeper part of who she was clung to the moment. She'd been numb, she'd been afraid, and she'd been hopeless.

Now she hungered.

Even so, when he laid her on the bed, vulnerability swamped her.

He straightened and tugged the shirt over his head, revealing a tattooed and battle-scarred chest. Some scars were old and faded to white, some new and still jagged; knife and bullet wounds cut into hard muscle and firm ridges. "Nothing happens you don't want," he said, his hands going to his belt buckle as he read her with impressive accuracy.

The sound of the streets echoed in his tone, the tenor somehow intriguing and full of warning.

Masculinity could be both beautiful and devastating in its brutality. She hadn't realized that before. Even after months of fighting and months of hiding, she hadn't seen the elemental nature of man at such a level. "I want you," she whispered.

He shed his jeans and reached down, with surprisingly gentle movements, to remove hers. She gasped at his fully erect, glistening cock. "Uh—"

"We've established you haven't been abused, and you're not exactly afraid of me right now, but I need to know, how long has it been?" he asked, dropping one knee onto the bed and sliding up her.

Her mouth opened and closed. He nearly enclosed her, pinning her to the bed, all heated male and lust-filled intent. Heated flesh slid against her, and she fought the urge to let her eyes roll back in her head. "How are you talking rationally right now?" she gasped.

He reached for his jeans on the floor and drew out a condom. "Losing control isn't an option. I asked you a question."

Yeah, but command filled every word. She slid her fingers through his thick hair and clenched. Her body burned, and her clit actually pounded for release. "Have you always been like this?"

"No." His grin transformed the harsh lines of his face into something almost sweet. "Believe me, I had a temper to tame. But now survival dictates we think before acting, and I'm sussing out the facts here. How long has it been?"

She amused herself by sliding her hands through his rough hair. "A year, I guess. Before getting infected."

"Good." He lay over her, elbows holding his weight, and lowered his head to kiss her deep. Question and intent filled his kiss, winding through her mouth and down to hit all the important spots on the way.

She widened her legs, gasping when his cock jumped against her clit. "Any chance you could get lost in the moment?"

He grinned against her mouth and leaned back, brown

gaze warm. "Green Eyes, if I got lost in the moment, you'd be bent over the bed, face in the pillows, begging to come with every fiber of your being. I'd make you promise everything."

Heat flared in her abdomen, and a shudder slid down her back.

He chuckled. "Don't tempt me." Before she could think again, doubt the moment, he reached down and slid his thumb across her clitoris.

Electricity sparked through her sex. She arched into his hand, and the sound she made would've embarrassed her had her mind not blanked. The feelings, so good, so natural, nearly threw her into an early orgasm. "Jax," she moaned.

"Enough talking." He shifted to the side and rolled a condom into place. Then he levered his body over hers, both hands capturing her face to hold firm. "Decide now. You want slow and building, or do you want fast and explosive? Want me to take you away?"

Heat rose from her chest to her face, burning in its intensity. She was already wet and primed for him. "Not slow."

His chin lifted, his gaze intense. "Say it. Tell me what you want."

She blinked, her body rubbing against his. Pride didn't mean a damn thing in the face of oblivion. Add in pleasure, and she truly didn't give a damn what she needed to say to reach temporary bliss. "Fast and wild. Make me forget."

"Forget what?" His biceps strained as if he held himself back with great effort.

"Everything," she whispered, spreading her legs wider.

"Fair enough." Raising up to plant one hand by the side of her head, he reached between them, positioned himself, and shoved deep enough to stop her breath.

Pain flared inside her, and she arched up against him, her breath catching in her lungs. One hand slapped against his chest, as if trying to ward him off. Feelings, raw and real, ripped through her. Pain hinting at an edge of pleasure.

He grabbed one of her thighs and pushed up, opening her further. "You're tight, sweetheart," he murmured, dropping his wet forehead to hers.

That simple act, one of intimacy, warmed her throughout. "I know."

He positioned the other thigh, opening her fully to him and whatever he wanted to do to her. The moment should've whispered for caution, but instead, her desire clawed higher. She couldn't move. Her internal walls relaxed around him, and her breath picked up.

"Hold on, Lynne Harmony," he said, dropping his face to the crook of her neck.

She slid both hands over his shoulders, feeling scars and bunched muscle. At her most vulnerable, with him inside her, holding her where he wanted her, a small part of her wanted to seek reassurance. To find in him something safe, something to cling to in the midst of hell. Instead, she shook her head back on the pillow and dug her nails into his flesh, taking what she could.

He growled low and slid out only to shove back inside again. Hard.

"Oh God," she moaned.

At the sound, at the acceptance, his hand clamped onto her hip, and he started to thrust. Hard, with precision, with determination, he pounded into her. The metal headboard slammed against the wall, but Lynne didn't care who heard.

Each hard thrust, each impact of his body inside hers, forced her to climb higher. Bliss, jagged in its reality, hovered just out of reach. More. God, she needed so much *more*.

She clawed into his back, her thighs trembling as he held them apart. The immobility, the forced vulnerability, spiraled her into an orgasm so wild she could only hold on and gasp. Her body contracted around his, holding tight, the waves burning through her. Her mouth hit his shoulder, and she clamped down, needing to find an anchor.

He growled low, grabbed her ass to lift her half off the bed, and hammered harder, giving no quarter. Finally, as her waves died down, he held her in place, hand across her butt, and jerked with his own release.

For the briefest of moments, he slumped against her, his heart beating against her blue one. A lazy swipe of his tongue across her wet neck made her shiver.

With a deep exhale, he slid out and removed the condom, tied it, and dropped it in the trash. Turning, he tugged her into his body, spoon style. "You okay?" He sounded sleepy and almost boyish.

Adrenaline and nerves sparked throughout her body, although her muscles melted into pure relaxation. "Yes." She couldn't stop a soft smile from lifting her mouth.

For a badass, dangerous killer of a soldier who had no problem wielding a belt, Jax Mercury sure liked to cuddle.

Chapter Nine

The human heart has hidden treasures;
In secret kept, in silence sealed; The thoughts,
the hopes, the dreams, the pleasures;
Whose charms were broken if revealed.

—Charlotte Brontë

Morning light awoke Jax, and he ran a hand down the very nice curve of Lynne Harmony's ass. Man, he'd slept an entire night. She lay on her stomach, her back rising and falling as she breathed, her head buried in her arms. Dots of sweat glimmered on her shoulders. The blankets had pooled at her feet. A contented sigh went through her.

He smiled, not guarding his expression since she couldn't see him.

Continuing his exploration, he traced a very light stripe from the belt he'd wielded. The woman bruised easily, and he'd need to remember that fact.

She yelped and shifted her hips, trying to shake him off.

He tightened his hold. "Knock it off. I'm playing."

"Play time is over, and you owe me an apology." She turned her head and opened one very green eye.

He lifted an eyebrow and traced her smooth skin. "For what?"

Her pretty lips tilted in an expression close to a snarl. She tossed the wild mane of her hair and glanced over her shoulder at the clear result of leather on flesh. "For those."

Truth be told, he didn't like marking a woman. Ever. But he'd needed to get his point across without really harming her, and she needed to know he'd follow through on any warning he made. The lines were clear, his thinking linear and unemotional. Even more so after the fever than when he'd been a soldier. Now his brain ruled far more than his heart ever had.

But as he kept his gaze stoic and faced that spitting green eye, something inside him shifted.

"How can you not apologize now?" she asked.

"Now?" he asked, lazy slumber in the tone.

"Well, yeah. You know, after." When the woman blushed, the color reached her bare shoulders. He watched, fascinated.

He didn't want to hurt her, but he needed to be clear. "The sex was great, and I'd love to be inside you again. But I meant it—just fucking. It changes nothing between the two of us except to provide an avenue to release some stress." Yeah, he sounded like a dickhead. But he'd rather be an asshole than a liar, and if she wanted to continue with him, she needed to make the decision with her eyes wide open. "You disobey me again, you put yourself or anybody else in danger, and I'll raise welts next time."

She turned her head, surprise sizzling in her stunning eyes. "You're kidding me."

"No." He kept her gaze, fairness dictating he show her the truth. His point had been made, and she'd think twice before endangering his people.

She rolled on her side to face him fully, anger sharpening her gaze. "Let me get this straight. Jax Mercury, the legend feared far and wide by rebel groups and Rippers, keeps his soldiers in line by threatening a good spanking."

Amusement swelled his chest, and he paused at the sensation. When was the last time he'd actually laughed? The idea of his spanking either Tace or Wyatt made him bite back a full-out laugh. "Not exactly."

"Meaning?" Even naked, after he'd fucked her nearly senseless, spirit and challenge filtered across Lynne Harmony's classic features.

He sighed. "If a soldier disobeys, he's out. I mean, if the screwup doesn't get him killed. Same with citizens. Those are my rules right now, in the name of survival, and if people don't like them, they can get the hell out." He wasn't policing anybody, and he didn't believe in martial law. People were all in or out right now; that was the only way he knew how to move forward. If they survived the Rippers and the local rebel groups on his ass, then he'd figure out a more democratic way of living in the future.

She punched him, not so gently, on the chest. "You didn't kick me out."

"Well now." He slid a hand through her hair, enjoying her involuntary shudder. "I can't let you leave, can I? You're too valuable and too dangerous. So I can either cage you, which I don't want to do, or I can make sure you understand, on a rather basic level, the repercussions of crossing me." He caressed down her flank to squeeze her firm ass, hiding a smile when she hissed. "We live in primitive times, darlin'. You won't challenge me again."

"But that's . . . I mean, that is—"

"Effective," he finished for her. "Are you going to cross me again?"

Her expression said *definitely.* "You may get more of a fight next time, you know."

"And you'll get more of a beating," he finished easily,

flattening his hand over one buttock. Heat filled his palm, and when she growled, he squeezed harder.

"You know, I don't think making battery perfectly okay is the way to start a new society," she mumbled.

Perhaps not. He continued his exploration to her smooth thighs, smiling at her hitch of breath. "I'm not trying for a new society—we're still in survival mode, baby." Hell. The last thing he'd ever be was a societal leader. His time as ruler, as commander, was temporary and born of necessity. "If it makes you feel better, you're the only woman I've battered."

"Except for the woman you choked out," Lynne snapped.

"True." But the two situations were different. Or maybe the two women were different. He frowned, not liking where his thoughts led. Lynne Harmony was different.

Not wanting to delve deeper into his motivations, he quickly switched topics, to one that had been eating at him. "Lynne?"

"What?"

"Who do you want me to kill?"

That quickly, she shut down. An impressive veil dropped over her expressive eyes, and her face went cold. "I'm not ready to share."

Interesting. "All right. Then how about you tell me why there's such a hurry to get to Myriad?"

She mumbled something he couldn't quite catch.

"You said there were people who wanted to destroy any hope for a cure," Jax continued, his heart beating harder.

"There are."

"Do they know about Myriad?" he asked, his instincts flaring.

"I think so," she whispered, pressing her lips together. "But as far as I know, nobody has the location. It has to be in the documents you took."

He shook his head. "With our luck, probably not."

She licked her lips and dropped her gaze to his mouth. Tension hummed around them.

Good to know they were on the same page, no matter how briefly. Grabbing another condom from his discarded jeans, he quickly sheathed himself.

She watched him, eyes alert, lips curved, no protest.

He rolled her over and flattened himself against her front, pinning her in place. Her lithe body, a bit too thin from traveling, nevertheless softened beneath him. Lust roared into his cock. "Why aren't you ready to share any of the facts you have, and especially the person you'd like killed?"

She snuggled her butt into the bed, cascading wetness across his balls. "I'm still weighing my options and haven't decided on the right course of action."

Now that sounded like the scientist he figured her to be. "Interesting. You think you actually have options?"

She met his gaze levelly, easily, so many secrets in her deep eyes, his instincts sprang alert.

His head lifted. "Lynne."

He'd spanked her, he'd seen her cry, and he'd fucked her into oblivion. Yet the woman eyed him with no hesitation, no caution. Admiration and warning ticked through him. He took a deep breath. "Have I given you any indication I'm somebody you want to take on?"

She stretched her back, elongating smooth muscles. "Have I given you any indication I'm afraid of you?" A quick blink of devastatingly intelligent eyes caught him up short. "I know you're in charge here in your little fiefdom, but I've survived more than your very worst, Jax Mercury."

Brilliance sizzled from her. In his time of war, in the fighting, he'd seen *might* win every battle. Yet looking in her eyes, in the absolute confidence she exuded, he suddenly remembered a time, not so long ago, when intelligence ruled. For now, he couldn't help but be intrigued—and challenged.

So he slowly, smoothly, slid inside her. Conquering in the

most primitive way. Yet as he reached home, as her internal walls gripped him with enough heat to make him grit his teeth, he wondered who'd been captured.

He'd dated tough women, really tough. On the streets and then in the service. And he'd dated a couple of really intelligent women. But the combination of so much brain and courage, he hadn't seen before.

Her hand flattened over the tattoo on his chest and down his left arm. "I see 20 in here, but there are so many lines crossing over the mark. Why didn't you just get rid of it?"

He glanced down at the dark lines. "Twenty is my past and has marked me, so I kept it but showed how I'd changed. The 44 is from my unit . . . something just we knew, and it changed me more than I would've thought possible." At least before Scorpius. "We can't erase where we've been."

"Ah. And the Vanguard tattoo?" She traced the lines across his other arm with her fingers. "The sword behind the shield has a scorpion for a handle." She tapped the heart in the center of the shield that held the word VANGUARD. "A scorpion?"

"I figured it fit, considering Scorpius has altered us all."

Her thighs gripped him, and she slid her feet around him to press her heels into his back. "I'm smart and I'm tough, Jax."

He paused, deep inside her, to focus on the hint of vulnerability in her voice as her words mirrored his thoughts. "I'm aware of that."

A pretty pink dashed across her high cheekbones. "Don't hurt me."

The plea, made as a statement, tunneled deep into him and planted hard. He closed his eyes. Of its own volition, his body began to move. He dropped his forehead to hers, skin to skin, heart-to-heart, and started to thrust. Slow and powerful, he shoved inside her, a sense of urgency and coming home surrounding him.

He altered his angle, and she gasped. His lips formed a smile against her damp skin, and he did it again. Caught up in the moment, caught up in the woman, he pounded harder, allowing them both to just feel. Enough thinking.

She broke first, his name a cry on her lips. The vibrations clawed into him, and he pushed deep, coming hard.

They panted against each other for the briefest of moments, their heartbeats slamming to the same rhythm.

He fell to the side, his gaze captured by the blue glow. Holding his hand over her heart, he counted the beats. "Amazing."

She shut her eyes and struggled for air. "That's one description."

"I've heard rumors of how the blue happened, but what's the truth?"

She rolled over onto her stomach and stretched her arms above her head, revealing her long, smooth back. "I don't want to talk about it." The pillow muffled her voice.

He had to get to work, but instead flattened his hand between her shoulder blades. Blue glimmered between his fingers. They should start at the beginning. "Did the Scorpius bacteria really come from a meteorite, or did the government create a biological weapon?"

She sighed and turned her head to face him. "Meteorite. A group of Stanford students went meteorite hunting in the Nevada desert, which was quite common. They found a meteorite that had probably fallen after the Scorpius comet passed by, and they cut it open, letting loose the bacteria."

So the CDC had been telling the truth. "The story seems impossible."

She shrugged against his hand. "Not really. NASA had been worried we're sending bacteria into space with every shuttle mission, and we've successfully experimented on bacteria living in space."

"Yeah, but really? Bacteria from outer space."

She snorted. "Everything on our planet came from outer space, Jax. All the bacteria here. It's totally plausible."

When she put it like that, he guessed it made sense. "The strain was instantly deadly? Without any mutations caused by the government?"

"Yes. Scorpius killed 99 percent of the people infected."

"Did you create the Scorpius strain that turned your heart blue?"

She shut her eyes. "Yes. My team at the CDC took the original strain and mutated it in an effort to find a cure—colored it blue. The mutated strain was special and one of a kind, and no matter how hard we tried to copy it, we couldn't."

"Why not?"

She sighed. "We used DNA from a rare squid, and it appears the little monster had a mutation of its own, and we were never able to find another one. Well, we didn't have a chance to find one before all hell broke loose, you know? I'm sure there are more out there somewhere, but now, how will we ever find them? And do we care? I mean, I'm not immune, and I don't seem to have any gifts except for a blue heart."

He nodded. "I guess. It seems like you have to be different, even if we haven't figured out why yet. So, what happened after you created the mutation?"

"A lab aide, not even my aide, purposely infected me before going on a rampage to spread the contagion."

"Was he crazy?"

"Yes. He'd been infected, was one of the people who'd become a sociopath. I mean, if he wasn't one already." She sighed. "Scorpius is capable of stripping the frontal cortex of a victim and turning him or her into a serial killer. We tried to figure out who and why, but as with any illness, it affects different people differently."

"Where is the guy who infected you now?" Jax asked softly.

"I have no clue. Zach was captured and secured somewhere to be studied by the government, and I don't know what happened to him when everything went south."

Jax caressed down to the small of her waist. Small. Definitely delicate. "Is Zach the person you want me to kill?"

She opened her eyes and seemed to stare through him. "If you ever run across Zach Barter, microbiologist, feel free to cut off his head. But no, he's not the one you bargained to end for me."

End? "Kill."

She blinked. "Excuse me?"

"If you're contracting for me to take a life, then you're not allowed euphemisms. *Kill*. You want me to kill."

Fire lit her eyes. "Yes. I want you to kill." No hesitation, no regret in her tone. But fear? Yeah, enough fear filled her eyes to amount to terror.

He pressed against her tailbone, his fingers extending across her waist. "I won't let anybody hurt you, Lynne." It was as close to a personal promise as he could make in his current situation, but he meant every word.

"I know," she said softly.

Even if they hadn't slept together, he'd protect her as one of his own. Sex did create a deeper motivation, and a smart woman would know that. He moved his hand. "Is that why you slept with me?"

She angled her head to better study him. "I've made it this far and this long without bartering my body, Jax. I slept with you because it felt good, and you intrigued me."

He grimaced. "Before the world disintegrated, no way would somebody like you and somebody like me end up naked together."

She rolled her eyes. "You don't know that. When I worked for the CDC, I met a lot of soldiers."

Yeah, but not one from the streets who'd done more killing by the time he'd turned twenty than anybody he'd ever met. "Nah. I would've asked you out, and you would've told me to get lost."

She bit her lip. "You would not have asked me out, and you know it. I would've been a little too, well, boring and studious for you."

Nope. He would've wanted her on sight, just like he had the day before. "Who did you date?"

"I didn't date."

Lie. The first lie she'd told him, and it was about whom she'd dated. Interesting. His back stiffened. "Please tell me you want me to kill somebody dangerous and infected by Scorpius and not some ex who betrayed you." Jax couldn't have read her that badly, could he?

She met his gaze levelly. "Everything is about Scorpius these days, isn't it?"

Good damn point. "Have you slept with the person you want dead?"

She didn't answer.

Well, shit.

A sharp rap on the door jerked up his head. "Saved by the door," he muttered. He maneuvered over Lynne and yanked on jeans he couldn't fasten with the semi hard-on still torturing him. Padding barefoot to the door, he glanced back to make sure Lynne was covered.

She lay in the bed, the covers at her neck, her hair mussed, looking like a woman who'd been well loved to within an inch of her life.

He grinned.

She rolled her eyes.

He turned to the door. "What?"

"Jax? It's Sami. I have news."

Jax slid open the door to one of his top soldiers, Sami, his only female lieutenant, handed him a hastily drawn map.

"C Team was out scouting near Pacific Palisades and found another food depot controlled by some unknowns."

He took the map and frowned, studying the rough lines. "We should get more intel before deciding what to do." He focused back on her.

Sami stared at his chest, her tongue darting out to lick her lips. About twenty-five years old, the former LAPD rookie had pinned her thick black hair in two braids hanging down her back. She had deep brown eyes and sassy freckles spattered across angled cheekbones.

This was the first time he'd seen her blush. "You okay?"

She swallowed. "Ah, yeah. Just never seen you right out of bed." Her gaze rose. "Want to go back?"

He stilled. "Um—"

She stiffened her shoulders and nudged open the door. "I'm serious, Jax—" Her voice caught as she took in Lynne. "Who the fuck are you?"

Lynne, naked and wearing razor burn on her chin, lifted an eyebrow like any three-star general questioned by a subordinate. "I'm unaware of that being any of your business. Who the hell are you?"

Sami sputtered and rounded on Jax.

He took a deep breath. At least two guns and three knives showed along Sami's fit form. "Can we talk about this later?"

She planted both hands onto trim hips. "No. Let's talk about it now. There's a strange bitch in your bed, and considering I'm in charge of take-ins, I'd like to know who the hell she is and why she's here."

Amusement, dark and annoyed, filled Lynne's eyes. "I'd get out of bed and introduce myself, but that would just piss off handsome here. And according to him, I don't really want to piss him off. You know. The whole 'you won't like me when I'm angry' kind of thing."

Jax shot her a look that would've immediately made a recruit piss his pants back in the service. While he appreciated her keeping the blue heart hidden, he didn't like the fury emanating from her well-kissed skin.

"Now, Jax," Sami ordered.

Oh hell no. He pivoted until her back was against the door. "She's none of your fucking business, Sami. When I want her properly taken in, I'll let you know. Get back to work."

The soldier opened her mouth to argue, and he stepped even closer, erasing all expression. She gulped. Her skin lost color, and she shot Lynne a hard look. Lifting her head, Sami sidled past him and stomped down the hallway. He shut the door and crossed his arms. "Was that necessary?"

Anger, bright and obvious, nearly succeeded in hiding the wounded look in Lynne's eyes. "I take it you fuck your way around your people?"

Shit. He truly didn't owe the woman an explanation, and having her believe he was a complete asshole suited his plans. But that hurt look did him in. "You're the only woman I've had sex with in the last year."

A frown furrowed between her eyebrows. "Bullshit."

He sighed and rested his head back against the door. "Listen, Lynne Harmony, and listen good, because I ain't saying it again. I haven't fucked anybody else and have no intention of doing so, because it creates an issue I can't afford right now. However, what happened between us already happened, so there's no going back. I like you, I enjoyed the hell out of being inside you, and I'd like to be there again. But the decision is yours." He lowered his chin to meet her gaze.

She studied him, her eyes clearing. "You also don't go around spanking people, now do you?"

He lifted an eyebrow. "No."

"You wear dominance like most guys wear boots." She rubbed her reddened chin. "Were you all into that BDSM stuff before Scorpius hit?"

He barked out a laugh. Damn. He'd smiled more in the last day than he had in months. "No, I wasn't into that BDSM shit. Labels have never worked for me. Although if I was with a woman, and she needed her ass reddened, I took care of it."

She sputtered.

Yeah, he liked that expression. A lot. With a brain like Lynne's, probably not many people had the ability to catch her off guard.

She shook her head. "You're unbelievable."

He shrugged. "Probably. Again, the decision on whether or not to continue this is yours."

She swept a bare arm around the small apartment. "Right. But I'm pretty much a prisoner here."

He grabbed a shirt from the counter and yanked it over his head. "Stay here for an hour or so while I talk to my lieutenants before announcing your arrival to the group at large." Too many people already knew about Lynne, and he needed to get out in front of the story. "You can look at research afterward."

She blanched. "They'll riot and want me kicked out."

"You stay." He softened his voice as he slipped into his boots and buttoned his jeans. "If they want to leave, they may do so. Period."

Her chin lifted. "What if I want to leave?"

"No." Keeping her against her will went against all the standards he was trying to establish, but she was valuable, and she was vulnerable. So she stayed put. "Sorry."

"You don't look sorry."

He gave a half nod in acknowledgment. With her knowledge, he finally had a chance of deciphering all the confiscated research, and with her in his bed, he had a chance to stay human. Maybe. She brought out dueling parts of him, but maybe she could help him remain sane. "We made a deal, Lynne." Although she still hadn't told him who his target was.

She pulled the sheet up closer to her neck. "I've escaped meaner guys than you, Jax Mercury."

Man, she was cute. Naked and fragile, spitting fire at him. He grinned. "Fair enough, and since we're being so honest here, feel free to make a break for it." He opened the door and tossed over his shoulder, "Only one of us is gonna like the result of that decision." The door closed on the echoes of her hiss.

Chapter Ten

We are going to have peace
even if we have to fight for it.

—Dwight D. Eisenhower

She had to get to those records, and now. After pacing all morning and trying to figure out a way to escape from Jax's room, Lynne tried to do yoga and create a plan. What in the hell had she been thinking sleeping with the man? Even as her mind rebelled, her body finally felt human again. There were health benefits to good sex, and she needed all the help she could get.

But time was working against her, and she had to find Myriad, even if it meant escaping Vanguard first. There was always an armed soldier in the hallway, so that route was out. The window, on the other hand . . .

She finished the Downward Dog pose just as the locks disengaged on the door. She had to fight to stay still. Man, she was a klutz.

Jax stepped inside and paused. Stress cut harsh lines into the sides of his mouth. "Yoga?"

"Yes." Heat flushed into her face, and she stood, trying to keep her balance. "Helps with brain activity, heart health, and general well-being." She sounded like a damn commercial. "Shut up."

He held out both hands. "I didn't say anything."

She tugged down the T-shirt over the yoga pants that had been left outside the door earlier. "Thank you for the clothes."

"Weren't mine." He glanced down at her ragged tennis shoes. "We'll go shoe shopping tomorrow."

Funny. She looked up to his face, and was swamped again by vulnerability, wanting the focus off her. She glanced at the picture on the wall and edged closer to the door. "Your brother?"

Jax rocked back on his heels. "Marcus. Four years younger than me." Pain. Definite pain echoed in his low tones.

"He's gone?" Lynne asked softly.

"Yeah." Jax's expression smoothed out into . . . nothing. "We called him 'Slam' because he was an amazing baseball player."

"He looks like you." Handsome and already strong at a young age.

"We had the same mom. Different dads and no clue who they might've been." Jax rubbed his chin. "When I went into the service, I wrote when I could and promised to come back for him. I failed to protect him."

Lynne shivered. "Nobody saw Scorpius coming."

"Marcus didn't die from Scorpius." Jax eyed her, the hard set of his jaw not inviting questions. "Want to get out of here?"

Yes. God, yes. Her body stilled. "And go where?"

"I thought I would take you to the nearest lab to meet Tace so you can start going through documents, after a slight detour."

She studied his veiled expression. "What detour?"

He gestured her into the hall. "Rumors about your arrival have surfaced, and I want to update my head soldiers now. Seeing you is the best way."

She gulped and wished for a power suit with high heels.

Her heart beat faster. Finally. She could finally get to those damn records and find Myriad. Hopefully before the people after her found where she was hiding. "Fine." Sweeping by him, she turned down the hallway toward the stairs.

He slipped his hand over hers.

Shock caught her breath. He wanted to hold hands? Because they'd slept together or just to keep her in line? Warmth engulfed her hand as if they were a normal couple walking together. She should probably tug free, but she didn't want to be cold and alone. Perhaps a few moments of feeling safe and normal wouldn't hurt, so she left her hand in his, uneasy with the pleasure it provided.

He led her down two flights of stairs, through a twisting hallway, and into an empty room littered with overturned milk crates. She only tripped once. Several industrial safes lined one entire wall, and boards covered the windows.

"This is my war room. It used to be attorney offices. I took out all of the walls except for the back office, which is where we use the ham radio." Jax tilted his head toward the safes. "Guns."

"Oh." Lynne followed him to what appeared to be the front of the room.

He kicked a milk crate closer. "Have a seat."

She turned and gingerly sat, biting the inside of her lip to keep from wincing.

He grinned. "Sore?"

"Fuck you," she retorted without enough heat.

"You already did." He pointed to the hand-drawn map on the far wall. "We have seven blocks of territory, and the soldiers are housed along the perimeter."

Lynne squinted and began memorizing the layout. "Most folks would have put the main headquarters dead center."

"If we're attacked, I need to get there fast, and if any enemy infiltrates to the center, we're fucked." He stepped partially in front of her as men and women filed into the room, all armed, all wearing dark and torn clothing with a multitude of guns and knives strapped to their bodies. A vigilante uniform.

Sami swept inside, next to a broad blond man, and immediately lost her smile. Her glare lasered past Jax to Lynne, and Lynne met her gaze evenly. If the small soldier thought she could intimidate Lynne so easily, gun or not, she was mistaken.

Jax waited until about twenty people had filed in. The last one, the huge black guy who'd covered Jax's back in the firefight, shut the door.

Everyone seemed to ignore Jax and focus on her. Her hands dampened, and she wiped them on her borrowed yoga pants.

"You're my head soldiers, and you get the information first. If you decide to stay, it's your job to relay the same information to your squads." Jax cleared his throat. "Listen up. I'm going to say this once, and then you have a decision to make. This is Lynne Harmony, she's under my protection, and she's staying here. You can stay, you can go, and you have one night to make your decision."

Dead silence, filled with tension, spread from one end of the room to the other.

Lynne remained perfectly still and tried to keep her expression clear. Her lips wanted to tremble, so she tightened her jaw until her teeth ached.

A redheaded guy with a long scar down his face stood in the back. "How do we know that's her?"

"It's her, Red," Jax said.

Manny, the guy who'd driven the car the other day, nodded. "I saw her heart. She's Lynne Harmony."

The big blond guy who'd covered Jax's back in the fight stood. "I'm staying."

Sami jumped to her feet. "I say we talk about this. The

woman is not only a carrier, but the distributor of a virus that killed billions of people."

Lynne stood. "Bacterium."

Sami whirled on her. "Excuse me?"

"Scorpius is a bacterium, not a virus." Lynne lifted a shoulder. "There is only one strain of Scorpius, no matter what rumors you've heard. I didn't create the strain, nor did I spread it, but I have survived it when others haven't." She kept her voice level.

"You seem all cut up about that," Sami spat out.

Lynne smiled. "You don't know anything about me."

"I know you're a carrier," Sami returned.

"I am." Lynne glanced around the group as a whole. "Anybody who has been infected and lived through the fever is now a carrier, and that's the truth. About one-third of the population before the illness carried staph or MRSA, and only people with wounds or weak immune systems caught those."

The blond guy smiled, his gaze warm. "Do you think there's a cure for Scorpius?"

Lynne faltered. She didn't want to lie or give false hope. "If there is, it'll be a long time before we figure it out."

A murmur fluttered through the room.

Jax cut a hard look over his shoulder. "There might be a cure, and we're going to keep looking."

"Absolutely," Lynne said softly.

Sami shook her head. "There's a reward on her head. We could get more vitamin B, guns, and food if we turn her back in to her own people."

"No." Jax crossed his arms. "She's our best chance for a cure."

Lynne tried to remain calm. If there had been a cure, it would've been discovered at the CDC months ago. She'd tried everything. The best they could realistically hope for was a way to ameliorate the effects of the disease. "As far as we can tell, the only sure way to be infected is to be bitten."

Sami hissed. "Looks like you have a good set of chompers."

"I have no interest in biting you," Lynne said dryly.

Sami's gaze turned sly. "Since you're sleeping with our leader here, he has a good chance of being bitten, and we wouldn't know it."

More murmurs.

The blond guy glanced at Jax and lifted both eyebrows.

Jax settled his shoulders. A vein swelled along his neck, and his stance widened. "I've already survived the fever."

A small roar whipped through the crowd. Several folks reached for weapons.

Jax's two pals in the back of the room whipped out guns, pointing them at the ground, clearly preparing to defend him.

"Hold on." Jax held up a hand. "There will be no shooting. The first person to lift a gun gets shot by me."

Nobody even twitched.

Whoa. So he could get to his gun and shoot somebody first? Lynne scanned the crowd. The people believed him, because not one raised a weapon. Even so, the tension grew so thick the air seemed clogged. Her heart sped up and adrenaline flooded her system.

The redheaded guy's mouth gaped open. "You never said a word."

Jax lowered his chin. "Have I infected anybody?"

"Well, no," Red said.

"See? If I don't bite you, you don't get infected. I'd bet more than a few of you have been keeping the same secret." He turned to the blond guy, who just shrugged.

Was he the main medical doctor? Lynne pursed her lips. "Even when a patient survives the infection, Scorpius remains in saliva, blood, and semen. Keep those to yourself, and you won't spread the disease."

Jax crossed his arms. "We're done talking about this. You have tonight to decide whether you're staying or going."

Sami pressed both hands on her hips. "I say we vote."

The air changed. The atmosphere grew heavy, and tension emanated from Jax Mercury.

Lynne swallowed and barely kept her knees from buckling. Why had she stood?

Jax settled his stance, threat and violence in every line of his hard muscled body. "If you're under the impression that this is a democracy, get the fuck out now. I'm in charge, and you'll follow my rules if you want to stay." His gaze swept the entire room. "Tace and Wyatt have already decided to stay with me. If any of you decide to go, you'll be given a backpack of provisions to take with you."

As he concluded, the blond guy and the broad black guy maneuvered toward the front of the room to flank him. Must be Tace and Wyatt.

Lynne found herself behind a wall of muscled men, their message perfectly clear. She peered around the side of the blond to see reactions.

The sound of milk crates scraping against concrete filled the silence, and soon people filed out. A seriously hot Native American guy was the last to reach the door, his movements graceful, his gaze not leaving her.

"That's Raze," Jax told her quietly as the man left. "I think he's on our side. Maybe."

Finally, the three men turned toward her.

"Tace Justice," the blond said with a Texas twang, holding out a hand. Sizzling blue eyes sparkled in a rugged face. "Former military medic and current only doctor with combat experience here." He frowned. "Of course, that's changing. More and more combat, you know."

She shook his hand. "Lynne Harmony, former head of the

CDC division of infectious diseases and current carrier of Scorpius. Only one with a blue heart, however."

The other guy held out a hand bigger than her great-grandma's apple-patterned roll platter. "Wyatt Quaid. Second soldier in command, I guess."

She smiled and shook his hand, appreciating his gentle touch. Had he been a soldier, too? "Nice to meet you. What did you do before all this?"

He blinked.

Jax chuckled, and Tace full out grinned.

Crap. "Not that it matters, I just—"

"He played football," Tace drawled. "Not well, but . . ."

"Super Bowl champ, asshole," Wyatt snarled. "Well, before I went to the Niners."

Oh, so he was famous. Lynne tried to smile. "I didn't much keep up on sports, to be honest, but I'm sure you were really good at the game."

He lifted one dark eyebrow. "Why's that?"

"Dude, you're huge," she burst out. Heat climbed into her face. "I mean, you move gracefully, and—"

Jax took her arm. "Quit while you're ahead."

She closed her lips.

"Did you watch any sports?" Wyatt asked, his lips twitching.

"Um, water polo," she admitted.

The three men all looked at her with identical expressions of surprise.

Jax coughed out first. "Water polo?"

She crossed her arms. "I went to Pepperdine as an under-grad, and water polo was big there. The combination of grace and muscle needed to play is impressive."

Tace snorted.

Wyatt grimaced. "Does Pepperdine even have a football team?"

She shook her head. "No."

"Geez." Wyatt turned and headed for the door. "When are we telling the medical personnel and civilians about our water-polo-lovin' scientist making her home with us?"

Jax sobered. "Tomorrow. I want a count of how many soldiers are staying before we tell the rest."

"Water polo," Wyatt muttered, disappearing out the door.

Lynne rocked back on her heels. "I can tell, your people love me."

Jax rubbed his whiskered chin. "They'll do as I tell them. Well, most of them besides Wyatt. I think you've blown it with him. He's a great soldier, and a good guy, but his ego and Super Bowl ring make him think everybody should know who he is. Or rather, was."

Tace chuckled. "I knew who he was, but I was a huge Dallas Cowboys fan. Took my nearly getting shot by a Ripper for him to like me." Tace jerked his arm toward the door. "How about we retire to the medical room, go through the records you requested, and talk shop?"

Lynne wavered. "Don't tell me. You'd like to take blood." It had been months since somebody had stuck her with a needle, and she'd enjoyed the reprieve.

Tace shook his head, his smile charming. "Gotta be honest in that we don't have the facilities to do anything with your blood. But I thought maybe you could catch me up on everything you know."

Jax pivoted to face them. "What about a cure?"

Tace sighed. "I've told you, pard. There's no cure at this point. There's the bacteria, the illness, and then the recovery. No cure."

Lynne blew out air, her foot tapping. She had to get to those documents. "Maybe. We never found a cure, Jax. Containment and treatment are the paths we ended up finding."

Jax and Tace shared a look Lynne couldn't decipher. "What?" she asked, her stomach roiling.

"We're out of B," Tace said softly.

Lynne gaped. "There are four research facilities near L.A. that were ordered to mass-produce B the second we discovered its importance."

Jax's head jerked back. "We raided Hyroden Labs, and Cruz raided Phillip Labs. Those are the only two we've known about."

"In the L.A. area, the CDC also contracted with Philter Drug Company and Baker and Baker Incorporated," Lynne said.

Tace's eyebrows lifted. "Baker and Baker was a shampoo company."

"Their parent company was Washington Pharmaceuticals," Lynne said quietly.

Jax ran a hand through his hair. "We need the location of Baker, as any place with *drug* in the name was raided almost instantly. What do you know about Baker?"

Lynne shook her head. "Just a name on a list. They had an impressive research and development program, and we ordered them on B immediately. I don't know how much they created or how much they shipped before shipping stopped. There may be nothing left."

"We have to try. Find out the location," Jax said, lips tightening into a white line. "You two do your thing in the lab and update me later. We go at midnight."

Tace shook his head. "We won't know who's with us until tomorrow."

"Small group, then. Wyatt, me, and Sami, if she stays. I'd like to take Raze and see what he can do."

"What about me?" Tace asked.

"Can't lose you, Doc. You're too important." Jax sighed. "We need to get a few more medical personnel somehow."

"No problem. I'll order a couple up on the Internet," Tace said.

"Asshole," Jax muttered without heat, moving toward the other corridor. "And, Lynne?" he asked, turning.

She turned her head. "What?"

"I have neither the time nor manpower to keep a guard on you at all times. Promise me that for at least the next twenty-four hours, you won't try to make a break for it." His eyes darkened to the color of warmed whiskey.

Her shoulders went back. He trusted her? "What makes you think I'll keep a promise?"

He lifted one broad shoulder. "Gut feeling."

She breathed out, her chest heavy with a sweet warmth she didn't want to examine. "I promise."

His grin flashed a dimple she hadn't noticed before. "Thank you."

With that dimple, with that trust, she suddenly felt bound to Jax Mercury with stronger ties than when he'd been thrusting inside her.

Chapter Eleven

*The inevitable conclusion for our species
doesn't mean we won't fight—and fight hard
to survive the unsurvivable.*

—Dr. Franklin Xavier Harmony

Jax jogged into the combat infirmary, his gut swirling. Three new victims had succumbed to Scorpius somehow, and right now they thrashed uncontrollably in makeshift beds in the inner hospital. They had to get more vitamin B, stat.

Darkness climbed across the sky, and his nerves settled as he planned the midnight raid.

He hustled around the corner to see Lynne and Tace in the makeshift lab, papers and graphs spread out before them. Discarded paper plates and bowls showed they'd spent all day working.

His mind had gone to her several times during the day, and he needed to knock that shit off. When he'd first found her on the deserted highway, so brave and alone, he'd instantly been drawn to her, but he hadn't considered that he'd genuinely like her.

If she was lying to him, if she was playing him, she was a master at it.

And she'd pay.

She glanced up from a graph, and her pretty green eyes focused on him. "What's the frown about?"

Tace reached for the gun at his side to check the clip. "That's Jax's normal expression. Haven't you noticed?"

She shrugged.

Jax settled his stance. "Tell me you found Myriad."

"Not yet." Lynne pushed back from the table and shoved hair from her eyes.

Damn it. He glanced at Tace. "Update me with what you do know."

Tace gave a mock salute. "Of course. We've mapped out known B manufacturing plants in California, Nevada, Oregon, and Washington. Some are under the radar, but Lynne knew about them, and if they still have stock, we have a chance to replenish our coffers. Baker and Baker still looks like the best bet."

Jax straightened. "If they don't?"

"We're screwed," Tace said simply.

Lynne fumbled through a stack of papers to give Jax a handwritten list. "Here's a breakdown of natural foods with heavy vitamin B content. I heard you say yesterday there's another food depot around here."

"Yeah, but I doubt we'll find greens or even meat," he said slowly.

"What about wild game?" Lynne asked. "Aren't you planning to move north at some point?"

"Not for a while unless we're forced to move. Right now, we're in the safest place to wait while Scorpius does its thing." By infecting the rest of the population and either killing, turning, or changing them. "I don't want to mess with the Mercenaries to the north, either."

She paled. "I see."

He wanted to reassure her, to appease the guilt flitting across her expressive face. But really, what words existed? While she'd been trying to cure the infection, the CDC had allowed the bacteria to spread. Accidental, sure. But his words wouldn't appease her guilt. Only survival would. He bent to look at the location of Baker and Baker. "One problem."

Tace winced. "Just one?"

"Yeah. According to this, Baker and Baker is located on the other side of Twenty territory." Jax stretched his neck, hissing as his vertebrae popped.

"Of course it is," Tace muttered. "Any chance they've already raided it?"

"Sure, but it's in the business portion of town, and they probably haven't gone raiding for shampoo. If we didn't know about the B, Cruz doesn't either."

"Probably," Tace said with a grimace. "If you're heading through or around Twenty, you need every trained soldier, and that includes me. If something happens, we have another doctor now at headquarters." He tilted his head toward Lynne.

Jax blanched. "No one knows or trusts her, Tace. Can't leave her as the doctor, and the doctors in the middle of the compound are overworked." Plus, he didn't know for sure she'd stay, now did he? If something happened to Jax, Tace would have to take point with her.

The idea of anybody else with her, in her bed, punched him squarely in the chest. Not that she'd sleep with Tace. Even so, the intensity of his reaction gave him pause.

He needed to get himself under control and now. "Any other news from the CDC files?"

"Not yet." Lynne gestured toward several boxes of papers lining the far wall. "We've just started going through the research. It's entirely possible you'll find some good information if you raid Baker and Baker. I can't imagine the labs were this close in proximity and didn't at least communicate with each other as well as with the CDC. To share supplies as things went bad, at a minimum."

Tace slammed his clip back into his gun. "Did you feed Marvin?"

"Yes." Jax tossed the paper back onto the table.

Lynne lifted an eyebrow. "Marvin?"

Amusement he didn't have time to enjoy tickled Jax's lips. "Marvin is a lion that apparently escaped from a zoo somewhere. We leave him meat around the perimeter, and I'm fairly certain he's eaten more than one Ripper trying to get in."

Lynne frowned. "A lion. Wow."

Running boot steps echoed in the hallway outside, and Jax turned to see Red Dolan barreling toward him. He half pivoted to protect Lynne.

Red lurched to a stop, his face flushed, his eyes wide. He'd been a redneck bar owner until Scorpius hit, but the guy could shoot and had good knife skills. "The Snyder kid has gone into a fever and convulsions."

The world narrowed in focus. Holy shit. The girl who Cruz had taken. "Cruz infected Haylee?" Jax spat out.

Red gulped. "Looks like it."

Holy fucking damn it. Jax moved and launched into a run, acutely aware of Tace and Lynne on his heels. "Where is she?"

"The soldiers scouting the interior didn't have time to get her to the main hospital, so they just put her here in the room by the back door," Red coughed out. "They went back to patrolling."

The makeshift triage area was usually used for wounded or ill soldiers. The main containment area for recently exposed victims was several blocks in, but he didn't have time to take the kid there. Jax ran down the hallway and hustled into a room on the left.

April Snyder sat by a bed, tears streaking down her face, a fresh bruise across her neck showing where he'd choked her out earlier. She looked about eighteen, pale and wan, and not old enough to have a teenage daughter. Her hand covered Haylee's.

The girl tossed in the fever, her cheeks scarlet, sweat pouring down her smooth skin. A series of low moans escaped her.

Tace elbowed past Jax with a knife in his hand. He lifted the girl's eyes to show the pupils dilated and red striations marring the red. "Where were you bitten, sweetheart?" He rolled up her sleeves and then cut open her shirt, finding nothing. He turned her over. Nothing.

Jax yanked off the sheet and slid up her leggings. A perfect bite mark—human—marred her right calf. Somebody in Cruz's camp, maybe even Cruz, had bitten her deep. Somebody who'd survived Scorpius. "Damn it. Why didn't she say anything?"

"Probably too scared." Tace wiped his chin. "We need B injections to slow down the illness. Now." He hustled across the room and grabbed a syringe of liquid—undoubtedly morphine. He pushed the stopper, and a little liquid spilled. "This will take away some of the pain, but nothing can help the headache that's about to occur."

Jax pivoted. "I'll get Wyatt and lead a team right now to hit the labs for B. You try to bring down her fever, if possible, and keep her here. No need to go inland." He glanced at Lynne.

"I can help," Lynne said. "We need ice, if there's any. If not, cool compresses."

April released her daughter to run for the door. "I'll see what I can find."

Jax shared a hard look with Tace. They didn't have cold water, much less ice. Maybe it was time to move north to a cooler climate, even with the Mercs waiting.

The girl groaned and rolled over.

Tace dropped to his haunches and smoothed damp hair away from her face. "It's okay, Haylee, we'll get you figured out."

Her eyelids shot open, and she grabbed his arm.

Jax moved as fast as he could, but before he could reach her, she jerked upright and sank her teeth into Tace's arm.

Tace howled and yanked free with such force he flew across the room and smashed into the wall.

Shit, shit, shit. Jax planted Haylee back down and reached for the straps placed out of reach beneath the bed, just in case of infection in a soldier. She fought him, gyrating and bucking, with more strength than a normal teenager should wield. Finally, he secured her in place.

Growls and inhuman sputtering ripped from her throat. Many of the newly infected tried to bite and infect others— it was part of the disease.

Jax turned and stepped over Tace's legs to pull him to his feet. Tace's arm bled profusely from a perfectly sized teenage-girl bite. "Fuck." He all but dragged Tace to the sink and dumped a standing pitcher of water over his arm. Rusty, dirty, trickling water.

Tace punched his arm. "That won't help, brother."

Jax ignored him and reached for the industrial soap, pouring it generously on the bite marks.

Tace winced and threw an elbow. "You know that won't help."

Jax swallowed, fear gripping his chest. He couldn't lose Tace. "I know." Without another word, he dragged Tace to the bed next to Haylee and set him down. Reaching for the hidden restraints, he quickly secured one of his best soldiers.

Tace didn't fight him or utter a word of protest. For some reason, that made the entire situation more painful.

"You're healthy, and you're updated on B, right?" Jax cinched the chest strap tighter.

Tace winced.

Jax paused, and heat exploded in his chest. "Are you fucking kidding me?"

"We ran out, pard," Tace said slowly. "I'm healthy, haven't

been infected, and thought I could wait for the next round. Plus, being updated wouldn't protect me from infection, although it might make the fever easier." He glanced at the girl thrashing on the bed. "Was stupid of me not to watch her closer."

A soft hand glided along Jax's arm, and he glanced down at Lynne.

Her somber gaze remained on Tace, but she leaned into Jax's side. "I'll take good care of him, of them both, until you return with the B. I promise."

His heart eased a tiny fraction. Who could he trust to watch her back while he was gone, now that Tace was down? He frowned.

She squeezed, and her lips turned down. "I won't make a break for it."

He blinked. She might be a badass survivor, but the woman was seriously sensitive. He hadn't been doubting her word. "You already gave your promise. My worry is for your safety."

She bit her lip. "I've been in danger before. Vitamin B is more important."

It really was, especially now. Tace needed that vitamin. As did Haylee.

Tace grimaced. "My gut feels like somebody just kicked me."

Lynne took a seat between the two patients. "Your head is going to hurt next. Do you have more morphine?"

"Don't waste it on me," Tace said through gritted teeth.

"In the drawer over there." Jax pointed. "We have the syringes ready to go just in case."

Tace shoved his head back on the pillow, and his body went rigid. "I don't want fuckin' morphine, Jax."

"Too bad." Jax stomped across the room and yanked open a drawer to return with a syringe. The least he could do was ease his buddy's pain. Why the hell hadn't he known Tace hadn't taken B? He should've double checked. "Suck it up, Texas." He smoothly slid the needle into Tace's vein and pressed the stopper.

Tace sighed, and his body went limp.

Lynne eyed him. "You're pretty good at that."

Jax exhaled slowly, gaze on his friend. "Not my first time, unfortunately." He tossed the empty syringe across the room and into a trash can.

April rushed back into the room with semiclean and damp towels. "We've been keeping them in the basement where it's kind of cool." She glanced at Tace, secured to the bed. "Oh no. What happened?"

Jax moved from Lynne to slip an arm around April's shoulders and escort her back to her chair. "Haylee bit him. I need you to assist Lynne while we're out securing more vitamin B."

April looked at Lynne, Tace, her daughter, and then back to Jax. "I need a gun."

Jax blinked.

"We might have a problem with Lynne, and I may need to protect her. In fact, we should both have guns." April's eyes hardened. "I'll do what I need to do to protect everyone in this room. You can trust me."

Jax reached down and retrieved Tace's ankle weapon to hand to April and then did the same with his own for Lynne. Both women glanced at the small guns, holding them in hands that shouldn't hold weapons.

He scratched his head. "April, you know how to use that?"

"Point and shoot." She shrugged. "I can do it."

"Lynne?" he asked.

Her gaze met his, filled with nightmares. "I've been trained, and I know how to shoot."

The pain in her eyes hit him right in the gut, so he focused on April again. "What did you do before, well, all of this?"

April snorted. "I was the head of the PTA, the softball team mom, and my husband's helper at his dental office. I did the books."

"Sounds like a nice life," Jax said.

She glanced at her daughter, her shoulders slumping. "It really was."

Jax had already heard the husband had died of Scorpius. "I'm going to shut the door, and you two lock it. Don't open it for anybody but me or Wyatt. I'll leave orders you're to be left alone, and since you have two patients here, people will probably give you a wide berth." He'd take Sami with him so she couldn't harass Lynne.

Here he was already worried about Lynne.

He needed to keep some distance from the wounded scientist or he'd completely lose perspective. If he'd been more on his game, perhaps Tace wouldn't be fighting the fever right now. Women and relationships complicated things, which was why he'd remained alone.

Yet even now, watching Lynne Harmony settle her shoulders, gun in hand, worry in her eyes, he couldn't help but be drawn to her. The urge to place a reassuring kiss on her forehead before he left had him turning on his heel and heading for the door. "Stay in here and stay safe," he said before shutting the door firmly behind him. He waited until the lock engaged before striding down the hallway to find Wyatt.

It was time to hunt.

Chapter Twelve

———◆◆◆———

There is no law
that declares the human species to be immortal.

—Richard E. Leakey and Roger A. Lewin

Two tension-filled hours after Jax had left, Lynne pressed a hand to Tace's sweating forehead, rubbing over the deep creases. His body fought against the restraints, stiffening until his back arched off the bed. Blood beaded on his lips.

Chances were, he was going to die. If he survived, he stood a good chance of going insane. It was hard to imagine the good-natured doctor as a crazy man. If she had vitamin B, she'd shoot him up. Unfortunately, there was nothing to do but ride out the fever and pray he didn't die.

She reached for a cup of water and held it to him. "Don't bite yourself," she tried to murmur in a soothing voice.

He coughed out the liquid, spitting blood.

She sat back, glancing sideways to check on Haylee. The girl had quieted to soft mutterings and incoherent spurts of crying.

Her mother held her hand, lines of fatigue and fear cutting into her face. "I can't believe this," she muttered.

Lynne wiped her brow. "I know. She'll be okay. She's young and in good shape."

April's eyes filled with tears. "I hope so." So much pain filled her voice that Lynne's heart clutched.

April dug out a rough angel figurine and placed it near Haylee. "Little Lena gave me this yesterday. Must've found it in one of the apartments inner territory."

"Lena?" Lynne asked.

April swallowed. "Lost seven-year-old who hangs around soldier headquarters and gives presents. Pretty petite blond who I've kind of taken in. You'll see her, and she'll probably give you some sort of present, although she doesn't speak. She loves Haylee."

Haylee seemed pretty lovable. "What was Haylee like before Scorpius hit?" Lynne asked softly.

April's lips trembled into a parody of a smile. "Amazing. Straight As, good kid, played shortstop on a competitive team." She chuckled. "We traveled all the time—every summer. Don used to say softball was our life, but he was so proud of her. No matter his schedule, he made it to every game."

"How long were you married?" Lynne asked.

"Um, fourteen years." Lynne sobered. "We had Haylee when we were only sixteen, and we got married after she was born." She shrugged. "Grew up in a farming town in the middle of Washington, and there were plenty of people who said we wouldn't make it. But we had Haylee, got married, and then Don went to college. I cleaned houses for a long time to help with bills."

Lynne nodded. "Sounds tough but sweet."

A sad smile lifted April's lips. "Yeah. Then about ten years ago, his dental practice took off, and I quit working. Became a full-time mom." Her brow wrinkled. "Wanted more kids, but it just didn't happen."

"I'm sorry."

"Maybe it's better, considering. We almost made it to the big fifteen year mark. We were planning to celebrate with a trip to the Caribbean." She glanced down at her loose jeans. "Believe it or not, I was working incredibly hard to lose twenty pounds before we hit the beach."

Life from now on, if humanity survived, would be measured as before and after Scorpius had infected the world. "Scorpius bacterium. The ultimate diet," Lynne said.

April snorted. "So true. Who knew?"

Lynne cleared her throat. "For the record, I am sorry about everything."

April rolled her eyes. "From what I understand, none of this was your fault. I mean, unless you're psychic and ignored the signs."

Lynne picked at a string on her yoga pants. "Not psychic."

"Besides, aren't you the one who figured out that vitamin B could help?"

Lynne's stomach recoiled. "Two of us figured it out. My best friend, Nora McDougall, and I studied the research on which medications were known to work on the brain. Which supplements. It was a shot in the dark, but we took a few of those."

April caressed her daughter's arm. "Where is Nora now?"

"I don't know." Lynne rubbed her chest. "Things went bad at the CDC, and she was out on assignment with her husband, and then all hell broke loose. I had to make a run for it, communications were down, and I haven't found her again. God, I hope she's okay."

"She smart like you?" April asked.

Lynne grinned. "Thinks she's smarter and probably is. More importantly, she's not alone. If her husband is still alive, and I'd bet on that Scottish bastard any day, then she's safe."

"Scottish bastard?" April smiled.

"Yes. He's got the coolest brogue even though he moved to the States as a teenager. Went into the service, and he's a badass. If anybody could keep Nora safe, it's him. He was appointed the leader of the Brigade right away, and I hope they're still alive somewhere."

"Do you think the Brigade is still out there?"

Lynne nodded. "I really do." The Brigade was created with top soldiers as the first line of defense against Scorpius, and they'd been working on securing nuclear plants and military facilities before communications went down. Lynne patted Tace's arm when he stirred. "I kind of blackmailed them into getting married. Made it a deathbed wish when my heart first turned blue."

April nodded. "You're a good friend."

"Nora wanted to kill me." Lynne slipped the sheet up over Tace's torso as he shivered. "But I was right, and she needed protection. Plus, it was so obvious they were in love and belonged together."

"Speaking of romance, what's up with you and our illustrious leader?" April squinted.

Lynne swallowed. "Nothing. I mean, he's intriguing and dangerous as hell, and we had a moment. Neither one of us can afford emotions right now."

April smoothed hair from her daughter's forehead. "If you say so. I think emotions have their own agenda, you know? If you can find something real in the hell we're living, you'd be a moron to let it go."

Lynne shook her head. She hadn't even leveled with Jax completely, and soon he'd want her gone. After she shared all she knew with Tace, if Tace survived, then the group would be a hell of a lot safer with her far away from them. She might not know Jax well, but she understood he'd sacrifice her for his people. It was his duty.

Haylee thrashed to the side and strained her feet against the restraints. Her eyes suddenly opened wide. She screamed, louder than any banshee, and kicked out. One small foot escaped, and she started kicking wildly.

Lynne jumped up and reached for her ankle.

The girl struggled with amazing strength, and Lynne dropped to the floor. Grunting, she stood back up and snagged the girl's foot, planting it hard on the mattress. April scrambled for the restraint and secured it around her daughter's ankle.

Haylee yelled and gyrated on the bed.

Damn it. Lynne rushed to the medical cabinet and drew out another syringe of morphine. Hustling back, she smoothly inserted the drug into the girl's vein.

Haylee subsided with a soft whimper.

April sat back down and exhaled loudly. A tear streaked down her face. "I can't believe this."

"I know." Lynne put the syringe in the garbage and returned to check on Tace. He'd lost all color, and his body shivered as it fought the fever, but he'd gone quiet. For now.

April wiped off her face and tucked her head against her chest. "I need to get out of my head for a minute. What about you? Before Scorpius, I mean. You were a bigwig at the CDC, right?"

Lynne stretched out on the floor, her back to the wall. Knots curved around her spine and her muscles pounded in pain. "Yeah. I was in charge."

"Type A personality?" April lifted her chin.

"Definitely." Lynne nodded. "Only child, enjoyed school, just loved science. The possibility of it . . . of what we could do."

"Your parents?"

Lynne shook her head, hurt echoing in her chest. "No. Scorpius got them."

"Mine, too." April scratched her leg through a hole in her jeans. "What's it like outside of Los Angeles? I mean, the world out there? Are we reorganizing civilization?"

Lynne took a deep breath and blew it out. "I don't know. What I saw was more refugee camps outside of cities. I haven't been into a city except here in three months, and even before that, I was pretty isolated and locked down."

April bit her lip. "What about our government?"

Lynne swallowed. "I, ah, don't know." Hell, she really didn't want to know, but she'd probably find out soon enough. "The military was regrouping and trying to secure vital areas, specifically with the creation of the Brigade, and since all troops were recalled six months ago, at least all our soldiers are here on our soil." Not that the soldiers had fought Scorpius any better than the civilians. It killed without discrimination. She chose not to mention the creation of the Elite Force to April. Maybe word hadn't spread this far.

"Oh." April smoothed the ragged edges over the hole in her jeans. "So. Did you have a boyfriend or anything? I mean, I watched a television special on you when your heart first turned blue and you came out of the coma, but the show focused on your career and the hope of curing Scorpius. It showed your picture but didn't talk about your life."

Heat flared down Lynne's torso. "No. No boyfriend. I guess I lived for my work." She cut her eyes toward April, unwilling to trust that much.

"Hmm." A frown settled between April's eyes and then understanding lightened them. "Okay."

For the next couple of hours, they kept the talk simple and impersonal. There were a couple of tense moments with Tace trying to escape his bonds, but Jax had tied them strong.

The night stormed outside, and in the midst of the inside quiet, a knock echoed on the door.

April lifted her head from where she'd laid it on Haylee's bed. "Who's there?"

"Red. Jax radioed in and said to bring you two some food."

Lynne lifted her eyebrows at April.

April rubbed her chin. "He's one of Jax's. We can trust him." Standing and stretching her back with a low groan, she limped to the door.

Lynne faltered. "Are you sure?"

April glanced back. "Well, pretty sure. Red has been with Jax for months."

Lynne crossed and reached the woman to draw her away from the door. "Jax said to only let in Wyatt or himself, and I say we listen to the big guy. I'm not that hungry—are you?"

April glanced back to her too-quiet daughter. "No. Not at all."

Good. Lynne raised her voice. "Red? Thanks for the offer, but we're going to pass. We're not hungry, and the two fighting the fever can't eat."

"Come on, let me in, Lynne. You can trust me, and I want to see Tace. I need to see my friend." Red's voice remained calm.

Not too long ago, she would've opened the door with an apology for waffling. But she'd been hunted, and she'd been terrorized. Now she went with instincts—screw manners. "Thanks, Red, but Jax ordered us to keep the door closed, and I'm sure you value his orders. I'd hate to cross the guy within a day of coming to camp."

"April? You know me, sweetheart. Now I'm getting worried what's going on in there. Are you all right?" Red asked, his voice muffled only slightly by the thick door.

"I'm fine." April tucked the sheet more securely around Haylee. "I agree with Lynne that we should follow Jax's orders. You know how he gets when defied." She winked at Lynne and gave a mock shudder, whispering, "Actually, that's kind of true. Not a lot of mercy lives in that man."

Lynne turned away from the door. Sure, Jax was a hard man, but she'd seen plenty of mercy in him.

A boom echoed, and the door plowed open. The blast hit Lynne square in the back, and she flew across the room to crash between the beds and drop to the floor. Pain flared through her shoulder and the side of her face. Her ears rang, and her vision fuzzed.

April screamed and moved to partially cover her daughter.

Red stomped inside, silver semiautomatic glinting in the dim light. "April, I'm sorry, but we have to get rid of those infected. They're a danger to us if they survive."

April's lips quivered, and she hunched over her daughter in a protective pose. "There are tons of carriers, Red. You can't kill them all."

"I can try," he said grimly. "Next I'll hit the three in the inner hospital." A man aged fifty or so stood behind him, carrying a shotgun. "We've had a little vote, and this is the only way. I'll give you a few minutes to say good-bye to your daughter, what's left of her, while I take care of Blue Heart here."

"A vote?" Lynne slurred, reaching for the mattress to haul herself up. "The two of you?"

Red pointed the gun at her chest. "That's all we needed."

She made it to her feet, her knees wobbling and her head spinning. "What about Jax? He admitted he's a carrier."

Red snarled. "He's betrayed us for six months by lying to us, and he's being taken care of right now."

Lynne straightened. Jax was walking into an ambush with his own people? Fear heated her veins to the point of pain. She tried to take several deep breaths to calm herself, to think rationally, but her side hurt. Bad.

April uncurled from Haylee and stood. "You've elected yourself our new leader."

"I have as much training as Mercury, even without being in the military," Red said evenly.

"I doubt that," Lynne returned, losing her hold on the bed and going down again. Concussion? Probably. Her ears still rang, and she couldn't catch a complete thought, although adrenaline ripped through her veins, trying to clear the cloudiness.

Her ass hit the ground, and Red laughed.

What a dick. She had to fight the terror and reason with him before he killed Tace or the girl. "How is Jax being taken care of?" she asked slowly, her fingers inching for the back of her waist, where she'd hidden her gun.

April eyed her and gave a barely perceptible nod.

Red stepped toward her, his gun steady. "Let's just say I'm not the only one ready for new leadership. Mercury will be taken out today before he ever leaves Baker and Baker."

There wasn't a way to warn him. Lynne tried to concentrate on the threat at hand. She'd have to worry about Jax later. The guy was trained and dangerous as hell. Now she needed to survive the next few minutes and save the patients. "Please think about this before you make a huge mistake." Her legs weren't steady enough to stand yet.

Red scoffed. "Did you think before you let loose a biological weapon that took out 99 percent of humanity?"

"Yes." She bowed her head. "I did think, and I tried to cure the infection. We tried to contain it."

"You fucked up," Red retorted. Sweat rolled down the side of his face.

She nodded. "I'm aware of that fact, but don't compound our mistakes by making a huge one of your own. You're not a killer."

"No, I'm a protector." He switched his aim to Tace, who lay unconscious. Sorrow glimmered in Red's brown eyes, and his hand shook. He used his other hand to steady the weapon, and his jaw clenched.

Lynne's fingers touched smooth metal, and she yanked the gun from her waistband to fire. Three bullets struck Red's chest, and he looked at her, eyes wide, his mouth dropping open like a clown at a circus. Blood spurted from his torso and bubbled through his lips.

His eyes rolled back into his head, and he pitched forward, face hitting the tile. His legs kicked up and then back down. Blood seeped from under him.

The guy behind him turned the shotgun toward her, and April fired, hitting the doorjamb and splintering the wood.

He growled and swung the gun toward her. Lynne jerked back and fired twice, striking him in the temple. He fell backward, the gun toppling uselessly to the ground.

Lynne swiveled to look at April, whose mouth opened and shut several times.

Glancing down at the gun, April shook her head and then set the weapon gingerly on the bed. "Oh my God."

Lynne shuddered. She'd killed somebody. Two some-bodies. Her vision hazed again. Panic ripped through her, and she crawled up the bed to her feet and tripped over Red as she shoved the other corpse out the door. Grabbing the handle, she used her undamaged elbow to close it. A hole gaped where the lock had been.

She looked around frantically and spotted a table holding supplies across the room. "Help me." Inching forward, trying to hold her aching ribs with one hand, she grabbed the table while April hefted the other side. Between the two of them, they managed to set it in front of the door. While the metal cart wouldn't keep anybody out for long, at least it'd provide some warning before the next wave of assassins hit.

Lynne made her way back to Tace and set a knee on his bed.

"You okay?" April asked.

"Yes. I'll be fine." The blackness falling over her vision won the fight as panic and shock triumphed. Lynne's eyes closed, and she pitched forward onto Tace, her face hitting his cheek. Her first thought as she succumbed to oblivion was that his fever had risen, and her last thought was that if she didn't regain consciousness, she couldn't handle the next guy who came to kill her.

Maybe it was finally time to die.

Chapter Thirteen

Now this is not the end.
It is not even the beginning of the end.
But it is, perhaps, the end of the beginning.

—Sir Winston Churchill

On the western side of what used to be Los Angeles, the shadows were long, the streets empty, and the wind desolate. A block of tall buildings that once held sparkling windows now stood silent vigil over a dusty land.

Jax gave Wyatt the sign to take his team north around the tallest building while he went south. They'd found Baker and Baker without much mishap, considering they'd left the truck a couple of miles outside of Twenty territory and had run the rest of the way. The moon cooperated for a dark mission, allowing itself to be covered by clouds.

Thunder had rolled, and now rain blasted down, masking their steps.

It was a hell of a storm, and the timing was perfect.

Sami and an ex–Utah State baseball player named Shawn Banks flanked Jax, while Raze and a former wild game hunter followed Wyatt. A team of six was low for the mission, but until everyone else decided whether they were in or out, it was all he had.

He jerked his head for Sami to scout an area of abandoned cars circling the three story building, and she sprang into action. Though young and impetuous, she had the markings of a great cop or soldier. If she'd just keep her personal shit out of the way.

During the mission, she'd remained professional while managing to glare at him several times in a way that didn't feel professional. They were going to have to talk about the mistake of her trying to kiss him months ago, and he really didn't want to go there.

Hell, truth be told, he might've kissed her back if he hadn't carried Scorpius inside him. Good thing he hadn't.

Although he knew better than to open the conversation with that gambit.

She'd finished the task and gave the high sign. He swept left and gingerly opened the glass front door while Wyatt's team came in the back.

Papers, shredded drawers, and overturned furniture littered the reception room. He stalked behind the desk and rifled through papers for a map of the building. Offices made up the first floor, while labs and testing areas comprised the second. Shipping and a loading dock were located one floor down.

Wyatt's crew silently entered the reception room, flashlights down. "Nothing but offices that have been picked over," he whispered.

Jax nodded. "You head down one level to shipping to see what you can find, and we'll go up to the labs. Look for vitamin B."

Wyatt loped toward the stairs. "It's awfully quiet out there."

"Hopefully the storm will keep Twenty indoors for the night," Jax said. Of course, good luck didn't exist. "But keep an eye out. They're trained and like to kill."

Wyatt led the way to the basement stairs. Raze easily kept

to his six, and Jax wondered at his training. Definitely special ops, but not Delta. The guy didn't feel like a friend, and he watched like an enemy. But at the moment, Jax needed him more than he needed to be cautious.

Jax found the stairs to the next floor and jogged up, keeping track of Sami and Shawn by the sound of their footsteps. She moved silently, and he moved like an elephant. He'd need to work on stealth in the next few months.

They reached the next floor, where several labs with glass doors lined the hallway. "Everybody take one and meet back here. Keep the lights low and away from the windows as much as possible." Without waiting for a reply, he opened the door to the first lab.

Beakers, counters, and nonfunctioning machinery lined the counters. A couple of useless dead refrigerators made up one entire wall. He yanked open the few drawers that hadn't already been ransacked and went through the entire room. No vitamin B.

A box of bandages had been forgotten in the back of one of the lower counters, and he fetched it before exiting and turning for the next lab.

By the time he got to the final unsearched lab, he'd found small samples of bandages, shampoo, instant noodles, shaving cream, and some toothpaste. Not a lot, but something. After securing the items in his backpack, he turned toward the door.

Shawn stood there, feet spread, Ruger pointed at Jax.

Jax froze and dropped the backpack to the ground. "Looks like you learned how to move quietly."

The kid shrugged, anger burning in his deep eyes. "Not really. You just made a lot of noise ripping apart that last cupboard. What did you find?"

"A stash of condoms," Jax drawled. "The good kind with lubricant and ribs. You know. For her pleasure."

Shawn snarled. "So you can continue to fuck the woman

who pretty much killed society? My mother? My entire family?"

Ah. Jax eyed the gun pointed at his gut. Safety off. Probably one in the chamber, and the kid's aim remained steady. "Scorpius was a bacteria nobody created or expected, and Lynne did her best to cure it."

Shawn cupped the gun with his free hand, steadying his aim. "Maybe, but the fact remains that you lied to us. You're a carrier and should be destroyed before you infect us all."

Anger tried to swell. Jax shut down all emotion and focused. "Who are you working with, kid? We both know this isn't your plan."

Shawn's chin with the barely there goatee lifted. "I could be workin' alone."

"You're not. Who's pulling the strings?" Jax leaned nonchalantly against a countertop.

Shawn's shoulders went down from around his ears, and his legs unlocked. "Red is our new leader."

"Says who?" Jax said softly.

"Says my gun," Shawn spat out.

How many people had voted to have Jax killed? His blood quickened through his veins. "What about Lynne?"

Shawn smiled, the sight garish in the odd yellow light. "Oh, that bitch is dead by now. Red has taken care of her and the infected."

Jax stiffened to keep from running through Shawn to get home. *Dig deep and concentrate.* "Red wanted to kill Lynne, Tace, and Haylee?"

"Anybody infected." For the first time, an emotion other than anger filtered through Shawn's eyes. "I liked Haylee, but either she'll be a Ripper or she'll be a carrier if she doesn't die from the fever. We have to protect ourselves."

"That's rather shortsighted, don't you think?" Jax asked.

"No." Shawn settled his stance again. "I really am sorry about this."

Jax dropped into a slide that carried him across the tile and into Shawn's ankles, where he twisted. Shawn fell hard, and Jax rolled him over, straddling his waist. Two hard punches to Shawn's jaw, and the kid flew into oblivion.

Sami ran up, her gaze wide, carrying several boxes of Kleenex and soap. "What the hell?"

"He tried to shoot me and wants Red as Vanguard's new leader." Jax stood and extended his smarting knuckles. "Kid has a tough jaw."

Sami tossed off her pack to load it with the goodies. "Please tell me you found some B." With her tennis shoe, she nudged Shawn's side. The kid partially rolled over but didn't awaken.

"No B. You?" Jax held his breath, shoving provisions in his pack. They had to get moving if they were going to have a prayer of saving Lynne and Tace, but he needed to load his pack first.

"None." She cocked her weapon. "Listen, I'm sorry about the scene this morning in your bedroom."

Could his life get any stranger? "No problem. We're colleagues and buddies. Right?"

"Yeah, but man, Jax. What about the rumors that Lynne Harmony is carrying a more dangerous strain of the disease?"

"She's not." Jax shook his head.

"If you say so." Doubt curled Sami's lip. "Just make sure that's your head and not your dick thinking."

Like he had time to think with his dick. "Knock it off. So we're good?"

"Yeah. Believe me, you are so not my type, and I see that now." Sami shook her head, stepping next to him. "What is it about you and death? You just love dancing with it."

Jax drew himself up short. "Excuse me?"

"Come on, dude. You were in a street gang and then joined the most dangerous unit in the army. Now you lead a vigilante group trying to survive a murderous contagion, and the first time you get with a woman, she's the deadliest of them all." Sami kicked Shawn harder. "It's like you dare death."

Did she just call him *dude*? "Whatever. We need to get back to headquarters fast."

Sami pointed at Shawn. "What about him?"

Jax shook his head. "He stays here."

Sami gasped. "If we leave him, Twenty will find him. It's a death sentence."

"I know." Jax hardened everything inside him. "I can't afford to have somebody trying to kill me or anybody else who's survived Scorpius. Shawn is an adult, and he made his own decision. Now he lives or dies with it."

"But—"

"Enough." He didn't raise his voice, but he put every ounce of command he had into it. "Start moving, Sami. Now."

She faltered but began moving for the stairwell.

Bile rose from his stomach, and he swallowed it down and followed her. Once at the stairs, he took point, gun out, and jogged down the two flights to find Wyatt and his team waiting in the loading dock. Rain churned up dust around them. "Well?"

"One box," Wyatt said, his lips tight. "We looked everywhere and only found one fucking box of vitamin B, but we did find a bunch of shipping records from Baker and Baker to other labs. They must've been cooperating with each other and sharing information. What did you find?"

"Nothing worth mentioning." Jax eyed his watch. "Dawn will break in a couple of hours, and that storm is ebbing. We need to get the hell out of here, and now. There's a problem at headquarters." He tried to stay calm, but his nerves were firing fast.

"Let's roll," Sami clipped out.

Two men, armed with knives, ran around the far corner. Dirty and disheveled, their clothes hung on thin bodies.

The first guy paused. "We own this block. Whatever you took, it's ours."

Jax stiffened. Clear voice, calm manner? "You're not a Ripper."

"Nope." The second guy, one with tats down the side of his face, shook his head, and his hair sprayed rainwater. "We just own this block." Then, faster than Jax would've thought, he dodged forward and yanked Sami against him.

Jax went still. They didn't have time for this shit.

Sami hissed.

The guy shoved his knife near her jugular.

Wyatt stiffened and started to move.

"No." Jax lifted a hand in warning. "If you pull the gun, he may slice her throat." Then he waited.

Sami seemed to relax as she waited.

"Kill them," the guy ordered, his body moving just enough. "This little bitch is staying with us."

Sami shot an arm between his, shoved out, and the knife moved away from her neck. One elbow went back, and she turned so fast, she was just a blur. She took the guy out with a punch to the throat and then a knee shot. He was out cold before he hit the ground.

In a truly beautiful spin kick, she nailed the second man in the temple. He dropped down. She followed up by calmly striding forward and grabbing his hair, plowing her knee up. The guy's jaw snapped shut with an audible click.

Wyatt winced. "Holy shit."

Yeah. Sami's moves were a work of art. Stunning. And deadly.

She grabbed the knives and quickly searched the bodies, coming up empty.

Wyatt blew out air. "That's beyond rookie police training." He glanced around. "Where's Shawn?"

"Didn't make it," Jax said shortly.

Wyatt hitched to a stop. "Then we take him back and bury him."

"He's not dead." Jax met his friend's gaze levelly. "We have to get moving. Now."

Wyatt took a deep breath. "Fuck, man, what happened?"

Raze moved to his side, gaze not revealing anything, although he now kept an eye on Sami.

Jax sucked in air and fought every instinct he had to go back and throw the kid over his shoulder. "Insurgents. They're willing to kill anybody who's been infected, including Tace." He kept his face stoic. "We can't be watching our backs at all times."

"Then he stays," Raze said flatly, no emotion on his sharp face.

Wyatt swallowed, his eyes hollowing. He shuddered. "All right. Let's get back."

Sami shook her head. "You agree with him that we leave Shawn here? I thought for sure you'd try to talk some sense into Jax."

Wyatt patted her hand, his huge mitt covering her past the wrist. "If Jax says he stays, then it's best for the group if he stays. We don't have the time, energy, or manpower for a prison." He slid an arm around Sami's shoulders and tugged her closer. "We don't live in a world of rehabilitation right now, sweetheart. It's all survival."

She blinked back tears. "I don't like this world."

This world fucking sucked. How the woman could go from knocking out two guys twice her size to being upset about Shawn bewildered Jax. He tightened his jaw. "It's all we have right now. We'll head out the back door. The front faces the east, and as soon as the sun comes up it'll be too exposed."

Wyatt lowered his voice. "Do you think Lynne and April could've protected Tace and the girl?"

"I don't know," Jax muttered. Lynne was smart as hell,

and she'd said she knew how to shoot, but knowledge and action were two different things. The woman probably hadn't deliberately killed before. "April is protecting her kid, so my money is on her. Let's move. Now." His stomach rolled, and he had to fight to remain calm. He led the way into the pouring rain, making sure the team crouched low and stayed behind cars, bricks, and crumbling buildings. At one point, he allowed everyone to catch their breath before they made a run for the truck.

Sami crouched next to him, gazing above a half wall. "Were you like this before Scorpius, Jax?" Sadness and more than a little fear filled her voice.

"Like what?" he whispered.

"A killer without remorse. A survivor at all costs. So . . . cold."

Coming from somebody who could fight so easily, the words cut deep. "Yes. I've always been like this." His blood hummed, and his gut roiled. Had Lynne survived?

Chapter Fourteen

Man's chief enemy and danger is his own unruly nature
and the dark forces pent up within him.

—Ernest Jones

A couple of hours after she'd regained consciousness, Lynne's head still pounded. Was death coming for her finally? For so long, she'd been ready to rest, and suddenly, she wasn't sure. Living held merit again.

She sat on the floor of the examination room, her back to the wall, her gun ready. The paint was peeling, and every time she moved her shoulders, flecks dotted her shirt. Tace slept uneasily to her right, his breathing labored, while Haylee slept silently, nearly too silently, to her left. April sat next to her daughter, resting her head on the bed.

The smell of illness and blood permeated the room.

God, what if somebody else came to kill them? She had a limited supply of bullets. Her heart thundered against her rib cage, and her breath panted out.

"Are you sure you're all right?" April asked in a high-pitched tone, her voice muffled by the blanket.

"Yes. I passed out from shock. No concussion." Lynne's ribs ached, and her temples pounded. She tried not to look at the dead man sprawled across the concrete floor. The congealing blood, turning darker with each minute, had stopped spreading.

April lifted her head and looked over her daughter's barely moving chest. "Have you ever killed anybody before?" She blushed, the red contrasting garishly with her too pale face. "I mean, with a gun?"

Lynne closed her eyes. "No." Her hands shook, so she flattened them on her yoga pants.

Outside, the wind increased in force, slamming debris against the building. Thunder bellowed, and she jumped. "You ever shoot anybody before?" Not that April had shot anybody now. The woman had missed by a foot.

"No."

Heavy boot steps clomped down the outside hallway, and Lynne reached for the gun again, pointed it at the door. Someone shoved, and the table moved an inch. Her breath catching, she scrambled to her feet.

"Lynne? April?" Jax snapped.

Lynne shared a look with April, and both women rushed for the table to move it. The door burst open. Jax stood next to Red's body, his gaze taking in the room. "Everybody all right?" he asked quietly, lowering his chin.

Lynne's lips trembled. Relief chilled through her, weakening her knees. Jax had survived. She wanted to barrel into his arms but instead stood in place. "Yes. We're okay."

Wyatt moved past Jax and focused on Red. He sucked air into his broad chest, and his shoulders slumped. "I'll get this cleaned up."

Jax exhaled slowly. "Wyatt? Call a Vanguard meeting for late tonight, and find out if anybody else is involved in this uprising."

"These two mainly stuck together," Wyatt muttered. "I bet they worked alone in this stupid plan."

"Agreed. But we need to make sure everybody understands

that if they choose to stay, the leadership in position remains in place. Make sure they know we shoot back and have no problem digging new graves."

Wyatt winced. "Got it."

Jax turned to Lynne. "It's still raining. Why don't you ladies go take a shower?"

"I'm staying here," April said, patting her daughter's hand.

Lynne frowned. The second Jax had arrived, her brain had fuzzed as if she no longer had to be vigilant. She could fall apart now. "Shower?"

Jax reached for Lynne's arm. "It's raining." His hand encircled her bicep, and she allowed him to lead her around Red and the guy who'd held the shotgun, where he nudged her toward a pale Sami. "Show her the showers." He glanced down at the dead body without expression. "I'll meet you in our quarters in thirty minutes for an update."

She stumbled toward Sami. The prospect of leaving the dead bodies held too much appeal to argue against Jax's high-handedness. "Did you find B?"

"Just a box," Sami said wearily. All fight seemed to have deserted the young woman, although her knuckles were bruised and swelling. "Come on. We don't know how long the rain will last."

Lynne began to move forward, only to be stopped by Jax's hand on her shoulder. "Gun," he said.

She glanced down at the silver in her hand—she'd forgotten it was there. Without looking at him, she handed back the weapon. Straightening her shoulders, she followed Sami through the hallway and outside to the left of the building to stand under an overhang. Cold slashed into her. Three makeshift stalls made of wood, metal, and what looked like various vehicle hoods stood in the middle of what used to be an alley. Rain pummeled down, pinging against the metal.

"Leave your clothes here so they don't get wet," Sami said, setting her gun against the building. She shrugged out of ripped jeans and her shirt without a hitch of modesty, putting them on top of an old trash can. Then she reached for a camping lamp and twisted the knob to get some light since the day still hadn't banished the darkness, although morning should be arriving soon. The dark clouds made it impossible to guess the time.

Lynne stripped, her brain still buzzing.

"Watch your feet. We cleared everything we could, but sometimes the wind blows in glass and debris." Sami ran for the nearest stall, all grace and weary muscle.

Lynne gingerly picked her way across cracked concrete, the darkness hiding anything dangerous. Finally, she reached a stall, and Sami set the lamp on the low wall between them. Lynne sighed, surprised to find a shelf with soap. Dish soap, but still soap. Lightning cracked overhead. Damn. Could she get electrocuted? Maybe. Did she care at this point? She wasn't sure.

Rain sluiced over her, chilly but refreshing. She quickly poured soap into her hand and lathered up, almost groaning at the decadence. "One box of vitamin B won't last long."

"I know. We'll have to raid the other labs soon."

"I figured more people would be out here."

Sami scrubbed her hair. "It's been raining all night. We're the last to shower, probably."

That made sense. "What happened on the raid?" Lynne asked.

Sami closed her eyes and lowered her head, allowing suds to drip down her face. "Shawn tried to kill Jax, and Jax knocked him out. Left him for Twenty to find."

Lynne blinked, her stomach turning. "Was Shawn dead?"

"Nope. Very much alive." Sami sniffed.

Lynne wiped soap off her shoulders. "How old is Shawn?"

"Old enough to know better. Probably nineteen." Sami shook her hair, sending water spraying through raindrops. "He just made a mistake, you know?"

Yeah, but if Jax couldn't trust him, how could he bring Shawn back? More importantly, what had it cost Jax to leave a nineteen-year-old in enemy territory? "I'm sorry."

Sami took a deep breath. "No, I'm sorry. About the way I treated you earlier. I was jealous."

Lynne scrubbed her legs. Had Jax been telling the truth about his no-touch policy? "Were you and Jax together?"

"No. I tried to kiss him once, after a fight, but that was it. He turned away—probably because he'd already fought Scorpius. Or maybe he just wasn't interested." Sami shook out her hair and lifted her face for more water. "You can definitely have him. I hadn't realized how empty he really is." She shivered.

Lynne stuck her leg out to rinse. Trembles wandered down her back from the chill, but who cared? She was getting clean. The cold was worth it. "I don't think he's empty." He seemed more like a volcano ready to erupt, with too much trapped beneath the surface.

"Oh, he's dead inside." Sami rubbed her nose. "I mean, I don't know you, but you seem smart. You get that he's using you, right?"

They were using each other. "There's more to him than you're seeing." Lynne blinked as the words came out of her mouth. What was she saying?

Sami spat out water. "Well, woman to woman, take some advice. Don't give him one hint of emotion, or he'll kick you to the curb so quickly your blue heart will shatter."

Lynne turned around in the miserable rain, allowing the feeling of clean to compete with the cold. She had no intention of losing her heart when she could barely hold on to her life. "Give me a break. I just met the guy."

Sami leaned on the divider, her eyes sober. "He doesn't get close to anybody, even the guys guarding his back. If you want to keep enjoying what I'm assuming is a pretty good lay, check yourself. That guy doesn't have a heart, and believe me, you can't save him."

Lynne shoved her hair away from her face. "I don't want to save him." She could barely save herself.

"Right." Sami shrugged bare shoulders in a clear *I tried* gesture. "You know, I'd probably kill to be able to jump in the ocean or even a lake. To just be submerged and, well, wet. You?"

Lynne coughed out water, memories crashing into her. "Hell, no."

"Why not? You can't swim?" Sami shook her hair.

Why not share? It wouldn't hurt anything. "I almost drowned when I was eleven, playing at the beach with friends. You know how you're not supposed to swim after eating?" Lynne winced as soap ran over a small cut on her arm.

"I figured that was an old wives' tale."

"It's not. I went in after eating, got a cramp, and sank to the bottom." She'd never forget the feeling of the water closing over her head and beginning to fill her lungs. "My dad saved me, but sometimes I still have nightmares." She'd never jump into a body of water again.

Sami spat out water. "The good news is that you probably won't get the chance, so no worries."

"What are you afraid of, Sami?" Lynne asked. If she opened up, perhaps the young cop could, too. Not that she was going to be there long enough to really forge friendships. The world wasn't made for friendships any longer.

"Getting shot. And, well, disappointing people." Sami shivered. "While we're chatting, do you mind telling me what's going on outside of Los Angeles? I mean, is there any organization forming in the cities?"

"I avoided the cities and just saw smaller outposts. There's a military, but I don't know how strong it is right now." Lynne spat out water, unwilling to trust the woman with the full truth. The most dangerous Ripper of them all was out there, and he was coming for her. "Sorry I don't know more."

Sami turned away and sneezed before moving back. "I figured. You done? I'm freezing."

Lynne ran back to yank on her clothing. "Remember the days of towels?"

"We usually have some towels here, but we're probably the last to shower. Somebody will replenish them for next time. Hopefully." Sami retrieved her gun and led the way back through the building, climbing the stairs and dropping Lynne off at Jax's door, which was unlocked. Sami opened it and took a quick glance around. "You're secure. Lock the door till Jax gets here."

Lynne touched Sami's arm. "I'm sorry about Shawn. And Red and the other guy."

Sami nodded. "Me too. Do you want me to get you anything to eat?"

"No. Thanks." If she ate, she'd throw up. Right now, she had to get on warm clothing and then get back to the lab documents. It was only a matter of time before the Elite Force caught up to her, only so long that she could hide from the team created specifically to hunt, find, and return her. "Thank you, though."

Sami gave a weak smile. "We can get to know each other over breakfast in several hours." She lifted a shoulder. "I need some sleep to get back on track, you know?"

"I get that." Though who wanted to sleep with nightmares so ready to strike? Lynne waited until Sami started down the hallway before locking the door. She finger-combed her hair into some semblance of order and glanced at a bunch of clean clothes on the couch. She sat and folded both men and women's clothing. Somebody had included her.

The thought warmed her, and she pressed a freshly folded shirt to her chest. Then she let routine take over, and she slowly folded most of the laundry.

After a while the locks disengaged.

Jax stepped inside, his hair wet, the scent of Dawn soap coming with him. "I talked to April. Sorry you had to shoot those men." He shut the door, honey-brown eyes lasering through the semidarkness, so many weapons strapped on him he could probably wage a war by himself.

"Thanks." She folded mismatched socks together. The sound of the gunshots still echoed in her head, and her body wanted to flinch. "I want to get back to the documents."

"Sleep first. You need it." He locked the door and began removing weapons and placing them on the counter. Heat swelled from him, and tight lines cut into the sides of his generous mouth.

She eyed him, her instincts flaring to life. "How did the talk go with your people?"

"Fine. I believe Red and Joe were working alone in trying to take over, but everybody else now knows without question that they either leave or they stay here under my leadership." The atmosphere charged with his frightening mood. "Did you eat?"

"Not hungry." She held still, feeling him out. Her eyes were gritty, and she probably did need a few hours of sleep before returning to work. The documents were complicated, and she needed to concentrate. For now, her attention centered on the warrior filling the apartment.

Tension, dark and angry, filled the atmosphere around him. Instead of frightening her, as it should have, the fierceness clawed through her abdomen. "Are you all right?" she asked.

"Fine." He slipped another knife from his boot and tossed it onto the counter. "Why?"

"I heard about Shawn."

Jax stilled. "I don't want to talk about it."

"I wasn't asking you to." Jax's pain, his fury, were palpable in the small room. The emotions, so raw and real, sped up her heartbeat and warmed her blood. She couldn't save him, she knew that, but something about his wounded desperation called to her. She felt it in her own abdomen, the pain of the night and the futility of continuing on. She'd killed. On purpose. There had to be a way to stop feeling the repercussions for now—to turn off her brain.

He pivoted, tall and powerful, strength among ruin. Sexy and masculine, and just as damaged as she. He eyed her, direct, and her body finally started to warm. She stood, breathless, and crossed to him.

"What are you doing?" he rumbled, sliding a wicked-edged knife next to a bowl.

She had no clue. Going on instinct? They'd both had a hellish night, and she was freezing. She just wanted to warm up.

Jax was all heat. Hurt glimmered in his eyes, and the sense of being torn apart sizzled on his fury. She could think of only one way to ease his pain and forget her own. So she stretched up on her toes and licked under his jaw. Whiskers bit into her tongue, and she moaned.

He stiffened. "Lynne, baby? It's been a really shitty night."

"I know." She pressed against him, enjoying the ripple of muscle as he tried to hold back. "I don't want to think about the night. Or talk about the night. Let's forget the night."

His hands clamped on her arms, and he held her at arm's length, studying her. "You want me to take you away?"

"God, yes." She unfastened his belt buckle.

Jax Mercury wasn't a guy to ask twice. "Gladly. Forget about Myriad, forget about vitamin B, and just be here in the moment." He slid his hands across her chest and down, tightening them over her breasts before reaching the hem and tugging the slightly damp cotton over her head. She shivered.

Big and warm, his hands molded to her breasts. "You're beautiful," he whispered. "In case I forget to tell you, you're beautiful."

Panic rippled through her abdomen, and her breath heated. She flattened her hand over the bulge in his jeans. "I don't want sweet, Jax." She didn't want emotion or feelings or depth. She squeezed.

He stilled. "You don't want sweet?" Something dark, a warning of sorts, deepened his voice.

She shivered again. "No."

"Fair enough." He moved faster than possible, lifting her, moving, and laying her on the bed. Another wipe of his hand, and her yoga pants flew across the room.

Fire lit her from within, along with a healthy dose of reality. Of caution.

"Jax?" she asked. What had she just unleashed?

He straddled her and reached for his belt, gaze intent. The sound of leather sliding through denim echoed loudly in the silent room, skittering a wary hunger down her spine. He smiled, showing his teeth in an expression that was anything but sweet.

Thunder roared outside, and metal clashed against the building.

Nude, beneath him, she was breathless with vulnerability. "I don't want scary, either."

His belt free, he leaned toward her face. "You sure about that? Maybe scary is exactly what you need." His thighs tightened, and he ran the leather down her neck and over her nipples. They hardened to sharp points and zipped electricity across every nerve. The memory of the leather against her flesh earlier assailed her.

She trembled, her mind blanking. "Uh—"

He grinned and grabbed her wrists in one firm hand. She struggled, and his fingers tightened. Awareness clipped through her on the heels of fear. Manacling her, he wrapped the belt around her wrists, securely binding them.

She gasped. "What are you doing?"

"Not being sweet." He yanked her arms up over her head and fastened the belt to the metal headboard.

She arched, fighting him, unable to move.

Lightning flared outside, illuminating the harsh lines of his face. Of his tight, strong body.

She caught her breath, struggling against the bed, her arms bound tight. He encircled her neck, gently, but providing a clear reminder of her fragility. Humming softly, he traced a path down to her breasts, where he tweaked both nipples. Hard.

Electricity, desperate and out of control, zipped from her breasts to her sex. She arched up against him, a craving for more rendering her mute. Her entire life she'd been in control, and losing it, to somebody like him, heated her up. Fast.

He chuckled and stood, dropping his jeans. Hard and ready. He slid back onto the bed, all smooth-muscled grace, and flattened his hand over her abdomen. "You ever been tied up?"

"No," she gasped, tugging on the restraint.

He chuckled, the sound dark. "I bet not. Brilliant, beautiful Lynne Harmony. I bet you had guys begging for a kiss. Nice guys."

Awareness, uncertainty, caught her voice in her throat. "No."

"Liar." He reached up and played absently with a nipple, adding just enough bite to make her gasp. Confusion fuzzed through her brain as her body hungered with an edge close to pain. "Did they ask you politely for a kiss? Inquire as to what you wanted? Wait for instructions on how to touch you?" He slid down, parted her labia, and scraped a nail across her clit.

Pain and pleasure flared together. She cried out, shoving against his hand, needing more. So much more, but she instinctively tried to press her legs together.

"Yeah. I bet they asked permission. Hell—*panted* desperately for permission. Lawyers and stockbrokers—no alley rats or foxhole hounds like me." He rolled on top of her, shoving her thighs wide and forcing her open with his hips. One hand held his weight off her, and his cock slid against her wet mound. "Nobody ever made you beg, now did they, baby?"

Heat flushed down her torso, and she closed her eyes. "No." Her voice cracked. She could smell the raging storm on him, just barely covering the scent of violence. His shower in the rain had merely taken care of the dirt and blood. The violence lived *within* him. She swallowed. "For a take-charge badass, you sure talk a lot."

He barked out a laugh, his breath heating her lips. "You've seriously miscalculated here."

Her eyelids flipped open. "How so?" she breathed, throwing a challenge into her gaze, unnerved by the glint in his eyes.

His focus held steely determination. "Sweet, you could've handled. Sure, there would've been emotion, and that's tough. But this way? My way?"

Even bound, even helpless, she tilted her head back on the pillow to raise her chin. "Yes?"

"This way, I'll own you."

Chapter Fifteen

Love is a strange master,
and human nature is still stranger.

—Edgar Rice Burroughs

Jax leaned over Lynne, his gaze right above her. Desire heated the air, and hunger glowed in her amazing eyes. But he needed more. "Say it," he said softly.

She blinked, completely helpless to him, pride and strength flickering across her face and holding her still. No fear. Only need filled her expressive eyes. "Say what?"

"Ask me." He lowered his face to within an inch of hers, covering her completely. The smell of fresh rain and woman filled his senses. "Beg me to release you." He wanted her begging, but he needed her bound. Controlled. The darkness inside him, so much deeper after the fever, demanded to be appeased.

Her jaw firmed. "No."

He stiffened. "No?"

She trembled against him, and inside, he roared. Just how far could he push? "This is your one chance. Ask now, and I'll let you free. Stay stubborn, and no matter how hard you plead, I won't release you. Until. I'm. Done."

If the devil had an expression, she gave it to him. Meeting

his gaze, pink skating cross her face, she slowly, deliberately, licked her lips. "Fuck you."

The coarse words spoken in such an educated tone spurred him as nothing else could have. He shot down the bed and buried his face in her cunt. Soft and sweet—so feminine. She cried out a sound of surprise and struggled against him.

Forgetting gentle, he palmed her thighs and spread them wide. Then he gave one long, slow lick into her.

Tremors cascaded through her legs. "Oh God," she moaned.

He smiled. The anger inside him, the emptiness, fought with humor. How did she do that? Could she appease him enough to halt the nightmares?

"Now you stop?" she moaned, bending her leg at the knee and nailing his ribs with her heel.

He instantly sank his teeth into her labia. Not hard enough to damage, but with definite intent.

She squawked and went still. Completely.

He lifted his head, resting his chin on her heated mound, the beast inside him waiting patiently. "You really want to play?"

Her eyes widened, and she slowly shook her head. As if sensing what he needed, her body softened into the bed.

Submission.

Yeah, he would've demanded it, but to have it given so freely by a woman with such strength made him relax. She watched him, eyes alert, lids half-closed.

He kissed her, right on her swollen clit. Her breath caught audibly. "You behave, and I'm going to make you very happy. Kick me again, move merely a muscle, and I bite." To enforce his point, he nipped her thigh.

She jumped and then stilled. "I, ah, said I didn't want to play."

He lifted an eyebrow. "You didn't ask to be released when you had the chance, so it doesn't matter what you want."

Her eyes flared at that, with challenge and heat. He waited

for her to say something, to object, yet she wisely remained silent. She'd probably ruled her little world until it had disintegrated, leaving her alone and lost. He could take her away for a while and get her out of her head, but she'd play the game his way.

"Any questions?" he drawled.

She narrowed her gaze and tightened her lips.

He chuckled against her clit, sending vibrations he could see through her abdomen.

She held still, stubborn woman, but couldn't help a low gasp. "Please, Jax."

Such a pretty *please*. He dropped his head and gave them what they both needed, going at her with focus and no mercy. She tried to hold still, she truly did, and he could feel the cost to her. But after merely a minute, she gyrated against him, moving with the fast rhythm he'd set. She broke with a low moan, her abdomen undulating, the waves riding her hard.

He prolonged her orgasm until her body stiffened against him, and then he rose lazily up her body. She blinked, eyes wide and slightly confused, satiated for the moment.

Grabbing a condom, he sheathed himself, grabbed her hip, and stroked deep inside her.

Her hips rose from the bed to meet him, and her mouth opened on a gasp. She struggled against the leather belt, her thighs slamming against his.

He paused, balls deep, and kept her attention. Waiting. She blinked, tugged hard on the secured restraints, and then stopped. Her hands wrapped around the leather. Keeping his gaze, she slowly released each muscle, her body soft and pliant beneath him.

Hunger roared through him, sparking his nerves, clawing deep. So many words rushed to his mouth, he bit his tongue. Not one could he say. Feelings, the real kind, would get them both killed. So he started to move.

Hard and fast, giving no quarter, he pounded into her. She

took what he gave, wrapping her legs around him, trust and a light he didn't want to identify in her wary eyes. The harder he thrust, the higher her hips met his. So he pushed down, keeping control, pinning her where he wanted her. Red flushed across her face, and her nipples sharpened even more against his chest.

He took her mouth, overcoming her, stealing even her breath. He took everything she had, knowing full well what he was doing, forcing her higher and higher. Her nails bit into the leather belt, and internal quakes grabbed his cock in an unreal heat. He released her sweet lips, levered himself up, and battered her clit relentlessly with each thrust.

Her body stiffened, and she opened her mouth in a high scream as he hurtled her into oblivion. It crossed his mind to cover her mouth, to kiss her deep, but he let her cry echo against the apartment walls and beyond—in a primitive display of possession. Let them all hear. Too far gone to care, he dropped his head to the crook of her neck and shoved deep, his entire body shaking as he came.

They panted against each other in the aftermath. He reached up and released her wrists. She lowered her arms with a pained hiss, rolling her shoulders into the bed. He pulled out of her and removed the condom. Without a word, he levered himself up and pushed her onto her stomach.

"What?" she murmured.

He planted both hands on her shoulders and started to knead. She moaned, the sound full of pleasure, and buried her face in the pillow.

He could admit, just to himself, that he didn't want her to see his face until he got himself under control. While he'd easily released the restraint around her, the ones trying to capture him, to bind him to her, were growing stronger.

He'd let down too many people in his life, and the Vanguard group deserved his full allegiance—no matter how sweet Lynne Harmony turned out to be.

* * *

Lynne sat at the wooden table in a sprawling middle room on the first floor, trying not to fidget in the afternoon light. After the wild bout of sex, she and Jax had slept for several hours. "What was this room before?" she asked Sami.

Sami glanced around. "A soup kitchen."

A counter ran alongside one wall holding food, and tables had been scattered throughout like a mess hall. The tables consisted of everything from lawn furniture to wooden planks set over concrete blocks. A doorway led out front to the deserted parking lot, and a sliding glass door opened out back to an empty street. The showers were over to the left, she thought. She leaned forward and blew on some soup heated over a makeshift fireplace outside. "I need to get to work."

Sami drank soup from a plastic Dora the Explorer cup. "Jax said to make sure you ate something and then take you to Tace's infirmary."

"How are Tace and Haylee doing?" Lynne asked.

Sami winced. "I heard both have slipped into comas, so we'll see if either one of them wakes up."

God, Lynne hated the Scorpius bacteria. She kept drinking her soup, trying to regain some strength. Jax had been gone when she'd awoken, leaving her oddly bereft. So they'd had sex. Wild, crazy, kind of intriguing sex. She could handle that. Yep. No emotions for her. That would be crazy. Plus, once she'd taken care of her agenda, she'd be free. Enough of this place, which was just another prison.

Two women, dressed in faded jeans and dark shirts, skirted their table and scurried across the room.

Lynne lifted her chin.

Sami rolled her eyes. "Ignore them. The blue heart is scary, and that's life."

"What. Are we becoming friends here?" Lynne downed her soup.

Sami shrugged. "Why not?"

Why not, indeed? "You didn't like me on sight."

"Geez, I apologized already." Sami sat back in a torn wicker chair.

Heat climbed into Lynne's face. "You're right, and I'm sorry."

Sami's brown eyes sparkled. "But you don't want a friend."

Lynne swallowed. "I don't, ah, want complications."

Sami threw back her head and laughed, the sound almost contagious. "Well, then it's a good thing you're banging Jax Mercury. That doesn't seem complicated at all."

Lynne snorted. "Shut up."

"You shut up." Sami sobered. "Seriously. You show up, offer to help, ask Jax for a favor, and then what?" Wisdom far beyond her years glowed in her eyes. "You done at that point?"

Lynne swallowed. "That's an odd question."

"That's not an answer." Sami played with a sliver on the makeshift table. "I know more than a couple of people who couldn't handle this new life and checked out. They had the same look in their eyes as you did last night."

Lynne blinked. "I hadn't really thought I'd make it this far, to be honest."

"Yeah, I get that." Sami rubbed her nose. "But you're here now."

Yes, yes she was. The idea of hope and a real future hurt, so she banished them. "What did you do before this?"

"Com . . . cop. I was a rookie here in L.A." Sami glanced down.

Lynne paused, her mind clicking. Interesting. "What's a com . . . cop?"

Sami laughed, the sound a bit more forced. "I burned my tongue."

Lynne leaned forward and waited until Sami met her gaze. "Whatever your secret is, I don't care."

Sami blinked. "I don't have a secret." She pushed her chair back from the table to look down. "I have to ask you—is there any truth to the rumors? That you're carrying a more deadly strain of Scorpius?"

Lynne dropped her head and then looked back up, frustration welling in her. "No. I promise—there's no deadlier strain."

Sami nodded. "That's what Jax said. You know, at some point I wonder if we'll have to separate people. You know, survivors from folks who haven't been infected."

Lynne shrugged. "I bet it'll get to that point, but even then, Scorpius will remain on surfaces. I think everyone will be infected someday, and only the survivors of the contagion will live on. But I could be wrong."

Sami rolled her shoulders. "Something to worry about for another day, right? I'll get us some water. With the rain last night and today, we can drink all we want."

Lynne watched as Sami strode across the room to a barrel of water, saying hi to people on the way. In society as it was now, who didn't have a secret or two? She turned and glanced out the square industrial windows out back. Rain still pattered down, turning an already depressing landscape gray. Jax and another soldier, one she hadn't met, strolled into her view.

Her stomach tingled.

Jax stood in the mist, ignoring the cold, tall and broad. Droplets caught in his thick hair and slid down the sharp angles of his face. The streets had stamped him hard, but he stood erect, like a soldier. Such an intriguing mixture in the man. The other guy tugged a gun from his waistband and pivoted to jog out of sight.

Jax stuck his hands in his pockets and stared across the empty street to a long building and beyond into the heart of his territory.

A little girl, with blond hair so light as to be white, and

wearing a wet pink dress, danced up from the shower area, ragged doll in hand, to grab his pants leg.

Lynne's breath caught, and she rose from her chair. The girl was so tiny.

Jax's face, even in profile, was transformed by a look that stuttered her heart. His dimples flashed and he dropped to his haunches, eye to eye with the little girl.

She held out her doll.

Appearing serious, his attention on the girl, he took the doll and turned her over. Then he put her to his ear. Finally, he grinned and handed the doll back. Whatever he said had the little girl smiling widely.

Tingles scattered throughout Lynne's entire body. Jax Mercury, on his own with no witnesses, was a sweetheart. Now what the hell was she supposed to do with that information?

The girl handed him something, and he placed it in his pocket. A female redheaded teenager ran up and grabbed the girl's hand.

Jax stood and turned to point inside.

The girls ran inside, bringing the scent of fresh rain, and hurried toward the soup station. They must've run out of food in the center. Or maybe the girls were visiting somebody at the main headquarters.

Suddenly, the blonde turned and stared right at Lynne, her eyes so dark as to be black. She smiled, jerked free, and ran toward Lynne to stop right in front of her.

"Hi," Lynne said.

The girl reached into her pocket and pulled out a smooth, round rock to hold out.

Ah. A present. Lynne took the rock. "Thank you for the gift. You must be Lena?"

The girl nodded and then turned to run for the soup counter. Lynne turned the rock over to see a rough 4 scratched into both sides. 44? Interesting. She glanced back toward the window.

Jax's gaze caught Lynne's and heated. She blinked, captured.

Then Wyatt jogged up, gun in hand, obviously coming from the rear exit of the infirmary. Jax turned toward his friend. Wyatt's lips were tight, and anger was carved into his face. Whatever he said to Jax cooled the expression in Jax's eyes until, yards away, Lynne shivered.

Jax took a deep breath, his gaze going out to the tumultuous day.

Lynne swallowed just as Sami returned, her eyes glimmering with tears as she left a whispering group over by the soup. "What?" Lynne asked.

Sami wiped her cheek. "Haylee Snyder just died."

Chapter Sixteen

—◆—

To be alive is to be vulnerable.
—Madeleine L'Engle

To the left of headquarters, past what used to be a busy street, lay two full blocks of vacant land fronting old business buildings that now stored weapons. Garbage, fragments of glass, and crack pipes had littered the weeds and dirt of the empty property before Jax had ordered it cleaned up to create a cemetery. The first grave had been dug six months ago, and since then, too many to count.

Or maybe he just didn't want to count.

He'd placed the graveyard across the road from the east side of his headquarters so he could see it every day. So he could keep track of the people he'd failed. Plus, he kept the area extra secure so folks could visit the dead.

When he'd set the time for Haylee's funeral, just hours after her death, Lynne had asked why he went to the trouble to bury people in the middle of chaos. Her tone had held curiosity, the genuine kind, and no judgment.

His only answer was that the dead deserved a good place to rest.

It was all he had.

Jax kept his hands together, his head up and gaze searching as others bowed their heads.

Wyatt's deep tone wound through the falling rain, some-how reassuring and hopeful in a prayer for everlasting life.

But the look in his eyes was one of fury. Pure, raw, unadulterated fury.

Jax nodded. Cruz had infected the girl on purpose, which meant he'd killed her on purpose. Soon, Jax would go hunting his old friend.

For now, good-byes took precedence.

Tace, his stance wide, kept point to Wyatt's left. His fever had broken, but now tremors visibly shook his arms. Yet he watched Wyatt's back, gaze alert and seeking.

The gratitude Jax felt at Tace's survival was only slightly marred by the uncertainty of Tace's future. Of his sanity. When Jax had been infected, he'd immediately begun the vitamin B regimen, which had hopefully helped him retain his sanity. There had been no immediate B for Tace, and the repercussions of that could be devastating, although now he was getting shot up. For now, Jax would take whatever good he could.

Lynne stood at Jax's side, tears falling silently down her face. Her body remained still, almost too much so, and not one sound emerged with her sorrow. The woman had learned to grieve in silence and alone, now hadn't she? No matter how tempted he was, how he knew she needed comforting, he couldn't reach out.

Wyatt finished the eulogy. How many had he given just during the last month? The guy had gotten his minister's license online before Scorpius as a joke so he could officiate a football buddy's wedding. But now, with death all around them, he was the only minister they had. Internet or not.

April Snyder watched the men pour dirt over her daughter's covered body, not crying, not saying a word. She'd gone pale as if life had left her along with her color. The wind whipped into her, lifting her hair.

Little Lena stood vigil nearby, a small doll-like angel in her hands. She'd been giving April angel related gifts for a month.

Jax shivered. The irony there had to be just that—irony. He focused back on the ground.

The grave was small. Jax jolted internally at the thought. So fucking small. Haylee had been only about five feet tall, young and thin. Way too fucking young to die or be buried. He'd seen death up close since childhood, and he'd seen more than his share of dead kids. But now, as the leader of their small group, he felt each death somewhere deep and dark. One day, he'd fall in there and never climb out.

Rain poured over him, but he didn't feel the cold. Hell, he didn't feel anything but fury.

Until one small hand slid into his.

The anger rioting through him quelled. Just enough so he could breathe. Lynne had slipped her hand into his, and he curled his fingers, holding her against his abs. He couldn't imagine how she'd dug deep enough to reach out, because he couldn't have done it.

But he held tight.

The sermon ended, and a couple of the teenagers spoke next. Lena, her white hair glimmering in the lost day, moved forward and handed April the angel before turning back to the teenager watching her. Then the group slowly began to wind their way back to the center of Vanguard territory and the apartment buildings, walking through puddles and over cracked concrete, their shoulders and heads down.

April Snyder didn't move.

Neither did Jax, Wyatt, or the soldiers flanking her. Jax thought about giving Lynne leave to go get warm, but the idea of relinquishing her hand made his gut clench. He'd seen parents grieve, and sometimes they stayed all night at the grave site. So he'd wait for April however long it took. He gave Tace the high sign to get inside, but his friend just stared back.

Stubborn bastard.

Without even a hint of warning, April Snyder dropped to her knees. Water and mud splashed up.

Lynne began to tug away to approach the grieving mother, but Jax held firm. The woman had to grieve in whatever way worked for her.

Silver suddenly contrasted with her black coat. She held a gun in her hand, the one Jax had given her.

Oh fuck. Jax shoved Lynne behind him. "April?" He began to move toward her, slowly, just as Wyatt approached from the other side.

She looked up, her gaze blank.

Shit. "April, honey? Look at me. Focus." Another two feet, and he could get the gun.

She twisted and put the barrel under her neck.

Panic tightened his throat. "April, don't do this. We need you. I know you're in pain, but we need you." He lowered his voice to soothing, edging closer, trying to connect.

Tears filled her eyes. Finally. "I can't." Her lips trembled.

"You can," he said gently, his hands shaking for the first time that day. "It almost kills you, but you can. The fight is all we have left."

A tear fell from her eye. "No fight left. They're all gone."

He scrambled for anything to get through to her. "You're religious and believe you have a purpose. Don't end your time here."

She blinked. "Or I'll go to hell?"

He didn't want to touch that one. "No, honey. Just please put down the gun and we'll talk," he said.

Her head tilted to the side as if becoming too heavy for her neck. Weariness and agony cascaded from her. "I'm already in hell."

"We all are, but we need you. We'll never get out if we

don't help each other." The gun pointed to her delicate head was fucking with his brain. Bombs exploded and screams echoed in his head—an immediate flashback to pain and death. To Frankie dying in his arms, surrounded by gunfire and devastation. He shoved himself back to the present. "Please, April." His voice shook. "Don't do this."

Her eyes focused. "It's too hard."

His eyes filled. "I know. God, I know." Slowly, so as not to spook her, he approached until he was close enough to grab the gun. "Please, put down the gun." He could probably take it, but she needed to make the decision to live, or no matter what he did right now, she wouldn't.

April focused on him, so much anguish in her eyes he wanted to yell. The toy angel dropped from her hand, and her gaze followed it. She stared at the now dirty angel. Her shoulders slumped. An anguished sob echoed from her chest. Finally, her hand trembling, she lowered the gun to the mud.

Wyatt instantly reached her, lifting her to stand and securing her weapon in his pocket. "Let's get you inside, sweetheart." April leaned into him, moving almost like a robot.

More flashbacks bombarded Jax, and he wavered, turning around.

Lynne eyed him, her skin pale, her lips shaking. But she held her ground.

He tilted his head to the side, watching her, not sure what he was seeing. Bombs kept going off, and his body jerked.

"Jax!" Raze's voice shot through him.

"What?" He turned, and his gaze dropped to the fresh grave. To the present and not the fights of the past. The day hazed. Dead kids. Too many dead kids surrounded him. "Why?" he breathed.

Nobody answered.

Raze cleared his throat. "I'll finish here and smooth things over. You get Tace and Lynne back to headquarters and out of the storm."

Storm? What storm? Jax settled, the hollowness inside him spreading until pain became everything. "No. You go. I'm not done."

"No," Raze said.

Jax jerked up his head. "I said, I've got it."

Raze's head lifted, and his somber blue eyes glowed through the gray. "Fine. Tace, take Lynne. I'll cover."

Tace moved toward Lynne.

"No, I—" She stopped speaking when Jax jerked his focus to her. Whatever she saw in his face had her backing toward Tace. Raze reached them and walked away as well.

Jax waited until they'd crossed the street and were halfway across the old parking lot fronting headquarters before grasping a shovel and patting the earth smoother around Haylee's grave.

When he finished, he leaned on the shovel, his entire body hurting. "I'm sorry," he whispered.

An hour after Haylee's burial, Lynne sifted through Tace's laboratory records, failing to find another source of vitamin B but refusing to give up.

She sat on an examination table with a box of papers from Baker and Baker. An hour later, her head hurt and her eyes burned. Yet she picked up a new box and moved on. Most of the notes in the first box were about vitamin B and different SRI inhibitors that might assist in slowing down the progression of the infection. Her mind quickly cataloged everything she'd read.

Her entire life, she'd been quick. Very smart. But since surviving Scorpius, her brain worked even faster and more efficiently. She'd remember everything she read.

Ideas began to form.

When she reached the third box, a list of shipping addresses caught her eye. Numbers lined up evenly. She bit her lip. What did they mean? She memorized them, her breath catching when she deciphered a very faded pencil line at the bottom. *Myriad*. The letters were scratched in and tilted, but they spelled *Myriad*. Shit. The sheet was about Myriad Labs. What did all of the numbers mean? Was it some kind of code?

Tace entered the doorway. "Dinner has been over for a couple of hours, but there's still food. You need to eat."

She slowly nodded, more than willing to take a break and let her subconscious take over with the code. After she ate something, she'd get right back to work.

Tace escorted her into the soup kitchen where Raze was already eating, and in a few minutes, she'd eaten a little dinner. Soon she held a chipped plastic cup next to her silent companions, Raze and Tace.

She hadn't spent much time with Raze and had yet to hear him speak a complete sentence. He'd tied his shoulder-length black hair at the nape, showcasing sharp features with definite Native American markers. His light blue eyes showed no sign of emotion, but he seemed to be on constant alert. She could ask him about himself, but forging another connection with a person, even so lightly as with general conversation, was just too much right now.

Dinner had consisted of some sort of bread meal mush that had actually filled her belly. The mood in the rec room remained somber, and death hovered all around. She cleared her throat and focused on the man she already kind of knew once her brain kicked back into gear. "How are you feeling?"

Tace rubbed his whiskered jaw. "Like I got run over by my granddaddy's farm pickup. Twice."

Yeah, that about summed up the fever. She needed the right words, but the time for niceties had passed. "You've been getting injections of B now, so that's good. How's your cognitive functioning?"

Raze lifted an eyebrow but didn't comment.

Tace tapped fingers on the table. "I don't know. I don't want to kill anybody or plan a mass murder, but . . ."

"But?" Raze asked.

"So you can speak," Lynne blurted out.

Raze cut her a look and focused back on the medic. "But what?" he asked.

Tace rubbed the back of his neck. "My brain processes seem . . . slow. Muddy and hindered."

Lynne breathed out. "You had a high fever, and your body is still reeling. It can take weeks to get back to normal."

Tace nodded. "I know, and if I get the urge to bite somebody, I'll let you know."

Raze shoved back from the table, stood, and stalked toward the outside door.

"Well, good-bye," Lynne said without heat. What an odd guy.

Tace smiled with a definite lack of humor. "He doesn't talk much."

They needed to get back to work, but for a moment, her eyes stung. So she stayed put. "What's his story?" Not that she cared. Sometimes the scientist in her reared up when she least expected it, and curiosity won out.

Tace shrugged. "Hell if I know. He walked into camp two weeks ago, fully armed, and said he wanted every member of Twenty dead. That was good enough for Jax."

Yeah, that would be. "Will Jax go after Cruz now that Haylee has died?" Lynne asked, trying to sound casual. She needed Jax Mercury alive and ready for the next battle. One he didn't even know was coming.

"Yes."

That made sense. Her body shook in a yawn, and her vision blurred.

"You're exhausted." Tace pushed back and stood. "I can

escort you to your quarters if you'd like?" While the suggestion was posed as a question, his manner said it was anything but.

Lynne stood. "So I'm still under house arrest?"

"I don't see that changing." Tace grabbed their dirty dishes to place in a hollowed-out tire near the food. "Sorry."

"I can keep working for a few hours." She swayed.

Tace shook his head. "Come on, Dr. Harmony. You know as well as I that sleep is necessary for brain function."

She regained her balance. A couple of hours would probably do her good. She should probably ask who did the dishes, but at the moment, she didn't really care. "Are we meeting in the, ah, lab tomorrow?" It was still early, but exhaustion lived in every one of Lynne's movements.

"Yes. Maybe the info from Baker will give us more information on inoculations or other businesses turned into production labs. For now, get some sleep." Tace escorted her out of the main hall. "I plan to do the same soon, but right now I need to go hash out the scouting schedules with Wyatt." They walked up the stairs, and Tace left her at her doorway.

Okay. She'd sleep on it and let her subconscious work on the code. If that didn't help, she'd get paper and pen the next day and try to decipher the numbers. If the numbers even related to Myriad. It was possible they had nothing to do with the lab, but it was all she had.

Lynne drew in air, opened the door, and slipped inside, only to draw up short. Apparently Jax had sought his quarters after burying Haylee. Chaos had touched down in the little efficiency apartment. Broken dishes, a demolished chair, and clothing littered the floor. Even the counter had been partially pulled from the wall. She quietly closed the door.

Jax Mercury, his back to her, stance wide, faced a broken window as Mother Nature pounded outside. He'd torn the wooden boards away. Shards of glass, covered with red and dripping rain, were scattered around his feet. Tension rode him, stronger than raging nature out the window. Muscles rippled down his back like those of a beast about to lunge.

Holy hell. Lynne faltered and swallowed. A year ago, she would've probably backed away and shut the door. Instead, she locked the door behind her. "When you throw a tantrum, it's a big one," she murmured.

His shoulders stiffened. "Leave. Now."

"No."

He turned in a gracefully slow arc that sped up her breath. His eyes had darkened to almost black, and an unholy wildness, one not quite human, glimmered in their depths. "Go."

"No." She tried to breathe out evenly to keep from having a stroke. She'd only been in camp a short time, but she could see the problem. Could he? "We don't have time for this. You don't have the luxury of this."

He blinked. Slowly. "Excuse me?"

The tone pulsed through her, igniting adrenaline. Flee. No fight. Her instincts bellowed to run. "I said, knock this nonsense off. The people here are sad and they're scared. Step up and help them."

His eyebrows lifted.

Good. She'd gotten through to him.

"Haylee is dead because of me," he whispered, the sound broken.

She shook her head. "No, she is not. She's dead because a bacteria was unleashed and Cruz purposefully infected a young girl. That's not on you. None of this is about you."

"I'm the Vanguard leader," he exploded, red shooting across his cheekbones. "It's all on me."

Caution screamed at her but she ignored it. "You're not their leader. You're their protector." She sucked in air, facing death. "They fucking need a leader, and it's time you stepped up." What the hell was she doing?

His head jerked. Those eyes focused. "What did you just say?"

"There's a difference between defending and leading, Jax," she said softly.

His lids lowered to half-mast. "Is there now? Is this about Shawn?"

Shawn? It took her a moment to remember Shawn. "The kid you left in Twenty territory?" Oh. So that was eating away at Jax, too.

"Yes. You think I should've brought him back." That quickly, any hint of being lost disappeared from Jax's hard face. "I made the right decision."

"Did you?" She truly didn't know. Would a true leader have brought the kid home to rehabilitate him? Or had Jax possibly saved the group from another attack? "Either way, it's done and time to move on."

"Move on? I've known that kid for months, through famine, pain, and war. I liked him." Jax shifted his weight, and glass crunched beneath his boot. "I left him for Cruz. I left another fucking kid for Cruz."

Another? They all knew what Cruz did to enemies. At the very least, he'd infect Shawn. "I know." Lynne sighed. Then her gaze caught on Jax's right hand, the one with white scars. Red dripped from his knuckles and between his fingers. "How many windows have you punched in your time?" she asked.

He lifted an eyebrow and glanced at his bleeding hand. "More than I can count, but the scars aren't from windows."

It wasn't the right time to ask him about the scars, that much she knew for sure. "The new ones will be, and you'll need stitches."

"Probably." Jax glanced around the apartment and then began striding her way. She tightened her leg muscles to keep from backing up. He reached her.

She stopped breathing.

Slowly, as if not wanting to spook her, he lifted his un-damaged hand and ran a knuckle down the side of her face.

Gently and with warmth. His arm dropped, and he moved past her to the door.

Her breath whooshed out, and tingles lit her abdomen.

He disengaged the locks. "I'll send somebody in to clean up."

The world tilted. She'd had enough of people for the night. "I don't want anybody here. I'll clean up."

He left without another word. When he locked the door from the outside, Lynne turned and sagged against it, her gaze on the demolished room. She'd made a huge mistake in seeking out Jax Mercury. He was damaged, and he was dangerous, but instead of wanting to flee, she wanted to heal him.

There was no healing for any of them.

Chapter Seventeen

Ideologies separate us.
Dreams and anguish bring us together.

—Eugene Ionesco

He shouldn't have punched the window, because he was still bleeding an hour later after doing weapons inventory. Jax swore as blood dripped through the rag he'd wrapped around his injury even as he moved to the next locker. At this rate, his guns would outnumber his ammunition ten to one by the end of the week.

He slammed the last door and hurried from the storage building, skirting the cemetery and keeping his gaze away from the new crosses. Just for tonight. Tomorrow he'd look again.

Rain slashed across his face, and he ducked his head, shoving through the back door of the infirmary. Voices alerted him, and he jogged faster.

Dim lanterns cast a yellowish light through the grimy room of the old kitchen, and microscopes with documents had been shoved to a far counter. Tace, Wyatt, and Raze sat around an old card table, half glasses of whiskey in front of them. Maps of the county were scattered across the table with circles drawn around future raiding areas.

"Figured you'd be out running all night, so we've been planning," Tace said.

"You're bleeding," Wyatt murmured, tipping back his drink.

Raze, as usual, didn't say anything. But at least he was spending time with the group. Perhaps he'd loosen up and start to earn Jax's trust.

Tace kicked a chair toward Jax and reached over his shoulder to yank out a drawer. "Sit down."

Wyatt dug another glass from under what used to be a working sink, poured whiskey into it, and nudged it across the table. "You'll want a drink first."

"You've dipped into our hidden reserve." Nothing wrong with stating the obvious. They'd found a couple of bottles while scouting homes to the east about a month ago.

"Life's the shits." Tace withdrew a sewing kit. "The needle has already been burned. I'm prepared." He threaded the needle and grabbed an old golf-bag towel to place on the table before settling a lantern close to it. "Hand."

Jax tipped back the whiskey and let it burn down his throat before placing his damaged hand on the towel. He held his breath when Tace dug the needle in. Jax forced his body to stop feeling, at least to stop registering pain. It was a trick he'd learned as a kid, and it had saved his life more than once overseas. "Where's Sami?"

"Training with some of the kids. They're angry and scared, and she's helping them fight through it. Literally," Wyatt said. "Said she'd be finished by ten-ish tonight and would drop by to check out the new schedules."

Raze frowned. "The woman can fight. Where did she learn those skills?"

"Dunno," Tace said, his face lowered as he stitched. "She won't talk about her past."

Wyatt watched him move the needle, gaze sober. Raze also watched but looked as if seeing needles drawn through flesh might put his ass to sleep.

"Are we boring you?" Jax asked Raze.

"Yes." Raze poured himself another shot and drank it down, the glass looking small in his hand. A series of scars scored up his arm in what appeared to be burns.

Agony flared between Jax's fingers when Tace hit a nerve. "I haven't asked for your story," he said.

"I know." Raze nudged the bottle toward Wyatt, who refilled all four glasses.

"Would you like to share?" Jax asked, trying to focus on anything but his hand.

"No." Raze tipped back his glass, his eyes glowing in the dim light.

Wyatt snorted. "You're such a fucking prince."

Raze didn't blink. "We're up." He stood from the table, drawing a nine mil from his waist.

Wyatt groaned and stood. "Great. I get patrol, in the fucking night, with Mr. Personality here."

Jax forced a smile. "Watch each other's backs."

Raze and Wyatt left.

Tace continued to stitch. "What do you think his story is?"

One of loss and pain. "I don't know or really care so long as he doesn't try to kill us." Because if he tried, he'd probably succeed. Jax shut his eyes and tried to relax his body. He'd lost the luxury of curiosity months ago. "Do you think I'm doing a good job here?"

"I think"—Tace slid the needle back in—"we'd all be dead if you weren't doing a good job."

Jax winced. "Haylee is dead." As was Shawn, probably.

"Not your fault." Tace tied the string tight. "We're out of antibacterial stuff." Without warning, he poured his shot of whiskey on the wound.

Agony ripped into Jax. "Fuck it, Tace." He breathed out, his eyes watering. "God."

"Sorry." Tace replaced the kit in the drawer and stood. "You really ready to go after Cruz?"

"I've wanted him dead for a long time, and he deserves to be gone." Jax's lips tightened. "I owe that bastard."

Tace's eyebrows rose, but he didn't push the subject. "We don't have full check-in from all the lieutenants until tomorrow night, but I can confirm everyone seems to be willing to stay here under your leadership, even if you are a carrier."

Jax scrubbed a hand over his eyes. "They don't have much of a choice, now do they?"

"Sure, they do. They trust you, and Lynne's stock went up a lot when she protected April and Haylee. They don't trust her, but they're willing to let her be."

Good, because he could only provide her so much cover, and he was stretched thin. "What else is going on?"

"Well, we lost all three of the Scorpius victims inner territory."

Ah, hell. "I'm sorry. What else?"

Tace sighed. "We've got two fevers at the main hospital, and an ear infection."

Jax stilled. "Fevers?"

"Not Scorpius. My guess? Strep or just the flu." Tace rubbed a hand over his hair. "Which is bad enough."

Jax tried to flex his pounding hand. "Yeah, it is. Do you think we'll have to separate into survivors and non-infected people?"

"Maybe, but the problem is we don't know who a survivor is, you know? Right now, that's not an immediate concern."

True. Thank goodness. Jax nodded. "How are you feeling?"

"Not sure yet, but I'll let you know. So far, I'm not right." Tace took one of the two lanterns. "For now, if I don't get some sleep, my head is gonna explode." He strode away.

Alone, Jax slumped in his chair and lifted his feet to the wobbly table. Tace wasn't *right*? What the fuck did that mean? Jax sighed and shut his eyes as his hand pulsed in heartbeats of pain.

Things had calmed down enough that he could finally go after Cruz and slice his jugular.

The whiskey and rawness of the day dug into Jax, and he finally relaxed, slipping into the slim world between wakefulness and sleep. He couldn't afford sleep, but he could drift.

Suddenly, he was ten years old, taking a beating against jagged concrete from Bast Ace, a kid from his school. He'd told his younger brother to run home, and for once, Marcus had listened. Thank God. But Jax had remained to protect his brother, and he was definitely losing the fight. The fists pummeling into his face didn't hurt as much as the old beer bottle glass cutting into his back. Suddenly, Bast stopped.

Jax blinked blood from his face and looked into the sun. Wincing, he turned just as Bast knelt down. "Your mama's a whore," Bast spit out.

Yeah, she was. "So is yours," Jax mumbled through split lips.

The punch didn't hurt this time, which was probably a bad thing. "You're a half-breed piece of shit."

Jax swallowed blood. "So are you." He shouldn't mess with the fourteen-year-old bully, but sometimes he just couldn't stop talking.

"Maybe. But you're half-white." Bast punched him in the gut.

Jax cried out and lifted his knees toward his chest.

Then suddenly, Bast lay face down on the concrete, with a boy pounding his face into the ground. Blood sprayed in every direction.

Jax spat blood and rolled over, struggling to stand on unsteady legs. Boys surrounded him, all older, all bigger. All wearing specific colors—all shades of purple. Twenty colors. The gang ruled the neighborhoods to the east.

Ruthlessly. Finally, when Bast was out cold, but probably not dead, the boy beating him stood.

Definitely Hispanic, tall, and a few years older than Jax, the kid had several kill tats already down his neck. "You Mercury?" he asked.

Jax spat more blood. He couldn't outrun all of them, and if they wanted him dead, they'd get him dead. So he held his ground. "Yeah."

"Did you help an old lady at Maker's Grocery yesterday?" the kid asked.

Jax wiped blood from his eyes. Death didn't much scare him, but he couldn't leave Marcus alone. The kid was only six years old, and Jax had vowed he'd protect his little brother until death. "Sí."

"English, puto," the kid spat out. "Speak English."

"Why?" Jax asked. Damn it.

The kid shrugged. "It's what we speak. Usually."

Whatever. "Yeah, I helped a lady. Two guys tried to steal her purse. She was an old lady." Mierda. Maybe those guys were brothers to this guy. Shit. He was dead now.

"She's my granny," the kid said, sticking out his hand. "Cruz Martinez."

Jax took the hand and tried not to wince when they shook. Maybe his fingers were broken. "Jax Mercury. I'm glad she's okay."

Cruz looked down at the fallen kid. "You need better friends, Jax."

Yeah. Yeah, he did.

"In fact, you need brothers." Cruz smiled. "Come with me."

"Jax?" a soft voice asked, yanking him from his memories and right back into the hell of the present.

His eyelids slowly opened, and he focused on Lynne Harmony in the soft light. Her eyes were wide and her movements hesitant. How badly had he scared her? "I'm under control, Lynne."

"I know." She moved closer to the table.

He reached over for a chair and pulled it out like a guy at a fancy dinner. "Sit down. I'm sorry about earlier."

"So am I." She slid onto the chair, a small woman with such a big brain. "I wasn't fair to you and had no right to judge."

"Doesn't mean you're wrong." He truly didn't know if he was leading or not, but so long as there was somebody to fight, he'd keep stabbing. "I thought I locked you in for the night. You should get some sleep."

"Sami finished training with the kids and dropped by to check on me. Then she escorted me down here before going out on patrol. My brain is working on a problem, and I'm not ready to sleep. It's not even midnight yet, anyway." Lynne eyed the whiskey bottle. "I'm not a prisoner."

That was exactly what she was. He nudged his still-full whiskey glass toward her. "Cheers."

She accepted the glass and lifted it to her nose, sniffing. Her eyes closed, her pretty eyelashes fluttering against her blushing skin. "Yum."

Hell, she looked like that just before she came. His cock sprang up, and he shifted his weight to hide the evidence. "Drink."

She sipped and then downed the entire shot. Sputtering, she wiped her eyes. "Wow, that's good."

Actually, it was shit whiskey. Bottom of the barrel. But a luxury nonetheless. "Want another?"

"No." She set down the glass and studied him. "Is Jax short for Jackson?"

"No." He eyed his new stitches. "My mama didn't speak English very well, and she meant to name me Jack."

Lynne smiled. "I like Jax. It suits you."

Could he even have a normal conversation like this? He

cleared his throat. The previous night, he'd fucked the woman until they'd both dropped from exhaustion. This nicety? Might be too much for him. "How did you, ah, get your name?"

Her slender fingers played with the shot glass. "My mother's sister was named Lynne." She shrugged. "Pretty simple."

Right. "Your parents—they were nice people?"

She smiled. "Yes. My mother was a veterinarian, and my father a professor at Harvard. Good people." She lost the grin.

Sounded like smart and successful people—definitely upper class and the opposite of his family. "Did Scorpius get them?" he asked.

"Yes." One word full of guilt and pain.

"I'm sorry."

She blinked. "Me too."

A rustle sounded by the doorway. Ernie Baysted, sixty-year-old retired marine, hitched his impressive bulk into the room. "I've got something. On the ham. A message being sent all around."

Lynne's breath audibly caught.

Jax stood and reached for her hand with his good one. For months, Ernie had manned the ham radio, trying to send messages, trying to receive anything. Could there finally be news? Maybe some sort of consolidated effort? He launched into a jog behind Ernie, trying not to run over the guy. Lynne moved at his side, albeit more slowly, trying to tug away.

He didn't know what her problem was, but he needed to keep her close.

She paled and fought him, and he turned on her. "What are you doing?"

Her lips opened and then closed. Thoughts, so many of them, scattered across her face along with fear. "I, ah, need to go to the bathroom." She eyed the outside door.

Awareness tickled down his spine. "No, you don't. Why are you afraid?"

She lifted her chin. "I'm not."

Definitely a lie, but he didn't have time to suss it out. "Good. Get a move on." Keeping a firm grip, he launched back into motion.

They hurried into the small room Ernie had set up, which used to be an office on the first floor. He slid down and turned dials. "The voice said a message would be forthcoming in a minute. It was a man." Ernie's faded blue eyes lit up. "A person. A real person."

Jax pulled Lynne in front of him. "Stay still," he ordered.

She shook her head. "I have a headache and should—"

What the hell was wrong with her? Jax wrapped his good arm around her waist and pulled her back into his body, both of them facing Ernie. "Just hold on a minute. I'll take you back after the message." Jesus. She was stiff as could be.

A loud squeak echoed, and Ernie adjusted a knob. A male voice became audible:

"Hello. To anybody hearing this message, hello. This is Commander Greg Lake of the U.S. Elite Force and the current vice president of the United States. We are the force created specifically by the president of the United States, and we are strong and in control—the Brigade and other military arms now answer to us. If anybody hears this message, please contact us. We have this message on a loop, but we are monitoring responses, and we will respond as soon as possible. We have food and medical supplies as well as protection from the Rippers."

Jax breathed out. Thank God. There was organized resistance out there.

Lynne trembled, and he drew her nearer. Was she so relieved she was shaking?

The message continued:

"The president has authorized us as a military unit under martial law, and we are here to help. Contact us with the numbers of your survivors as well as location, and we'll send troops as soon as possible. The president is also issuing a warning to anybody coming in contact with Lynne Harmony, the woman the world knows as Blue Heart. She is a carrier of a more dangerous strain of the infection, and she is a Ripper with a deadly plan. If anybody has seen Lynne Harmony, contact us immediately."

Jax froze.

Ernie slowly turned around, his eyeglasses askew.

What the hell? Jax grabbed Lynne's arms and yanked her around. "Anything you want to tell me?"

She'd gone so pale her lips matched her blue heart. "Remember that promise you made to me?"

He slowly lifted his chin, keeping her gaze. "Yeah. You finally going to tell me who you want dead?"

She swallowed, her green gaze meeting his evenly. "Yes. You promised to kill the president of the United States for me." Her shoulders went back. "Why don't you get on that now?"

Chapter Eighteen

———————⊰◈⊱———————

*There's no fiercer creature on earth
than a woman protecting her own.*

—Dr. Franklin Xavier Harmony

As soon as they were inside their apartment again, Lynne slowly backed away from Jax and fumbled to twist on the lantern. Earlier, she'd tidied up the best she could, but the orange counter still hung drunkenly from the wall, so she had to be gentle with the lantern in the center. "Thank you," she whispered.

"Don't thank me." He leaned back against the door and crossed his arms. "I told Ernie to hold off on doing anything until I returned. I plan to respond to the military tomorrow morning."

Then she had about six hours to get the hell out of there. "Okay."

He studied her. No expression, no hint at the passion she knew lay within him. None of the anger, either. A chill swept down her spine. Jax was scarier in full control than in a fierce temper. "Care to explain?" he asked. His tone hinted she would explain, one way or the other.

Exhaustion pummeled down on her with a strong dose of

futility. She crossed to drop onto the bed. "Bret Atherton is a Ripper."

Jax coughed. His brow wrinkled, and his chin lowered. "You're telling me the president of the United States is a serial killer?"

Lynne lifted a shoulder. "You know he started out as Speaker of the House, right?"

"Yes, but then the president died of the fever, and the vice president died of a heart attack. The Speaker was third in line."

How fucked up was that, anyway? "Nobody voted for the guy." She clasped her hands together in her lap. "And the vice president didn't die of a heart attack. Bret Atherton killed him."

Jax blinked. Slowly. He opened his mouth to speak, and somebody rapped on the door. "What?" he asked.

"We have a problem." Wyatt's voice came through the door, strong and filled with stress. "There's a scavenger team missing."

"Goddammit." Jax pushed away from the door, then looked down at her. "We're not done. I'm putting a guard on the door until I get back."

Lynne didn't flinch. She knew Jax well enough to guess that he'd reach out to the closest thing to a military that still existed, thinking he could control the outcome. But not even Jax Mercury could outmaneuver pure evil. There had to be a way for her to get free. "Just please don't let Ernie respond until we finish our talk." Thunder bellowed outside as if in agreement.

"He'll have to wait until the storm passes anyway. Tomorrow morning, Lynne." Jax unlocked the door and stepped outside, closing the heavy metal with a slight nudge. Several locks quickly engaged.

Lynne dropped her head. She'd figured Bret would find her, but not this quickly. Not until she'd had a chance to find the location of Myriad. Before he did. Jax Mercury had been a distraction she shouldn't have allowed, and he'd been even smarter about keeping her contained than she'd figured. She'd underestimated him.

Lightning zagged sharply outside, lighting the room. She desperately needed a few hours' sleep, but then she'd have to find a way to escape. Rain beat against the boarded window, but without the glass, droplets slid down the wall. With a sigh, she stood and pulled the bed away from the wall so the blankets wouldn't get wet. Then she curled up, her head on her hand.

The thrum of the angry weather outside and the meager lantern light inside lent a sense of coziness to the barren room. The fear she'd lived with for so long surrounded her. She'd rather get the battle over with and stop running, but first she had one more job to do. One more hope to chase. Or rather, one more duty to fulfill. Hope had disappeared too long ago to regain.

She replayed the canned message in her mind. The president of the United States. The person hadn't been named. If he was third in line, who was fourth? Secretary of State? Hopefully not. Though even that crackpot would be better than Bret. Anybody would be better than Bret Atherton.

Had she ever loved him? There was a time, before Scorpius descended, that she had felt the giddiness, the sheer excitement, of what might've been love. Bret was the blond golden boy with an edge who had intrigued her. From a wealthy broken family that had kept up appearances, he'd excelled in school and then in the House of Representatives with sheer genius and stubborn will. He'd been ambitious, dedicated, and determined. She'd liked that in him. There was no subterfuge or hidden agenda, just a balls-out approach that had quickly propelled him into the Speaker position.

But she hadn't committed fully to him.

Something, call it instinct, had whispered for caution. Every once in a while, a phrase would pass his lips that gave her pause. A view of women, no doubt colored by his drunken mother who'd worn genuine pearls and a fake smile. But Lynne had told herself that everybody had issues.

Muttering about issues, Lynne allowed sleep to pull her under.

The dream, she knew well. Most people found darkened alleys and faceless attackers in their nightmares. Not Lynne.

She stood in the Oval Office, surrounded by splendor and symbols of power. Her elbows and wrists ached, as usual, from the vials of blood taken daily for the previous three months. In the early days of Scorpius, every survivor who didn't become a Ripper was treated like a lab rat. There were so few of them, and her blue heart had made her even more worthy of study than the others.

The president sat across from her at his desk. Pale and wan, his gnarled hand trembled when he spread out papers. "According to Vice President Atherton, you're no more contagious than anybody else who has had the fever." The president had nodded at Bret, who sat next to Lynne. "Including the vice president himself."

Lynne turned and smiled at Bret. He'd been infected somehow, yet he'd survived the contagion. Nobody had attacked him, but the bacteria could live on surfaces as well as within people, and he'd come in contact with it. Her feelings were a little hurt that he hadn't confided in her during his illness, but that was the least of her problems right now. "I'm so glad you made it," she murmured.

"As am I." Bret reached out and took her cool hand in his warm one as he turned to the president. "I asked the Secret Service to bring Lynne here so you could see she's no more

contagious than anybody else and should be allowed her freedom."

Lynne tangled her fingers in his, holding tight. The CDC, her former colleagues, had pretty much kept her locked down for the last three months in the emergency triage hospital created in D.C. While she'd continue to help them find a cure for Scorpius, she still wanted her personal freedoms. "Thank you."

The president rubbed his eyes. "Millions are already dead, soon to be billions, and I have what amounts to serial killers running amok. In addition, our enemies abroad haven't been hit as badly as we have by Scorpius, so there's talk of a foreign attack coming. I'm sorry, Dr. Harmony, but I don't have time to worry about your personal freedom. Much of the world blames the CDC for failing so spectacularly, and many of our enemies believe we're hiding a cure. That you, with your blue heart, are the cure."

A pit opened up in Lynne's stomach. "That's not true."

Bret shook his head. "Keeping her prisoner is against everything we are fighting for right now."

The president nodded, his eyes bloodshot and rimmed by dark circles. "I know, but I have no choice." He cleared his throat. "We have to make the difficult decisions now."

Bret stilled. "Then you should make the choices and stop sitting here being a coward."

The president gasped, and his nostrils flared.

Lynne frowned, the hair on the back of her neck standing up. "Bret!"

"The world is crumbling, and we need to make a stand. We need to impose martial law everywhere and take out the enemies we can right now," Bret said.

"You've lost your mind," the president spat out.

Bret stood. Since the fever, he'd somehow filled out even more, although he'd always been in good shape. He held a bound set of papers and moved around the desk. "I have the newest intelligence reports, and North Korea is about to strike."

The president fumbled for his glasses and placed them gingerly on his nose.

Then Bret struck.

Faster than Lynne would've thought possible, he clamped his hands around the president's neck and yanked him to the ground. The prestigious leather chair crashed against the wall.

"Bret!" Lynne leaped around the massive desk and jumped on his back.

He didn't even twitch. Instead, as the president struggled beneath him, ineffectually kicking out, Bret choked the life out of him. Spittle flew from the elderly man's mouth, and then his lips went slack in death.

It happened so quickly.

Lynne scrambled away from Bret, her gaze on the wide, unseeing eyes of the president. Shock rocked through her. She opened her mouth to scream, but Bret was on her, taking her down.

He slapped his hand over her mouth, and his body flattened hers. "Not a word," he ground out, his face an inch away, his blue eyes hard.

She blinked. What had just happened? His hand pressed down, and her teeth ground against her lips. Tears sprang to her eyes, and she nodded. With him on top of her, she couldn't move.

His eyes warmed.

Her entire body chilled.

"He was weak, and we need strength in this office. We're at war on several fronts," Bret hissed.

Panic stopped her breath, and she started to struggle, shoving against him.

He removed his hand. "Stop fighting me."

Slowly, she shook her head. A tear slipped down her face. Who was this man? "You killed him."

"Of course," Bret said. "There's important work to do, and it's life or death."

Lynne breathed out, trying not to move against him. He was stronger than she was, and she was weakened by having given blood again that morning. "The fever affected you, Bret." Did he see that?

He slid his lips against hers. "I know, but I'm not a Ripper. I'm just more focused than before. It's possible different individuals can be affected different ways."

She tried to push her head back against the floor. He was showing no regret for killing the man next to them. "Yes. But you just killed the president." She tried to eye the door to the Oval Office. "The Secret Service isn't going to let you go."

Bret flashed his teeth. "The men outside the door are mine."

"You have your own men." Lynne blinked. Terror froze her body, but she could still focus. "This isn't you," Lynne snapped out. She glared at him. At the man she'd considered planning her life with, at the man she'd trusted.

"Yes, it is, and I'm making the difficult decisions." He shoved both hands in her hair and pulled it back from her face. "You're mine, Lynne. You and I are going to heal this nation and lead it into the next phase of history. We're going to protect and defend our people by any means necessary."

A soft knock echoed on the door, and an agent stepped inside. "Mr. Vice President? We need to get moving. Now."

Lynne's mouth dropped open. Should she ask for help?

Bret stood, drawing her up. "Lynne Harmony, meet Greg Lake, my new head of, well, everything."

Greg, his eyes darker than midnight, gave a short nod. "Ma'am."

Lynne didn't move. The president lay at an awkward angle, dead in the Oval Office. "What now?" she asked.

"We make a speech to the country, to the world, about the tragic passing of the president, and I step up." Bret caressed her arm.

She had to get out of there. "I need to work. In fact, I have to go check in with the outlying labs. You still want a cure, right?" Did he? Maybe he no longer wanted a cure.

"Of course. We need the power and control a cure will give us, no matter what. America will lead the whole world if we have a cure." He turned and pinched her chin with affection. "I'll have you escorted to the labs at the CDC, and as soon as I take control and put everything in place, you'll stay here."

She could feel the blood drain from her face. "I have a bacteria to beat." There were some promising results from using nanoparticles to destroy the toxins caused by Scorpius, so perhaps she could still save Bret. Turn him back into the man she'd thought he was.

He smiled. "I'll have guards on you."

She forced another smile while warning skittered down her spine. "I appreciate your trying to keep me safe." Her voice trembled, and she couldn't meet his eyes.

"We're working together, right?" More demand than question lived in his words.

She no longer knew the answer to that question. "Of course. I have too many enemies." Which unfortunately was true. Her blue heart made her a target.

He must've heard the doubt in her voice. With unreal reflexes, he grabbed her throat and yanked her face toward his, which had contorted into harsh lines. "Don't make me one of them."

She swallowed, hindered by his hold. Her knees tried to buckle. "I won't."

* * *

Thunder ripped across the sky, yanking her awake and back to Jax Mercury's bed in the present. Tears cooled her face. She'd trusted a man once, and the fever had destroyed him. Or perhaps it had merely brought out the sociopath that had always been lurking inside him. Now she'd made her bed, literally, with another soldier, another strategist, another deadly man who'd survived the fever. A man raised on the streets who fought dirty and would do anything to follow whatever path he decided was just.

Trusting again would be foolish.

She took several deep breaths. Her subconscious had gone to work while she'd slept, despite the nightmare. The numbers, the ones she'd memorized, flitted into a pattern. A simple pattern. Numbers one and two combined into the first number of a city block. Numbers three and four equaled the next number, and then so on. Coordinates. Holy crap. She could find Myriad. Probably. If she did, and if she found the information about vitamin B there, she'd have something to bargain with. Something strong.

But going out into the storm—going into the city alone—would be stupid. Really stupid. So her only chance lay in negotiating with Jax. If he wanted the location of Myriad, he had to vow to refrain from calling Bret. Or he had to let her go before he did so.

Now she had something with which to negotiate. This time she had to stand firm—they were going to do things her way for once. Whether he liked it or not.

Chapter Nineteen

———— ❈ ————

*No man chooses evil because it is evil;
he only mistakes it for happiness, the good he seeks.*

—Mary Wollstonecraft Shelley

President Bret Atherton stiffened in a leather chair once used by the owner of the three largest Las Vegas casinos. The impressive mansion overlooking a now overgrown golf course housed the unit traveling with him, while he'd taken over the small guest house next to the pool. Although the water had evaporated, the bottom had been painted with a trio of sparkling mermaids that amused him. He could use a generator on the house if he wished, although he needed to conserve gas, unfortunately.

It was spring in Vegas, which meant milder temperatures and perhaps a bit of rainfall. Or not. Any day his men would find Lynne Harmony, and then they'd return to his power base in D.C.

She'd ripped out his heart when she'd left him, and he wanted an explanation. Everything he'd done was to protect her, whether she liked it or not. And he needed to find Myriad before she did because only God knew what she'd do with the data there. The woman had been unstable since being infected with the bacteria, and he'd failed to help her.

When she'd run, he'd created the Elite Force to find her and bring her back.

A knock sounded on the double-paned glass door.

"Enter," he said, shifting his weight and shoving closer to the massive desk he'd had placed in what used to be the living room of the guest house. It was after midnight, but he didn't require sleep like he had before being infected.

Greg Lake, the leader of the Elite Force and his first in command, strode inside, all but standing at attention. "Mr. President."

"Vice President Lake," Bret returned, having sworn Lake in immediately after he'd become president. "Have a seat and report."

Lake glanced at the leather guest chairs, and his upper lip curled. "As you wish, sir." He took a seat, his posture ramrod straight.

Bret wanted to ask, not for the first time, if there was an iron bar up the guy's ass. Sitting down seemed to insult him. "Do you have a report?"

"Yes, sir." Lake was in his late thirties and had been a rising star at the Secret Service before Scorpius wiped out most of the agents. "The Elite Force is continuing to track Lynne Harmony to the west and is closing in."

"Do you have her current location?"

"No."

Damn it. Bret fought to keep his face calm. "Continue."

"We have forces defending key forts and protecting sites as well as gathering weapons throughout the country. They're reporting in to us but not really taking orders."

Bret bit back a sharp retort. Society had gone to hell, and he desperately needed an active military to rebuild the United States. He had to shore up his own power base, add to the Elite Force he'd created to hunt down Lynne, before getting everybody back in line. "What about Deacan McDougall?" The man had been personally appointed by the former president as the leader of the Brigade, the first line of defense against Scorpius, and much of the military answered to him. If Bret could get McDougall in line, he'd regain the power of a true presidency.

"McDougall is up north dealing with NORAD last I heard," Lake said. "He hasn't reported in for several days, but he will. McDougall is a patriot."

Whose wife was best friends with Lynne Harmony, yet another reason Bret needed to get Lynne under his thumb. The Brigade and the Elite Force hadn't worked together before, and the time was coming for them to combine. "Any reports since we reached out to the public about Lynne?"

"We have the message continually looping, and we've received many responses. An interesting one came from a co-op in northern California."

"A co-op?" Bret lifted an eyebrow. "Like a farming co-op?"

"Yes." Lake smiled, revealing stark white teeth. "They sound like a bunch of farmers with a ham radio, so we could easily take their food."

Bret rubbed his smoothly shaven chin. "Hmm. We're going to need food, and they know how to farm. We might have to implement some sort of tax that requires their trading food."

"For what?" Lake asked.

"Their lives. We allow them to live, and they do as they're told." Bret didn't have time for niceties, and he no longer had an IRS to take taxes. "We're under martial law, Congress is gone, the Supreme Court is gone, and only the executive branch is left. I think this time we might take a lesson or two from feudal England."

Lake chuckled. His pure blue eyes contrasted with his sharp buzz cut in a way that made the man look like a knife. "Yes, Mr. President."

The perfect soldier. Bret smiled. "Are you sure you haven't been infected by Scorpius?"

"I have not, sir."

Interesting. Lake had the rare characteristic of lacking a moral compass to mess with his life, and Bret could appreciate that fact. A part of him wanted to infect Lake just to see what he could become, but another part counseled caution. First, he didn't want to lose the man who'd walk through fire for him, and second, he didn't need Lake any stronger and smarter than he already was. "You are a true soldier, Greg," Bret said.

Lake's chin rose. "Thank you, Mr. President, although so far I'm failing you in the most important mission, considering I personally chose the men for the Elite Force."

"Yes, but that's not entirely your fault," Bret said, tugging on a small USB drive he wore on a black cord around his neck. His Harmony USB drive. All of her research as well as Nora McDougall's research was on it. He understood most of their findings and knew more information was at the damn Myriad Labs. Why the former president had kept it top secret was beyond him, and more than a little frustrating, considering Bret had killed him before gaining the information.

The flash drive also held Bret's pictures of Lynne, and if he wanted, he could get somebody to rig an old laptop with a generator just to see her. Although he had plenty of pictures in his paper file, which he looked at nightly. "Lynne's uncle was a retired cop, and a damn good one. Obviously, he was also very good at disappearing. Not every soldier can be that, ah, effective."

Lake's jaw hardened, and a vein stood out in his neck. "I will make sure we find her, sir."

"I believe you. She has been steadily traveling west, and if she continued her trajectory, she has to be somewhere between Arizona and the Pacific. We will find her." Bret tapped his fingers on the desk. "She's heading west to find Myriad. Are we any closer to locating it?"

"No. The only intel we've gathered is that Myriad is in California."

Another knock rapped on the door.

Lake instantly shot to his feet and stood at attention.

"Enter," Bret said, eyeing the canister of Scotch on the far counter. He hadn't had a drink all day.

A young soldier entered. "Sir? We've had contact with a community just outside of Lake Havasu City in Arizona. Five families, basically scavenging to live."

Bret sat back. "So?"

"They helped Lynne Harmony for two nights," he said.

Lake pivoted around. "Are they sure?"

The soldier swallowed. "Yes, sir. She was by herself, no doubt recovering from our shooting her uncle in Tucson, and they gave her food and shelter. On the second night, one of them caught the glow from her heart through her shirt, so she ran. They haven't seen her since, but after our message, they're afraid they've been infected with the stronger strain of the Scorpius bacteria."

There was no stronger strain. Bret fought the heat of fury at hearing Lynne had escaped once again. His temperament hadn't returned to normal after the infection, and he had to fight to control himself. "You know we invented the rumor about her in order to get people to call us back, right?"

The kid widened his stance. "Yes, sir."

Bret focused on Lake. "How many men do we have with us?" He'd had to spread his new units out across the country gathering intel, food, and weapons as well as protecting crucial resources.

"We have twenty-five on this mission, sir," Lake said.

"Good. Send three seasoned men to meet with the families and get all information they might have. By any means necessary." Bret played with a pure silver letter opener that would look beautiful piercing a traitor's throat. "Then kill them."

The kid at the door sucked in air. "They're just families, sir."

"You're excused," Lake snapped.

The kid wobbled and then disappeared.

Lake shook his head. "The kid can shoot but lacks mental strength. He was a college kid before Scorpius."

Bret gripped the letter opener. "You can strip him down mentally and retrain him. I have confidence."

"Yes, sir." Lake's head lifted at attention. "About the five families. At some point, we're going to rebuild society, and we'll need, well, civilians. For the menial work."

True. Bret sighed. "To imagine that one year ago, the United States had more than 300 million citizens." Scorpius had truly thinned out the herd. "Now we have, what? Much less than 1 percent of our population survived; even fewer have not yet been exposed to Scorpius. At our last guess, we still have maybe five hundred thousand citizens spread throughout the country." Many of them farmers who were off the grid and far enough from cities not to be infected. "We can take out five families who dared to help Lynne Harmony." They were lucky he didn't order them tortured first.

Lake nodded. "Yes, sir. Speaking of countries, any news from abroad?"

"No." Bret swallowed. "We have no idea of the status of North Korea, Russia, or even the Middle East. They closed their borders when Scorpius began to spread, and I haven't heard whether they were successful or not." He needed more troops and now. "We have to assume they contained the bacteria better than we did, and at some point, they'll attack us."

Lake shook his head. "With all due respect, I don't believe anybody contained Scorpius. At least we have several pilots and secured planes."

"I know, but fuel and maintenance are issues." Bret twirled the letter opener. "Scorpius swept through our military bases as quickly as it did the cities. We were not prepared." Now that he was president, he'd do a much better job of keeping his people alive.

There was a reason he'd lived when so many others had died. He'd fulfill his purpose. He was born for this.

He reached for a map to spread on the desk, eying the circles around various known survivor groups. "These are the groups we know have some sort of leadership." And fighting ability. "When we have time to focus, we should take out the Mercenaries."

"Yes." Lake glanced down. "After we secure Lynne Harmony, we'll double our efforts to reach out and start rebuilding the rule of law. Right now, these rogue gangs are living under their own leadership. That must stop."

Bret tapped a finger on Los Angeles. "Any news about L.A.?"

Lake nodded. "From our ham radio contact, it seems the same. Several rebel groups vying for food and resources, the most powerful still being led by Jax Mercury."

Ah, the special-ops soldier who had banded together a group in L.A. while there was still television and Internet. Known for his skills and brutality dealing with the enemy, he'd become almost a folk hero in less than a month, and everybody had been warned to stay out of L.A. if they didn't want to join his Vanguard group. Bret rubbed his chin. "After we find Lynne, we should reach out to Mercury. He's still in the service and will follow orders."

"Yes, sir."

Bret eyed the door. "Dismissed."

Lake made a perfect pivot and marched from the room.

Bret stood and reclaimed the letter opener while igniting a lantern as he moved. He might not have Lynne yet, but he did have a woman to deal with. His boots clomped on the dusty tile as he walked through the kitchen to a small doorway for a storage room for pool items.

Now a woman sat in the corner, a chain around her ankle, her hair falling into her face. She lifted her head when he set down the lantern, hazel eyes blinking awake.

He let the letter opener glint in the muted light. While he didn't like this part of his job, he'd do whatever was necessary to lead the country. "Did you have a nice nap, Vivienne?"

She didn't answer. A bruise spread an angry purple and yellow across her cheekbone from when he'd lost his temper the day before.

He peered closer. When he'd kidnapped her, she'd been wearing a gray suit with skirt and red high heels. The shoes she'd lost, and the skirt was more brown than gray now. Yet he left her in it as a reminder of who she used to be. "Are you ready to tell me where Lynne Harmony is?"

"Fuck you," Vivienne said without much heat. Exhaustion lined her dirty face, and scratches marred her bare legs.

"Okay." He smiled and stepped closer.

Her head snapped against the brick wall. "Lynne Harmony, Lynne Harmony, Lynne Harmony."

His dick instantly went limp. Fury bit into him with the heat of a thousand fires. "You fucking bitch." He kicked out, nailing Vivienne in the calf.

She cried out and drew her legs closer, but triumph glittered in her eyes. "Oops."

Smart. She'd figured out right away how to keep from getting raped. He smiled. "My heart might be with Lynne, but I could have ten soldiers here in a minute to fuck you to death."

"Your penis, not your heart, is obsessed with Lynne." Vivienne coughed. "I'll tell your men you can't get it up."

That was only one of the reasons he'd spared her, but at some point, he was going to shackle her, spread-eagled, and watch every single man in his command take her. For now, he'd continue his campaign to break her. He glanced at the bucket in the corner serving as her toilet. "Where's the Bunker?"

She snorted. "The Bunker is a fantasy invented by loons. There's no Bunker."

Bullshit. He'd seen enough hints in the documents he'd found in the Oval Office to know that there was a Bunker out there, one safe from the outside and fully stocked . . . with the cure hopefully. But that knowledge had been in the former president's head, and Bret hadn't realized it until too late. "The Bunker exists."

"Huh." Vivienne blinked.

He grimaced. "Don't you want out of here?"

"I don't know," she murmured, her pink lips twisting. "I'm seeing the charm of the place."

He studied her. Even after a month of containment, of his messing with her head, of sparse showers, she was beautiful in a tragic way. Long blond hair, blue-green eyes, aristocratic facial features. Although feminine, she had the spirit of a fine soldier. Too bad she wasn't Lynne. "If you just tell me what I want to know, I'll let you go. Anywhere you want."

She snorted. "Bullshit. Even if I had the ability to find Lynne, and I don't, you'd kill me the second you found her." Vivienne lowered her chin. "I know you think I'm psychic, Bret, but I'm not. Never have been, and never will be."

Oh, she was. "I've read your file, and I've seen you work. Before the fever, you had abilities beyond the norm, and you will tell me what I want to know."

She rolled her eyes and settled her head back on the wall, her movements weary. "Listen, jackass. I was a profiler, and a damn good one, which was why they brought me in when Scorpius first started changing people's brains. I'm just good at profiling. There's nothing psychic about it, and I've never even met Lynne Harmony, so I can't guess what she'd do."

He shook his head, his hand tightening on the silver letter

opener. "You're lying. You solved several murders for the FBI before Scorpius hit, and your abilities were beyond normal even then. Nobody is that good." His arm jerked with the need to jam the letter opener into her leg. "You survived the fever, so any skills you had should be enhanced. In fact, I read how the CIA used you to trace the path of the contagion through the military."

She blinked.

His chest heated. "Yeah. I have those files. Nobody should've been able to figure out those stats, and yet you did."

Her lips tightened.

"Scorpius changes brains, and it changed yours. Now tell me where Lynne is. Or I will kill you."

"Go ahead," Vivienne whispered, shutting her eyes.

Ah. He was getting closer. "I have new plans for you."

Her eyelids opened. "You're a Ripper, and that's a fact. You know that, right?"

He shook his head. "Wrong. The fever reorganized my brain and increased my intelligence, much as it rewired your brain and gave you new skills." Based on the research he'd studied, it was more than possible.

Her fine eyebrows arched. "Oh, you're definitely a crazed killer. There are several types of serial killers, and you're the more organized kind. Those whispers in your head telling you I'm physic or that you're special? Yeah. They're lying to you."

The woman was a good liar, but he'd seen what she could do. Bret backed away from her. "We'll know soon enough."

She stilled. "Meaning what?"

He grinned. "I sent men to a former CIA location a couple of days ago, and they'll be returning with drugs you won't be able to beat. Finally, you'll tell me the truth."

"You are a damn nut," she whispered. "Why don't you just kill me and be done with it?"

"I'll let the drugs do that." He rubbed his chin.

For the first time in weeks, real fear glittered in her eyes. Yet she didn't speak.

Yeah. He was finally getting her attention. He grabbed the lantern and turned for the door, leaving her in the dark. He had to get to Myriad in time to stop Lynne, and then he'd take her home. Soon.

Chapter Twenty

———◦◦◦———

Monsters are real, and ghosts are real too.
They live inside us, and sometimes, they win.

—Stephen King

The rain continued to batter the earth, and only the lightning periodically piercing the cloud cover lit the way through the inner city as they searched for the missing scavengers.

Broken and empty buildings lined their way until they reached the warehouse district. The smell of the ocean, salty and briny, filled the air.

Jax kept low to the chipped concrete, his baseball hat shielding his face, his bulletproof vest hopefully protecting his chest. He'd been shot more than once, and at some point, the vest would just fail. He reached the south side of a building on the planned scavenger list for the night and put his back to it.

Wyatt appeared next to him, his breath panting out. "We need more vests."

They needed more of everything. "We're sure this was one of the scheduled locations tonight?" Jax asked.

Wyatt gulped in air. "Yes. We sent a team to scout this area of the warehouse park, looking for anything. Preferably fuel and food. Guns and ammo. Per usual."

The team hadn't returned by the appointed time, so Jax had ordered sets of two out to the known targets. "I don't like sending kids out, Wyatt."

Wyatt nodded. "Pete and Laurie are eighteen, but I get what you're saying. Have you met them?"

Jax peered around the corner at the entrance to the warehouse. "Sure."

"Yeah? What's Pete's last name? His story?" Wyatt asked.

Jax slowly turned to eye his friend. "Why would I know?"

"Exactly." Wyatt cocked his gun and straightened his shoulders.

Jesus. Not Wyatt, too. "I'm sorry. Am I supposed to sit down with everybody in our little montage of a community and share? Bond?" Fuck. Jax was doing his best to keep everyone alive. He didn't have time to get to know more than five hundred people.

Wyatt lifted a Super Bowl–sized shoulder. "Why not?"

A clatter echoed inside the medium sized metal building. Jax froze. "We go in fast and hard."

"Copy that."

Jax jogged around the building, bunched, and kicked the door in square. It flew open, and he ran, gun sweeping out. A man in a ripped gray suit turned, his fingers wrapped in the long blond hair of a severed head, his mouth covered in blood. He chewed and lifted the head to his mouth again.

Holy fuck. Bile rippled up Jax's throat, and he swallowed ruthlessly. Lifting his gun, he fired three shots between the eyes.

The Ripper fell back into several barrels, sending them scattering. More barrels scattered around the nearly empty metal building, and water dripped somewhere in the back.

Wyatt leaned over at his side, puking onto the concrete floor.

Shit. The blond was Laurie. Her headless corpse lay at an odd angle, half hidden by more barrels.

Jax shut down and jogged toward the nightmarish scene.

He kicked the Ripper, who rolled over onto his back, eyes unseeing and dead. Blood coated the ground, adding the smell of copper to the stench of unwashed flesh and death. Turning, Jax scouted the one-level building. Mainly empty except for the barrels; only one room stood off to the side. Probably what used to be an office.

He waited for Wyatt to gain control and then started for the office. Before he reached the door, another man, this one wearing a torn and filthy baseball uniform, stumbled out dragging Pete. Blood dripped from a gaping hole in Pete's neck, where his jugular had been bitten away. A white bone, the spine, stuck out at an odd angle.

"Jesus," Wyatt muttered, taking aim and hitting the Ripper center mass in a kill shot. "Two Rippers? Working together?"

"Probably just temporarily with two victims." Jax had seen wild, crazed Rippers as well as methodical, organized Rippers. "I'd give my left arm for a shrink or one of those FBI profilers from television." He needed to know more about what he was dealing with.

Lightning lit up the night outside the open doorway.

Wyatt sighed. "We burning them?"

Jax rubbed his aching chest. "Did either of the kids have family?"

"No more than the rest of us."

"Then we burn them here." Carrying the bloody carcasses through the violent weather and then all the way back to the group didn't make sense. "I'd rather nobody else saw them like this anyway."

Wyatt stalked across the bloody ground and hefted Pete in one big hand and the Ripper in the other, dragging them both to the other bodies. "The Rippers were probably decent people at one point, too."

Jax lifted an eyebrow. Wyatt had a way of seeing beyond the obvious, beyond the division between friend and enemy, into reality. "I'm glad you're here," Jax said.

Wyatt grimaced at the pile of death, his full lips set in a hard line. "I'm not."

Fair enough. Jax reached for a small canister of lighter fluid to spray on the bodies. Then he stood back. "You're the preacher."

Wyatt sighed. "At some point, you're gonna have to make a speech or give a eulogy, you know?"

"Not with you around." Jax folded his hands and shoved down the urge to gag at the smell. "I lead with action, not words."

"You need both." Wyatt lowered his head. "God, please accept these four victims into your arms, and maybe send us some help while you're at it. Amen."

Jax swallowed. "Amen." Was help coming? He needed to finish his discussion with Lynne before returning that message to Greg Lake.

Wyatt fumbled with a match.

"I've got it." Jax held out a hand. Wyatt faltered and then dropped the match into his palm. Jax leaned down and struck the match on his boot, igniting fire, which he dropped on the piles. Laurie's hair ignited first. He let out a low growl and then turned around. "Scout around and make sure there's nothing here to take back."

Wyatt went for the office, while Jax looked in the empty barrels and tried to ignore the stench of burning flesh. Finally, they met up at the door, both empty-handed.

Smoke billowed out. "Let's take cover the hell away from here," Jax muttered, leading the way into the storm and around several warehouses, most with open doors. Finally, he reached the overhang of a boat storage facility that looked out into the dark vastness of what used to be the city of Los Angeles. He hunkered down. "The rain should pass in a few minutes."

Wyatt slid to sit beside him on the concrete, shaking out

his wet baseball cap. "Maybe we should send larger scouting parties out."

Jax nodded. "Yeah. Who's in charge of that?"

Wyatt turned, and heat glimmered in his eyes. "You are."

Jax blinked. "No—"

"Yes, man. That's what I'm trying to tell you. Whether you like it or not, you're in charge of everything, and you have to know people to do it right." Wyatt inched the hat back on his head.

"I know my soldiers." Jax hunched his shoulders.

"I know, and that's why our soldiers are still alive. But you haven't taken over the rest of the camp. The entire group needs a leader, not just the fighters," Wyatt said.

Jax's throat tightened. "Wyatt—"

"I know." Wyatt flicked a rock away from his hand. "It's hard. Getting to know people now, caring about them, it's hard. Because most of us aren't going to make it."

Jax exhaled slowly. "You think I'm a pussy."

Wyatt grinned. "No. I think you're the toughest guy I've ever met, and I owe you my life. Without question. But I think you need to step up fully, to take over the entire group, for us all to survive. It's time."

Jesus. Why couldn't somebody else cater to the civilians and scouts? "Tace is usually the one trying to get me to open up."

"Tace isn't here." Wyatt leaned his head back against metal. "We should talk about him. He's worried."

"If he's worried, then he's fine." Jax stretched his legs out. Something poked his thigh, and he reached in for the newest gift from Lena.

Wyatt's eyebrows rose. "That's an odd rock."

"Yeah." Jax twisted the heart-shaped rock around in his hand. Blue dots, made by markers, formed a heart within the heart. "She's always giving me rocks with a heart somehow cut or drawn on them."

"Blue hearts?" Wyatt asked.

Jax stilled. "Sometimes." No. No way. He shook his head. "Doesn't mean anything. She's a little girl who likes hearts, most do, and her favorite color is blue." The girl had never spoken a word, and he truly had no idea who'd named her. "It's a coincidence." A chill skittered down his back.

"If you say so." Wyatt stretched his neck. "She always gives me watches or clocks. All broken."

Jax shuddered and glanced toward his buddy. "That's kind of creepy."

"Maybe, maybe not. Perhaps I remind her of a guy she knew who wore a watch." Wyatt picked up a pebble to toss across the vacant area. "Or Scorpius messed with her brain and those rumors about possible psychics are true." He grinned.

"You've never had the fever?"

Wyatt shook his head. "Nope. Not yet, anyway."

All right. So. Jax cleared his throat. "How is April Snyder doing?" He couldn't imagine losing a kid.

"Not good, but she's trying. Is working at organizing the scavenging parties."

"Good. Um, did you have family? Before Scorpius?"

Wyatt chuckled, the sound deeper than the storm. "This is you trying to connect?"

"Fuck you." Jax glared at the darkness.

"Sorry. Okay. Yeah. I was raised by my mom, who was a paralegal. Smart as heck. The fever got her." Wyatt rubbed his chin. "Before that, she was so damn proud when I graduated from Stanford and went to the NFL."

Stanford? Man. Jax had fought next to the man for months, and he hadn't known he'd gone to Stanford. "I figured you more for a Michigan State or Notre Dame guy." Both had great teams.

"Yeah, but I wanted to stay in California close to my mom." Wyatt shifted his feet.

"No wife or kids?" Jax glanced sideways at one of his friends and a man he should know a lot better than he did.

"Nope." Lines cut into Wyatt's face. "I was dating this woman, a cheerleader, and she was pretty cool. Gorgeous and smart." He cleared his voice, and his chin dropped. "She, ah, got pregnant."

Jax stilled. "Oh."

"Yeah." Wyatt grasped another rock and side-armed it across the pavement. "I was, unsure, you know? Worried about how a kid would affect my life." He shook his head. "I was an asshole."

"I doubt that." Jax shook his head.

Wyatt breathed in. "One day, I met her at the doctor's office for one of those ultrasound things? Saw a baby move." He rubbed his chest. "My baby."

"Yeah?"

"Yeah." Wyatt smiled, his lips trembling. "I thought it was a girl, but Margie thought a boy." He swallowed several times. "We never found out who was right. She caught Scorpius, and neither of them made it." He rubbed his eye. "I wanted that kid. After I saw her on that screen, I wanted her." He shrugged. "Although now I wonder. If I'd been more sure, if I'd—"

"No." Jax slapped an arm around his friend. "There are no ifs. Scorpius took them out, and there's nothing you could've done. You know that."

"Yeah." Wyatt shuddered. "I would've liked to see my baby girl."

Jax sighed. "Let's hope she would've had her mama's looks."

Wyatt chuckled, his chest moving, while one tear slid from his eye. "God willing." He pushed to his feet. "Let's get back. I don't mind bad weather."

Jax stood.

Wyatt frowned. "You have family?"

Jax's gut clenched. "A mom and a younger brother. They're both gone."

"Sorry." Wyatt peered into the empty land.

"Me too." Jax jogged into the rain, not feeling the chill. Maybe he didn't talk much, and perhaps he hadn't made much of an effort to talk to people or get to know them. But he'd sacrificed enough, damn it.

The run home took longer than he'd expected, thanks to the angry storm. The wind fought them, rain battered them, and debris chased them. Finally, they reached the outskirts of the protected area. He stopped and whistled a low tune. An answering whistle relaxed his shoulders. After checking in with the sentries, he ordered Wyatt inside while he scouted the outside to make sure all was well.

He hadn't figured out what to say to Lynne yet. True, he'd made a promise to kill, but he hadn't known he was promising to kill the president. If Lynne spoke the truth, and Atherton had turned into a Ripper, then he needed to be taken out. If Lynne was lying, Jax couldn't tell.

Sleeping with her had been a mistake. It was fucking with his head.

He paused at the south side of the building, looking up in time to see Lynne Harmony near the entrance. Her arms were crossed, and he could feel her gaze on him. Her posture was ramrod straight, and her chin was high.

Tension ticked down his spine. Instinct whispered he was about to have a hell of a fight. He reached her in long strides, his temper prickling. "Why the hell are you outside?" Had his people become so lax they just let her wander around?

She lifted an eyebrow, looking every bit the educated sophisticate. "I was waiting for you. It's time we talked."

"About what?" He put his hands on his hips and crowded into her space.

Fire flashed in her gorgeous eyes. "I know where Myriad is, and I'm willing to trade that information for your cooperation."

He studied her calm façade. The woman was trying to shake him down? Irritation clawed down his throat. "If I don't cooperate?"

"Then you don't get the information." Her delicate jaw hardened. "No matter what you do."

He'd had a rotten night, and now the woman he'd fought his own people to protect was practicing extortion? *Oh, hell no.* "Let's test that theory." Ducking his head, he tossed her over his shoulder.

Chapter Twenty-One

---◦◦◦◦◦---

The supreme art of war
is to subdue the enemy without fighting.

—Sun Tzu

Lynne coughed out, upside down over Jax's powerful shoulder. Shock kept her immobile up the stairs and into the apartment. The door clicked shut and he bent, putting her on her feet.

"What the hell?" she spat out.

He faced her fury, aggression in every line of his body. "You sure extortion is how you want to play this?"

She stopped breathing. Maybe it had been a bad plan, but now she was committed. "I'm sure we can work out an agreement."

"Sit down."

Anxiety bloomed in her chest, and her knees wobbled. Sitting down might be a good idea. There was no way she could get through him and out the door. So she backed away to perch on the sofa, wrapping her arms around her knees. "Are you going to sit?" she asked. Even across the rickety coffee table, he loomed.

He sat on the threadbare chair, the movement both graceful and intimidating, his gaze never leaving hers. "Now talk."

She bristled. "Stop ordering me around."

He extended his long legs onto the table and crossed one combat boot over the other. No expression marked his strong features, but the white scar along his jaw stood out in the meager light. "Lynne, I've had a shitty night. The only reason I'm not covered in blood and soot from burned bodies is because I've spent half the night running in a rain cold enough to pierce bone. Stop fucking with me, because I'm done."

The chill ticking over her skin had nothing to do with the rainy night. "Who died?"

"Two kids out scouting and two Rippers who might've been decent guys at some point."

Life sucked. "I'm sorry," she whispered.

"I don't care," he said evenly, revealing not a hint of the passionate man who'd taken her away the past night. "Now you're going to answer every damn question I have, and we'll end with the location of Myriad. First, why do you want the president dead, and why is he saying you're carrying a new infection?"

She exhaled, noting her racing heart rate. If she just seized right now, if her heart would finally burst, then all of the hell would be over. Yet her heart, blue and damaged, kept on ticking. Way too fast. Challenging Jax had been a bad idea. Cooperating was her only logical choice. Right now, anyway. "Fine. Bret is a Ripper with the power of the presidency behind him, and I saw him murder the sitting president."

"You were lovers."

"Yes." Heat climbed into her face. For goodness sake, she was a grown woman.

"You saw him kill a former president, and yet, nobody did anything." Jax didn't twitch a muscle.

"Right. Bret already had his people in place. They took me back to the temporary CDC in D.C. afterward, and I started planning my escape that day." She shuddered. "I stole a phone from one of the labs and called Uncle Bruce, who had already gathered supplies. Getting out took over a month, but we finally had the opportunity, which I already told you about. The second I got free, Bret created the Elite Force out of men from the Secret Service, the FBI, and the army to hunt me down. The EF's sole purpose for now is to find me."

Jax lifted his chin. "Why?"

"Bret says it's because he loves me, and because of my research on a cure for Scorpius. But what he really wants is to hurt me." God knew what he'd do to her if he actually caught her.

"So it's personal." Jax gave no indication whether he believed her or not, his voice remaining level and distant.

"Yes." Was it ever personal. "After the fever, he changed, became obsessed with power." Hell. Obsessed with her, too.

"Once and for all, are you carrying any sort of new infection?" Jax asked.

She shook her head, plucking a string on her worn pants. "Of course not. There's no new infection. That's just a ploy to get people to turn me in."

"Last I heard, the Brigade was the first line of defense against the Scorpius disaster."

She nodded. "Yes, but the Brigade is putting out fires all over the country by protecting nuclear supplies and other situations like that. The EF is a singular purpose or mission organization, and right now, I'm their target."

"Is the Brigade working with the EF?"

"No, I don't think so. When the EF caught up with us and killed my uncle, the Brigade, or rather, the McDougalls, weren't anywhere around."

Jax watched her like a hawk eyeing a defenseless field mouse. "Where is Myriad?"

She sighed, her shoulders slumping. "I think I found the coordinates of Myriad Labs in the data you secured from Baker and Baker."

Tension filled the space with a heaviness she could feel in her flesh.

Jax crossed his arms. "Why not just tell me instead of trying to force my cooperation?"

She hugged her legs. "I was afraid you'd turn me over to the Elite Force. I've got to get to Myriad before Bret does."

Jax lifted his chin, his gaze scorching. Did he believe her? "The president is going to Myriad?" he asked.

"He wants the records and tests at Myriad that may lead to a cure. If he has a cure, or even a way to help people survive the contagion better, he'll be able to control every nation in the world. Hopefully he doesn't know where I'm heading. But I know he's been tracking me," she murmured. "He confiscated all of my research notes, and I really need to get them, but I don't know how. I remember my research, but there were so many tests and so many different concoctions, I can't remember everything, even with my brain working better than before."

Jax rubbed his chin. "Tell me everything you know about the research that was being done at Myriad."

She lifted a shoulder. "Promise you won't turn me over."

"No. Talk now, Lynne."

Damn it. She really didn't have a choice. Somehow, she had to convince him, and maybe the truth would do it. "Fine. They'd managed to synthesize vitamin B in the lab in concentrated amounts, and I think their results showed promise. Enough to investigate further." She gestured with her hands as she spoke. "Bret was busy consolidating power and didn't pay much attention to my work or contacts at that point. He'd already survived the fever by then, and he'd changed. I didn't realize it at the time, though."

"His focus went from dealing with the crisis to consolidating his own power?" Jax asked.

"I guess."

Jax rolled his shoulders against the door. "You haven't seen him since he supposedly killed the sitting president?"

Supposedly. So much for trust. "That's the truth." Enough of this crap. Either Jax believed her, or he didn't. She shouldn't care. But her stomach hurt, and her temples pounded. Tears clogged her throat, but no way would she let them fall.

"Where's Myriad located?" he asked.

She settled. "If I have the coordinates right, it's in Century City."

"Good. I want those coordinates."

"Fine. What happens then?"

He watched her, no expression, filling the entire world with Jax Mercury. Even the atmosphere altered with his mood. "I haven't decided."

The constant fear living inside her slowly abated. If she died, she died. "Make me one promise."

"What's that?" he asked.

"If you decide to contact Bret, and he comes, kill me before he does." Without question, death at Jax's hand would be a hell of a lot less painful than letting Bret have a go at her.

"No promise."

She coughed out a laugh. Well, that sucked. Would Jax trade her to Bret to save his people? To obtain more vitamin B and medical supplies?

"Did he attack you?"

"No," she whispered. "I'm done sharing my story with you."

"You'll share whatever I want you to share," Jax said evenly.

That quickly, that easily, the fear disappeared. Completely. Realization dawned through her. Jax wouldn't sacrifice her— it wasn't who he was. She blinked. "I'm sorry."

His head jerked up. "For what?"

She rested her chin on her knees. "I'm not scared of you. It'd help a lot if I were, I think. But I'm not." He'd been inside her, and he'd been gentle. She'd seen him be kind to a little girl, and she'd seen him mourn at a grave site. "You won't hurt me."

His eyes finally softened.

She breathed out.

"You're underestimating my vow to protect my people, Lynne." His lip twisted. "I don't like myself much, and I'd hate myself if I hurt you. Yet I'll do exactly that if it'll get the job done for good."

Her breath stopped again. Not because of Jax's words, but because of the regretful tone. He meant it. Or at least, he thought he meant it. "I don't find you very self-aware," she murmured.

"How is there one ounce of naïveté in you after what you've gone through?" he asked. "Much of the blood permanently staining my hands is that of people I cared about. From childhood friends, to my fellow soldiers overseas, to my younger brother. Even the two kids I burned last night. You might want to keep that in mind."

Not a fact she'd likely forget. "We made a deal. If I told you everything I know, which I have, you promised to kill Bret. I've kept my part of the bargain, and I've even given you Myriad, which might hold a cure."

"You left out a couple of facts, darlin'."

"Just because he's the president—"

Jax's cheek creased, but his half-smile lacked any semblance of amusement. "Yes. Killing the current president of the USA, Ripper or not, is an important fact. Don't you think?"

She jumped in. "I've read your file. The military one without any redactions."

He froze. Even his chest stopped moving. "Excuse me?"

She swallowed, holding her knees again, instinctively trying to make herself as small as possible. "A friend at the CDC had a friend in Intelligence, and when all hell broke loose, files were easier to obtain. You were a legend already, taking over L.A., and I needed to know more."

Anger flared through his bourbon-colored eyes. Was anger better than nothing? Suddenly, she wasn't sure, yet she pressed on. "You were Army Special Forces, nicknamed Delta Force, a real badass. You've killed high-ranking officials before. Maybe not ours, but still." She'd sought him out for that fact as much as anything else. Bret was almost untouchable, and she'd needed a legend with a file like Jax's.

"What was in the file?" he whispered.

She flinched as if he'd shouted. "Everything. Your background, your training, and your missions. Even your past relationships, but not why you entered the military." He'd shared that with her willingly. Heat shot into her face. "I had to know before trying to escape the CDC." Her gaze dropped to the faded scars running up his hand and arm. "I know how you got those."

Fury lit crimson across his cheekbones. "Do you, now?"

She bit her lip to keep from apologizing. That would probably just set him off. "Yes. You were a hero."

If possible, he looked even angrier.

She tried to calm him. The man had the worst case of survivor's guilt she'd ever seen. "You couldn't save them all, Jax."

His head lifted, and his eyelids lowered, giving him a predatory look. "You don't know what you're talking about."

"Yes, I do," she said gently, like she would with any wounded animal. "The bomb exploded, and you were thrown free of the Humvee in Afghanistan." Yet instead of running away, instead of ducking for cover, he'd run straight back to the burning metal and shoved his arms through shards of glass to reach for his men, ripping his skin apart. He saved two of the men, but a soldier named Frankie Blake didn't make it. "You tried."

He didn't answer, just kept staring at her.

A shiver cascaded down her body. "The psych reports said that you and Frankie were good friends, and that you blamed yourself for his death."

"He re-upped because I had the year before."

"A bomb isn't your fault."

Even sitting, Jax Mercury was all threat. "He was the first friend I made in the military when I was a scared, angry kid from the streets. I owed him, and I failed."

"No—"

"And not any of this, not one thing of it, is any of your fucking business."

She blinked. When she'd read up on him, when she'd pried into his private life, she hadn't known they'd end up being together. Even so, the harsh words hurt. "Then let me go."

"No." He stood. "I told you that you were staying with Vanguard, and you should've listened to me."

A whimper tried to rise up her throat, and she swallowed it down. Releasing her knees, she shoved to her feet. If he was going to restrain her, his balls would be inside his body before he finished.

Oh, she wasn't delusional enough to think she could take Jax Mercury in a fight, but she'd make sure he lost the ability to ever reproduce. She bent her knees and lifted her arms, closing her fingers into fists.

"What the fuck are you doing?" he asked.

She blinked. "I thought we were, I mean . . ."

His brows drew down, and his expression, although unreadable, made her feel like a complete dumbass.

She lowered her arms. "I'm confused."

Amusement, for the first time that night and definitely at her expense, lit his eyes. "We're heading to the war room where the maps are so you can show me the location of Myriad."

"Oh." She wiped damp hands down her pants.

His amusement disappeared. "You're going to be honest and show me everything. Deviate from that order, even an inch, and I ain't gonna be gentle, Lynne. Get me?"

She slowly nodded, reminding herself that she wasn't scared of him. Nope. Not at all. "I get you."

"Good."

"I caught some sleep last night, but you didn't. You should sleep." She cleared her throat.

"I'm fine." He turned to open the door and stilled. "Has Lena, the little blonde girl, given you anything?"

Lynne stared at his back, her curiosity blooming. "Yes. A rock with the number four scratched into both sides."

His head lifted. "Two fours? Like my tattoo?"

"Yes. Why?"

He turned and pulled open a kitchen drawer to reveal a pile of rocks.

Lynne leaned closer to see the rocks all had hearts drawn or scratched into them. Blue hearts. "What in the world?" she breathed.

He shook his head and opened the door, walking into the hallway. "Mystery for later?"

She swallowed, more than happy to forget rocks for the moment. "What about Bret?"

"I'm returning that message. After that point, what happens depends on him." Jax widened the door. "Let's go. Now."

Chapter Twenty-Two

All wars are civil wars, because all men are brothers.

—François Fénelon

Jax led Lynne down the stairs to the main vestibule of the building. Morning light finally filtered through the glass doors, hopefully marking the end of the storm. After the shitty night with the headless corpse, his mind kept trying to return to Afghanistan and one of the worst days of his life, but he shoved the panic attack and pain away to be dealt with later. Now wasn't the time.

They reached the door to the war room. Something caught his attention, and he turned toward the outside door. His breath caught. Instinct flared down his back, and he stilled.

The world exploded.

Glass blew out of the truck windows. He tackled Lynne to the ground, covering her, ducking from flying glass. Another explosion rocked the earth, and metal parts flew through the day.

A scream came from outside. "Stay here." He turned and ran out into the smoke and kept going through the first line of vehicles to reach a downed guard—a woman named Heloise.

"Shit," he muttered, feeling for and not finding a pulse.

"I'm sorry, Jax," Lynne said, shoving hair from her face. The damn woman had followed him.

Another explosion pierced nearby metal, and he jumped over her, taking her down. He crouched onto his knees, got a good hold of her shirt, and lifted. Her hands and feet scrabbled against the mud. Staying low, he carried her around the closest barrier. "Report," he bellowed to Raze, who was running through the barrier, gun in hand, Sami on his six.

Another explosion echoed, and an engine part flew through the air. Fucking grenades.

His soldiers, armed with guns and knives, flowed out between the two barriers. A Molotov cocktail landed next to his feet, and he leaped for Lynne, throwing her away. The blast knocked him off his feet, and he landed hard. "Damn it." He shoved himself to stand in the mud. "Fucking Cruz."

"You sure it's him?" Tace asked, tossing Jax a semi-automatic weapon.

"Yes." Fucker loved Molotov cocktails. "Take defensive positions," he yelled, watching as the soldiers ranging from former teachers to golf instructors to marines fanned out as he'd taught them. He stalked over to Lynne and lifted her up.

She was wide eyed and trembling, with mud covering her entire right side. He pushed her toward Wyatt, who'd finished setting sentries into position. "Get her inside and secure before coming back out."

Wyatt grabbed Lynne's arm. "I've got you, Lynne." He turned and pulled her toward the openings in the minivans. Automatic fire spattered through the day, pinging off metal. Jax ducked and crouched behind the semi already on its side, turning to aim between broken shards of glass. Purple, the color of Twenty, filled his view, and he started firing.

More shots pinged around him, and a cry of pain, low and dark, jerked up his head. He turned to see Wyatt fall, knocking Lynne over. Lynne scrambled and planted her hands over Wyatt's neck. Blood welled between her fingers. She ripped off her shirt and held it against the wound, grabbing Wyatt's hand to cover it. Without missing a beat, she grabbed his gun and positioned herself in front of him in a crouch, barrel pointed toward Twenty members.

"Somebody get him behind the vans," she yelled, pulling off three shots.

Wyatt shrugged her off and dragged himself to sit, his back to the minivan on its side. Keeping one hand on his neck, he reached for another weapon in his boot, pointing beyond the trucks.

Purple caught Jax's eye, he turned and fired, hitting his target in the chest. Gunfire erupted all around them. A spray of gunfire blazed out from a window in the top floor of the building across the way. Jax ducked back, down on his haunches. Mud splattered all around Wyatt.

Shit. Jax had to get him to safety and get that neck wound taken care of before it was too late. "Raze? Take my position."

Sucking in air, Jax waited until Raze took his spot and then zigzagged toward his friend and tucked his gun in the back of his waist. He reached down and grabbed Wyatt by the armpits, dragging him up and pulling him around to the other side of the minivan. Fuck, he weighed a ton. Lynne followed, scattering bullets, covering his back.

It was the fucking bravest thing he'd ever seen.

He yanked her to his side to catch his breath. Blood caught his attention. He looked down at the river of red covering his torso. Had he been shot?

"Jax?" Lynne asked, her voice rising. "Oh, God." She grabbed the bottom of his shirt and yanked up.

Nothing. He glanced down at his skin. No wounds. Realization slapped him. Almost in slow motion, he turned toward Wyatt, who lay gasping for breath. A black shirt covered Wyatt's huge torso. Dark material didn't show blood.

Jax reached for the hem and drew it up to reveal several

holes in Wyatt's gut. Blood spurted, and part of an intestine hung out. "Holy hell," he muttered. The air whooshed from his lungs. He glanced frantically around. "Tace Justice? Now!" He lowered his voice. "It's okay, Wyatt. It's okay."

Blood bubbled out of Wyatt's mouth and dribbled down his chin.

Lynne patted Wyatt's arm, her eyes filling with tears.

No. Oh, hell no. "Tace?" Jax bellowed.

Tace ran around the other side of the minivan as gunfire pierced the day. He slid onto his knees and reached Wyatt. "Neck?"

"No." Jax drew up the shirt made heavy by blood.

Tace lifted his head and swallowed. The sound he made defied description but felt like agony. "Wyatt."

"Fix him," Jax said. "Now."

Wyatt coughed and winced. "It's okay, Jax." He reached out and grabbed Jax's head with one strong hand. "Remember what I said. They need you." He coughed again, and blood spurted over Jax's chin to mingle with the rain.

Jax gripped Wyatt's arm and turned to Tace. "Fix him," he repeated.

Tace's blue eyes cut through the smoke, full of sorrow. Regret. Jax had seen the look before, he'd felt the look in a desert hell across the world. He hadn't thought he'd see it now.

"Wyatt, you're a good friend," Tace said somberly, leaning toward the former football star. "I never told you this, but I found one of your trading cards while out scouting one night." He reached for his back pocket to draw out a worn and weathered card of Wyatt in his football uniform. "I was gonna give it to you for your birthday."

Wyatt grinned bloody teeth. "You were a fan," he gasped out.

Tace clasped his other arm. "I am now." His eyes filled. "I'm sorry."

"No!" Jax exploded. "No sorry. Fucking fix this."

Wyatt's chest heaved, and his hold tightened. He closed his eyes and then reopened them. He tried to speak, but only bubbles of blood slid out.

Pain ripped through Jax's chest, compressing his lungs. He looked in Wyatt's steady eyes. "You're a great friend and soldier," he said.

"Jax," Wyatt whispered.

Jax leaned forward, tears falling from his eyes, turning his ear to Wyatt's mouth. "What?"

"Do-don't do this . . . a-lone," Wyatt whispered, his breath already cold against Jax's skin. "Life. Not worth it . . . a-lone."

Jax straightened, his vision blurry, and nodded.

Wyatt smiled, his eyes unfocusing. "I'm gonna see my baby girl, Jax." He stiffened, a groan billowing up. His body convulsed, once and again, and then went limp. A death rattle cleared his lungs, and he went still. Eyes staring at the sky, he ceased to be.

Jax coughed back a sob. His hand shaking, he reached forward and closed Wyatt's eyes. "Wyatt." Jax yanked his buddy close, holding him tight, his hands fisting in the back of Wyatt's shirt. "I'm sorry." Gently, with as much care as he could muster, he laid down his fallen friend. His head lifted. Rage warmed him until the burn filled his entire body. Turning, he grabbed the picture, the trading card, from Tace. "Okay?"

"Yes," Tace said, jaw firming.

Jax shot to his feet. "Cover me."

Lynne stood and grabbed his shirt. "Wait a minute—"

He manacled her biceps and lifted her up on her toes. "Get inside and tend to the wounded. Now." Turning her, he shoved her toward the building. Then he looked at Tace. "I'll take the east opening and then head to the apartment building across the way. Make sure I'm covered."

Tace reached down and took Wyatt's automatic, his face losing all expression. "I've got you."

"Hey buddy," Cruz called out through the gunfire. "Don't tell me I just killed another brother of yours."

Jax stilled. Everything in him quieted. "He'll die for killing both Marcus and Wyatt."

Tace coughed out. "Marcus? Cruz killed your brother?"

"Close enough. Recruited him for the gang, where he died." Jax crouched and ran along the line of minivans and downed trucks, passing his soldiers at their posts, firing. He tried to shove away all emotion, but the feeling of Wyatt's hand still tingled on his neck. As a football player, Wyatt had been a role model. As a soldier, he'd been a hero. As a friend, he'd been a conscience.

No more.

Jax reached the edge of the fortifications, where a rusted red pickup rested on its side against the compound, providing a shield. He kicked the tire closest to him and created a small opening. Enough to get through.

Thunder bellowed across the sky, and the wind hurtled clouds into a darkened mass.

Tace braced his legs and set his arms across the truck, pointing at the building Twenty had taken over. "If you stick low, you'll be able to get around the building and take Twenty from behind," he murmured.

Jax nodded. "Good plan. Don't fire and draw attention unless they see me."

"Copy that." Tace's aim remained steady. "Go."

Jax breathed out, slowed his heartbeat, and focused into the moment. He waited for a sporadic firefight to become more localized in the center, and then he ran. Low and fast, he went full bore for the back of the apartment building. Mud splashed up his legs, but soon he panted, his back against rough brick, hidden from the fight. Tace hadn't needed to fire a shot.

Jax turned for the back just as two men in purple rounded the corner. He ducked and then fired two shots, hitting each man between the eyes. Shock filled their faces as they fell. Jax jogged toward them and peered over their dead bodies around the corner into the dark alley running behind the building.

Abandoned single-family homes, their backyards empty save for old garbage, lined the other side of the alley behind the still-standing apartment building he'd been unable to take down. Even before Scorpius, despair and futility had smothered the neighborhood.

He turned and quickly frisked both bodies. Three knives and two guns were quickly concealed in his clothing. Then, keeping his left shoulder to the building, he ran around the corner and went full bore to the back entrance. In its heyday, the bottom floor had been a halfway house for newly released prisoners, while the second floor held apartments the locals knew housed hookers. The fifteen minute kind.

Jax had purchased his first joint from an ex-con living on the second floor.

Gravel scraped. "Where the fuck is Sal?" a low male voice said just as a twentysomething Hispanic kid in full purple turned the corner.

Jax was on him before he could open his mouth, taking him to the concrete and wrapping him in a choke hold. A hard snap, and the guy's neck broke. Jax yanked the body behind a Dumpster overflowing with water and old fast food containers before sliding inside the back door of the building. Knowing Cruz, the bastard would be on the top floor spraying bullets.

Creeping silently, Jax found the rear stairs and inched into the stairwell while the fire fight continued outside. He jogged up, pausing at the second-floor landing. Cruz had purchased him a blow job from a local hooker for his fifteenth birthday, and they'd met on the landing. His first blow job. He shoved down memories and peered up.

Silence in the stairwell. Cruz had always had more balls

than brains. The stairwell should've been secured instead of having everyone shooting all their bullets at people behind trucks and minivans.

Jax stilled and listened at the landing, which was missing the stairwell door. Hell, it had been missing the door for twenty years. He stayed down a step and ducked, peering around the corner. A sentry stood guard in the center of the hallway. Right. Jax settled back into place, holding his breath. The second another spray of firepower was unleashed, he jumped into the hallway and took out the sentry with a hit to the temple. The man fell to the side, dropping his weapon.

Jax powered forward, sweeping rooms right and left. Nothing. Cruz must've had his main force on the ground floor, ready to go if Jax made a frontal assault. Shit. Ten years ago, and he would've done just that.

The military had changed him in more ways than one.

He reached dead center of the hallway, where a closed door stood between him and the ping of bullets. Crouching, he felt for a pulse, already knowing the man in purple was gone. A quick frisk revealed nothing but the Glock the guy had carried. Weird choice, the Glock. Jax shrugged and slid the gun in the back of his waist.

Standing, he stood and waited until more firepower was unleashed so he could kick open the door.

The cocking of a gun behind him stopped his breathing.

"My old friend," Cruz said quietly.

Jax lowered his gun to his side and turned around. Cruz emerged from the next room down, gun pointed at Jax's head. "Looks like you underestimated me."

"Apparently so." Jax jerked his head at the closed door behind him. "Who's the shooter?"

"New kid. Recruit that's a decent shot." Cruz kicked his fallen man over. "This guy, I hoped you'd take out."

Figured. It had been too easy. Jax's fingers settled on his gun, and he slowly released each muscle. Cruz never had given a shit about most of his followers. "You should be careful. There aren't that many recruits out there."

"Oh, I don't know. You keep leaving them for me."

Jax stilled. Shawn? Had Cruz actually let Shawn live? "Why did you infect the girl?"

Cruz, his face lined from drugs, booze, and being a prick, smiled. "For fun. I didn't have time to really use her, but one good bite ruined her just the same. Tell me she died."

Jax kept his expression lax. "Sorry. She had a bad fever and it was close, but now she's knitting sweaters. You know, in time for winter."

Cruz's eyes narrowed until they were almost all black. "You're lying."

"No, I'm not." Jax lifted a shoulder. "Did you bite her?"

Cruz snorted. "No. I'm not a carrier, but I keep a couple of Rippers chained in the basement. They bite when I tell them to bite."

Bile cut through Jax's gut. "You're fuckin' sick."

"Drop your gun."

"Sure." Jax dropped the gun, and it bounced once on the torn carpet. "You know what I don't get?"

"Women?"

Jax barked out a laugh. "Besides women. I don't get why you're coming after me. L.A. is a huge place, and we don't have to lose people fighting each other."

Cruz stepped closer. "You betrayed me by leaving me here, mulo."

Jax rolled his eyes, his muscles tensing. "Bullshit. I left because I needed to leave."

"Brothers choose prison and not the government. Not the fuckin' army."

They would never see eye to eye. "Nice boots, by the way. Three-inch heels?" Cruz was under six feet tall, and it had always pissed him off that Jax, with his white daddy's genes, had gotten so tall. "Are those girl boots?"

"Fuck you." Cruz stepped in and shoved the barrel of the gun against Jax's throat.

Pain pricked his larynx. "Not my type."

Cruz lifted his head, hatred in his eyes. "No? Your brother liked me just fine."

Fire roared through Jax's head. "I told you to leave him alone. He didn't belong in Twenty."

Cruz leaned in, his face a mere inch from Jax's. "He was the best enforcer I've ever seen. Killed like a motherfucker."

Jax grit his teeth and tried to shove out words. "Marcus didn't kill anybody."

Pure delight glimmered in Cruz's wild eyes. "He killed more than anybody I ever knew. Was a fucking genius at it." Cruz sighed. "But Marcus had to go. Too . . . what's the word? Charismatic."

Everything inside Jax stilled. Went dead. "He had to go?" he asked evenly.

Cruz smiled, his red lips tipping in almost a snarl. "Yes. The drive-by? Well, too many of my men, my followers, were looking at your little brother. So he had to go. Even his nick-name, Slam, was charismatic."

Jax had suspected. Without any evidence, even a hint of the truth, he'd wondered. He'd even stood at the grave site and asked for answers, but his mother had already died before Marcus had, so there were no answers. "You're gonna pay, Cruz."

"No, I'm not." Cruz leaned back while keeping the gun flush against Jax's throat. "After I kill you, I'm going to take apart your little fiefdom. Starting with Blue Heart."

Jax jerked. What the fuck?

"Yep. My new recruit was all full of info. Shawn gave me her location so I'd allow him to live." Cruz chuckled, low and deep.

Fuck. "The kid lied to you."

Cruz's lips brushed Jax's ear. "Ah, you never could lie to me, brother. The woman? She stays in your quarters."

Heat compressed Jax's heart. Cruz would destroy Lynne and enjoy every second. "You're misinformed," Jax ground out, his heart pounding.

"I don't think so. Now you die so I can go get my hands on the woman. It won't be the first time I've used your left-overs."

A bullet flew by Cruz's head, and he jerked back.

Jax ducked and punched up as hard as he could, throwing Cruz against the far wall. He turned to see Tace coming at him, gun firing. "What the hell?" he asked.

Bullets shot through the door behind Jax, and he leaped to the side and into Tace. Tace grabbed him in a bear hug and hurtled them both into an empty room across the way.

"What the hell?" Jax repeated.

Tace ran for the window. "I decided I didn't want to lose Wyatt's picture. Give it back."

What?

The gunman swept inside, spraying bullets. Fuck. It was Shawn. It was true. Cruz had recruited instead of killed him. Smart.

Jax hit the ground.

Tace turned and calmly plugged the kid between the eyes. Red mingled with purple, and Shawn took his last breath.

Jax stood and turned toward his friend. A week ago, Tace wouldn't have tried that shot. He would've negotiated, especially with a kid he'd known personally. "Man, we gotta talk."

"I know. Let's get out of here first." Tace threw an arm into the window, shattering it out.

"No." Jax grabbed a knife from his boot and ran into the hallway, hurrying west and ducking into the next room. It was time to fulfill his vow, even if it was his last act. Cruz began firing. Jax ducked, bunched, and shot forward to hit Cruz's midsection, throwing them both into the window.

They impacted it with harsh grunts, flying through glass, and then falling. Jax manacled Cruz's shirt. They hit the ground with Jax on top of Cruz, and he could feel it as Cruz's ribs shattered.

Not enough. Not nearly enough. Gunfire erupted around them, and they both rolled in opposite directions.

Tace landed next to Jax, rolled, and kept firing. He grabbed Jax's arm and started to yank.

"No," Jax yelled, spit flying from his mouth, scrambling to go after Cruz. A blow to the head sparked stars behind his eyes, and then darkness crashed through him.

Chapter Twenty-Three

The noir hero is a knight in blood-caked armor.
He's dirty and he does his best to deny the fact
that he's a hero the whole time.

—Frank Miller

Lynne shivered, once again in the makeshift graveyard many hours after the world had blown apart in the morning. They'd had to restore their defenses before turning to the dead. She'd never seen a mass grave before, and the thought brought bile into her throat. Night was beginning to fall, and they'd need to take cover under darkness soon.

Jax stood on the other side of the grave, his left arm cradled against his stomach, bruises and cuts deepening on his face. It had been too long since he'd slept, and exhaustion glimmered in his dark eyes. Tace and Sami flanked him, while Raze circled the group, scouting out, looking for threats. Sami cried freely, but neither Jax nor Tace showed any emotion. Any hint of an expression of pain.

All of the bodies, all seven of them, had been wrapped in whatever old sheets had been available and then placed in the hole.

Seven. They'd lost seven of the group, and at least five

more were too wounded to leave the infirmary. Most of the damage had come from the early grenades.

Several men started piling dirt on the bodies until only a mound remained.

Tace looked at Jax, who didn't move.

Lynne stiffened. Wyatt was gone. Who would speak?

She waited and then caught Jax's gaze. He blinked. She tilted her head, trying to convey sympathy and support. This wasn't his bailiwick, but he was the leader.

Fury lit his eyes, but she kept his gaze. Finally, he stepped forward, his voice gravelly low. "These were our friends, our people, our soldiers. They fought hard, and they died well. We will miss them all."

Jax turned his focus to Wyatt's grave. "Scorpius made you a soldier, but you made yourself a friend. We disagreed about what's next after life, and I hope to hell you were right and I was wrong. If so, rest in peace, and send some help our way. Hooah, my brother." His voice cracked.

Tears clogged Lynne's throat as Jax stepped back.

Other folks talked about the dead, and then Sami said a short prayer.

The group attending the funeral, about fifty people not needed in protection, security, or anywhere else at the moment, turned toward the inner compound. Lynne moved around the mound until she reached Jax. "How badly are you hurt?" Rumor had it he'd fallen out of a second-story window.

"I'm fine. Go back with Sami, and we'll talk later." He glanced over his shoulder at Raze. "I need help with a job."

Raze jogged toward him.

Tace's gaze remained on the mound. "I'll come help you burn the Twenty bodies."

So enemies got burned while friends were buried. Lynne wasn't quite sure which was better. "I can help."

Jax shook his head. "The doctors are all overwhelmed,

and I need you at the headquarters infirmary." He turned and focused on Tace. "We need to talk, too."

Tace's chin lifted. "About me or about you?"

Jax's jaw clenched. "You shouldn't have knocked me out, and I'm definitely gonna return the favor, but for now, we're talking about your brain."

"I know. Tomorrow when we're clearheaded," Tace said. "You haven't slept in too long."

Lynne frowned. "Let's go, Tace." She pivoted and sloshed through the mud to the concrete, trying to wipe off her shoes on the cracks. Tace strode next to her, scanning the area around them. "You knocked out Jax?"

"Bullets were whizzing at him, and he was trying to run into them to get to Cruz." Tace spoke matter-of-factly. "I had to knock him out to get him to safety."

Yeah, she could see Jax holding a grudge, although he hadn't said anything all day while directing the cleanup after the attack. "What else does Jax want to talk to you about?" she asked.

"I'm turning into a Ripper." Tace stretched his neck to focus on the former soup kitchen. "At some point, he'll probably have to put me down."

Lynne tripped, her mind fuzzing. "You're a Ripper?"

"Yeah, I think so. I'm not feeling anything, and I was fine plugging Shawn in the face this morning." Intensity rolled off Tace. "Before the fever, I would've balked at that."

Lynne tried to shove down fear. "Any big urges to mass kill or obsess about anybody?"

Tace rubbed his chin. "No."

What she wouldn't give for an MRI or PET scan of his brain. "Then don't ask Jax to kill you quite yet. Perhaps your brain has changed, but that doesn't mean you'll be a danger." Right? If Tace became a danger, how would they know if he decided to hide it?

Tace lifted a shoulder. "The weird part is I don't really care, you know?"

"Part of that could be shock. There's been a lot of trauma." Lynne followed the group into the front entrance and then wound around to the makeshift infirmary.

Tace nodded. "You should know. Cruz killed Jax's brother and Wyatt, and now he's coming after you. He knows about you."

Nausea rolled through Lynne's stomach. "He's going to have to stand in line to kill me."

Tace followed and went to check patients one by one, relieving the nurse who'd been on duty. Well, she'd been studying to become a nurse, so good enough. Lynne slipped on gloves and assisted, careful not to touch anybody who looked terrified by her. The group had slowly begun to accept her, and most seemed to believe she couldn't harm them, but every once in a while more than fear or indifference filled their eyes. A couple loathed her.

Finally, she stood and stretched her back, the muscles protesting. Or maybe the bruises. When Jax had tackled her during the first explosion, she'd hit pretty hard.

They'd patched up folks and sent them on to the main hospital, which used to be a school. Somebody brought them a box of granola bars, which had stood in for dinner.

Tace approached her from the other side of the room. "We're good here. Why don't you take advantage of the rain, take a shower, and get some sleep. Unless you have any injuries?" At her shake of the head, he pointed to a bucket in the far corner. "Drop your gloves in the bleach over there. We have to reuse them."

The mere idea of reusing hospital gloves made her stomach lurch. "I hope we have a lot of bleach."

"We don't."

Great. She gingerly tugged off the gloves.

Tace sighed and leaned back against the wall. "It's Friday night. Before Scorpius, what would you have been doing?"

Was there life before Scorpius? She paused. "Probably working. But I did have a boyfriend, and we tried to meet up on weekends. I was in Atlanta, and part of the year he was in D.C. So we hit bed-and-breakfasts up the East Coast." While she hadn't completely known Bret, he'd had a romantic streak he liked to share. "I also, ah, played poker."

Tace snorted. "Poker?"

She grinned. "Yeah, at the retirement home. My Mema was in the home, and they had weekly games. Those old broads could make a bundle, usually from me." Too bad Mema hadn't survived Scorpius. Lynne needed her wisdom now. "What about you?"

Tace closed his eyes and breathed out, crossing his arms. "On a Friday night? Well, in Afghanistan, I was just trying to survive and tie off blurting arteries. Before that or on leave?" He smiled, revealing startling white teeth. "I was a ladies' man. Would put on the cowboy hat, the boots, and say ma'am a lot." He chuckled. "Women loved it."

Lynne rubbed her tired eyes. "I bet you could dance."

"The two-step is a work of art."

A man coughed in pain across the room. Danny? Or Denny. Lynne turned toward him. The guy had been shot in the upper chest, but the bullet had missed the heart.

"I've got him. Go." Tace shoved away from the wall and strode through the odd configuration of beds.

Lynne was too tired to argue. Skirting several cots, she reached the doorway and dropped her gloves into water that appeared almost clean. The faint, very faint, scent of bleach wafted up. Swallowing unease, she wandered into the darkened soup kitchen and made her way to the exit by the showers, which were empty. Apparently anybody who'd wanted to shower had already done so.

Night had fallen and the storm had ebbed, leaving only a soft pattering of rain. Lynne shivered, looking outside. She was already cold, but also muddy and bloody. Yeah, she needed a shower. She toed off her shoes and socks inside, wanting to keep them somewhat dry. What she wouldn't give for a hot shower. Or even a lukewarm one. Shrugging, she stepped out of her clothes.

If anybody showed up, they could just feel free to check out her bruised and battered body. At this point, who cared?

She slipped outside, and the wind instantly assaulted her. Goose bumps rose on her skin. She ducked her head and ran for the shower, immediately reaching for the soap. The scent of lemon surrounded her, somehow comforting in the dark night. A weak moon peeked through the clouds, offering enough light for her to see the soap.

She washed as quickly as possible and hurried to the stack of worn and ripped towels. But at least they were clean. She hurriedly dried off and grabbed her destroyed clothing, keeping the towel wrapped around her body. She hit the edge of a table in the soup room and hissed, slowing down to reach a lantern on the table. Nobody stopped her as she walked up the stairs and to the quarters she shared with Jax.

She hurriedly dressed in one of his shirts that reached her knees and finger-combed her hair.

The door opened, and Jax stepped inside with a towel wrapped around his waist, the scent of dish soap coming with him. He must've been just behind her.

She swallowed. "You okay?"

"Fine." He dropped wet clothing and boots on the floor, reaching for a pair of black boxers.

Right. He'd just lost a friend, had failed to kill Cruz, and turmoil all but glowed in his eyes. They hadn't had a chance to talk since the attack earlier that day. Lynne bit her lip and eyed the bed.

"Get in bed, Lynne. We both need sleep, and we can talk tomorrow morning about your blackmail attempt." The towel hit the floor.

Lynne swallowed and padded across the room to slide under the covers, scooting as far as possible to the other side. Her heart rate picked up, just from the tension. She wouldn't win a fight with him, and right now, as tired as she felt, she wouldn't win an argument. Sleep was a good idea.

The mattress sagged when he lay down, and instant heat spiraled her way. She stiffened to keep from scooting into that warmth. Real warmth.

He sighed and wrapped an arm around her waist, dragging her into his hard body.

Heat. Blissful, amazing heat. She couldn't help but snuggle right in with a soft moan.

"Fuck, you're freezing," Jax breathed into her hair, sliding a leg over hers.

She sniffed. "I know." In the darkness, in the intimacy of the room with the rain pattering outside, she could feel his pain, deep and dark. Reality tortured Jax Mercury. Every ounce of her, everything feminine and soft, needed to offer comfort. She turned around, almost surprised when his grip lessened enough to let her. Slowly, gently, she cupped his whiskered chin, careful of the fresh bruises. "I'm so very sorry, Jax."

He closed his eyes, and his broad shoulders shuddered. "Me too."

"Wyatt was a good man," she said softly.

"Yes." Jax's eyes opened. A small grin almost lifted his upper lip. "Did you know Wyatt had a foundation?"

"No."

Jax swiped a hand down her back in a gentle caress, spreading tingles. "Yeah. He ended up with a bunch of money from football and created a foundation for kids with diabetes. His younger sister grew up with it, so instead of spending his money on himself, he decided he'd aid others with the disease."

Lynne smiled. "That sounds like Wyatt."

"Yes."

She lost the smile and slid her leg between his. The warmth made her groan. "I heard what you said. That Cruz killed your brother."

Jax stiffened. "Cruz killed Marcus on purpose because Marcus was special and probably challenged him."

"I'm sorry." Lynne leaned even closer, her hand flattening on Jax's chest. "We'll get Cruz. I promise." She glanced toward the wall. "You don't talk about your mom."

Jax stiffened. "She wasn't that good a mom. Not horrible, but not great. Slam and I were on our own, and that's okay with me." He stroked down her arm. "You need to know, I'm contacting the Elite Force tomorrow. We have to reach out for help. Twenty isn't the only gang out there, and we're almost out of supplies."

Lynne sighed. "I figured. You'll let me go first?"

"No. When we get the research from Myriad, I'm counting on you to figure out how to help everyone survive the contagion. We need you." Jax rested his hand on her hip. "But I won't let anybody hurt you, and I won't let them know you're here. I'll just ask for supplies."

Now that was a promise he probably couldn't keep. He'd try, but somehow she needed to find a way to leave on her own. For now, she wanted heat and to offer comfort. It was all she had. She licked her lips and pressed them against his.

He remained still. "Lynne, you don't have to sleep with me for protection."

She breathed in, her mouth curving on his. "I know. I want you, you need me, and we have right now." She kissed him, cuddling closer. "Let me help you for once."

Chapter Twenty-Four

The tragedy of war is that it uses man's best to do man's worst.

—Harry Emerson Fosdick

Jax settled back, acutely aware of the soft body pressed against his—of the curve of her waist cradling his hand—of the compassion she was trying so hard to hide. At her core, Lynne Harmony was a healer, a nurturer, and now she offered herself.

Maybe not even consciously, not completely.

Yet she'd sensed his pain, somehow realized his turmoil, and she gave up the only thing she could.

Her body.

And she didn't realize he saw that. Hell, he saw her. Sure, she'd been keeping secrets, but he understood and didn't blame her.

So he caressed up her ribs, over her arm, and cradled her head. Damp curls wound around his fingers. "Go to sleep."

"No." She shoved him over and rolled on top of him. "Sleep is overrated." She wiggled against him, her breasts brushing his chest through her worn shirt. "I don't want anything but tonight from you, Jax. No expectations."

The words hit him like a punch to the solar plexus, and he

breathed out, sliding both hands into her hair to cup her head. "Not true, Lynne Harmony."

She blinked, caught. "I mean it."

"Do you?" he whispered, dragging her down to his mouth. Her lips opened to his, and he went slow, pouring emotion he couldn't express into the kiss. He was so fucking lost, needing to hold on to something. To somebody. Deep and soft, determined, he overtook her lips, the taste of her nearly drugging him.

Without releasing his hold, he rolled them back over, pinning her to the bed. He swallowed and leaned up. His cock hardened.

She blinked rapidly, her mouth forming a bemused *O*.

"I can't use you tonight," he said. After losing Wyatt, after failing to kill Cruz, after trying to go numb, he couldn't be the guy just fucking a body. "I can't do it, Lynne." His voice cracked. Jesus. His vision blurred. Losing Wyatt brought back every devastating moment of losing Frankie in Afghanistan.

Shock covered her face.

Then a tear dropped onto her cheek. His tear. Shame roared through him, and he moved away, mortified. More wetness coated his cheeks.

She struck out, grabbing his neck, stilling him. Realization dawned, widening her eyes, moving her mouth silently. Her eyes softened to the green of a spring meadow, filled with regret. Then sorrow. Finally acceptance. "Jax," she whispered, her knees sliding up to cradle his hips, and her arms tugging him down.

He fought her for two seconds, and then he broke. Allowing her to settle him, he buried his face in her neck, his body rigid, one low sob escaping him before he could stop it.

Pain clawed through him. She wrapped herself around him, arms and legs, much smaller than he but holding so tight. One hand ran down his hair, offering comfort. She murmured soft words, sweet words, words lacking meaning but providing peace. Somehow.

He closed his eyes, allowing wetness to flow silently onto her skin.

"You're all right," she murmured.

He was anything but all right. For several heartbeats, measured in more than just time, he allowed her to comfort him. Her scent began to fill his head. His dick stirred against her sex, and he breathed out.

That was that, then.

He lifted and let her see his pain. Then he took her mouth, going deep, losing himself in the taste of Lynne. She opened her mouth on a sigh, taking him in, returning the kiss.

Pain turned to hunger, scoring him.

He cupped her jaw, gliding his thumb across her smooth skin. So soft, almost unreal considering the harshness of the world. How had something so delicate, so fragile, survived? Releasing her mouth, he kissed her nose, her cheekbones, her forehead. Getting lost, he licked his way down to bite her earlobe.

She moaned and arched up into him.

"So pretty," he said, drawing her shirt up and off. Her breasts sprang free, her pink nipples already hard and waiting. He licked across them, sucking one into his mouth.

Her grip tightened in his hair.

Yeah. He suckled and nipped, worshiping her, caressing every inch.

"Jax," she breathed, a protest in the sigh. A protest against emotion and gentleness.

He couldn't heed the protest, too far gone to draw back. He wouldn't allow her to hide, to retreat, to make them less than they'd just become. "I'm sorry," he whispered, tracing a path down her abs, kissing along each rib. She gyrated against him, sweat slicking her skin, her legs restless. His fingers found her, ready and wet.

Heat burned his lungs.

He ran his thumb across her clit.

"Jax." She arched into his hand.

Jax. The way she said his name, as if only she had the key to him. He moved up her body, kissing and licking on the way, his mouth finding hers. He grasped her hip, lifted her, and powered inside her with one strong push.

Tightness, wet and burning hot, coated his cock. He dropped his forehead to hers, his hand encircling her nape. Then he slid out and back in, the feeling as close to heaven as a killer like he would ever find.

She dug her nails into his shoulders. The small bite of pain spurred him on, and he started to thrust. Harder and faster, he tried to get so far inside her, he'd feel whole. Her hips rose to meet his, her neck arching as she pushed her head back on the mattress. His lips enclosed her jugular, her very life, and he held on. The headboard slammed against the wall, and the blanket fell to the floor.

Only Lynne mattered. Jax grabbed her ass and held her tight, shoving deep. She exploded around him, cascading ripples along his dick, her mouth opening on a silent scream. He hammered harder, prolonging her orgasm, until she went limp with a muffled sigh. Then he shoved deep and buried his head in her neck again. His balls drew tight, and electricity ripped down his spine. He held himself tight against her as he came, finally dropping them both to the bed.

She pushed halfheartedly against his shoulder. "Breathe. Can't."

He rolled off her, yanking the blanket off the floor to wrap around them both. He spooned her and kissed the top of her head.

"Um," she murmured sleepily.

"No talk." He curled her closer, keeping her warm. "Sleep." Her breathing evened out before he'd finished the order.

He kissed her again on the top of the head, and then he closed his eyes.

In what seemed like mere seconds, morning light filtered between the rough boards of the window, awakening him. Aches and pains flared to life along his entire body, but he hadn't moved an inch in sleep. Neither had Lynne. His sleep had been peaceful, without even a hint of his usual nightmares. He blinked. Hell. He hadn't had a nightmare since Lynne had taken over his bed.

She slept quietly, her body lax.

His groin stirred, and he bit down desire. He'd lived in a lot of different places, and for the first time, he had found a home. With one small, brilliant, dangerous scientist. Slowly, so as not to awaken her, he slid from the bed and tucked her back in. He made no sound while moving around the apartment and yanking on somewhat fresh jeans and a shirt.

He tucked a gun at his back and a knife in his boot, heading for the door.

"Are you all right?" she asked softly.

He turned to see her curled toward him, head on hand, hair wild with curls. Her green eyes were sleepy, her cheeks rosy.

"I'm fine," he whispered. "Go back to sleep. I'll have Sami come get you closer to breakfast time, and then you can help Tace check the wounded before going through documents again."

She blinked. "We, ah, didn't use protection last night."

He stopped breathing. Holy fuck. He'd totally forgotten in the urgency of the night. In fact, he wasn't even sure they had more condoms. "Um, are you—"

She sighed. "Cycle-wise, I'm probably just fine. But we both got lost, and that can't happen again."

"Agreed." He'd cut off his head before bringing a kid into this world. "I'm sorry."

She shrugged. "We're safe, Jax. I know that I'm just the one here. In your bed."

He lifted his chin. She thought she was interchangeable? Man, she really didn't understand what had happened to him last night. He might not be able to put it into words, but he figured she was a helluva lot smarter than he was and could work it out. "You're just the one here?" he repeated.

She closed her eyes, snuggling farther into the covers. "It could have been anyone," she murmured.

He barked out a laugh, loud enough that her eyelids flew open. "No, Lynne." If he had time, he'd get back into bed and make her eat those words. Something to look forward to doing later. "There's only you. From day one, the second you marched into my camp, there's only been you." Hell. It was *her* before he even knew of her. He turned on his heel and left the room, rather enjoying the surprise on her pretty face.

Or was that panic?

Lynne finished bandaging Raze's ripped rib cage as he sat like a statue in the headquarters infirmary with full morning sun streaming inside. The bleached gloves made her skin ache, but she didn't complain. "That's better. Next time you get cut, you get it cleaned and bandaged right away." She bit her lip. "You can't afford an infection, Raze." Sitting back, she met his dark gaze. His eyes were so blue they appeared to glow. "Got it?"

He reached for the ripped T-shirt next to him on the bench. "Thanks."

"Sure." She squinted to better study the striations of the bruise beneath his eye. "Looks like you took the butt of a gun to the face."

"Foot. One of the Twenty members had some training." Raze slid off the bench.

Lynne stepped back. Her stomach rumbled from the over-cooked oats she and Sami had eaten for breakfast hours ago. She'd been feeling off all day, and she needed coffee.

Something warm before she finished here and returned to her documents. She shivered. "I'd suggest ice, but we don't have any."

"You okay?" Raze asked.

Lynne blinked. "Um, yeah." Had the super-silent soldier just asked about her well-being? "What does Raze stand for, anyway?" she blurted out.

He grinned, and a shocking dimple appeared in his left cheek for the briefest of moments. "Razor." Turning on a combat boot, he started for the door.

Interesting. Lynne turned to the last patient, a thirtysomething man with a perfectly shaped brown goatee.

He held up a hand. "Don't fucking come near me. I want Tace."

She faltered. Man. She'd forgotten. For the entire morning, her head had been filled with Jax Mercury, and she'd forgotten her freaky blue heart. "Okay. Tace will be with you in a minute."

"You shouldn't be here," the guy spat out, stepping toward her. "Blue-hearted whore."

Without even a wisp of sound, Raze suddenly stood between Lynne and the man. "Go inner territory to the main hospital," Raze said, looking down. Way down.

"I need a bandage," the guy whined, stepping back.

"Too bad. Go. To. The. Hospital." Raze's back filled Lynne's vision, but if his face looked half as scary as his low voice sounded, she'd be running.

The guy stomped off, shoulders down, anger in his wake. Raze turned. "You good?"

"Fine." Her voice shook, and she cleared her throat. "Thanks."

"Welcome." Raze turned and left.

Tace glanced up from across the room. "You have a friend."

And several enemies. Lynne forced a grin and moved to clean up the cluttered counter. "Raze does talk my ear off."

Tace frowned and then his face cleared. "Funny." He

finished stitching a soldier's arm and slapped on a bandage. "Stay out of firefights, Buck."

The soldier nodded, dressed, and hustled from the room.

"I made a joke, too," Tace muttered.

"It was funny." Lynne threw bandages in the garbage and turned to view the medic. "You feeling, well, anything?"

He shrugged. "Not really. Is the president really a Ripper?"

Lynne gaped. "Jax told you?"

"We had a meeting this morning—Jax and his inner lieutenants. With Wyatt gone, that just left Sami, Raze, and me. Looks like Raze is part of the inner circle now. Besides Jax, he's the only one who really knows his way around weapons." Tace shrugged. "Jax told us the entire story about the president and about your finding another lab called Myriad."

Lynne's chin rose. She would've liked to have been at the meeting, considering her ass was on the line. Her chest ached. "What did Jax decide?"

"He hasn't decided about the president, I don't think, but he's going to lead a mission to Myriad for the records tomorrow morning, which gives us today to plan as well as recuperate a little bit." Tace stood and winced. "You strong enough to shove a shoulder back into place?"

Breath whooshed from Lynne's lungs. "Your shoulder is out?"

"Yes. Happened this morning after the meeting when I was training with Sami, and it's my left one, so I haven't needed it much." Tace rubbed his chin with his healthy hand. "I don't feel pain like I used to."

"Sit back down." Lynne hustled toward him, faltering when he sat on a lawn chair. "You know I'm not a medical doctor, right?"

Tace leaned his head back onto the dingy wall. "Yes ma'am. But you did study some anatomy."

"Sure." She gingerly reached for his shoulder.

"What's going on?" Jax asked from behind her.

She jumped and whirled around like a teenager caught with a bottle of tequila. "His shoulder is dislocated."

Jax frowned and crossed the room. He tilted his head to the side and then placed one hand on Tace's clavicle and the other on his back. "One—" He popped the shoulder back into place.

Tace's face lost all color. "Thanks."

"No problem." Jax straightened up and held out a hand for Lynne. "We need to talk."

She looked down at his hand and then back up at his rugged face. "About what?"

He lifted an eyebrow, his face hard and set.

Her knees wobbled. They didn't need to hold hands, for goodness sake. Sleeping together was one thing, and public affection another. She'd already been called a whore once that day.

"Lynne," he said.

Tace's lips twitched. At least the jackass could feel amusement. At her expense.

She glared at Jax. Fine. It wasn't as if she could get past him. Straightening her shoulders, she slipped her hand into his as casually as she could. His hand closed, providing instant warmth and a skittering of warning through her belly. She bit her tongue as he led her from the room, across the soup kitchen, and into his war room with the ham radio.

"Where's Ernie?" she asked.

"Getting tea." Jax settled her into one of the four chairs in the room. "We're going to reach out to Greg Lake and the EF today, and I thought you'd want to be here."

Fear detonated in her stomach, and she tried to stand.

Jax clamped his hands on her shoulders and sat her back down, sinking to his haunches so they were eye to eye. "Take a deep breath and listen to me. I meant what I said last night.

I won't tell them you're here, but I have to reach out. We need everything from food to medical supplies."

"So let me go," she whispered. She could probably survive on her own. Uncle Bruce had taught her well.

"No." Jax brushed a curl off her cheek. "Trust me. I won't let anything happen to you."

Her temper snapped. "Trust you? You're about to call the one person in the world who would like to carve me up like a turkey dinner." She struggled against Jax's hold, but he didn't relent. Tears filled her eyes, and she batted back the frustration.

Jax waited until she stopped moving. "You have my vow nothing will harm you."

Her shoulders slumped. "I have too many enemies here. While you'll lie for me, they won't."

Jax's face hardened. "They will. I promise."

Ernie ambled in, a cup of something steaming in his hand. "We ready?"

Lynne swallowed, glaring at Jax.

Jax drew a chair nearer and sat, folding one hand over her thigh. "We're ready."

Chapter Twenty-Five

There is no hunting like the hunting of man,
and those who have hunted armed men long enough,
and liked it, never really care for anything else.

—Ernest Hemingway

Jax tried to keep his hold reassuring, but his hand clamped onto Lynne's thigh to secure her in the chair. He could've called without her there, but it would be better if she heard the entire exchange. Her leg trembled beneath his palm, and his jaw tightened. She was frightened.

Ernie fiddled with dials and every once in a while stopped to speak, to say he was returning the call of the Elite Force. The sixty-year-old former marine had been retired and totally into the ham radio world when Scorpius had descended. Jax had found him wandering the rubble near the Hollywood Walk of Fame months ago.

Thirty minutes passed, and then an hour. Lynne continued to sit, every muscle tense, not looking at Jax. Maybe they wouldn't be able to find the EF. Maybe Jax had waited too long. A surprising mix of disappointment and relief filled her.

Static echoed over the line.

Jax straightened.

More static, and Ernie leaned forward to twist a dial just a smidge.

"This is Vice President Greg Lake, UT980 near Vegas, calling out."

Ernie jerked his chin at Jax.

"Thanks, Ernie." Jax leaned toward the old machine, drawing the microphone toward his mouth. "This is Jax Mercury in Los Angeles."

"Master Sergeant Jax Mercury, we've heard of you," Lake said, his voice coming through tinny. "Please give your location."

Lynne tried to rise, and Jax tightened his hold on her leg. "If you're as good as I hope, you know my location," Jax returned.

"Master Sergeant Mercury, I am ordering you to give your location," Lake said evenly.

Jax's lips twitched. "Well now, Vice President Lake, we have a problem. Because first of all, the army has disbanded. Secondly, and this is the big one, I have no proof or clue you're who you say you are. Provide proof, and I'll follow orders." He covered the mic. "Is there any way for us to know where he is, other than Nevada?"

Ernie shook his head. "Nope—not that I know of, anyway."

Jax nodded. "If I had troops and was heading west, I'd be in Nevada close to the Hoover Dam." Rumor had it Las Vegas still had electricity. "If they manage to keep the dam going, all electricity won't be done forever." The rest of the country had lost electricity when power plants had shut down for various reasons, all stemming from there not being enough trained people to keep them running properly. Although, before Scorpius, only about five thousand people had the knowledge to keep a dam running. How many of them had survived? Probably not enough.

Lake cleared his throat. "Unless we meet, there's not much proof I can offer."

"Copy that. How about we meet at the California and Nevada border the day after next at fifteen hundred hours?"

"We could meet tomorrow," Lake said.

Jax shook his head. "I require more time. The first I can meet is the day after next."

Lynne frowned.

Jax leaned toward her ear to whisper. "I want the info from Myriad in my hands before I meet with the president or any sitting government."

She nodded, her body still trembling.

Lake sighed. "Affirmative. I will speak with the president and get back to you with a more specific location."

"Who is the president?" Jax asked, wincing as Lynne stiffened even more.

"Bret Atherton," Lake replied. "Do we have a plan?"

"Affirmative." Jax sat back. "Where are you?"

Quiet reigned for a few minutes as Lake probably spoke to his group. "Close by."

Jax frowned. "Do you have any air support?"

"Negative."

What Jax wouldn't give for a crop duster or two. "What type of force have you been able to mount?"

Static crackled over the line. "We'll update in person. Do you have any intel on the location of Lynne Harmony? Our sources say she was heading to Los Angeles."

"Negative. If Blue Heart was in L.A., I'd know about it. At least by rumor." Jax ignored the tightness of Lynne's body. If she didn't breathe soon, she was going to pass out. He patted her leg.

"How many do you have in your force?" Lake asked.

"We'll update in person." Jax repeated Lake's hedging.

"Fair enough. Let me remind you, Master Sergeant Mercury, you are still a United States soldier under orders."

Hell. Could he be considered a deserter? Probably. Jax

leaned forward. "Actually, I'm not sure there's still a United States. Are you?"

"There is, and you're still a soldier," Lake shot back.

"Not if there isn't a country or service," Jax said. "For all I know, you could be the leader of yet another renegade group out to steal my meager resources, and I have to tell you, if that's the case, you're gonna be disappointed."

"Because you've amassed such a strong fighting force?" Lake asked.

Jax snorted. "No. Because we don't have shit for supplies, food, or trained people. We're a group of civilians barely making it, Lake. So if you're looking for loot, go elsewhere."

"We'll see."

Jax cleared his throat. "Tell me about the Elite Force as well as the Brigade."

"The Elite Force is mission specific and answers directly to the president. The Brigade is still our first line of defense right now, and it is part of the United States government," Lake said.

Did the guy sound defensive? "Where's McDougall?" Jax asked.

"McDougall is leading the Brigade, and right now he's securing nuclear plants before they are taken over or, worse, melt down."

Jax winced. Was Lake lying? "I'd like to meet him."

"I'll see what I can do. Lake signing out."

Jax had Ernie cut the line.

Ernie turned, his double chin wobbling. "That's too bad. About air support."

"If he's telling the truth." Jax released Lynne's leg. "In the last six months we've lost billions of people, and in the riots, many of our airports and bases were bombed or destroyed by crazy-assed Rippers or home-grown terrorists who wanted to take us down and saw an opportunity. But if Lake has managed to put together a security force, somebody has to be able to fly a damn plane." It was unthinkable that every plane or helicopter had been destroyed. Of course, the lack of fuel might make it impossible to put birds in the air. When Scorpius had hit the world, the flow of fuel had stopped.

"He didn't believe you," Lynne said woodenly.

"It's his job, if he's who he says he is, to doubt me," Jax said.

Ernie cleared his throat.

Jax lifted an eyebrow. "You got something to say?"

Ernie rubbed his white beard. "Last time Lake said Lynne was a carrier of a new disease. I figured that was untrue and a way to scare folks into turning her in. She hasn't infected anybody new here, so that's probably right."

Lynne tilted her head. "You want me to reassure you?"

Ernie squinted faded blue eyes. "I wouldn't mind."

She breathed out, and her body finally relaxed. "There's no new strain or illness, I promise. They want me for personal reasons."

Multiple lines fanned out from Ernie's eyes and deepened when he frowned. "Personal?"

"Ripper, serial killer, obsession," Lynne said wearily.

"Oh." Ernie nodded.

Jax shook his head. Jesus. What kind of a world were they living in where that series of words explained everything? "Thanks for keeping quiet, Ernie."

The older man straightened. "I fought in 'Nam, Jax. We're on the same side, and you're our commander, government or not. I can follow orders and keep a secret."

"You're a good man." Jax stood and tugged Lynne to her feet. "Tomorrow at dawn, we're going on a mission to get more information on a possible cure. I'll go meet Lake the following day. Until then, please keep this under your hat."

"Understood." Ernie turned back to his dials.

Lynne swallowed and stumbled as Jax drew her from the room. He glanced down at her. "Take today to get your strength back. How do you feel about going on the mission to Myriad tomorrow morning?"

She lifted an eyebrow. "Why? Because you don't trust me to stay here, or because you want my help at Myriad?"

Both, actually. Jax glanced down at her weary green eyes, and something softened deep inside him. "Maybe I just want you with me." Oddly enough, that too was true.

President Bret Atherton waited until the ham radio operator packed up and left the office before lifting an eyebrow. "Waiting until the day after next gives us time to prepare for the meeting. What do you think about Mercury?"

Lake rubbed a hand across his razor-sharp buzz cut. "I think Mercury is lying about the forces he's amassed. He took over a food distribution center immediately, so he probably also raided anywhere he could find weapons at the same time. He's smart and he's strong, and he would've been training people from day one to fight."

Bret nodded. "Do you think he's a Scorpius survivor?"

"There's no indication he was ever infected," Lake said.

Yet instinct roiled in Bret's gut. To move that quickly and become such a legend in a short amount of time spoke of a higher intelligence, one Bret believed came to a fortunate few who survived the bacteria. "I read his military record, and before Scorpius, he was impressive."

"Delta Force members usually are," Lake responded dryly. "Lynne Harmony is a smart woman, and she was well aware of Mercury's reputation. No way would she seek him out unless she had something to barter with him. In that scenario, his protection, especially from our forces, would be appealing to her."

Bret blew out air. "Lynne has always played it safe. My guess is that she avoided L.A. and the rioting gangs there, unless she discovered that Myriad is in L.A." Which is more than he'd known. Why Vivienne wouldn't just tell Bret what he wanted to know was beyond him. As a psychic, surely the woman could tap into the universe or whatever the hell they tapped and give him the information.

"Even so, sir, I'd like to follow up on this lead. Send an Elite Force scouting team to L.A. to just observe Mercury's forces." Lake remained at attention.

Bret blinked. He'd had a dream the night before of Lake saying those very words. Perhaps his brain was still evolving and he'd be psychic soon, too. His instincts started to hum, and his parietal lobe tickled. "No. Let's wait until we have more information before you leave on a mission."

Lake didn't move. "Understood. I just sent out two contingents of six men—one to Boise to confiscate the weapons of the militia gathering there, and the other to a newly discovered lab in Wyoming. That leaves only thirteen men here, and I would prefer to cover your back."

"Agreed, although let's keep our ears to the ground. Perhaps your thought about Lynne being with Mercury is on track. I mean, even if she didn't seek asylum, his men might've found her and taken her in."

Lake's face twitched in a slight frown. "The intel on Mercury's group is that women are protected and not used or bartered for."

Bret rolled his eyes. "Propaganda, I'm sure. Smart, too." He played with the USB drive on the black cord around his neck. Lynne's USB drive.

"Yes, sir. I'll scout the best place to meet Mercury so we have time to secure the area, and I'll give him instructions that only allow for enough time for him to arrive."

"Good."

Lake's shoulders somehow went back even farther. "The men have finished emptying the water truck." His tone remained level, but Bret could sense the disapproval.

"The water is important to me, and it's the last time I'll use such resources." Bret had ordered his men to find a water truck, which they had, and then fill it from one of the indoor pools in the casinos, so nobody could drink the water, anyway. The usage of the gas alone had made Lake tense all day. "Trust me. I need the pool filled for Lynne." His back stiffened. Hell, he was the president of the United States and didn't need to explain himself to anybody.

"Yes, sir."

"Excused."

Lake pivoted and left the room.

Bret eyed the set of syringes and vials on his desk, wondering if Vivienne could take any more. So far, no matter what he'd pumped into her blood, she hadn't given up Lynne's location. Whistling, he filled a vial with what Lake had assured him was a potent truth serum and strode from the room. So far, the stuff hadn't done anything but make Vivienne goofy.

He hummed and kept hold of both the syringe and the lantern as he walked into the room. Vivienne sat, shackled to the wall, mumbling.

Damn it.

Bret walked to her and kicked her ankle.

She giggled, spit sliding from her mouth. "You're such a dork."

He grimaced. Hell. He glanced at the syringe in his hand. Well, he couldn't waste it. Crouching, he slid the needle into her exposed arm and pressed the plunger.

She gasped, and her chest filled with air.

He slapped her face. "Tell me the truth about Lynne."

"You're gonna die soon." Vivienne's head lowered, and she sang the words. "I am psychic and I know that to be true."

He grimaced. "You stink." When was the last time he'd allowed her to shower? Of course there was no running water, but they kept barrels in the garage. Soon they'd be out of water and would need to leave the desert.

Her head lagged, and she began to sing a Garth Brooks song an octave too high.

He sighed. "Where's the Bunker?"

She stopped singing. "Under the ground, of course."

His heartbeat picked up. "Where?"

She opened her mouth and started singing "Jingle Bells."

Damn it. Drawing a key from his back pocket, he unlocked the shackle around her leg and jerked her over his shoulder.

She protested with an oomph, her legs dangling uselessly against his chest. He easily stood and stalked out of the small storage room. How much did she weigh, anyway? He hadn't kept close track of feeding her, but she felt like a bag of bones. Another country song, one he thought was by Trisha Yearwood, mumbled from Vivienne's lips as he crossed through the guest house to the sunlit yard outside.

She stopped singing and moaned as sun hit her legs. "Psychics don't see what isn't there," she muttered.

The woman was losing her mind. He eyed the sparkling mermaids at the bottom of the now full pool. Pretty and shimmering. Without exerting much effort, he ducked and tossed Vivienne into the shallow end of the pool.

She hit with a splash and then screamed.

Interesting. Bret studied her. Pain creased into her face in harsh lines. Ah. The chlorine probably burned the raw flesh around her ankle where the shackle had been. He strode to a small table and grabbed a couple of hotel shampoo bottles. Vivienne could sit with her head above the water. Otherwise, with the drugs in her system, she'd probably drown.

He squirted shampoo into his hand and dropped it on her hair. "Wash yourself."

She blinked, confusion filling her face.

Maybe he shouldn't have given her another dosage today. He snarled. "Now."

She shook her head, obviously trying to concentrate, and lifted her hands to her hair. "Where am I?"

Yep. Too many drugs. He sighed. "Vegas. Where is Lynne Harmony?"

"Dunno because you don't dunno. Dumbass." All of a sudden, Vivienne's eyes focused. "I hope I'm there when you die." She shrugged out of her stained jacket and slowly started scrubbing her hair back to blond.

He smiled. "I have a destiny to fulfill first. Believe me, you'll die long before me." He focused as Lake stepped out of the house. "What?"

"We reached a rival group in L.A. on the ham. They're calling themselves Twenty. You're going to want to hear this," Lake said.

Chapter Twenty-Six

Between the idea and the reality,
between the motion and the act, falls the shadow.

—T. S. Eliot

Her knees still shaking from listening to Vice President Lake on the ham radio, Lynne followed Jax from the small office into the main war room. Someone had wheeled a whiteboard into the far corner, complete with markers. "Nice," Lynne breathed.

Sami rubbed bloodshot eyes. "There was a school a few blocks away, and when we made our home here, we raided the place. Too bad there wasn't more canned food."

Lynne sat next to Sami. Tace sat on her other side, and Raze loped inside to sit next to Lynne.

Jax shut the door and stood by the whiteboard, grabbing a blue marker. "I've asked Lynne to sit in on this meeting because she'll be going on the mission to Myriad tomorrow morning, which we think is in Century City, based on her calculations. My hope is she'll see the documents we need to take as well as identify compounds and medical shit to bring back."

Lynne clasped her hands on the table. Hopefully she'd

find *medical shit*. Her life had gone crazy. Nobody protested her presence, so she sat back.

Jax drummed his fingers on the table. "I hope we're back before the president calls, but if not, Ernie can make the arrangements for a meeting. I want the Myriad information in my hands before we meet."

Lynne nodded. "I agree."

Jax focused on his soldiers. "This morning I finished hearing reports from all the squadron leaders, so I'm well versed on what's happening with the entire community. Let's get your reports out of the way now, starting with Tace."

Tace leaned forward, elbows on the table. "We have the one box of vitamin B, and that'll last through another month. Then we're in trouble. No current cases of Scorpius. Far as I can tell, and while most don't admit it, we probably have many survivors of the fever and probably a few hundred who haven't contracted it yet. The total number of folks in our little slice of heaven is just over five hundred, so I'm totally guessing about statistics."

"All right. I've heard a couple of rumblings about folks wanting to separate into two communities, one for Scorpius survivors and one for the uninfected. How serious is it?" Jax asked.

"Not so much yet, because mainly nobody knows who's been infected and who has not." Tace shrugged. "That's a worry for another day, if you ask me."

Jax nodded. "Agreed. Is that it for your report?"

"No. We have several cases of what my doctors think are just colds, ten still wounded by the Twenty attack, and one pregnancy."

Jax's head jerked up. "Who's pregnant?"

"Jill Sanderson," Tace replied.

Jax frowned. "Which one is she?"

Tace's lips turned down. "You should know that, leader.

She's sixteen and helps out with the orphans and the kitchen, very often in the headquarters kitchen right here."

Jax went still. "Who knocked up a sixteen-year-old girl?"

Tace sighed. "A seventeen-year-old boy."

"Well, fuck." Jax scrubbed his whiskered jaw.

Lynne leaned forward, her heart beating faster. "Have either of them been infected with Scorpius?"

"I don't think so," Tace said, his gaze sharpening. "Why?"

Lynne swallowed. "We, ah, don't know of any successful births since Scorpius spread."

Jax sat back. "What?"

She nodded. "Any pregnant woman who contracted Scorpius died, as far as we could track." She played idly with a pencil, her temples pounding. "Anybody becoming pregnant after surviving Scorpius lost the baby at some point . . . based on medical reports from all over the world."

Sami shook her head. "But communications went down so quickly. There might be plenty of pregnant women out there due in a few months."

Lynne nodded. "I know." Scorpius had spread only six months before, so it was too early to really know if a recuperated woman could give birth. "The early results didn't look good."

Jax breathed out. "So you're telling me Scorpius may kill us off no matter what."

"Yes." Sure, some folks hadn't been infected, but the bacteria was strong and sturdy and would always be around. "Some of the research into vitamin B focused on successful births, and I'm hoping we find that at Myriad."

"Your research just became more important than ever." Jax glanced around. "For now, where are we on condoms?"

"Almost out." Tace shrugged. "We're almost out of all medical supplies. Hopefully we'll find some on this mission."

Lynne nodded. "We're going into the heart of Century City, all workplaces and no residences, so it's possible we'll find supplies. When the fever hit, it all happened very quickly, and people flocked to their homes. Scavengers and Rippers haven't been organized, so there are still many places untouched by humans after Scorpius spread." Hopefully. She cleared her throat, her stomach aching. "Do either of the kids, the ones having the baby, have family here?"

Tace settled back in his chair. "No. Hardly anybody has family here."

Made sense.

Jax twirled the marker in his hand. "Sami?"

Sami scratched her wrist. "April is doing a good job directing scavenging missions as well as providing some sort of organization for the civilians in Wyatt's absence. She's hurting but is throwing herself into action, which I guess helps."

"She's healing like the rest of us," Tace said slowly. "Let's keep her really busy."

Sami nodded. "Little Lena is sticking close to her, and since they've already bonded, that seems to be helping, too. We're low on food. Maybe six months' supply left if we don't find a way to replenish it." She played with a chewed-up pencil on the table. "Morale is down. Way down. Wyatt was the counselor, the person everybody went to with problems or issues or just to talk." She lifted her head, brown eyes burning. "You need to step in with some sort of reassurance."

Jax blinked. "Reassurance? About what? We have Twenty regrouping now, two more radical groups in L.A. wanting our resources, the Elite Force on my ass, and a group population where some folks haven't contracted Scorpius and many other people are carriers of it. What the fuck do you want me to tell them?"

"Anything," Sami whispered, her gaze dropping. "Give them some sort of hope."

Bewilderment filled Jax's eyes along with a healthy dose of anger. "Hope about what?"

Lynne's heart hurt. "If you have no hope, why do you fight so hard?"

Jax switched his powerful gaze to her. "Because there's something to fight, and those people can't survive on their own."

Lynne blinked. If he didn't know the people, why fight for them?

Jax slipped the marker in his pocket. "Wyatt?"

The room stilled. Pain, nearly palpable, filled the air. Jax cleared his throat. "Sorry. I meant Raze. Report."

Raze's stoic expression didn't twitch. "Ammunitions are way down. We wasted too many rounds fighting Twenty, and the civilians need better training. Fuel is low, and it's time to send scouts out with screwdrivers and gas cans."

Lynne breathed out. Her uncle had taught her how to pierce a gas can and empty the tank in less than two minutes. "I'm actually pretty good at that."

Raze lifted an eyebrow.

Jax shook his head. "We need you on the Myriad documents and materials once we get them. Your brain is the key to Scorpius, and that has to be your focus."

Her concentration was on getting the hell out of the area before Bret showed up. "I understand," she murmured.

"Good. Tace and Sami, you can stay for the briefing if you want, but you're remaining here to secure the compound tomorrow morning." Jax took the lid off the blue marker. "Raze, Lynne, and I will scout Myriad. I think we should take Byron. The kid's a genius with computer stuff, and maybe he'll see some wires or components we could use."

Raze nodded. "I'll have him suited up and mentally prepared."

Tace tapped his fingers on the table. "Byron is the father of the baby, by the way."

So much for being a genius.

Jax snarled. "And he couldn't figure out to sheathe his dick? For fuck's sake. We trust that kid with the ham radio."

"He's seventeen," Raze said simply.

Lynne winced. "You should probably talk to him, Jax. Reassure him that it's okay. He'll need that, as will Jill."

Jax lifted an eyebrow. "I'm not his mom."

"His mom is probably dead," Lynne shot back.

Jax turned toward the board, anger vibrating down his back. "My focus is strategy. We leave at first light, so let's get a plan in our heads." He began to draw.

Jax left Lynne with Sami to eat what looked like broth and smelled like old socks. The cooks did their best, but spices had run out eons ago. At some point, he was going to have to move them all north to a place where they could both farm and hunt. In L.A., the only thing to hunt was people. For now, he had a seventeen-year-old's ass to kick. As much as he hated it, with Wyatt gone, he had to talk to the kids—at least the ones working in headquarters.

He found Byron in the back storage room near the ham radio, cutting apart wires that might've gone to a speaker at some point. "What the holy fuck were you thinking?" Jax exploded, slamming the door behind him.

Byron jumped, and his wire cutters spun across the room. Swallowing audibly, he stood. "I wasn't."

Jax coughed out a laugh. "That's fucking obvious."

The kid kept his gaze, although his body was braced to stand up to somebody bigger and meaner. At seventeen, he was about five foot nine with sandy hair and skinny arms. "I love her."

Oh God. Fucking goddamn fucking kids. Jax leaned back against the door and tried to cool his temper. "If you love her," he began evenly, "you'd protect her and not knock her up when we're in a fucking war. Do you have any idea how vulnerable you've made her?" The irony of the question wasn't lost on him. He'd been worse than a horny teenager the other night with Lynne and hadn't taken precautions.

The idea of her being pregnant weakened his knees, but she'd been pretty sure of her cycle. Thank God.

"Yes." Terror filled Byron's eyes. "I know exactly how vulnerable I've made Jill. Them." His shoulders slumped. "She's all I've got."

Oh, man. Jax rubbed his chin, his gut churning. "Not true. You have more than her." A baby. So far, the youngest survivor they'd brought in was at least six years old. Where the fuck was he going to find baby food? "You have all of us, but get this." He stepped in and looked down. "You are now responsible for both her and the baby. There's no finding somebody else, no thinking it's too much, no trying to escape. They. Are. Yours."

"I know." Byron slid his glasses up his nose.

Jax breathed out. "Good. Have either you or Jill been infected by Scorpius?"

"Yeah. We've both survived it." Byron frowned. "Why?"

Well, shit. No need to scare the kid yet, and Jax didn't have to wonder about sequestering Jill from Scorpius exposure now. "Just asking. You're coming on the mission tomorrow morning, scouting for shit like this." He gestured around. "Then you train every day for two hours in hand-to-hand, guns, and knives. Every day."

Byron swallowed, his Adam's apple bobbing. "Yes."

"You just said good-bye to your childhood, kid." Jax turned and opened the door.

"Jax?"

"What?" Jax asked, not turning around.

"I said good-bye to my childhood when I buried my parents and baby sister five months ago," Byron said.

Jax closed his eyes. "I know," he said softly, exiting the room. He checked on Tace in the infirmary and then stalked into what passed for a kitchen to find Jill Sanderson scrubbing a pot while several others cleaned and put away dishes. He recognized her when he saw her. Long black hair, dark eyes, Korean features. Tiny girl—too tiny. He cleared his throat. "Jill? I'd like a moment, please."

Her eyes widened and she dropped the pot. Terror crossed her face.

Manny turned around, suds up to his elbows, hands in another pot. "Leave her alone."

Jax sighed out. "She doesn't need a mother hen, Manny. Trust me."

Manny took his measure, eyes sober, and then he nodded at Jill. "Go with Jax, sweetheart. If he's mean to you, I'll kill him in his sleep."

Jax wanted to smile, but Manny was probably telling the truth. "Follow me." He turned and crossed through the rec room/dining hall to the small war room.

Jill followed him, not making a sound, and then took a seat at the table, her gaze down.

He faltered and shut the door, dragging a chair to sit on. Wyatt would normally do this shit, but Wyatt was gone. The sharpness of the pang in Jax's heart caught his breath. He slowly released his lungs. "Are you all right?" he asked quietly.

Her head lifted, and her lips trembled. "Yes?"

That's what he'd figured. "Listen, honey. I just want to make sure you're feeling okay and you know you can reach out if you need help. I've never had a kid, so I can't offer advice, but a lot of people here have, and you might need help. I'll find baby food somewhere." They had nine months, right?

She nodded, her hands clinging to each other. Tears filled her eyes. "We didn't mean to."

Yeah. Words spoken by teens for eons. He shifted in his seat, uncomfortable as hell. "Well, you know how it happened? Right?"

Her head jerked, and she giggled. She slapped a hand over her mouth, but mirth filled her eyes.

"Jill?" he asked.

She moved her hand, her face pinkening even more. "I know about sex, Jax. We had classes on it and everything."

Now heat filled his face. He cleared his throat. "Um, okay. Good." Did he have to worry about sex education for the younger kids? He rubbed the back of his aching neck. Tension. Too much tension. "I just, ah, wanted you to know that you weren't alone. You'll be okay. You and the baby."

"I know. I love Byron. It'll be fine."

Nothing was going to be fine, and young love was about to make Jax's life a lot more difficult. "All right. Good talk." He stood and walked to the doorway, where he turned around. "Do you mind if I ask why you looked so terrified when I wanted to talk to you?"

She bit her lip and shrugged. "I don't know. It's just, that, well, I don't know you. I just see you with guns and knives telling people what to do." She smiled. "But now I'm not scared of you."

"Okay." He opened the door, his mind reeling. "Make sure you up your rations of dried milk and protein. I think you need more of that stuff now."

She nodded. "Okay. Thanks, Jax."

Jax left the room, rubbing his chest. God, he missed Wyatt.

Chapter Twenty-Seven

*I know not with what weapons World War III
will be fought, but World War IV will be fought
with sticks and stones.*

—Albert Einstein

Jax topped off the disastrous talk with horny teenagers by
scouting outside and making sure his barriers were in place.
When Los Angeles had begun to fall to looters and survival-
ist gangs, he'd immediately gathered any allies he could find
and had taken over the food distribution center with the
crappy slum apartments next to it. He'd sent groups to gather
weapons, fuel, and medicines. Then he'd created two surrounding lines of defense, the first with downed Mack trucks,
and then an inner circle of overturned minivans. They'd
spiraled inward, creating barriers as they went.

The air was cool but finally dry. He checked the line, signaled to the guards at post, and finally reached the eastern
end, where a truck met headquarters. Marvin padded by,
turned his massive head, studied Jax, and then moved on.
Obviously he'd already eaten.

Raze leaned against the brick wall, odd blue eyes cutting
through the darkness. "That's a lion. A real lion."

Jax nodded. "Name is Marvin."

Raze shook his head. "Marvin. How was the heart-to-heart with the kids?"

"Completely sucked." Jax noted Raze's alertness even while lounging. "How good are you, anyway?"

"Pretty damn good," Raze countered. His broad chest expanded and slowly relaxed as he let out air. "I haven't had a chance to tell you that I'm sorry about Wyatt."

The name sliced into Jax's gut, and he fought a wince. "Thanks."

"Seems like he was the heart around here."

Jax nodded. "Yeah. Well, he and Tace were both full of heart." Now Wyatt fed the worms and Tace searched for his humanity. "Lynne is a sweetheart, but people don't trust her, so she can't take that role. Sami is fighting her own demons, whatever they are, and she doesn't reach out to others. And we both know you're here for reasons of your own."

"Yep."

"Most special ops guys don't share much."

Raze twirled a knife end over end. "I never said I was special ops."

"Like you needed to." Jax crossed his arms. "You're not army."

"Nope." Raze cocked his head to the side.

"Not Green Beret or Secret Service." Jax rubbed his chin. "Beyond a SEAL." He smiled. "SEAL Team Six, were you?"

Raze lifted an eyebrow. "No such thing."

Right. "How did you end up here, man?" Jax asked.

"A story for another day." Raze slid the blade back into the sheath at his belt. "I knew you needed to take out Twenty, and I had a score to settle, so I figured I'd help out."

Jax rolled his neck. "I appreciate the help. Is there any chance you'll take a more active role around here?" He could really use somebody with Raze's training.

"No." Raze eyed the gathering dark clouds. "Why are you doing this?"

"Huh?"

Raze settled again. "With your skills, you could've headed into the woods and just lived off the land. You don't have family, you didn't have friends, and you didn't have a woman when you gathered this hodgepodge of a group together. So why?"

Jax frowned. "We were under attack, by first the bacteria and then rival gangs, so I just reacted. There were people to save." He lifted a shoulder. "I've been fighting ever since, and that's all I know. Now I've vowed to end Cruz for my brother." And he'd promised safety to a woman, one who needed protection more than any other person on earth. "To be honest, I always figured we'd find a cure, regroup, and then the government would step in." Was it too much to hope that might still happen?

"It's funny. With all the stories about you, almost making you a legend, nothing hints that you're such an optimist."

An optimist? Jax snorted. "I'm not even close."

"You think we're going to survive Scorpius and go on? I mean, as a species?" Raze asked.

Jax paused, his mind clicking. "Yes. Don't you?"

Raze scratched the stubble on his chin. "No. I think we're tilting at windmills right now."

Jax studied him. "Then why fight?"

"I've got my own reasons." Raze pushed off the wall.

"I got that the second you walked into camp," Jax said easily. "You might be quiet, but this isn't my first rodeo. I read you day one. I just don't know what your agenda is."

"I figured."

Okay. Jax made to go. "Well, good talk. While you're being helpful, I wouldn't mind if you helped train some of the civilians." He'd gotten sucked in with friends; maybe Raze would, too.

"Happy to help, but, Jax?"

"Yeah?"

"I'm not a group activity type of guy."

Finally, they were planning to go to Myriad in the morning. She was so close. Lynne tried to focus while working in the headquarters infirmary after dinner, taking note of a soldier with an infected cut. They needed some antibiotics. She wondered how many kids in the center of the territory had infections, ear or tonsil, that weren't getting better. "I'd kill for some amoxicillin," she said to Tace.

"People already have." He finished organizing their meager supply of bandages. "Why don't you head on up and get some sleep? When Jax says we're leaving at first dawn, he means it."

Her eyes ached, and her temples pounded. While she wouldn't sleep, lying down and shutting her eyes for a minute couldn't hurt. "Okay." She dodged through the rec room and up to the apartment, shoving open the door.

She stilled at finding Jax inside. Moonlight, weak and waning, cut through the boards over the window to light the area. "What are you doing?" she asked, glancing at a pile of clothing and weapons on the couch.

"Come here," he said, tugging a pair of jeans from the bottom of the pile. "Put these on."

She hesitated at the door. "I like my yoga pants."

"Too bad. You'll need jeans, something sturdier for your legs and weapons, tomorrow." He held out the denim. "Try these on."

Great. Jax Mercury in full bossy mode was too much at the moment. She approached the couch, kicked off her shoes, and added a shimmy to her ass when she dropped the yoga pants. Trying to appear innocent, she held out a hand for the jeans.

His lids dropped to half-mast, and he handed over the denim. Masculine tension filtered through the room and took over the atmosphere.

She slid into them, shaking her butt, sucking in her stomach to button the top. They were tight but would loosen upon wearing.

Jax slid a gun belt around her waist and tightened it, dropping to his haunches to attach the two strips to her right leg. "I've seen the way you can shoot." He shoved a black gun into the weapon holder, his face near her midriff.

"Yes." She settled her weight to keep balanced, her abdomen heating. "I practiced with my uncle as we made our way here." Talking about Bruce hurt somewhere deep in her chest.

Jax glanced up, his hands going to her thighs. "Your uncle was trained?"

"Yes. He was retired NYPD," she said, sadness hollowing out her stomach. "Helped me get out of the CDC, as you know, and then we ran."

Jax's brown eyes softened. "How did your uncle die?"

Lynne swallowed and bit down rage. "The Elite Force caught up with us in Arizona, and it was ugly."

Jax breathed out and stood. "They killed your uncle?"

"Yes." Tears sprang to Lynne's eyes, and she batted them back.

"Give me the story," Jax said, reaching for a pair of black leather boots. "But first things first. Try these on."

She slipped her feet into the boots, which were only a size too large. "They're okay. I can find socks." Then she sighed. "We were camping outside Tucson with a nice community led by a retired sheriff, and word came in that government soldiers were nearing. A sniper took out Uncle Bruce right beside me." She'd never forget the shock and slice of instant pain.

"How did you get away?"

She winced at the ache in her heart. "The sheriff had booby traps everywhere, and he kept the soldiers busy while I took off on a dirt bike." Hell, she'd almost crashed into several trees, but she'd made it. "I moved at night and stayed with a nice group of people for a couple of nights in Lake Havasu City. Then I kept on running, trying to get here, taking back roads or no roads at all." She'd been so scared and alone.

"I'm sorry about your uncle." Jax placed a knife right inside each boot. "Did he train you in knives?"

"Not really."

"Okay." Jax removed a knife and put the handle in her palm. "Strike here, here, or upward here." He pointed to his thigh, beneath his breastbone, and under his chin. "Just remember your knowledge of anatomy, and you'll be fine. Go for the softest entry and the ones with major blood vessels or arteries."

She hoped she didn't get close enough in a fight to use a blade. "Understood." Her hand shook when she replaced the knife in her boot.

Jax grasped a worn bulletproof vest and secured it over her chest. "This is the best one we have, but try not to get shot."

She gulped.

He sighed. "Okay, so I want to work on hand-to-hand, but first we need to change your mind-set."

The vest lay heavy over her chest, much heavier than she would've thought. How did soldiers and cops run with so much weight, in addition to weapons and supplies? "My mind-set is clear. I can kill if needed." In fact, she had. She'd killed Red and his friend just the other day.

Jax slid a hand through her hair, holding her in place.

"You've killed in self-defense. We need to change your mind-set from survival to attack mode."

She blinked. "I don't understand."

"I know. Right now, you're prepared if somebody comes at you. You'd attack in the name of getting to safety, right?"

She ran the words over her tongue. "Right."

He shook his head. "This isn't about keeping safe or defense. This is offense. If it's you and the darkness, *you're* the scary thing out there. You're hunting, not trying to hide. Get it?"

Kind of. "I think so."

Jax leaned in, his gaze intense. "Your whole life, you're a good girl. Smart and strong—you know you can defend yourself if necessary. A guy breaks into your house, maybe you shoot him, maybe you get to safety to call the cops. Right?"

"Right."

"Now"—Jax leaned in—"you're the guy breaking in. There's no safety, and there's no cops. *You're* the predator."

Okay, that was a shift in thinking. "Is that how you do it? Fight wars?"

"Yes." He released her and stepped back. "Your reasons may be honorable, and your purpose for fighting a good one, but in the heat of the battle? You have to be the one feared. Period."

Lynne shrugged out of the vest and allowed Jax to remove her weapons belt. "Is that how you've survived?"

"Yes. Being the worst thing in the dark always means survival." He dropped her weapons onto the couch. "How are you in hand-to-hand?"

"Terrible." Traveling so much, they hadn't had much time to work on those skills. "I know to strike first and try to debilitate my enemy so I can run. Hand-to-hand, with a guy trained like you, my best recourse is to get away."

Jax nodded. "If you can't get away, you get brutal. It's the same mind-set. They should be scared of you and not the other way around."

"I understand." Of course, that was with humans. Rippers didn't get scared, and neither would Bret. He had seemed to thrive on the fear around him. Lynne tried to force a smile. "How did it go with Byron and Jill?"

Jax winced. "She was scared to death of me. I had no idea."

Wow, he was clueless with people. Yet somehow so sweet in how hard he was trying. Lynne leaned in and pressed her hands to his ripped abs. Even through the cotton T-shirt, powerful muscles filled her palms. "I'm sure she's better now."

"Maybe." Jax ran his hands down Lynne's arms. "I don't have protection. Forgot to ask Tace for it."

Lynne lifted her head to look in his eyes. "Did you think I was making a move?"

He smiled, transforming his face into dark masculine beauty. "I guess I was hoping."

Man, she'd like to surprise him for once. So she dropped to her knees and reached for his belt.

His sharp intake of breath spurred her on, giving her confidence. "Lynne?" he asked, his voice rough.

She unzipped his jeans and tugged them down, humming at his already erect penis. "What I have in mind doesn't require condoms."

Chapter Twenty-Eight

Humanity and technology
don't necessarily go hand in hand.

—Dr. Franklin Xavier Harmony

Jax peered out the windshield as dawn rose over the horizon. The truck was old but sturdy and full of gas. Lynne rode shotgun, while Raze and Byron followed in a battered Ford pickup. He hated using the fuel and being seen in vehicles, but they'd need the cargo room if they found anything.

They passed between a series of old markets, where a group of cats scoured the area, searching for food.

Stress crackled across the truck, coming from his woman. She'd been tense all morning. "Do you understand what to do if we get separated?" he asked.

She huffed out air, nerves all but shooting from her. "For the love of all that's holy, yes, I understand. I have an IQ well above normal, and I get it. Stop giving me orders."

Okay, definitely tense and nervous about the mission.

While he could sympathize, he needed her to focus. He drove around a downed red Ferrari, heading into the heart of what used to be L.A. "I give orders, and you take them. Period." On missions, he couldn't allow for any back talk.

She rolled her eyes. "You are so cranky."

"I am not," he returned, wincing when he ran over a monstrous pothole. "I just don't like leaving the compound or using fuel, so we need this raid to go right."

"Whatever." She turned to watch out the window. "Most guys are at least halfway in a good mood after a blow job, you know."

He blinked. It had been a hell of a blow job, and then he'd returned the favor before they grabbed a few hours of sleep. "Focus, Harmony."

"Yep," she muttered to herself. "Great mood."

He skirted piles of debris. "The blow job was excellent, but if you did it for me, you missed the mark."

Her head swung full force toward him. "Excuse me? If I did it for you? No, Jax. Believe me, we women wake up wanting more than anything to suck cock. In fact, I woke up that morning thinking, man, I'd love to suck on Jax's dick until he comes down my throat. Yep. Big dreams there."

He gave her a look, his mouth twitching. "I meant that if you wanted to decrease my tension, it's impossible right now. But I did like your mouth around my cock."

"Nice, Jax. Geez." Her shoulders moved down from around her ears. "Last night wasn't planned, and I didn't have any ulterior motive like to ease tension. It's just, well, I wanted to."

"Thank you." He kept his gaze on the road. Should he have thanked her the night before? Hell, he'd gone down on her, truly enjoying himself, and made her orgasm twice. "In fact, you owe me one."

She chuckled, and sounded surprised. "Shut up. We are done talking about blow jobs."

Good thing, too. His pants were becoming too tight in the groin, and he needed to focus.

"Besides, we don't have a relationship," she muttered.

He glanced along the broken store windows. "What else would you call it?"

She kept silent.

Yep. He wasn't sure, either, but it was more than sex, and more than convenience. In fact, not much about Lynne Harmony was convenient. "Now you tell me about Bret, your uncle, and the last time you met up."

She stiffened. "No. Need to concentrate on the mission."

"With the safest route, we have a couple of hours in the car. Time to multitask." He kept his voice low, but she would talk, and she would tell him everything. "Don't mess with me, Lynne."

"You have *got* to stop threatening me."

Unfortunately, he didn't have time to be gentle, and he was losing the patience needed to use reason. "How long after Bret killed the president did you escape?"

She held the gun in her lap, one hand over it, as if she didn't want to pick it up. "About a month. Communications went down, and the Internet failed because of all the hacking." When she thought, her lips pouted just a little. "Although the Internet would've failed at some point anyway. Not enough people to man the servers."

"I know."

"After I figured out Bret was a Ripper and that the CDC would soon shut down because we were losing people right and left, I stayed for about a month to gather as much information as I could find. We'd printed out all reports coming in throughout the world on Scorpius, figuring we might lose power at some point, so I just read and made notes."

"Where are your notes?"

"Bret had his contacts in the CDC confiscate my records. But I have a pretty good memory, so I've been doing my best to reconstruct them."

Jax swallowed, not wanting to ask the next question. "During that month, what about you and Bret?"

Her hand tightened over the gun. "We were both very busy. He had to get sworn in and up to date on everything presidential, and I had intel to gather and more blood to give. Even though I was a test subject, I was also a key researcher."

"You were the head of infectious diseases for the CDC before Scorpius unleashed itself, right?" Jax asked, turning down a side alley that looked fairly clear.

"Yes." She ran her fingernail along the gun's safety. "Bret couldn't be seen with me, even though news coverage was spotty. But ultimately the CDC reached its end, and the buildings in D.C. and Atlanta were blown up—but I'm not sure about other locations."

That's right. He'd heard about the explosions. "The two facilities were blown up on purpose?"

"Of course. Once the power grid failed, we had to incinerate all the infectious diseases still present. We couldn't have them getting loose without safeguards." She swallowed, and her hand trembled. "I was to move to the White House that night."

"So you called your uncle?" Jax asked softly, watching some shadows in the crumbling apartment building to his left.

Lynne leaned over to look out his window. "Rippers?"

"Maybe. You called your uncle?"

Lynne settled back in her seat. "We'd met up at my parents' funeral months before and had kept in touch. The second Bret killed the sitting president, I called Uncle Bruce from a lab phone. Phones were still working at that point. We had a plan in place."

"Your plan was to get to me." That still didn't make sense.

"My ultimate plan was to find Myriad, to prevent Bret from getting their research. Once I discovered Myriad was in L.A. somewhere, you became a necessary stop because if I could get your help, I could keep Bret off me long enough to get there. And I'd hoped through your raiding that you'd found the location of Myriad, even if you didn't quite know what you had. Which was what happened, really. Although I certainly didn't expect to lose Uncle Bruce, and I didn't expect to choose to be in your bed."

Choose. It was an important distinction. "I'm glad you did."

A half-smile played around her mouth. "So am I." She cleared her throat. "Make me a promise."

"Another one?" he asked, warning tickling the base of his neck.

"Yeah. My chances of longevity aren't good—either from enemies or from this blue heart we haven't figured out. When I, ah, go . . . don't regret us. Okay?" She kept her gaze out the window and not on him.

The words hit his chest harder than a hammer attack he'd lived through once. The woman didn't want to be a mistake in his life. Every once in a while, she showed a sweetness that flayed him through and through. "I won't regret us, and I'm not letting you die." He hadn't connected with a woman the way he had with Lynne, well, ever. It didn't make sense, and they sure as shit didn't make sense, but he wasn't letting anybody kill her. "You can trust me."

"I do," she sighed. "I wish I didn't, but I do."

"So you and your uncle made it out of D.C."

Lynne set her head back on the torn headrest. "Yes. At first I was trying to find my friend Nora, because I thought she might help me get to you. But when there was no sign of her, Uncle Bruce and I headed west."

"Who's Nora?"

"Nora McDougall. She's a microbiologist and my best friend. When Scorpius got bad, I brought her in to help with the research."

Jax frowned, memories surfacing. "McDougall? Any relation to Deke McDougall?" He had been the president's first choice for military defense against Scorpius and had briefly given a frightened nation hope with his Brigade.

"Yes. Deke is her husband." Lynne snorted. "I forced their marriage when I was in a hospital bed. To protect my friend."

Jax remembered seeing McDougall on television while there still was television. The guy was a huge former soldier with a Scottish accent. "Any idea where McDougall is now?" If Lake was speaking for the president, it didn't look good for Lynne's old friends.

"No." Lynne sighed. "But Deke is one of the toughest guys I've ever met, and he would do anything to protect Nora. She's alive. I just know it."

"Okay." Jax doubted it, but why take away any ounce of hope? He pulled over in a deserted parking lot and waited for Raze to draw up alongside, both rolling down windows. "We can probably get on the freeway. What do you think?"

Raze frowned. "It's risky. Even if we find an on-ramp that's not blocked by abandoned cars, once we're on the 405, we could get stuck. A lot of people tried to make it out of the city and abandoned their cars when they ran out of gas."

"Then finding an off-ramp with maneuverability might be a problem." Jax glanced around the empty neighborhood, his instincts humming. "But sticking to back roads opens us up to Rippers and small gangs. We need to get to Myriad and back home before darkness falls." He calculated the risk and reward. "We're going for the 405. Follow me." He waited for Raze's nod before rolling up his window. "It's our best chance," he said to Lynne.

"Your instincts are good," she said.

Shit, he hoped so.

He drove the truck back onto the road and skirted several abandoned cars before reaching the nearest on-ramp. Cars and trucks littered the side, but if he drove slowly, he could maneuver between several. Just as he reached the top, his gut boiled. A line of silver compacts barred the entrance.

"Damn it," he muttered.

Gunshots echoed, and metal tinged.

Adrenaline blew through his veins. "Get down." He grabbed Lynne's head and threw her onto the floor.

She yelped and held her gun, breath panting out.

Jax gunned the truck straight at the cars, shoving himself down in the seat. Gunfire sprayed the truck. The back window shattered, and glass cut the back of his neck. He clamped a hand on Lynne's shoulder, shoving her down farther and trying to keep her somewhat stable. "Hold on, baby," he muttered, pressing his foot to the floor.

He plowed into the intersection of two cars, sending them both spiraling away. The impact threw him back into the seat. Even with his hold, Lynne's head smacked into the glove box. Releasing her, he slammed both hands on the wheel to keep the truck from fishtailing. More bullets pinged into the back of the truck.

If they hit the tires, he was screwed.

He barreled through the cars and swerved far to the right so downed cars covered his ass.

Holding his breath, he punched the gas and kept an eye on the rearview mirror as Raze followed in his wake, smashing into the sides of vehicles like a ball in a pinball machine. But he kept going, even as bullets impacted the side of his truck.

"You okay?" Jax asked Lynne, swerving around a crumpled Buick.

She gulped, shoving herself up into the seat. "I think so." Her voice was thick with what sounded like tears.

He reached over and gingerly fingered the back of her head. "You're gonna have a bump."

She winced and jerked away. "My vision is clear. Stop poking at my head." She leaned forward and turned to use her sleeve to wipe away glass from the demolished windows. Cool air rushed inside, but at least the front window was intact. "Who was that?"

"All I saw was gunfire and a black van." He glanced back to make sure Raze was keeping up.

"Will they follow us?" she gasped.

"Doubtful." One van wouldn't try to take on two trucks

without the element of surprise. Raze was still shooting out his window, so the attackers would know they were armed. "My guess is it was either Rippers with guns or bastards trying to get our fuel and cars." And women, probably. But on this mission, there was just one woman.

His.

Chapter Twenty-Nine

During the next millennium there is a significant chance that civilization on Earth will be destroyed by an asteroid, a killer plague, or a global war.

—Paul Davies

The coordinates for the secret Myriad Labs led to the corporate office and research labs for a cereal company called Chester's. The company was located on the outskirts of Century City, close enough to share in the glitz but far enough away from the Fox Plaza Building to have more space and reasonable rent.

It made for a great confidential lab, and Lynne considered how many more were out there. She'd been spot on with the coordinates, and for the briefest of moments, she wondered how advanced her brain would become. Was it still changing?

They parked the trucks in the underground garage because Jax figured it'd be better to be hidden than be able to make a fast getaway.

Lynne hadn't offered an opinion. The guy knew what he was doing.

She read the kiosk of the building's layout against the corner wall and then glanced at the dead elevators with what felt like unnatural longing. The vest was heavy, and it was hard to maneuver with the knives in her boots. "The offices take up the fifteenth floor, and the research labs are on floors three and four," she said, following Jax into the stairwell. "We'll need to go through all three of the floors, and I'd like to start with the fourth."

Byron followed on her heels, while Raze took the rear.

"I don't get why there'd be a research place here," Byron whispered.

Lynne glanced at the already peeling wallpaper. "It's not the CDC. They were researching how to make cereal crunchier or tastier without sugar. We didn't have them researching anything dangerous until there was no choice." Even so, the labs had been state of the art. She glanced at packing invoices scattered across the reception desk. "It looks like the manufacturing plant for the cereal is north of L.A. County."

Jax started up the stairs, sweeping a thick flashlight back and forth, a big gun in his other hand. "At an industrial distribution center?" he asked.

"I don't know where it is—just that it's north. There may still be food at the manufacturing center, since it's an unusual place. We can find the physical address in the offices, probably."

Jax reached the first-floor landing and turned to point the light on the stairs for the other three. "If there's food out there, we need to get to it." He waited until everyone reached the landing. "Lynne and I'll take the fourth floor, and you two head up to the fifteenth floor to see what you can find. First look for anything on Scorpius or manufacturing plants, and then go through every desk for supplies." He loped into a jog, and Lynne followed to the fourth floor.

Jax nudged open the door and swept between an elevator bank. He gestured for her to follow him, and she tried to match her steps to his. How did he move so silently? The guy barely seemed to touch the dusty tile floor with each step. The elevators led to a double-glass door with CHESTER CEREALS branded across the middle. He shoved open the door and stepped inside, his head up and his body still.

Lynne instinctively stopped behind him.

He waited a couple beats and then clicked off his flashlight. Wide windows fronted the entire north wall, and plenty of sunlight illuminated the area. "I don't hear anybody."

A wide reception desk took center stage along with a quaint waiting room. She followed Jax behind the desk and waited until he'd drawn out all the drawers. A couple of cup-of-soups instantly went into his backpack, along with a bottle of aspirin and some cough drops. A picture of a pretty blond with two kids, twins around four years old, sat by the phone. Lynne swallowed. Hopefully the woman and her kids had survived.

Probably not.

"Let's move," Jax said, coming around the desk and turning the knob of the door. "No go." He sighed. "When the electricity went out, the lock didn't disengage." He cocked his gun. "Cover your ears."

Lynne slapped her hands over her ears just as he fired. A second later, he planted a boot near the doorknob. The door flew open.

Jax ducked inside, gun sweeping. He slowly straightened and gestured her forward. Sunlight cascaded in from windows on the far walls. She moved inside to see four marked doorways, and she pointed to the one on the far left. "Let's start in the Vitamin Research department." She turned toward the door.

"Lynne? I want your gun in your hand and the safety off," Jax said evenly.

Her chest felt heavy, yet she drew the gun.

"Safety off," he repeated.

She faltered. "You sure? I may shoot you."

He grinned, intense and somehow sexy. "I saw you cover

Wyatt the other day. Woman, you're a champion in battle. I trust you."

The heaviness gave way to warmth. She nodded, although her breath still came too fast. "Okay." Centering herself, she clicked off the safety. "Let's go."

Lynne sucked down warm water from a bunch of bottles found in a Chester Cereal break room, sweat pouring down her back and her leg muscles wobbling. They'd searched the floors and had taken all the research she deemed important, carrying cartons and boxes down the stairs more times than she could count. She leaned against the doorway of the last lab on the third floor.

"One more lab," Jax said easily, not showing any wear from the day.

She sighed. As she'd skimmed to determine what to take and what to leave, more than once he'd had to hurry her up as she'd started to really read, telling her she'd have all the time in the world once behind safe walls again. So far, from what she could tell, the researchers at Myriad had been on to something with the research into vitamin B, but had had to halt the experiments when the power grid failed. "Okay."

He moved into his easy lope and headed into the last lab of the day. "We have about three hours of light left, and I want to be on the road in one hour."

She followed him inside a room set with five large glass refrigerators, all dead. Vials of every color filled them, and she hesitated.

"What?" he asked.

"These are the specimens." All of the other labs had held documents and excellent equipment that she'd helped to carry down the stairs, but the actual specimens were stored in this lab. She approached the nearest fridge and slowly opened the door. "Can I borrow your flashlight?"

Jax stepped closer, bringing heat and his unique scent. Male, aggression, and the forest. The smell, both familiar and wild, slid through her skin. She cleared her throat.

"I've got it," he said, pointing the light inside the fridge.

The first row of vials appeared black and coagulated. Lynne peered closer to read the label. LYNNE HARMONY. She drew back. "Huh."

Jax peered around her. "That's your blood?"

"Apparently." She shivered. "The CDC sent samples to all the labs working on Scorpius, so it makes sense." When the power went down and then the backup generators ran out of gas, the blood was ruined.

Jax shone his light to the next shelf. "Kind of creepy seeing your blood like that. Right?"

"Yes." She counted out breaths as her legs forgot they were tired and itched to run. The next level held blue vials and green vials. She peered closer. "These might be okay. Not all specimens need refrigeration like blood." She took a pair of gloves off the nearest counter. "Let's take everything that doesn't include blood." What she wouldn't give for a biohazard suit.

Jax rubbed his head. "Any chance those could kill us?"

"There's always a chance, but nothing is airborne because this lab isn't set up for it. So everything here would only be dangerous if we somehow got it into our bodies." She gingerly tugged an empty box toward her with her foot.

"Like Scorpius," Jax said grimly. "That one wasn't dangerous at all, now was it?"

Lynne swallowed. "That's a good point, but they were working on a cure here, not trying to create anything dangerous. We're safe if we follow protocols."

"Humph," he said, grabbing another box. Thunder bellowed

outside, and he breathed out. "Excellent. Let's hurry and go while it's storming. That'll mask the sound of the trucks."

She got to work.

Nearly two hours later, they finally finished and met Raze and Byron in the parking area.

Raze finished shutting the back of his truck. "We found more microscopes and other medical stuff. Brought it all. We can go through it back at the base."

Byron scratched his chin. "We also found a fully stocked break room with paper plates, coffee, and instant food. Not a lot, but some, as well as a bunch of wires I need." He rubbed a bruise on his arm. "Did you find the cure for Scorpius?"

Lynne shook her head. "I don't know. There's some interesting data, and we grabbed samples, so hopefully I'll know more as soon as I can dig in and figure out what they'd found." If they'd found anything. She also needed her data and Nora's data from the CDC, which hopefully Bret had.

"In the desks on the fourth floor, we found aspirin, bacterial wipes, condoms, and female, ah, products," Jax said. He glanced out at the waning light. "We have to hurry if we're going to get back before nightfall."

"The deluge will mask the sound of the trucks," Raze said.

"Roger that." Jax jumped into the truck. "Move, Lynne."

She hurried around the truck to get inside and secure her seat belt out of habit.

"Off," Jax said, igniting the engine.

She hesitated.

"If we need to move fast, you can't have the belt on. You would've been shot had you been wearing it earlier." A vein stood out on his neck.

She unclasped the belt. "You're not accustomed to explaining your orders, are you?"

"No." He glanced over his shoulder and then pushed the gearshift into DRIVE. "We found a map in a deserted delivery truck near the entrance, and there's an alternate way back home. We need to avoid the on-ramp where we had the problem and will get off the 405 two exits earlier. I need your gun out and ready to fire, just in case."

She unholstered her weapon as Jax drove into the rain. "The first time I shot anybody was when I shot Red."

"I know."

She winced as Jax gunned the truck out of the parking garage. "In a hurry?"

"Yes. If we don't get back by nightfall, we're screwed." His jaw clenched again.

She tried to stretch her aching legs. "We have lights on the truck."

"We can't use lights. It's bad enough we're using engines, but at least the storm will mask the sound. If we used lights, we'd be attacked immediately." His gaze seemed to see everywhere at once, although his head barely moved.

Fear roiled through her stomach. "How many, um, gangs do you think are out there?"

He lifted a shoulder. "Probably only a few with our numbers and organization. It's the roving bands of Rippers and just plain assholes I'm more worried about. They kill first and just scavenge."

She swallowed over a lump in her throat. "Yeah. My uncle and I ran into a few of those, but we managed to get by them without being hurt." Why did some people try to establish rules and laws, and others tried to hurt people? It wasn't just Rippers, either. "You're a good driver."

"Part of my military training." He flashed a smile, easily veering around a series of crumpled motorcycles. "If we had more time, we'd syphon gas. Next time, though." He braced himself as they reached an on-ramp. "Hold on." Just as he pressed his foot down, an older van ripped in front of them. "Shit." Jax swerved to the left, hitting a dented Kia.

Another van, this one black with a purple 20 emblazoned across the side, careened behind them to block the way they'd come.

"Fuck," Jax said. "It's the guys from earlier—I didn't see the other side of the van. They must've followed us this way and waited until we showed ourselves again. Hold on." He put the truck in REVERSE just as gunshots echoed through the storm. "Brace yourself." He hit the van full on, sending it spinning. Then he shifted into DRIVE and flipped to the side, punching the gas. The truck roared into motion.

Lynne stopped breathing, one hand on the dash and the other gripping her gun. She turned wildly. "They're coming."

"Duck." Jax grabbed the back of her head and shoved down.

She yelped.

Bullets went over her head to pierce and then shatter the front windshield.

"Shit." Jax grabbed her shoulder and tugged her toward him. "I need you to drive."

Her mouth dropped open. She couldn't breathe. Her vision fuzzed. "I can't."

"You can." He jerked her up and onto his lap. "Wheel."

She dropped her gun onto the seat and grabbed the steering wheel, her foot pressing on top of his. "Oh God."

He slid out from under her, turned, and aimed through the shattered back window. "Keep it steady."

She pushed on the gas pedal and dodged around bricks and blocks of debris. Jax jerked toward her and grabbed the handle above the door to stabilize himself.

"Sorry. Do you think it's Cruz?" she gasped.

"Not personally, but the idea that he has enough forces to stake out the local on-ramps concerns me." Jax took a shot. "Especially since he knows about you."

A pile of what looked like burned street signs blocked the middle of the road. "Hold on," she yelled, yanking the wheel to the left and jumping the curb. Metal scraped and sparks flew as the truck lanced along the sidewalk. "Shit," she muttered, swerving to get back on the road. The truck landed with a bump.

She looked into the rearview mirror to see the van on their ass. "Shoot them!" she screamed.

Jax gave her a look and braced his arm on the back of the seat. He lowered his chin and pulled the trigger.

The van jerked to the side, drove up a small Celica, and lifted into the air, spinning end over end to plow into an old movie theater. An explosion rocked the afternoon.

"Yeah," Lynne yelled, hitting the gas again.

Jax turned around. "Drive steady." He lifted his leg and kicked the rest of the windshield out of the way. Then he frowned. "Keep going and turn left into a residential area as soon as you can."

Wind blasted into her face, but she could see better. Kind of. Dusk was falling, and soon they wouldn't be able to see anything without using the lights. She gulped down fear, and her body began to shake as the adrenaline faded. As soon as she could, she took a sharp left, nearly slowing to a crawl in order to maneuver around a bunch of railroad spikes scattered across the concrete.

Without warning, her door was jerked open, and rough hands ripped her from her seat.

Chapter Thirty

*When it comes down to the fine-edge of a moment,
the moment, a hero always reveals himself.*

—Dr. Franklin Xavier Harmony

"Lynne!" Jax's fingers brushed Lynne's vest, but he couldn't catch hold as she was dragged away. In one smooth motion, he twisted the keys out of the ignition and launched himself from the truck, his boots landing hard and splashing water.

Lynne's wide eyes begged for help. A man standing well over six feet tall held her by the neck, her back to his front. The guy wore a ripped powder blue suit covered in muck and what smelled like shit. His eyes were a wild blue, and dried blood coated his full beard. "Girl," he growled.

Lynne winced and stood up on her toes, obviously trying to breathe.

A darkened bar rose up behind him, occupying the entire block. Dead silence came from within. The opposite side of the street held an old tire store, also abandoned.

Another man, this one with long blond hair, crawled out from a pile of rocks in the alley next to the bar. He was buck-assed naked and covered in bruises and cuts. He whimpered and snorted like a dog.

"Listen," Jax said evenly, "I don't know what kind of a

shit show we just walked into, but let the girl go, and I won't shoot you in the head."

The guy on the ground barked.

Jax kept his stance relaxed and his hand near his weapon. The beast holding Lynne could probably snap her neck or crush her larynx in a heartbeat. "I have food," Jax said. "Granola bars." A whole case, actually.

The blond guy whined like a collie begging for a treat.

Bile rose in Jax's gut, and he swallowed it down. "We can reach an agreement." Could the guy in blue even understand his words?

The guy grunted and buried his head in Lynne's hair. "Pretty," he growled.

Fuck. The weight of the blade in his boot had Jax sliding one foot back so he could move fast.

The guy lifted his head. "Gun. I want it."

Jax glanced down at Lynne's hip. Good. She'd dropped hers in the truck when he'd made her drive, so his was the only gun visible. "Okay. Let go of the girl, and I'll give you the gun."

The guy smiled, revealing broken and black teeth. "No. Give gun now."

Jax clenched his teeth. "Listen—"

The guy yanked up under Lynne's chin, lifting her. She cried out, her head thrown back.

"Okay—" Jax called out. He wiped rain off his face. "Okay." He gingerly took his gun and held it out.

"Throw," the guy ordered.

Death glimmered in the Ripper's crazy eyes, but Jax didn't have much of a choice. "Fine." He tossed the gun and pretended to yelp as it slipped from his grasp and landed a few feet from the Ripper.

The Ripper hissed and gestured to the one on the ground. "Fetch."

"Sit!" Jax ordered.

The blond guy whined and looked back and forth between the two.

"Stay!" Jax commanded. How fucked up was that?

The Ripper holding Lynne howled. Keeping hold, he dragged her over to the gun. The second he leaned over, Jax lunged toward him. He slid one hand beneath the grip on Lynne and pushed, hitting her with his hip. She flew toward the guy on the ground.

The Ripper in blue bellowed and swung a fist, connecting with Jax's temple. Lights exploded behind his eyes, and he dropped to one knee on the crumbling concrete.

"Yesssss," the Ripper hissed, grabbing the gun. His face contorted, and saliva dribbled from his mouth to mingle with the water flowing over his face. "Bad girl," he said, turning and pointing the gun at Lynne.

"No!" Jax leaped up just as the weapon fired. The impact hit him square in the chest, in his worn vest, throwing him into a cement guardrail. Pain exploded through his body, but he shoved it down and propelled himself toward the man. Jax ducked his head and plowed into the stomach of the Ripper, throwing them both yards away to land in the middle of the street.

The Ripper punched and kicked. Jax connected with a solid jab to the guy's nose. Blood sprayed. He grabbed the gun and pressed the barrel under the guy's beard.

The guy's eyes widened and his body relaxed. "Death good."

Jax fired.

Blood squirted up his chest and across his chin. The Ripper's head jerked once and then fell back to the ground. The corpse went lax.

Jax turned in a crouch to see Lynne standing, bewilderment on her face, with the blond guy licking her hand. "Jax?" she asked.

He stood. Agony rippled through his torso, and he had to

concentrate to keep his steps even. Had the vest protected him at all? He reached Lynne and tugged her close, pressing a kiss to her wet hair. "Get in the truck, baby," he whispered.

As if in a dream, she moved woodenly, stepping over cement blocks to slide across the front seat. Jax turned and blocked her view with his body.

The blond guy looked up and panted.

Nausea boiled in Jax's gut. "I'm sorry." He placed the barrel on the guy's forehead and pulled the trigger. His own body jerked with the sound, and more blood splashed across his vest. The Ripper fell to the side, dead before he hit the ground.

Jax turned and strode through the rain to the truck, sliding the keys into the ignition. "We have to find shelter for the night." Hopefully Raze and Byron had found their way home or to a safe place to hole up. For now, he had to get Lynne out of there. The gunshots would bring more Rippers and possibly gangs. Twenty was definitely out scouting for them, probably in droves at this point. They had about fifteen minutes to find safety.

If there was such a thing.

Lynne kept quiet, her arms around her knees, her body trembling as Jax somehow drove through the darkness without hitting anything. Finally, miles away from the dead Rippers, he pulled into the weed-riddled driveway of a faded yellow clapboard cottage. Empty flower baskets lined the front windows, and a sign hung on the door, proudly proclaiming that the Hernandez family lived there.

"Hold on," he said, jumping from the truck and lifting a weathered wooden garage door. He returned to drive the truck into the tidy garage. "Stay in the truck until I check it out." He didn't wait for an answer but jumped out of the truck to shut the garage door and then entered the single-story small home.

Minutes later, he returned and held out a hand. "Let's try to get warm, sweetheart."

The gunshots echoed in her mind, and the sadness of the Ripper who'd acted like a dog descended on her. Tears filled her eyes.

Jax reached for her, drawing her across the seat. "I know." He was warm and strong, and she allowed him to help her out.

Her mind replayed the fight. Jax had jumped in front of a bullet and then fought a huge crazy guy to protect her. Then he'd done what had to be done without burdening her. She swallowed and wiped blood from his chin. "Are you hurt?" she asked, the idea unthinkable and frightening as hell. Jax couldn't be hurt. Not because of her.

"No." He drew her into a dusty kitchen with dim yellow countertops and older white appliances. Three candles burned, lighting the space. "We're in an area of town where people didn't have much, so it hasn't been completely looted yet." He gestured toward the heavy blinds. "I've drawn all the shades, and we should be okay tonight."

She grabbed a candle to follow him into a living room with a sofa and matching floral chairs. No pictures adorned the wide mantel above the quiet fireplace. "They must've fled the city." People always packed pictures first. Unfortunately, they'd probably also taken all the food and medicine.

"I'll be right back. Need to head outside and wash off the blood." He walked through the kitchen and slid open a glass door, disappearing out back.

She dropped to sit on the couch, too overcome to do anything else.

Several minutes later, he returned, still dressed, wet and no longer bloody.

Jax approached and knelt before her, a candle in his hand. "Let me see your chin." His fingers were gentle as he probed, but pain rippled across her jaw. He winced. "You're going to have quite a bruise."

She blinked and reached for his wet vest. "Let's see what damage you have." Slowly, she released the Velcro and dropped the vest before removing his wet shirt. "Whoa." Purple exploded across his ribs in perfect striations. She gently felt along his ribs, biting her lip at his sharp intake of breath. Relief buzzed through her. "You're bruised, but I can't feel any breaks. There might be a crack or two."

He nodded. "I figured."

She leaned back, studying him. Strong muscles, masculine contours, unreal power. "God, you're beautiful," she breathed. The contusion only enhanced his deadliness.

He wiped something off her cheek, his touch gentle. "I'm sorry I let him get you out of the truck."

She blinked and shook her head. "Jax, you screwed up."

He sat back on his haunches. "I know, and I'm sorry."

Heat roared into her head. "No. That's not what I meant." When he became sweet, he stole her breath away. "You didn't think, throwing yourself in front of a bullet. The group needs you a lot more than me. You can't sacrifice yourself like that—not for me. You're more valuable." Life was hard, and they had to be logical.

His chin lifted. "I couldn't do anything else, Lynne."

She sighed. "Listen. I know I have the blue heart, and I know you think there's a cure for Scorpius, but there isn't. I'm definitely not the cure, so you can't sacrifice yourself for me. For anybody, really. Survival is all that matters, and the group needs you to go on."

He smiled, his lip lopsided and kind of sad. His hand slid up her chest to flatten over her heart. "I didn't jump in front of that bullet because your heart is blue, Harmony."

Her breath caught, and tension skittered through her abdomen. "Then why?"

He leaned in and brushed his lips across her aching neck. "I jumped because your heart is mine."

She blinked and tried to shove back, only to find her hands spread over his impressive chest. Panic tried to rear up, but his gaze caught hers, and the fight was over. "You said— you said just fucking," she whispered, fear squeezing her heart.

He smiled, slow and sad. "I know." His thumb brushed her cheekbone. "We've both lost too damn much to take a chance on getting close to anyone."

She frowned and instinctively leaned toward him. "I agree." A new panic mingled with the fear. What was he saying?

"It's too late not to." He rubbed his thumb over her lips, sending tingles through her entire body. "At least for me." Sighing, he sat back on his haunches, his gaze remaining sure and steady. "I know I'm difficult. I spanked you, and I tied you up with a belt." His bare shoulder lifted, rippling muscles. "I'll probably do both again."

The words jolted her. "Hey." Her hands fell into her lap.

He shrugged. "Well, I will. Might as well be honest about it. I am who I am, and you're, well, you."

Her head snapped up. *I am who I am?* "Listen, Popeye."

He barked out a laugh. "Cute." His hands manacled her wet jeans around her thighs. "You're smart and spirited, and I never thought I'd meet anybody like you. If there are bullets, I'm between you and them. If you get taken, I'm hunting you down till my last breath. And if you end up in hell, I'll storm the fucking place until the fires go out."

Everything inside her—the good and the bad, the strong and the terrified, the feminine and the scientist—all turned over. An ache for him, one with a sharp edge, filled her throughout. Her mind tried to take control. "You don't even know me."

"Don't I?" he asked, gaze dark and so male it stole her breath away.

"No," she breathed, her hands fluttering over his.

He flipped his hands over and captured hers. "You're the woman who walked by herself into hostile territory, knowing there was a good chance you'd get your head blown off. Or worse." He leaned in, brushing warmth across her skin. "You're a woman who took and gave what she wanted with me, not playing games, not trying to manipulate me. You're a woman who has worked in the infirmary with people who hate you, and you've sacrificed yourself to get to Myriad in the slim hopes of saving a humanity that probably doesn't deserve saving." His eyes softened to the color of warmed bourbon. "And you're the woman who put her body between my best friend and certain death, trying to protect him."

She tried to tug away, and he held her tight. Tears pricked the backs of her eyes. "Jax, I can't—"

"I'm not asking for anything from you, Lynne. I know who I am, what I've done. I'm a kid from the streets who got out and still killed, and now I'm just surviving until I take a bullet to the head." He brushed her lips with his. "I'm just telling you how it is."

Desire blasted through her from just that simple kiss. "Man, you really don't see yourself," she murmured. How could she not open herself up to him? The guy had already walked through hell for her. "You're a hero, Jax. You fight for people and don't even know why, but you keep going." She leaned in and kissed him. Hard.

His mouth opened over hers, and he took over the kiss, as she'd known he would. He leaned back and tugged her shirt over her head. "You need to warm up."

She smiled and then faltered as blue reflected on his face. A glance down showed the neon blue across her chest, spreading into blood vessels before blending into her body.

He placed a hand over her heart and waited until her gaze lifted. "I like the blue."

Those words. Four simple words, and they stole the fight right out of her. She closed her eyes and then opened them, reaching for his belt buckle. "I'll protect you, Jax."

He smiled and tugged her to land on top of him, shucking her wet jeans in one smooth motion. Weapons and clothing hit the floor, and soon she lay on top of him, his skin finally warming her. "You going to take up arms for me?" he asked, kissing her deep, sending her world spinning.

She caressed over his broad shoulders. "No. I'll just protect you." It was all she had to offer, and she gave it to him. She licked along his jaw to bite his earlobe.

He rolled them over, his gaze darkening with understanding. "You're a sweetheart, Harmony."

The dim candlelight flicked over his sharp features, highlighting the wildness living inside him. He rose above her, so male and powerful, yet so damn human. "The world wouldn't agree with you," she whispered, sliding her hands through his thick hair.

"Fuck the world." He leaned to the side and yanked a condom from his jeans. "Today's raid was a success, at least in one area."

Lynne chuckled. They'd found an entire box of condoms in an exec's desk. Apparently the guy was prepared at work. Jax ripped open the foil and quickly unrolled the rubber. He poised at her entrance and slowly eased inside her, stopping several times for her to relax and accept his size.

"Fuck, it's like coming home." He lowered his head and took her mouth, pressing her back against the carpet, his tongue claiming her.

She kissed him back, her body rioting, feeling more than filled.

He gripped her hands and pressed them above her head, entwining her fingers with his. Holding her in place. "Wrap your legs around me." Even gentle, even sweet, Jax was all control.

She obeyed, arching against him, groaning at the contact. Not only did she not have to be in control, but as usual, he wasn't giving her the choice. That lit her on fire in a way she never would've imagined. He started to move, slowly at first and then with speed. Magma boiled up, sharpening her nipples, igniting a craving only he could satisfy. She lifted her hips, meeting him, taking all he could give.

A tear fell from her eye and rolled down her cheek. He kissed it away, murmuring her name.

Her breath caught and she held it in, fighting to reach the pinnacle, so much emotion bombarding her that she closed her eyes.

He altered his thrust, pounding her clit, and she detonated.

Whispering his name, she held on to his hands, her thighs gripping his hips hard enough to hurt. Passion took her over in powerful waves, crashing into her, destroying any protective walls she'd tried to keep up. He ground against her as he came. His body vibrated against hers, and his lips settled over her shoulder, his teeth digging in.

The bite shot pain through her, and she climbed again, orgasming so hard her eyelids flew back open. She gasped, taken over, and finally slumped to the floor.

He stayed inside her and leaned back, his gaze on her pounding wound. "I bit you." Not an ounce of doubt or surprise filled his face. Only pure, definite, male satisfaction. He met her gaze. "Mine."

Chapter Thirty-One

*With violence, as with so many other concerns,
human nature is the problem,
but human nature is also the solution.*

—Steven Pinker

They'd waited until dawn to take back roads to headquarters, and the tension in Jax's shoulders still formed knots as he finished giving orders for his crew to unpack the two trucks. After dawn had arrived, he and Lynne had searched the entire neighborhood, finding some canned goods, bathroom necessities, and even medicine folks had left behind before fleeing or dying.

Now Lynne tried to keep a stoic face, but the woman nearly hopped around with joy at all the lab equipment they'd taken from Myriad. Even though most of it wouldn't work unless they used a generator, she was almost giddy.

He'd gone and fallen for a complete geek. A sexy one, but nerdy nonetheless.

"Why are you smiling?" Raze asked, rubbing an impressive black eye.

"I'm not." Jax heaved out a breath, turning toward the war

room. "Let's go update, and you can fill me in on that face of yours."

"It's from my mama's side. They were the good-looking ones."

Jax almost stumbled. "Did you just tell a joke?" he asked over his shoulder.

"I'm funny," Raze said. Even walking through the rec room, in the midst of allies, the guy didn't make a sound.

"Most special ops guys are hilarious," Jax returned, striding into the war room.

Tace frowned. "What happened to your face?"

"Bat wielded by a member of Twenty. Well, a former member. Had to kill three of them," Raze said easily. "Did we miss anything here?"

Tace shook his head, his eyes unfocused. "Vice President Greg Lake called on the ham, and when Jax wasn't here, he got pissed. Said for Jax to call him if he was serious about meeting the president."

Jax lifted an eyebrow. "I'd rather wait and call once we know what we have with the Myriad research. Lake and the president can wait a few hours. Anything else?"

"Yeah. Sami's a shitty shot. Did you know that?" Tace took the chair next to Jax. "We tried out a couple of the guns stolen from Twenty to make sure they worked, and she couldn't hit shit."

Jax frowned. "No. I've seen her shoot, but not in practice, so I haven't watched. She was LAPD, right?"

"A rookie," Raze said. "Maybe she just sucked at shooting."

Sami stormed into the room. "I heard that."

Jax kicked a chair her way. "Were you or were you not with the LAPD?"

"I was." Pink rose over her high cheekbones as she sat. "You've seen me grapple."

He had. The woman was tough as Justice in hand-to-hand.

Better than some soldiers he'd served with. Apparently she hadn't had the time to get good at shooting, although it was surprising she'd become a rookie. "You start practicing target shooting every day until Tace says you're perfect."

"We can't spare the bullets," Sami returned.

Shit. Good point. "Figure something else out, then." Jax rubbed his chin. "You're one of my top soldiers, and you need to be able to shoot." Just how well did he know the woman, anyway? Lynne was right that he needed to get to know his people better. "Tace? You crazy yet?"

Tace blew out air. "Well, maybe? I'm not feeling much, including concern over whether or not I'm becoming a Ripper. That's probably not a good sign." His white-knuckle hold on his weapon belied the casual nature of his statement.

"I saw a Ripper bark like a dog yesterday, so I'm thinking you're all right so far." Jax waited until Tace relaxed his hold. "Seriously. Talk."

Tace set his gun on the table and sat back. "I just feel different. Not better and not worse but different." He chewed on the inside of his cheek. "I miss Wyatt, and I'm cut up that he's gone, but it's more fury than sadness, you know?"

"That's normal," Raze said. "I'm always pissed."

Tace lifted an eyebrow, and Sami swung toward him. "You never look mad," Sami said slowly.

"If they see your emotions, they win," Raze said. He jerked his chin at Tace. "Maybe you just got stronger. It's possible."

"I'm not sure lack of emotion is a mental strength," Tace said slowly. "But I like that idea better than my becoming a cannibal."

Sami leaned away from him. "Do you, I mean, wanna eat people?"

Tace snorted. "No. Not at all."

Jax shook his head. He didn't have time to worry about Tace's mental state. "If you get urges, tell us. Other than that, let's keep going the way we are." He really couldn't afford to lose his head medic. Lynne knew anatomy, but she was no medical doctor.

"Just put me down before I hurt anybody," Tace said.

"No problem," Jax returned. The fact that Tace worried about harming other people said more than any brain scan ever would. "We have information about a manufacturing plant of cereal and granola bars that might be far enough off the grid to still hold food." He grabbed an old map from his back pocket and stuck it to the whiteboard. "We'll have to send a team out, but I want to wait until we call the president and his Elite Force. Raze and I will meet them." He hated using that much fuel, but there wasn't a choice.

"I want to go," Tace said.

"Sorry, no." Jax shook his head. "I need you here, Doc. You're the best doctor I have—the only one with combat experience."

Sami sat up. "What about me? I missed the last mission."

Jax lifted an eyebrow. "You're not going anywhere until you shoot decently." He softened his voice. "Plus, I need you to continue with the hand-to-hand lessons and grappling practice. At some point, we're gonna run out of bullets and will need both knives and combat skills to survive."

She sat back, mollified. "Fair enough."

Tace turned toward her. "You never talk about your life before Scorpius, which is fine, because neither does Raze. But no way did you learn to fight like that just training with the police."

She swallowed, her dark eyes turning hollow. "No. My dad owned a kenpo studio, and my uncle owned an inner-city boxing club." She shrugged and smiled. "I trained both places. When I went to college, I studied wrestling to round out my knowledge." Silver glinted when she pulled a serrated blade from her back pocket. "Dad wanted boys and he got two girls. So he trained us, and it was actually a lot of fun. I'm still learning blade fighting."

"What happened to your sister?" Raze asked.

Surprise rocked through Jax. Had Raze just expressed interest?

Sami's mouth dropped open and then quickly closed. "She was stabbed in the riots when Scorpius got bad and didn't make it. Our parents died before that from the disease." She rubbed her nose. "I couldn't save her. I should've."

It struck Jax once again how little he knew of the folks around him. "When the riots got bad, I gathered the people I knew and took over this place and the food distribution center next door. Then we started letting people in, so long as they followed my rules." He glanced at the old map and back. "We were in fighting mode from day one and have never stopped."

"We can't stop," Raze returned.

"I know, but shouldn't we know more about each other than how well we each can fight?" Sami asked. "We lost Wyatt, and he was the one who shared the most."

Tace leaned forward. "I share. You know all about me."

"That's true," Sami said. "You all know my past except about my sister. Now you know that." She elbowed Raze in the ribs. "You and Raze are the ones who don't share anything."

"Maybe we don't have anything to share," Raze countered.

Jax scrubbed a hand through his thick hair. He needed to find somebody who could give a decent haircut. "You all know I grew up in Twenty, went into the army, and came home to discover my brother had died, so I set out to avenge his death. Then Scorpius got bad, and here we are."

"What's going on between you and Lynne Harmony?" Sami asked.

Raze shook his head. "We are not turning into a knitting group here. So long as whatever is going on doesn't fuck with my life, I don't want details."

"Man, you're a prince," Sami breathed, rolling her eyes. "Why are you here, anyway?"

Raze turned his head, slowly, to meet her gaze. "For now, I'm here to go on missions and fetch granola goodness." He focused back on Jax.

Jax lifted his head. Fuck, he was tired of the secrets. "What exactly is your plan, Raze? You're a great soldier, and we've needed you, but you definitely have an agenda." Something told him it had nothing to do with Twenty. "Do you really want Twenty wiped out?"

Raze lifted a shoulder. "Twenty is a blight on L.A., and Cruz is a bastard who terrorizes innocent people, especially women. Sure, I want them wiped out."

That didn't sound personal, though, did it? Saying he wanted Twenty demolished had instantly put Raze and Jax on the same side. Had he been so blind he was that easy to manipulate? Even so, Raze had held his own and covered Jax's back more than once. He didn't owe Jax anything.

Jax studied his group of closest confidants, his mind settling. He had an excellent doctor who might be turning into a Ripper, a former LAPD officer who couldn't shoot worth shit and wanted to gossip more than fight, and a former special-ops killing machine with an agenda he wouldn't share. Not to mention a woman in the other room who'd stolen his heart and wore a bull's-eye on hers. "Do you ever just stop and wonder how the hell you ended up here?" he asked.

"All the time," Tace and Raze said in unison, while Sami just nodded.

Jax shook his head. "Whoever's working with Manny on the kids, make sure there's a box of the condoms we just found available to them. Somewhere they don't have to ask or be embarrassed." All he needed was another teen pregnancy. He lifted an eyebrow at Raze. "Speaking of soon-to-be fathers, how did the kid do on the mission?"

Raze grinned. "Kid did great. When we had to speed away from Rippers, he shot out the window and actually nailed a tire. Explained the shot in mathematical terms, but he's got good instincts. We should train him in more than the ham radio."

Jax thought of plans for the kid. "Good. You need an apprentice."

"No," Raze said.

"I'll take him," Tace said.

"Yeah?" Jax asked.

Tace kicked back in his chair. "If Byron is that smart, I could train him in medical procedures as well. We need as many medics as we can get."

Good idea. "Sami, any report on Twenty?"

Sami straightened. "Yes. We scouted their territory, and they're regrouping. They're focused on you and on Lynne. They know she's here."

"Even if she wasn't, we killed several of their members, and Twenty needs to avenge those deaths. It's the code, and Scorpius or not, they'll follow it." Jax's neck muscles ached from tension.

Raze reached for Sami's gun. "You need something lighter." He glanced up at Jax. "We took out at least fifteen of their members. How many more do you think they have?"

"A lot," Jax said. "They were the first to regroup when the riots started, and several other surviving members of other gangs joined Twenty." When he'd burned bodies after the last fight, he'd seen a multitude of different gang tats. "Cruz has the gift of recruitment."

"Great," Sami said. "We could use their forces. Any chance we can split them and then convert a few soldiers?"

Jax eyed her. The woman was smart and had an eye for strategy. "I like the way you're thinking, even if you don't sound like a cop."

"I was a cop," Sami snapped.

Touchy, wasn't she? Jax looked back at the map. "After Lake and his Elite Force contact me, maybe I should go alone. I can't afford to lose any of you, just in case it's a trap."

"I'm backing you up with the Elite Force," Raze said, no expression on his face.

Jax shook his head. He needed Raze to help secure the compound. "No."

"Then I follow you." Raze shrugged. "Your choice."

Jax glanced at Tace, who was frowning. Yeah. The guy had good instincts, and right now, Jax's were flaring to life, too. "The EF interests you, Raze?"

"Yes."

"Why?"

Raze shrugged. "If there's a government out there, I need to know."

Jax swallowed. Could he trust Raze? The guy hadn't told the truth since he'd arrived. Of course, he hadn't lied, either. He just didn't talk much. "Do you know anything about the president? If he's a Ripper?"

"No." Raze slid Sami's gun back to her. "The president doesn't interest me, but I said I'd have your back, and I will."

Jax studied the soldier facing him. In a fight between the two of them, it'd be close. "We come up with a plan, and you stick to it."

Raze stood, his height putting them eye to eye. "You have my word."

Chapter Thirty-Two

------ ◈ ------

*He who fights with monsters might take care
lest he thereby become a monster.
And if you gaze for long into an abyss,
the abyss gazes also into you.*

—Friedrich Nietzsche

Midmorning, in the small combat infirmary, his home base, Tace Justice finished organizing the meager antibiotics Jax had found on the Myriad raid. Since Scorpius, he couldn't stop organizing everything by height and weight. He only had two pairs of shoes, and if they were out of order, he couldn't sleep.

Fucking Scorpius had given him OCD.

Lynne had been busy all morning trying to set up the microscopes and new equipment. Most of it was useless without a generator, but the woman set up the pseudo lab as if she still worked at the CDC. After muttering to herself, she'd gone in search of tape.

Time was short, and they both knew it. The threat of Lake and the president hung over them all.

He continued to put things in order, his movements smooth and fluid. Smoother than before the fever, actually.

Footsteps alerted him of Sami approaching the room.

Even his hearing had sharpened to the point he could discern individual footsteps from the next room. He turned and tried to smile.

"You smile differently," Sami said, a Lady Smith & Wesson in her hand.

He quit trying. "I feel a smile differently." Hell, he didn't feel a smile at all. "You listened to Raze and found a lighter gun."

Sami shrugged. "Yeah. I figured he knew what he was talking about. For once. I mean, since he said actual words." Her grin was genuine. She'd secured her black hair into two sassy braids, making her look about eighteen. With her sparkling dark eyes and creamy skin, she could've easily been a model. Well, a short one.

Tace leaned back against the counter. "A cop would've known the best gun for herself."

Her chin lowered. "Six months ago, we didn't have much to choose from."

True. They'd emptied more than a couple of abandoned pawnshops in addition to homes during that time. "I don't really give a shit if you're lying, and I've lost any sense of curiosity." Tace rubbed his whiskered chin. He needed to find a razor without rust on it.

"I was a cop," Sami shot back.

"How?" Tace asked, not really caring.

She lifted her chin. "I slept my way in."

He studied her. Her pretty face, posture, tone of voice—definite sarcasm.

She frowned and stepped back. "You're not envisioning me on a plate for dinner, are you?"

He scoffed, surprised at the hint of humor bubbling inside him. "No. I was just noticing your facial tic when you lie. I wouldn't have caught that before the infection." Maybe his intelligence had increased. It was too bad they didn't have access to either an MRI or any sort of intelligence test.

Of course, he'd never taken one before Scorpius, so there'd be nothing to compare it to. "Stop lying. Don't tell me the truth, but stop talking. Be Raze." Perhaps that's why Raze didn't talk—the guy didn't want to lie. Interesting.

Lynne Harmony hustled into the room with tape in her hand. "I found tape from the office raid." Smiling broadly, she grabbed a printout of the Scorpius bacterium to tape to the wall. "There's the little bastard," she murmured, stepping back.

Scorpius was a big blue blob with spikes spreading out in every direction. The news, while there had been news, had played picture after picture of the contagion, so anybody who was old enough to see and comprehend knew exactly what Scorpius looked like.

"Did you get Jax to agree to the use of a generator for some tests?" Tace asked.

"Not yet," Lynne said. "We need more of a plan before I even try, and I think we need more gasoline. Aren't you guys planning another raid into Bel Air soon?"

"Yeah," Sami said, shoving her new gun in her waistband. "When do you want to train today?" she asked.

Lynne shrugged and looked up at her new artwork. "Maybe later. For now, I need to go through all of these documents and figure out if Myriad found what they thought they'd found."

"A cure?" Sami breathed, doubt wrinkling her forehead.

"Yes, or maybe," Lynne said.

Sami nodded. "Fair enough. I'm going to teach a class on basic hand-to-hand. Tace, let's meet up later to shoot before the next raid." She crossed to the door and then turned. "If we get the generators to work, is there any chance we could use a computer?"

"Maybe, but why? The 'net is down," Lynne said.

"I know. But what if we went to where the servers are?" Sami shuffled her feet. "Is it possible?"

Tace shook his head. "I don't see how we'd generate enough power, even with solar panels as well as generators."

Sami sighed. "That's harsh, Tace."

"It's the new harsh me," Tace returned, the truth slamming him in the gut.

Sami left without another word.

Lynne glanced at him. "You're still dealing with the aftermath of the most dangerous bacterial infection to ever attack humans. Give it time."

Tace eyed the woman he'd only known as Blue Heart until recently. Intelligence and weariness shone from her deep green eyes while dark circles marred the smooth, pale skin above her cheekbones. A dark bruise, purple striated with yellow, spread over her slender throat from the Ripper attack the day before. She moved carefully as if on alert and ready to flee at the slightest sound. "You've seen some shit," Tace said slowly.

She focused on him. "Who hasn't?"

Good point. "You know if we find positive results in those ten boxes of papers you brought, we might have to rig up a lab somehow."

She lifted her chin, resignation curving her pink lips. "I know."

"Are you ready to give blood if necessary?" He'd seen her arms and couldn't even imagine how much blood had been already taken. She'd lined up the blue, green, and pink vials of different liquids on the counter even though they didn't have refrigeration. Not all compounds needed to be cool, yet he didn't like the idea of mutated Scorpius being so close. "I'm just a medic," he said slowly, his gaze on the bright vials.

"I'm ready." She wiped grime off the table. "And you're not just a medic anymore. Now you're a medic, soldier, and lab tech. Like the rest of us."

He wasn't like anybody else, not anymore. He might have survived the fever, and he might not want to kill anybody, but

Scorpius still thrived inside him, turning him into somebody different. Somebody new. Who, he had no clue. But for the first time, he lacked the internal compass he'd used his entire life. What was good and what was bad?

The line had disappeared.

Jax finished training a group of girls in knife fighting and hustled across the road to the infirmary, his mind clicking possible raiding locations into order. He needed ammo and gasoline, and it was time to hunt. Although it was only mid-morning, he'd given Lynne and Tace enough time to go through boxes.

It was time to call the president.

Lynne worked in the makeshift lab, where several pictures of Scorpius decorated one wall.

The damn blue blob looked fucking harmless, didn't it? "Pretty pictures," he murmured.

Sitting at a small round table, she glanced up from a stack of papers, her gaze slowly focusing. "You said you liked the blue." Her voice came out scratchy.

"I like the blue inside your body because it's inside your body, and I like you naked." He looked at the macabre artwork. "I do not like the bacteria."

She looked up at the pictures, her face pale and lines of stress tightening her pretty mouth. "You have to admire its strength. So small as to be invisible, it divides and conquers humans, who are so much more advanced and have heart and intelligence."

He didn't admire shit. "All I see is the enemy, which I'm going to take down without mercy. There's no time for admiration." Striding forward, he dropped to his haunches. "Let me see your neck."

She batted away his hand. "It's just a little bruise." The hoarseness of her voice belied the statement.

"Humph." He ignored her movement and slid his fingers into her hair, gently tipping her head to reveal the bruise on her neck. The sight pricked his temper, so he softened his voice. "Looks painful."

"It's fine." She planted a hand in the center of his chest, slamming pain into his ribs, and he bit back a snarl. "How's your injury?" she asked.

He met her gaze and released her hair. "Surface damage with no problems breathing." If he could breathe, he could fight, and that was all that mattered. He pointed at the stacks of paper. "Find anything yet?"

"No, but all of it's out of order, so I'm flying in the dark here." She tapped the nearest pile. "This is research I actually sent to Myriad, but they made notations in several areas, so I'm reading those." Several more boxes lined the floor by the far counters, and she pointed at them. "I'm hoping Myriad printed hard copies of all their research, but we don't even know that for sure."

He glanced around, restless with tension. "We're under a time crunch."

"Yes. The box of vitamin B won't last long, and people like Tace really need a full six months of shots as Scorpius goes to work in their bodies. If we don't find more B or a way to help the body produce the vitamin in larger quantities, we might lose Tace."

Fuck. Jax couldn't put down an insane Tace. His heart thumped at how hard Lynne was working for people she didn't even know. He set his hand on her thigh, wanting to touch. "I've always liked smart girls."

Her eyes lightened with a smile. "Have you, now?"

"Yep." Seeing the genuine amusement in her eyes warmed him, and he stopped worrying about her bruise. She'd heal.

She shuffled papers in front of her, her gaze catching. "Wait a minute."

He stilled. "Huh?"

She scrambled for a page toward the bottom. "Oh my God."

His breath caught. "Explain."

She reached for a pencil and began scribbling quicker than he could read. "They found something." Her voice rose in pitch. "They have a formula for synthesizing vitamin B in the human body."

He blinked. "A cure?"

She lifted her head, her eyes focusing. "No, not a cure. Not yet, anyway. But the formula includes simple compounds mixed with my blood—heated and mutated. Ingredients we may be able to find . . . and my weird blue blood from squid."

His heart thundered. "Is it doable?"

She chuckled, joy in the sound. "I think so. I mean, if their math is correct, and once we see if any of this new lab equipment works, I may be able to create an injection that synthesizes vitamin B. It uses the actual Scorpius bacterium, which we can obviously easily get, mutates it with heat, mixes with my mutated blood, and creates a new form of the bacterium that interacts with our cells."

"No more injections?" he breathed.

"No." She blinked and looked back down at the papers. "The interaction, if it works, makes the body produce B like it would with antibodies and vaccines. Our kidneys and liver actually take over. We really found something at Myriad. It's here. I can do this."

"Good." His tone of voice must've alerted her, because she leaned back and focused on him. "I want to contact Lake and Atherton now to set up a rendezvous. When Raze and I go to meet with them, if something goes wrong, and we don't make it back, Tace is taking command."

Her eyebrows lifted.

"I know, but even infected, he's the best I have right now, and I can't leave Raze here."

"Why not? You still don't trust Raze?"

"No, I don't." Jax shook his head. "I like the guy, and I have to believe he'll have my back, but I don't know him, and he has his own agenda." Part of the reason Jax was allowing Raze on the mission was to keep an eye on him. "I trust Tace, even with Scorpius haunting him. He'll protect you if it comes to that. The bacteria changed me, too, and I'm still fighting for the right side. I think."

Her gaze softened. "You are. I'm sure of it."

"Good, because it's time for me to go call your ex and arrange a meeting."

Chapter Thirty-Three

The battlefield is a scene of constant chaos.
The winner will be the one who controls that chaos,
both his own and the enemy's.

—Napoleon Bonaparte

Jax left a pale Lynne reading documents in her lab and hustled down to the closet where Ernie fiddled with dials.

"I want to call Lake and Atherton," Jax said. It'd just stress Lynne out to listen, so he wanted to call out and make a plan while she kept busy, although he'd had to warn her out of fairness.

The older man was pale, and his right hand trembled.

"You okay?" Jax asked, shutting the door.

Ernie twisted another dial. "Yeah. Ran out of my heart medication about a month ago, and I've gotten the shakes." Even his voice quivered.

A knock sounded on the door, and Byron poked his head in. "Are you calling out soon?"

"Yeah." Ernie kept his gaze on the buttons. "The sun disappeared a week ago, and I haven't been able to charge the batteries with the solar panels, Jax. If you want power, we're gonna have to use one of the generators and gas."

Jax scrubbed both hands down his face. "How long will it take?"

Byron straightened. "Not long at all." He loped inside and went behind the desk, messed with a bunch of wires, and ignited the generator. The thing hummed like a quiet bird. He grinned. "I tweaked it yesterday."

Jax nodded. The kid was impressive. "Get to it, Ernie. We want to cut off the generator as soon as possible." Shit, he hated using gas like this. "You've got their frequency, right?"

"Yeah. High frequency and it will bounce off the iono-sphere." Ernie fiddled again. "This is Ernie Baysted, NS789 calling Greg Lake, UT980 near Las Vegas."

Static echoed, and a voice came over. "This is President Atherton. I don't know the call sign bullshit, but we've been waiting for you. Is Jax Mercury there?"

The hair on the back of Jax's neck stood up, and fire rushed through his gut. He was about to speak with the man who'd harmed Lynne, if it really was Atherton. Jax dug deep for training and took the hand-held microphone from Ernie. "This is Jax Mercury, Mr. President. Are you ready to meet?"

"Yes. We'll meet at Franco's Casino along I-15 on the California-Nevada border at three this afternoon," Atherton said.

"Affirmative. Fifteen hundred hours at Franco's," Jax said. He needed to get moving.

"How many will you bring with you?" Atherton asked.

"Just me," Jax lied easily. That afternoon worked for him—the sooner the better. "Our forces are down and the gang wars have continued, so I can't afford to bring any men."

"Understood," Atherton responded. "We have reports that Lynne Harmony, the woman known as Blue Heart, is heading toward California. Have you made contact with either Dr. Harmony or anybody who has had contact with her?"

"Negative," Jax said, his heart thrumming. "Your lieutenant mentioned before that Harmony is infected with an even stronger version of Scorpius. Can you confirm?"

"Yes. The blue took over her heart, mutated, and created an even deadlier form of the bacteria. She's gone crazy and is trying to take out the human race." Atherton cleared his throat. "How many people are in your, ah, community?"

Jax leaned back. "We'll discuss my people in person."

Silence crackled. "I'm the president of the United States," boomed over the line.

Jax lifted an eyebrow. "So you say. I'll believe you in person."

"Very well. At that time, Master Sergeant Mercury, I expect you to cooperate and bring your people into the fold."

"Fair enough. See you at fifteen hundred hours. Mercury out." He took great pleasure in hanging up on the president. "Hell." He might have to kill the bastard. He glanced over at Byron. "What are you still doing here?"

The kid's Adam's apple bobbed. "I have a compact ham radio for traveling—created it from a damaged radio and a bunch of old parts. I think I should go with you, just to call out, in case."

Good damn idea.

Ernie shook his head, sending wispy gray hair across his shoulders. "I'll go. You need to stay here with your girl." He kept his gaze down, and his shoulders trembled.

Jax clapped him on the back. "Are you sure? You don't look so good."

Ernie nodded. "I'm sure. I don't have a lot of time left. The kid stays here to protect his own."

Fair enough. Jax stood. "Be ready in half an hour. I want

to get there early and scope the place out." The drive should take about four hours.

"If it's really the government, do you think they have medicine and food?" Byron asked, his eyes wide behind the wire-rimmed glasses.

"I hope so," Jax returned. "Find Raze for me, would you? Tell him we leave in thirty."

"Yep." The kid disappeared.

Jax loped out of the closet and jogged through the rooms to reach the lab, where Lynne was once again hunched over documents, her back to him. Blue glowed from beneath her thin T-shirt, and he had the oddest thought of wondering if the glow would go out if she passed. Would her heart still be blue? His shoulders went back. No matter what, he wouldn't let Atherton hurt her. If he had to take the guy out that afternoon, he'd do so after determining the status of the military.

"Lynne?" Jax touched her shoulder.

She gasped and jerked around, eyes wide.

"It's okay." He kept his voice low, soothing. "You're safe."

She settled down, green eyes softening. "Sorry. I was lost in research."

He leaned over and kissed her, going deep. "I didn't mean to scare you. Okay now?"

"I'm good." She reached up and ran her palm along his unshaven jaw. "How are you?"

He leaned into her touch. "I'm good. Raze and I are leaving shortly for the border to meet with Atherton."

That quickly, the peace fled her eyes. "He's crazy, Jax. Don't trust him."

"I won't." Hell, Jax wasn't even sure he was dealing with the real Atherton. "Tace and Sami are in charge until I get back, and if anything happens, follow their lead. We have escape routes in three directions."

"I know." Lynne pushed papers out of her way. "We've already had drills."

Good. His people were doing their jobs. "I've left you two guns on the counter in our apartment, and I want them with you at all times. You stick close to Tace or Sami for now."

She nodded. "If you get the chance, Bret has my research somewhere. All of my notes and formulas, as well as Nora's, I hope. We need them—just in case the Myriad research isn't as complete as it looks."

"My guess is that he won't bring much but guns and men to meet at the border."

She looked both delicate and delicious in her own environment with lab equipment and documents surrounding her.

There was so much he wanted to say, but he couldn't find the words. He'd always been much better with action than with speech. "I need you here and safe for when I get back."

She smiled, her lips settling into an enticing curve. "You mean a lot to me, too."

He didn't have time for emotion, and he didn't have the need for somebody in his life, but it was too late. Here she was, and he wasn't letting her go anywhere. "I'm not good at this." Taking her hand from his jaw, he pressed it against his heart. "You're in here. Stay safe."

A shudder wound through her body. "Sounds serious, Mercury."

He met her gaze evenly. "It is."

"Me too." Her hand remained over his heart. "This doesn't mean I need to get your name tattooed on my ass, does it? With the former gang affiliation, with the military, and the new group, I'm unaware of the protocol."

His heart lightened as a laugh rumbled through him. "You're a smart-aleck, aren't you?" He leaned in and kissed her again. "I'll mark your ass later. For now, just promise you'll stay safe."

Color fused her cheekbones, and desire hinted in the air. "I promise I'll stay safe and be here when you get back. You be careful and don't trust anybody."

"I rarely do." Releasing her, he stood. "Weapons at all times."

"Yes, Jax." She reached for a different stack of papers.

He strode toward the door and turned around, his muscles bunching. "Last time I left, you were attacked by Red and Joe."

She glanced over her shoulder at him. "And I shot them both and protected myself."

Good damn point. Many of the group had accepted her, but fear still lingered about her blue heart. He didn't like leaving her. "Don't hesitate if you need to shoot again."

"Go on your mission, Jax. You get extra points if you somehow find chocolate out there."

Extra points. "Now that's a deal." He exited the room before striding through the compound and finding Raze loading a box van near the main exit. A minivan had already been moved to the side, leaving a path between two downed Mack trucks. Raze was helping men load empty gas cans into the back.

"I figured we'd fill as we went," Raze said.

"Definitely." Jax scrutinized the van. Bare tires, rusty metal, dented sides. An emblem on the side proudly proclaimed SNIDER'S BREAD as the best in the city. The scent of yeast and sourdough wafted around, and his stomach growled.

Raze tossed him a granola bar. "Figured you'd missed breakfast."

Jax caught the bar. "Are we bonding now?"

"No." Raze slid his hand through his thick hair, shoving it off his face. "We need to raid that cereal place when we get back."

"One thing at a time, but I agree." They needed food. The sun shone down as he crossed to the cab of the truck to see a collection of guns and knives already in place. What he wouldn't give for an explosive or two. "I see we have provisions."

Raze shrugged and gestured for a man to draw down the back of the truck. "Couldn't sleep."

"Been there." With the exception of the night before, Jax had slept better with Lynne than he had in his entire life. "You need a woman."

"A woman is the last thing on earth I need," Raze countered.

Jax raised an eyebrow. "A guy, then?"

Raze shook his head. "I like women, Jax. Just don't want the complication right now."

That Jax understood. He frowned as Ernie ambled out of the building, two fairly small boxes in his hands. Pale and panting, the older man neared. "You okay to go?" Jax asked.

"Yes." Ernie patted the boxes. "Byron did an excellent job with the portable ham radio, and this smaller battery is charged and will work. We should be able to keep in touch with headquarters as well as reach out to the president."

Jax nodded. "Okay. You're going to have to ride in the middle so Raze can scope out the window in case we need to shoot."

"I figured." Ernie hitched himself up and into the cab of the van.

Jax turned to find Lynne standing at the entrance, Sami flanking her. He lifted his chin.

Lynne raised a hand and gave him a smile. He returned the wave and jumped into the truck. Now that was a nice sight. Then he sobered and tucked another gun along his boot and ignited the engine. It purred like a lazy kitten.

"Byron tweaked it," Raze said.

The kid was becoming more and more useful. Jax glanced in the side mirror to see Lynne still watching him.

He'd promised to protect her, and he would, but he needed to discover if there was a military, and what his obligations to it were. Not to mention he had to figure out if there was a president of the United States and if it truly was Bret Atherton, and whether the man really was a Ripper.

Then he'd have to make a plan. At the moment, even without necessary information, he was seriously between a rock and a hard place. Yet he put the truck into DRIVE, maneuvered between vans and trucks, and headed for the I-15. "Watch for Rippers and gangs."

"Copy that," Raze said.

Chapter Thirty-Four

Security is mostly a superstition.
It does not exist in nature, nor do the children of men
as a whole experience it. Avoiding danger is no safer
in the long run than outright exposure.

—Helen Keller

The four-hour drive to the border took nearly six hours. Just getting out of the city had required Jax to prod vehicles out of the way with the van, but when they'd finally gotten out of Los Angeles, the I-15 hadn't been a problem. If the lanes were clogged, he just went off road and then got back on. Defunct vehicles littered the entire way, and by the time they'd neared the dead casino, he and Raze had started a contest of speed with siphoning gasoline.

Jax inched under an Escalade, pierced his screwdriver into the gas tank, and watched gas flow into the can he'd placed beneath. As soon as the flow stopped, he scooted back out to the warm sun. "Time."

Raze smacked the ground near a truck on its side. "This tank is full."

Jax shrugged and carried his can to the back of the truck before returning and going through the vehicle. Most of the abandoned cars had been cleaned out when the owners had left them, but bodies littered the desert around them, so those folks hadn't taken anything. He'd found several bottles of painkillers, some food, and some water during his quests.

Raze had found other medicine, so they'd cleaned up as scavengers.

Ernie sat quietly in the truck, a little pissed off. The radio had worked during the first hour they'd checked in, and then the battery had gone dead. He was sweating in the warm desert, and his face had taken on a flushed red hue. Yet besides bitching at the radio, he hadn't complained.

Jax finished his search by claiming several hair ponytail things somebody could use. He tossed them in the van and opened his door. "We're about fifteen minutes out," he said.

Raze screwed the cap onto his plastic container. "I'll go on foot from here." Stretching his shoulders, he walked around to deposit the can before shutting the door. "Give me a little time." He checked his weapons and glanced up at the sun.

"Yep." Jax paused. "And, Raze? Thanks."

"You're welcome." The soldier glanced at him, gaze steady. "Atherton's forces are stretched thin, and he usually travels with a squad of twenty-five or so. Many of those should be out on local missions. See you there." He mock-saluted Ernie and then turned to jog into the desert to approach the casino from the back.

Jax watched him go, his mind spinning. "How the fuck did he know that information?" Something to ask Raze at the nearest opportunity, to be sure. For now, he had work to do. Jax spent the next thirty minutes going through empty vehicles and then finally climbed back into the driver's seat. "You ready?"

"Yes," Ernie mumbled, his head against the back of the seat, his eyes closed.

Hopefully the guy wouldn't kick the bucket on the mission. Jax started the van and wove through several more cars before finding a clear road. Waiting fifteen minutes, he reached Franco's Casino. It rose from the desert, no longer shining with lights but still impressive and large. A ten-foot tall metal dollar sign stood strong and steady in the center of a sprawling parking lot littered with abandoned vehicles. Two men, fully armed, guarded the glass doorway. A vestibule was clearly visible through the many panes of glass. Inside sat a man flanked by two more guys with guns.

Besides the casino, the only other building within half a mile was a gas station to the left. Jax watched as Raze moved up behind a sniper on the station's roof and put him out of commission. God, the guy was good. Keeping secrets, but damn good at that, too.

Jax glanced at Ernie as he pulled up near the front door. "You okay staying in the van with your gun out the window?"

"Yes." Ernie nodded, his hand trembling on a shotgun. "I'll shoot if you give the signal."

Jax took a deep breath, his shoulders relaxing. Raze would be able to see through the floor-to-ceiling windows, and he had a sniper's rifle. This was going better than expected. He pushed out of the van and made his way to the soldiers at alert.

"Weapons," the first one said.

"Yes, and you can't have them." Jax smiled.

The guy turned and shoved Jax face first into the window. Jax let him and allowed himself to be frisked. "I didn't say I have the weapons on me," he said dryly as the guy pulled him back around. He wasn't crazy enough to carry weapons while possibly meeting with the president of the United States.

The soldier roughly grabbed him and opened the door to shove him inside.

Without the air-conditioning, the glassed-in room shimmered with too much heat.

"Master Sergeant Mercury," a blond man said from a

settee in the corner. He gestured to a seat across a marble table. "Please, sit."

Jax eyed the guy. Sharp blue eyes, clean shave, fighting shape. Yep. Bret Atherton. He'd seen clips of the former Speaker of the House on television. "Mr. President." He moved forward and took a seat, angling his body to keep an eye on the two interior guards. Raze would have to watch the guys outside.

"It's nice to meet you in person." Atherton reached into a basket and drew out a bottle of water he passed across the table.

"Thank you." Jax didn't move to take the water, his senses attuned to the rest of the building, which remained quiet. "Where is Greg Lake?"

"Busy elsewhere."

Jax straightened. "All right. What is the status of the government?"

Atherton smoothed his white button-down shirt. "We're reorganizing."

Ah. Jax studied him, noting the charisma and intelligence. A primitive beast rose within Jax to claim Lynne publicly. The woman was his and would remain so. Right now, he had to tamp down on himself and think.

Oh, he believed Lynne that Atherton was a Ripper, one of the controlled, organized ones, but the question was, should the man stay in power? If Atherton died, what would happen then? Maybe anybody in power with some logic, even a Ripper, would be better than chaos. Especially if outside threats still existed. "What are your forces?"

Atherton smiled, all charm on what was probably considered a handsome face. "I've consolidated all branches of the military beneath the Elite Force for now, and my numbers are around several thousand, all working right now to recruit and gather our forces."

Several thousand? "Please define several," Jax said.

"More, many more, than you have under your command." Atherton met his gaze levelly.

Fair enough. "Do we know about outside threats?"

"Not yet." Atherton lost his smile. "There's a chance of foreign attack at every moment, which is why I need my best soldiers in place. You're good. Damn good."

Yeah, but he couldn't work with a man who wanted Lynne dead, and the mere thought clenched Jax's fingers in a need to strike. "Thank you."

Atherton leaned forward, and a USB drive on a cord slipped free to rest on his shirt. "How many forces do you have?"

"Not many," Jax said honestly, unwilling to give a number. "What's with the USB drive?"

Atherton grasped the flash drive and fingered it with a low hum. "Lynne is on here." His chin lowered, and his chest moved. "Memories of a sort, as well as research. She really is the best, you know."

Jax leaned back, nausea mixing with a rapidly growing anger in his gut. "Nope. Never met any Lynne. I'm assuming that's Blue Heart?"

Atherton rolled his eyes, making him instantly more approachable. "For goodness sake, I know you have her in your compound. I've known for a while."

"I don't," Jax said easily.

Atherton pressed his lips together. "According to Cruz Martinez, Lynne Harmony has been with your group for days."

Jax stilled. "Cruz is a liar."

"Of that, I have no doubt." Atherton's nostrils flared as he inhaled. "You're not the only group in L.A. with a ham radio, Master Sergeant Mercury. We're also in contact with Twenty, and we're impressed by their forces. However, I'd rather not do business with gangs."

"Meaning what?" Jax asked softly, his body tensing naturally in case he needed to strike.

Atherton picked a piece of lint off his dark jeans. "Meaning I need forces, and I need allies. I'd much rather work with you, a soldier in our military, than a criminal who just wants to kill. But I need soldiers."

Yeah. That made sense. "Say I do have Lynne, what do you want with her?" Jax asked, having no doubt Cruz had reached out to the president. It was a smart thing to do, and Cruz was no dummy. But he was a criminal, and he wasn't trained like Jax or his forces. The president had to know that fact.

"She's infected with a more dangerous strain of Scorpius."

"Bullshit. Try again."

Atherton studied him and then smiled. "Fine. That was a story to gain cooperation from citizens in finding Lynne. The truth? I need her back at work," he said. "I have her research on this USB, and we can rig a laptop with a generator so she can return to her research."

Jax eyed the innocuous flash drive. "Did she find a cure?"

"Not yet, but if anybody can, it's Lynne." Atherton rubbed the USB drive.

"So you want her back for research reasons," Jax drawled.

Atherton leaned back, relaxing. "Of course I want her back for her research skills and knowledge. The woman is brilliant." He exhaled slowly. "And yes, I want her back for personal reasons, too. When I first recuperated from the fever, I scared her, and I regret that. It took a while to gain my, well, balance back."

Jax studied him, fighting the urge to punch the guy who used to date Lynne. However, Atherton's statement about the fever was true, and Jax could relate. "You killed the sitting president of the United States."

Atherton blanched. "I know. Not my finest moment."

Jax tried to hide his surprise. "So you do admit it."

"I do." Atherton shook his head. "Of course, he was weak and wasn't working for the country. She told you that, right?"

Jax kept his expression stoic. "I know everything."

"Good. Going forward, we have to be honest with each other. The president was weak, desperate, and he was hurting the nation. He'd put our soldiers at great risk, and somebody smarter needed to step up." Sorrow, deep and glimmering, filled Atherton's eyes. "I reacted quickly and without any finesse, trying to protect my country." His gaze narrowed. "What would you have done?"

Jax didn't flinch. "I don't know," he said honestly.

"Now I have to live with what I did, but all I can do is go forward from here. I wasn't quite right after the fever for a while. You know?"

Jax nodded. He still didn't feel like himself. "Lynne is afraid of you. Thinks you want to hurt her."

Atherton's head jerked back. He blew out air. "I guess I don't blame her, but shit, that hurts." He turned and looked out the window. "If I stay away from her, just communicate through intermediaries, do you think she'll come back to work for the government to head research? We need her. Bad."

"I don't know. How about you give me the USB drive, and we find out?" Jax asked.

Atherton shook his head. "No. You have to understand that I need to consolidate and keep the research, right?"

Yeah. It's what Jax would do. "No. If I can get it to Lynne Harmony, then you should give it up."

Atherton lifted his chin, blue eyes glittering with questions. "I'll rephrase the language, but Cruz said you and Lynne have started a relationship."

Jax lifted an eyebrow and forced a half-smile. "Cruz makes shit up."

Atherton studied him for several moments, and Jax returned the stare without blinking. "She's a beautiful woman," Atherton said slowly.

Jax shrugged even though his heart started to pound against his rib cage. "I'm more interested in her brain," he said. "Other than that, I don't have time for entanglements."

"Smart. In your position, you can't afford to be manipulated by emotion." Atherton steepled his fingers under his chin. "Even though I have feelings for Lynne and have for quite some while, I'm not blind to her brilliance or ability to manipulate people. One can't get to her position in life at such a young age without having those abilities."

Jax tried to look bored. Was Atherton just reminiscing, or was he trying to mess with Jax's brain? Either way, enough. "You said you had medical supplies and food."

"I do." Atherton leaned forward. "Any chance you'll trade Lynne for both? I can give you enough to sustain your entire group for two years."

Two years? That'd be enough time to hang tight, let the gangs kill each other off, and plan for the move north. *Trade* her? "You'd take her unwillingly?"

Atherton sighed. "No. I want her willing to help. But how can I talk to her, convince her that my initial response after the fever wasn't me and that I've changed, if she keeps running from me? If I could just talk to her, I could explain."

Jax eyed the guards standing at attention. "I don't know you, and I don't trust you. However, I'm not sure there's anybody better waiting in the wings to lead the country right now." He slowly stood. "I actually don't have Lynne Harmony, but I know where she is."

Atherton blinked. "She's not with your group?"

"No. We traded her for weapons and ammunition, including land mines and grenades." Jax lifted a shoulder. "I don't have the laboratory resources necessary to use her knowledge, and weapons are more useful to me than the former head of the CDC infectious diseases department, blue heart or not."

Atherton's nostrils flared. "Then where is she?"

Jax smiled as he lied his ass off. "I'll reach out and then be back in touch with you. If I'm able to get her, or rather the folks who have her, are willing to work with you, I expect compensation."

Atherton stood, his gaze darkening. "You have twenty-four hours to reach out, and then I'll go find her myself, and I'll start with dismantling your community, just to make sure."

Was the president pissed because he'd lost Lynne, or was he actually angry Lynne had been traded somewhere else? The guy was impossible to read.

Atherton gestured toward the door. "You're dismissed. And, Mercury? If Lynne has been harmed because of your actions, I'll put a bullet in your head myself."

"Fair enough." Jax shoved open the door and reached the truck without mishap, driving nearly a mile before catching sight of Raze waiting by the road. Was the man even human?

Raze jumped inside, and Jax gave him and Ernie a run-down of the meeting.

"Did you see anybody besides soldiers around?" Raze asked quietly.

Jax glanced his way. "No. Why?"

"Just asking." Raze kept his gaze outside the window.

"Someday you're going to level with me," Jax returned.

Ernie snorted. "Neither one of you is an open book, you know."

Jax swerved to avoid a partially decomposed body in the middle of the road. "Lake wasn't here, and that concerns me."

"You'd think meeting you would be of top importance. If Lake isn't here, then something bigger is going on." Raze kept his gun pointed out the window. "What now?"

Now? Now Jax needed to talk to Lynne and feel her out. Atherton had admitted the killing, and he might still be the best bet to run the country. And Lynne had forgotten to mention a few details. "If I don't at least get Lynne in touch with Atherton, he's sending soldiers our way." The last thing in the world Jax wanted was to fight the legitimate U.S. military, considering he was army himself. "We don't have much time."

He hadn't considered that his meeting with the president might result in having to choose between his duty and his woman. Where would that leave Vanguard? The people who trusted him, who needed food and medical supplies? "This sucks," he muttered.

"True that," Raze returned, his focus remaining on point outside the window. "Either way, we'd better get prepared for war."

Jax eyed the area for threats. "I've been doing that ever since Scorpius hit." Now he had even more to lose.

Chapter Thirty-Five

Courage is not simply one of the virtues,
but the form of every virtue at the testing point.

—C. S. Lewis

Lynne tried to concentrate after Jax had been gone for nearly an hour. Bret was smooth and charismatic, and he knew how to lie. Would Jax believe him? God, she hoped not.

She finished reading through the Myriad files, her mind spinning. "They were on to something." Her heart began to beat rapidly against her rib cage. "This experiment, the blue one, has serious possibilities."

Tace glanced up from across the small lab, his gaze focusing. "So it's still looking good?"

"Yes," she murmured, standing and crossing the empty room. "I was right—Myriad was a huge payoff. There's data about permanent B as well as pregnancy protection, but I'm not sure how far they took the research. But this is great."

Tace stilled. "Do we still need your earlier research?"

"If possible." Her shoulders slumped. "No way will Bret give that up."

Tace patted her arm. "Jax can be very persuasive."

Yeah, but Bret was bat-shit crazy. "I know, b—" An

explosion ripped through the peaceful day, jolting the building. Lynne grabbed on to the counter to keep from falling. Papers and a couple of vials rocked to the floor.

Tace yanked the gun from his leg holster and started for the door. "Stay here."

Lynne fumbled for the gun stuck in the back of her waist and tripped behind him. They were down Jax and Raze, so another gun wouldn't hurt, as long as she stayed out of the way. "Do you think it's Twenty again?"

Sami ran from the rec room, gun in hand, eyes wild. "Sounded like it came from east of headquarters."

People screamed, soldiers geared up, and civilians rushed kids down the stairs to the basement. Tace nodded grimly. "Lynne, you stay behind the door. If it's Twenty, they know you're here and want you."

They reached the doorway, and smoke billowed from a demolished minivan. The gate hung open with a hole blown in the center.

Lynne jerked back. Where had Twenty gotten explosives strong enough to throw a minivan across the road?

"Lynne Harmony? We know you're here," a male voice called out calmly.

Lynne blinked. Terror stopped her heart.

Tace stood in front of her. "Who the fuck are you?"

Two men stepped out from behind a van, both dressed in camo, fully armed, stances sure. One with a razor-sharp buzz cut held Jill Sanderson in front of him, a towel around her shivering body, a gun pressed to her neck. It was Greg Lake, the man who'd come into the Oval Office right after Bret had killed the president. Lynne would never forget his face. They'd waited until Jax and Raze were gone before attacking.

"I have something of yours," Lake said.

Lynne stopped breathing. How the hell had he gotten to

Jill? Soap suds slid from the pregnant girl's hair. So the soldiers had gone around back, somehow secured Jill, and then returned to the front to make things explode? They were obviously well trained and had a plan. Bret had set the attack in motion while Jax was still traveling toward Nevada. Bastard.

"Let the girl go," Tace said, settling into a shooting stance.

Lake smiled. "No."

Tace calmly plugged the other guy in the leg.

He cried out, going down, his weapon skidding across the asphalt. "Lake. Help."

Lynne wiped her eyes free of the smoke.

Lake glanced with disgust at the fallen man. "You get shot, you're on your own." He shoved the gun harder into Jill's neck, and the girl cried out. "We know Lynne Harmony is here, and unless she comes out right now, my sniper across the way will start shooting, and I'll kill this pretty girl."

"No!" Byron ran out of the building, and only Sami's grabbing his arm halted him. "Let her go."

"I'd love to. Send Blue Heart out," Lake said.

Byron faltered. "Lynne Harmony isn't here."

Lake sighed and gave a signal. A gun fired, and Byron hit the ground with a low groan. Blood pooled around his leg.

Panic rippled through Lynne. "Byron."

Sami ducked and grabbed his shoulder, dragging him inside. She glanced down at his leg. "That was a warning."

Lynne scrambled for him, yanking his belt free of his pants to tie around the wound. He'd gone pale, his lips tight with pain. But he still grabbed the wall and pulled himself up to stand, reaching for the gun he'd dropped. Civilians and soldiers both took position inside, guns trained on Lake.

"The next one goes through somebody's head," Lake said conversationally. "The men with me are trained, and they're ready to kill. We also have forces of hundreds ready to descend upon your little community here, and we'll take you all out without blinking. We know Blue Heart is here because we're in contact with Twenty and somebody named Cruz Martinez. Ham radios all around."

Lynne sucked in air. There was no reason to hide. Hell. If Bret knew she was with Jax, he might just kill Jax in Nevada. What should she do?

"All right. I guess I start shooting," Lake said.

"Wait." Lynne stepped into the sun, squinting. "Let her go."

Sami scrambled to grab Lynne and shove her back inside, but Lynne held firm.

Lake's head went back, and his jaw tightened. "Walk over here, and I'll let the girl go and call off the soldiers headed this way right now."

Tace stepped directly in front of Lynne. "No." His back visibly vibrated. "Get back inside, Lynne."

She slid to his left. "I have to go or they'll keep shooting. They have explosives, and he'll definitely kill Jill." Lynne took a step forward. "When Jax gets back, he'll come for me." Her body settled into that truth. Whether he made it in time was another matter. "Tell him, no matter what, that I wouldn't trade my time with him for anything."

"Jax walked into a trap, obviously. We don't know if he's alive or if he's injured." Tace manacled her arm. "I can't let you go."

She shrugged free. "There's no choice. This is our only chance. I'll try to stay alive as long as I can." She could handle any amount of torture from Bret if there was a chance to see Jax again. She should've told him all the words she'd been trying not to say. If he'd walked into a trap, if he was dead, then there'd be no rescue, and she'd join him soon. "Please, Tace. This is all we've got." They couldn't fight forces of trained soldiers coming their way, and she had to prevent the attack. Only she could do so.

He said something low and released her. "Fucking stay alive."

She straightened her shoulders and walked straight for Lake, trying not to note the tears falling from Jill's terrified eyes. Lynne tripped over a series of rocks and quickly righted herself to keep moving. A foot away, and she stopped. "Let her go."

Lake tossed Jill to the side and grabbed Lynne, dragging her into his muscled body. He pressed the gun beneath her chin and turned. "Anybody moves, I'll blow her head off." He peered down at his fallen comrade. "Get moving."

A shot echoed, and Lynne jumped. Blood spurted across the downed soldier's chest, and his eyes fluttered shut. She looked to the side to see Tace's gun pointed and his gaze direct. Whoa.

Lake chuckled. "I could use a guy like that." He turned and maneuvered quickly toward the Mack trucks.

Lynne coughed and tried to keep up without tripping. If she fell, he might accidentally pull the trigger.

Fear filled her, and her vision hazed. She'd known at some point she'd come face-to-face with Bret again, but she hadn't figured on having so much to lose, or having regained a strong will to live. Jax had to still be alive.

After long hours on the road, Jax smelled the smoke before seeing the demolished soccer-mom van smoldering ten yards from where he'd placed it outside headquarters. Several soldiers bustled around, rebuilding the barrier. Tension rode down his arms, and his hands tightened on the steering wheel until his knuckles turned white. Silence reigned in the box van for a moment.

He shut off the ignition and bulldozed out of the van, barreling for the front door.

Tace met him, blood splattered across his neck and white T-shirt. "They took Lynne, and we don't know where," he said without preamble.

Anger, raw and hot, thrashed through Jax. "When, how many, and which way did they go?"

"It was Lake." Tace wiped his chin with the back of his hand. "Two for sure, probably a few more, just an hour after you left this morning, and they went east."

So Atherton had just been fucking with him and keeping him busy for the ambush. Damn, the Ripper was good. Jax frowned, calculating whether to take a car or a bike. He was way too many hours behind her. "Are you hurt?"

"No. Greg Lake shot Byron in the leg, but it was a through and through." Tace nodded in acknowledgment to Raze as he maneuvered closer. "The blood's from one of Lake's men. I shot him in the leg and the shoulder."

Jax rocked back on his heels. "You've been operating on him?"

Tace's eyebrows drew down. "No. I patched the holes and have been questioning him, trying to find out where they took Lynne."

Raze coughed. "You, ah, have been torturing Lake's man?"

Tace's eyes hardened past blue. "Yeah. Isn't that what you'd do?"

Jax breathed out, studying his friend. "Yeah, but I'm not a doctor, and I'm trained to withstand torture, thus understanding it." The bacteria had definitely changed the medic.

Sami rushed from around the building, her eyes wild, dried blood on her jeans. "The south is secure, and soon the front will be resecured." She swallowed. "I'm sorry about Lynne. Greg Lake had Jill, and Lynne went out to trade herself. It was the bravest thing I've ever seen. She was terrified."

Everything inside Jax revolted. "Has the prisoner told you anything?"

Tace frowned. "Lake's taking her to a mansion in Vegas at 2111 Putter Drive."

Jax didn't hesitate. If he had a chance to save Lynne, he had to move now before Atherton could get more soldiers in place. So when he turned, the last thing he was prepared to deal with was the myriad of people, soldiers and civilians, spilling outside beyond the courtyard and waiting for him. He swallowed.

Tace shrugged. "Everyone wants to go with you."

He blinked. "Huh?"

A pretty teenager stepped forward, her chin quivering. "They took one of us, and we want to help get her back. We've been practicing shooting and stuff."

And stuff. God. Jax wiped a hand over his forehead. "Thank you, but Raze and I are quicker on our own."

Tace shook his head. "I'm going."

"Me too," Sami said.

"No. I need you here, just in case." Jax tried to step to the side.

Everyone pushed forward. About a hundred people faced him, giving their allegiance to Lynne. So much emotion roared through him, it burned. They were his people. All of them.

He took a moment and let the reality hit him hard. Exchanging a glance with Tace, he jumped up onto the hood of a car and held his hand up for silence. The people, a ragtag group of different ages, experiences, races, and nightmares, all looked up to him.

How the hell had he ended up here? Standing with gasoline staining his shirt, his mind rioting, his gut aching.

He cleared his throat. "Thank you for offering to go, but this is a fast op, and it's dangerous. There's no time for training, and I can't worry about anybody."

Byron limped forward. "It's the president, and he has soldiers. You can't go in alone. If the worst happens, we'll be okay with it."

Jax blinked.

Sami lifted her chin. "We're going regardless, Jax. You can't take on trained men just the two of you, especially with the weaponry they probably have."

Jill Sanderson slid her hand into Byron's, her other palm on her still flat stomach. "Your best chance for saving Lynne and returning safely is to take backup. We can handle things here."

An emotion, full and pure, vibrated through Jax. The people, the ones he barely knew, were giving him their faith and possibly their lives. They were right about the odds. "All right. We can afford to take twenty-four soldiers, led by Raze, Sami, Tace, and me." That would leave enough trained soldiers to protect the community on all sides, but it was thin. Really thin, and he hated to use that much fuel. They'd need three trucks and a few bikes.

Lynne had been right—the people needed him to lead. Not just shoot and fight. He cleared his throat as he looked around, really looked at the people he'd been shielding. "Thank you for your support and for being part of this community. I, ah, have been a soldier of one type or another my entire life. I've dealt with life and death on a daily basis, and I've known many different survivors. We, here, as a group are the strongest I've ever seen."

A rumble went through the crowd.

"Scorpius has scarred us in ways we never imagined, taking almost everything from us. But we're here, and we're standing up, as only human beings can. We're small in number, but we're fierce in our fight to survive." His voice cracked on the end. "I'm proud to know all of you, and I'm honored to lead you." He jumped down, his voice rising. "We will return, and we will rebuild."

The group exploded into clapping.

He stalked for the doorway.

Raze paused as they walked outside. "What the fuck was that?"

Hell if Jax knew. He'd finally given in to his position, and he'd needed to leave them with hope. "Pep talk."

Chapter Thirty-Six

―――⊷⟨⊙⟩⊶―――

"You forget," said the Devil, with a chuckle,
"that I have been evolving too."

—Sir William Ralph Inge

Anxiety fluttered through Lynne with heated wings, and she tried to remain focused. After traveling for about six hours, they reached an oddly tidy Vegas residential neighborhood after a too-silent and too long drive. With no water, the lawns of the stucco houses around them had turned brown. Greg Lake had promptly tied her hands, shoved her into an empty gardening shed, and locked the door. Hours ago. She'd tried everything possible to get loose, finally sitting in the cool dirt with heat swirling around.

Finally, he opened the door.

She blinked and stood, kicking straight for his balls. He pivoted and yanked her into the night.

"Sorry about the delay, but we had a bunch of preparations to make for what should be quite the battle later tonight," Greg said, dragging her over a weed-covered concrete walkway to a sprawling mansion.

"What battle? With Jax?" She had to hold on to hope that he was still alive. He had to be.

After staying in the shed for so long, she was more than

a little parched. Plus, menstrual cramps ached through her back, and she'd start her period within hours. Just great. A thought, unbidden and sad, slipped through her of the unprotected sex she'd had with Jax. Sure, she'd figured nothing had probably happened, but still, the oddest sense of loss pricked her as she now knew for sure.

The sun had gone down, so at least she wasn't hot any longer. She tried to kick Lake, but he kept moving past the mansion to a smaller house, a pool house, where he opened the door.

Bret Atherton stood just on the other side, his sandy blond hair swept back from his cleanly shaven face, dressed in dark jeans and a white shirt.

She tried to swallow.

A smile, slow and scary, lifted his lips. "Lynne."

Her stomach turned over. She tried to yank away from Lake.

Bret shot a hand into her hair and pulled her into a room filled with floral couches, a quiet plasma television, and a pool table empty of balls. "Please set up outside like I asked, and we'll debrief in the morning," he said to Lake, shutting the door in the man's face.

Pain clicked along Lynne's scalp, and she stopped struggling. Several lanterns lit a room holding a sofa and chair as well as a massive marble desk.

Bret dragged her over to a settee and shoved her down. "How was your trip?"

She tried to regain her balance, her hands tied in her lap, her eyes gritty. "Are you joking?"

"No." He tugged his pants up and sat in a matching chair. His blue eyes gleamed in the muted light. "I told Lake to take good care of you. You're important to me."

"I've been in a fucking shed," she spat out.

"Yes, sorry about that. We had preparations to make, and I wanted Greg to concentrate fully on those."

Fear settled like a rock in her gut, yet she kept her face stoic. "So he's a Ripper like you?"

Bret leaned forward. "Neither of us is a Ripper. I'm enhanced, and believe it or not, Lake has never been infected. He's just incredibly focused."

"So are you," Lynne shot back.

Bret studied her like a bug under a scope. "I could feel you drawing away, even before Scorpius changed everything."

She faltered, trying to glance around nonchalantly for a weapon. Any type of weapon. "That's not true."

"Sure it is. I think you thought you were smarter than me, and you probably were . . . before I survived Scorpius." His head tilted to the side. "Why wouldn't you move in with me?"

She tried to remain still. "We only dated a few months."

He drew a USB drive secured by a cord out of his shirt. "I filmed you sleeping. Did you know that?"

"No," she whispered. "You have me on that flash drive?" Her heart kicked into gear.

He nodded. "Films of you, pictures of you, everything of you."

"Even my research?" she asked, her hands digging into her thighs.

"Everything. I really cared for you and thought we had a future, but you wouldn't even think of committing to me."

"Perhaps I had commitment issues," she said, not seeing even a stapler on the desk. He was bigger and definitely stronger, but she was a survivor and could fight. There had to be a weapon close by.

"I don't appreciate the sarcasm." He leaned toward her, almost casually, and backhanded her across the face.

Her head jerked, and pain shattered through her cheek.

She turned back toward him, gasping for breath. "What is wrong with you?"

He looked down at his pants, which were tenting. "Apparently nothing, now."

Acid burned the back of her throat, and she tried to swallow. Okay. Talk. Get him out of his head. Maybe ridicule would work. "Why? Have you had problems getting it up?"

He hissed and kicked her in the calf.

Agony spread down to her ankle, and she bit back a groan.

His eyes glittered, and he smiled. "The more I hurt you, the harder I get."

She had to stop reacting. No matter what he did, she couldn't show pain. Would that get him to back off or try harder? Either way, the asshole was feeding off fear, so she rolled her eyes. "Did your dad hit your mom? I've seen her picture. So much makeup over her pretty face. Hiding something?"

His face contorted. "Shut up. Don't talk about my mother."

Lynne leaned back and tried to appear relaxed. "Okay. Why are you broadcasting that I'm carrying a new strain of Scorpius?"

He rubbed his hands down his slacks. "I figured somebody would turn you in."

Good plan. She glanced at a sprawling world map on the wall containing a smattering of colorful pins, searching for anything to draw his attention. "Are you in touch with the rest of the world?" If she could keep him talking, then hopefully he wouldn't keep trying to hurt her.

He frowned and looked up. "Not really. I'm afraid there's a chance Scorpius didn't spread across the world the way it did here, and at some point, we could face attack. Which is why our military is so important."

She stiffened. "Speaking of military, where's the Brigade?"

"Up north dealing with NORAD."

Thank God. Nora and Deke McDougall were still alive. Lynne kept her face stoic.

A woman's scream rent the night.

Lynne jumped. "What the hell?"

He shrugged. "That's Vivienne. She's in a storage room off the kitchen."

Lynne's head jerked toward what looked like a small kitchen. "Why is she yelling?"

"She's a complete bitch. Wouldn't help me to find you." He sighed. "Now that you're here, I can finally kill her."

"Who's Vivienne, and why would she know where I am?" Lynne asked, shivering. The scream had been tortured.

Bret absently rubbed his arm. "She was a top-level FBI profiler, and now she's a psychic, but she just refused to help me. So I've pumped her full of drugs from the CIA." His eyes glazed. "She survived Scorpius, and it gave her strength, like me. Otherwise, how the hell could she beat the drugs? She's half-crazy now, and yet, she still won't break."

Lynne tried to breathe, but her lungs had seized. Somehow, she had to save the woman as well as herself. "Now that I'm here, if she's so strong, maybe you should let her go." How crazy had Bret gone?

"No. I've wanted to slice her open like a trout for about a week now, and I'm going to do it. You can watch, if you make me happy." He reached out and clamped a hand over her knee to squeeze. "First, I have to know the truth. Have you been fucking Jax Mercury?"

Lynne flinched. "No."

Rage darkened Bret's eyes. "You lying whore. I can see the truth on your face. You fucked him."

Lynne bit her lip. The truth would get her hit, but it also might screw with Bret's head. How in the world had she thought herself in love with him at one time? Was Scorpius to blame for all of this, or had Bret somehow been deficient before? "You and I broke up when you murdered the president, and my love life is none of your business."

He threw back his head and laughed. "You said love. Do you really think a soldier, a cold-blooded killer like Jax Mercury, is capable of love?"

"Yes," she spat out.

Bret chuckled. "I always did think you were cute. Do you know, I've had the most interesting fantasies about you since you ran from me?"

She twitched. "You are totally grossing me out."

He snatched her up, one hand in her hair. "Then you might dislike what I have planned next."

She threw a shoulder back into him, fighting, her knee hitting the corner of the table and nearly tripping her.

"I'd forgotten what a klutz you are," Bret said, shoving her in front of him toward the door.

Her mind fuzzed, and she shot her elbows back. "Jax will come for me, and he'll kill you," she yelled.

Bret yanked her back into him, his mouth at her ear. "I'm counting on Mercury coming for you."

She stilled. "How so?"

"Twenty," Bret whispered. "We're surrounded by Twenty members, all ready to kill your lover. That's what took so long to arrange today. I have forces heading this way right now, in addition to having ten of my own men, the best trained members of the Elite Force, ready to defend me. Master Sergeant Mercury won't know what he's walked into when he tries to find you."

Fear dropped like acid and burned her stomach. "Fine. You have me. Let's get out of here." If there was a way to save Jax, no matter what it cost, she'd do it.

"I've been planning this moment for so long. Just wait until you see what I have arranged for you. It's lesson time." He opened the door and propelled her stiff body in front of him.

Oh God. All heat deserted her body, and she shivered. Candles and lanterns lit a pool that shone in the moonlight. She couldn't help a soft sob, her eyes locked on the water.

Bret leaned in, his breath heating her cheek. "I remembered how much you like the water."

Terror chilled through her, and her knees locked. Water. She couldn't go near a body of it like this. It was so deep. He'd actually gone to the trouble to truck water in to mess with her head. How crazy he must be to find water and have it brought to the mansion just to terrorize her. To waste water and fuel to transport it in such a manner. Bat-shit crazy. "Bret—"

"No." He pushed her forward. "When you told me of your fear, how you'd almost drowned as a girl and couldn't go near water, I thought it was sweet. Driven and successful Lynne Harmony couldn't swim." Without losing a step, he jumped into the shallow end and pulled her along.

She cried out when her feet hit and water splashed up her legs. It smelled like chlorine, brine, and algae. Then she took several deep breaths, but her lungs wouldn't work. "I'm not scared of the water anymore. Not at all."

Bret smiled and dragged her toward the deep end. "Let's test that theory."

Panic seared through her, and she bucked against him, trying to kick through the water.

He laughed and grabbed her shirt to haul her against him. "I've dreamed of this. Of screwing you in the water while you drowned." His sharp teeth sank into her lip. "Don't worry. I'll bring you back so I can do it again."

Her lips ached and blood dribbled down her chin, but only the deep water filled her mind. "Bret, please," she whispered.

He sighed and pushed her down.

She went under, the water overtaking her and sliding down her throat. Her mind sparked in pure terror, and she fought back, her lungs compressing.

He lifted her by her hair, and she rose, coughing out water. The chlorine burned her throat, but she gulped in air, trying to breathe. He grabbed her close, his body tight. "Don't worry, you're not going to die. This is a short lesson, and you'll learn it well. Then you'll live with me and continue your work on Scorpius."

Fire lit her, and she clutched his dick through his pants, squeezing as hard as she could.

He yelped and released her.

Sucking air, spitting out water, she shoved for the other side of the pool.

"You bitch," he shouted, tackling her from behind. She fell again, his weight on top of her, her face smashing against the tiled bottom of the shallow end. Her mouth closed, trying to keep the water out, and her lungs started to burst. Her last thought was a picture of Jax Mercury running a knuckle down the side of her face, his expression so gentle her blue heart hurt.

Chapter Thirty-Seven

I'll follow you into the depths of hell,
and if I can't get you out, I'll quash the fires.

—Jax Mercury

Jax waited until Raze, Tace, and Sami ditched their bikes and met him by the side of the too-quiet road. "We're ten minutes out from the subdivision. Something feels off."

Sami nodded. "Moonlight is good, but there's no sound in the desert. No wildlife. It's as if everything is on alert."

The woman had good instincts. "Raze?" Jax asked.

"My guess is that Atherton called his forces in, and they've spread out. Waiting for us." Raze rolled his shoulders. "Feels like we're walking into it."

Yeah. The three trucks lumbered to a stop, and soldiers jumped to the ground. Some trained in combat, some just trained since Scorpius, all serious and carrying weapons. Fifteen men and nine women in addition to Jax's central four.

He gestured everyone around and started drawing in the sand. "If this is the house where Atherton is, I'd expect resistance here, here, here." He continued marking spots. "We don't know how many soldiers are here, but we have to prepare for the worst." Then he set up contingents of four to spread out and infiltrate from every direction. "Raze and I will infiltrate behind enemy lines and reach Lynne."

The soldiers fell into step and headed through the subdivision, all fairly quietly.

"They've been trained well," Raze said.

But well enough? Not against real military, if that was what the president had amassed.

Five minutes in, and the night lit up. Explosions echoed all around.

A blur of purple sprinted out from behind a stucco wall, and Jax reacted instantly, slicing his knife into the gang member's gut before dropping him to the ground. Holy fuck.

Raze took down the guy's partner, snapping his neck.

Jax turned, breathing heavily, his gut burning. "Twenty is here."

Raze stood, his lips forming a grim line. "Smart. Atherton recruited Twenty to increase his forces against us. We don't have enough people."

No, they didn't. "Grab everyone and head back. I'm going in," Jax said.

Raze clasped his arm. "No. Your people made the choice to enter this fight, and it's one they believe in."

Jax whirled until they were nose to nose. "If I let them go into an ambush like this, I'm no better than Cruz." Cruz had been willing to sacrifice any member of the gang, any brother, to follow his own agenda. Jax wasn't that guy.

"No. They followed you willingly, and they're fighting for Lynne. Let's do this and trust the training." Raze released him.

Jax swallowed as fires began to burn around them, the smoke turning the moon a dingy yellow. Raze was right. They needed to find Lynne and end this. "Stay on my six." He broke into a jog, watching the shadows. Around them battles raged, and cries of pain filled the night. Jax flashed back to a battle years ago, one across the world, and his body shook with each boom.

The blood across Frankie's face, the wound in his neck just spitting more blood. The scent of death, more powerful than the stench of fear. The sound of Frankie's breathing, which somehow drowned out the patter of gunfire erupting around them.

His short dark hair burned with embers, and his too-pale face seemed devoid of any life.

Jax's arms shook with the remembered pain of punching through heated glass and trying to pull his dying buddy's body free. His one real friend in the world. A guy who'd never asked for anything but friendship.

Jax had failed so completely, even his gut hurt.

He jerked back to the present, trying to fuzz the past. And he kept on running, even as his arm ached with remembered pain. He couldn't fail again. Not Lynne.

Now that he knew Twenty was near, he knew what to look for and avoid. He and Raze made it inside the subdivision and to the center as the fighting went on around them. He attacked on the way in, noting Raze doing the same, while their forces disabled vehicles and fought around them.

Jax smoothly sliced the neck of the third soldier and waited for the telltale thump of a body from a few yards away. There it was. Man, Raze was good. They'd taken out four sentries already, which left eight soldiers as well as Atherton on the property—if the intel was good, and he'd bet his life the soldier Tace had tortured had given him everything. Of course, they had no idea how many Twenty members were fighting as well.

He hustled around the other side of the mansion, ready to go in the back at the signal. He'd given Sami a gas-filled bomb, rag, and matches. Taking a deep breath, he counted in his head.

An explosion rippled through the night, and then the sound of gunfire took him back to the service.

A splash behind him caught his attention, and he turned. Rapid water sounded, and then running footsteps. Somebody had been in a fucking pool? He bulldozed through a bunch of overgrown bushes to the pool and then stopped dead. Lanterns and candlelight complemented the moonlight around a large pool. Lynne floated in the middle, facedown, her hair billowing out.

The smell of chlorine burned the air. He stopped breathing. God. Lynne! He leaped across the concrete and jumped in, grabbing her and hauling her to the side.

Raze was instantly there, while the firefight continued on the other side of the mansion. He yanked her up and laid her flat.

Jax jumped from the pool and shook her. "Lynne?"

Her face was whiter than the concrete, and she was still. Too still. He pressed his ear to her chest.

Nothing.

Raze pivoted and fired into the bushes, but Jax could only see Lynne.

He set her down and blew into her mouth before starting chest compressions. He counted them out, then breathed into her mouth, and then counted again. Raze fired three more times.

Tears filled Jax's eyes. He thumped hard on her chest, noting the vibrancy of the blue had died down. "Lynne, wake up." He grabbed her in a hug, his face collapsing into her neck. She lay limply in his arms. Gone.

The pain cut sharper than any blade ever forged.

Heat rushed through him. "God, no." He set her back down and thumped her chest, then breathed into her mouth. "You wake up right now. You're not leaving me." She couldn't leave. Not after she'd taught him to feel again. Not now. He sobbed and hit her chest again. "Damn it, Lynne. Fucking wake up." He pinched her nose and breathed everything he was into her mouth.

She jerked. Her eyelids flew open. Water spurted from her mouth, and she coughed, panic lighting her eyes.

He shuddered and turned her on her side. "It's okay, baby." His butt hit the concrete, and he patted her back. "Let it out. You're okay." Thank God. His damn hands shook.

Raze dropped to a knee, shooting him a look of pure relief.

Lynne stopped coughing, and Jax turned her to pull her up and into him. "You okay?" he whispered.

She spit out more water. "Atherton."

"I know." The wet footsteps. Jax gently laid her down. "Raze is going to cover you, sweetheart. I'll be right back."

She nodded, her chest moving.

"You got this?" Raze asked.

"Yeah." Jax stood and jogged around the pool, following the footsteps. Atherton wouldn't ever stop coming, and with his resources, he would always be a threat to Lynne. Jax tracked him around the pool house, through a neighbor's yard, and onto an overgrown golf course.

A bullet whizzed by his head.

He ducked and rolled, coming up just as a boot connected with his cheek. He dropped and then looked up.

Atherton stood in the weeds, the moon shining brightly down on him, his gun pointed at Jax's head. "She's dead, you know," Atherton said.

Jax wiped blood from his cheek. "No, she's not. Mouth-to-mouth saved her. My mouth."

Atherton's hand shook. "My mouth was on her first."

Jax met his gaze directly, calculating the distance between them. Not good. "My mouth will be on her last."

"You lughead," Atherton spat out. "She's not worth it. Not even close."

Jax arched his foot to pull the weight off his knee. "We disagree there."

Atherton rose to his full height. "You'd really die for her?"

Jax smiled. "Die for her? That's the easy part, pal. I'm willing to kill the president of the United States for her." He pushed off his back foot, rising and lunging, catching Atherton around the waist.

The gun went off, and a piercing pain ripped through Jax's shoulder. He punched out and sent the gun whipping through the weeds. Atherton punched him in the wound.

Shock waves scorched Jax's shoulder, and a roaring filled his ears. His hold weakened. Atherton flipped them over, drawing a silver letter opener from his back pocket. He lifted his hands high.

Jax gasped for breath, his body going numb. Then he thought of Lynne. Of the people waiting at home for him. Of his life.

Atherton struck.

Jax caught his wrist at the last moment, the letter opener pricking his larynx. Digging deep, filled with resolve, he punched up hard.

Atherton rolled off him, holding his throat.

Jax staggered to his feet, struggling to focus. Arms grabbed him from behind, holding tight, stealing his air. Pain lanced through the bullet wound in his shoulder, making him gasp. His vision hazed.

"Hello, brother," Cruz whispered into his ear.

Lynne coughed out more water and sat up with Raze's help. Burning cinders wafted around them, and smoke billowed up into the sky to turn the moon blood orange. The sound of gunfire pattered intermittently through the night. She wiped off her lips. "Thanks."

"No problem." Raze scanned the area around them. "Let's get you out of the open." Slipping a hand beneath her arm, he hauled her up.

Purple burst through the bushes, and two gang members ran through, already shooting.

Raze hissed in pain and dropped to a knee, yanking her down while also firing into the neck of the first gang member. The second kept running beyond the house and toward the golf course.

She gasped and turned to Raze, who remained on one knee, his head down. "Raze?"

He lifted his head and then fell to the side. Blood poured from his leg.

Lynne scrambled toward him and yanked off his belt, taking a look. "You're okay," she soothed, pushing him over.

He groaned and bit his lip.

She breathed out. "Bullet went right through." She secured the belt and drew it tight, steeling herself against his hiss of pain. Then she helped him scoot his back toward the side of the house. "I need to help Jax." He wouldn't see Twenty coming, and Bret was already out there.

Raze lifted an eyebrow, pain etched into his angled face, warning in his eyes. "You should stay here."

"I have to go," she croaked out, standing.

Raze stopped her with a hand on her arm. "Secondary weapon, left boot."

She reached down and drew a small Colt from his boot. "Thanks."

"Shoot first and talk later," Raze said.

Lynne nodded. "If help comes, there's a FBI profiler, a woman, in a room off the kitchen who needs to be rescued."

Raze's gaze sharpened and narrowed to the point she shivered. "Who?"

Lynne shrugged, heading around the pool and toward the golf course. "Somebody named Vivienne." Even with her mind focused, she didn't miss Raze's quick indrawn breath. Her shoes squished out water and her lungs still burned, but she crouched low and angled around bushes and a couple of trees to what looked like the green of hole number seven.

Cruz held Jax against his chest, immobilizing him, while Bret smiled in the garish moonlight, gun out.

Lynne skidded across the grass, pointing at Cruz and then at Bret. She tripped and the gun went off.

Bret ducked, but blood spurted from a graze on his arm. "Your clumsiness is going to kill me."

Lynne gulped down air. "Let him go."

Cruz laughed out loud.

She tried to gauge Jax's status. Blood flowed from his shoulder and cascaded down his face from a forehead wound. His eyes were unfocused, but his muscles were clenched. He struggled against Cruz, who had a good hold. But if Cruz's arms were around Jax, he couldn't hurt him, so she concentrated on Bret. "Tell your buddy to let Jax go, and I won't shoot you."

Bret smiled, his body somehow relaxed. "Come on, Lynne. You don't do the dirty work, and we both know it. Let us finish with your boy toy here, and then you and I will talk again."

She settled her stance. If she shot Bret, what would Cruz do? Could Jax break free? "We can all still walk away." And figure it out another day. Right now, surviving mattered more than winning. The fight continued around them, and at some point, more Twenty members or soldiers would find them. She only had a short window to get Jax out of there.

Bret eyed her. "You can't shoot me. You love me."

Lynne slowly shook her head. "I never loved you. Not even before you became a Ripper." She glanced at Jax, who'd stopped struggling. "Now I know the difference."

Bret hissed. "You love that jarhead?"

"He was army, you dumbass," Lynne said quietly. "And yes, I love him." With everything she had. If these were to be their last moments, she needed Jax to know the truth.

"Well, now he's dead." Bret lifted his gun.

Lynne squeezed the trigger, just like her uncle had taught her. The bullet struck Bret's shoulder, and he fell onto the overgrown grass.

She froze in place for a moment, almost waiting for him to get back up. Then she scrambled toward him and ripped the USB drive from his neck before moving several feet away, her breath panting out. Her gaze slowly swung to Jax.

He moved suddenly, bending and throwing Cruz over his head. Jax followed him down, and the two rolled on the ground.

A knife flashed.

Chapter Thirty-Eight

I like the blue.

—Jax Mercury

Jax rolled on top of Cruz on the rough grass, trying to avoid the knife angled at his throat. Lynne was covering them with the gun, and he had to get her out of there before more soldiers showed up. The gunshot could've been heard for a mile.

Cruz punched him in the shoulder.

Jax gasped, pain lashing through the bullet wound. "Fucker." He shot a hard punch into Cruz's nose. Cartilage cracked and blood sprayed.

Cruz reacted instantly, slicing across Jax's thigh.

The cut felt deep but the pain took a second to register. Nausea filled Jax's stomach, and his ears rang. Agony cut through the nerves in his leg. Trying to dig deep and stay conscious, he shot an elbow down into Cruz's gut.

From his peripheral vision, Jax caught a soldier with a buzz cut hauling up a groaning Atherton. Lynne pivoted to shoot again, and the guy threw a knife. She cried out, clutching her shoulder, falling down.

"Lynne," Jax bellowed.

Cruz grunted and grabbed the back of Jax's head, pricking

the knife into Jax's throat. Jax grabbed the handle, his hand shaking.

Jax stilled. Eye to eye with Cruz Martinez. "We were never brothers," he muttered, blood dripping from his face onto Cruz's. Jax had been a lonely, scared kid, and he'd sought solace and protection where he could. "I was just protecting myself."

Cruz spat out blood, his shoulders bunching as he tried to shove the knife home. "We weren't brothers. But Marcus, Slam Mercury, is loyal to me, not to you," Cruz gasped.

Jax's palm was slippery with sweat, and his arm vibrated with the fight for the knife as he looked down at the fucker who'd killed Marcus. Blood flowed from his neck. From the corner of his eye, he could see Lynne shifting to the side, struggling to stand. Atherton and the other guy had disappeared into the tree line. "Lynne, hold still," he barked.

She stopped.

Tightening his hold on Cruz's hand over the knife handle, Jax let all pain flow away. People counted on him, and he had to live. Had to protect Lynne. Digging deep, filled with resolve, he reached into his boot with his free hand, struggling with the sharp blade at his throat. "Why did you kill my brother?"

Cruz smiled with bloody teeth. "He took to heart your bullshit letters about honor and doing something good and was actually convincing younger members there was a better way in life than running drugs. The kid needs to die."

Pride and sorrow mingled with the pain inside Jax until the words sank in. "*Needs* to die?"

Cruz started laughing, blood bubbling up. "The world is a little fuzzy."

Jax focused, digging as deep as he could. "You motherfucker. Marcus isn't dead, is he?"

Cruz lowered his chin, hatred glowing in his eyes. "Oh, I

shot the fucker, but we never found the body. Buried a bunch of rocks."

God. Marcus had gotten away. Was he still alive? Had he beaten Scorpius, too? A new hope, one he tried to control, filled Jax. "Marcus beat you."

"No, not possible. And I'll keep looking till I find him."

"No. You won't," Jax whispered, striking hard with his own knife. "For Slam and Wyatt."

The blade pierced Cruz's throat and kept going through his mouth. His eyes opened, and blood gurgled between his lips as he dropped his blade. Shock cascaded around him. "My brother," he sighed.

"No. I have real brothers now." Jax shoved harder until only the hilt remained visible. Cruz spasmed beneath him and then went still in death. Jax coughed, his shoulder on fire. With a grunt, he used his good arm to free the blade. As much as he'd love to leave his knife in Cruz's throat, they needed all the weapons they could find.

Staggering, Jax eyed the silent tree line. The damn president had gotten away this time. "Fucker," he muttered. "Always hated politicians." He turned to look at Cruz Martinez one more time. Cruz's eyes were open, dark with death. "Fuck you, too," Jax said.

Lynne ran forward and slid a shoulder under his arm, her gaze on the dead man. "We killed one monster, and we'll get the other one soon," she murmured.

Jax placed a kiss on the top of her wet hair. "Your shoulder?"

She glanced down at her bleeding arm. "Just grazed me. Isn't bad."

Thank God. "Gotta move, Harmony."

She helped him around the building to where Tace and Sami kept point outside the house.

"Status?" Jax barked.

Sami wiped blood away from her mouth. Bruises marred the side of her face, and she was leaning on one leg. "We lost six people, have seven injured, we have secured the area. There might still be Twenty members around, but they're either hiding or waiting to strike."

Tace rose to peer at Jax's torso. "Where?"

"Shoulder," Jax returned. Six dead? He'd lost six, and he felt each one in the center of his chest.

Tace grabbed him away from Lynne and turned him around, making his entire body ache. "Was a through and through. There are probably bandages here."

Sami stretched her neck, still favoring her leg. "I've checked the downed soldiers and haven't found Lake, per your description of him."

Damn it. "Lake got Atherton to safety, but we'll take them out when we regroup." Jax glanced around. "Our mission parameters were to save Lynne, and we saved Lynne. Plus, we're gonna raid this place. All weapons—everything we can find." He grimaced as Tace poked his shoulder again. "Where's Raze?"

"Went inside to fetch a woman." Tace nudged Sami. "Let's go find medical supplies."

Sami followed him, stopping by the bushes. "Lynne? I'm glad you're okay."

"Me, too," Lynne said, her voice scratchy. She turned to Jax. "Thank you for finding me."

Jax tucked her close, his world centering. His brother might be alive, and the next day, he'd start looking. But now he needed to focus on Lynne. She was everything he didn't deserve, everything good, and he'd make sure she stayed safe for the rest of her life, no matter what he had to do. "Are you sure you're okay?"

She kissed his jugular and leaned back, her blue heart glowing brightly. "I am. You will be, too."

Jax shuddered as relief rushed through him. Life had turned into hell, but he'd found heaven. Somehow, he'd been given a gift beyond what anybody deserved, and he'd hold her close forever. "Good. By the way, Harmony. I love you, too."

Lynne cuddled next to Jax as he drove the truck while Raze held a babbling Vivienne on his lap. The woman was in a worn and wrinkled pencil skirt and tank top, her wild blond hair falling in a tangle down her back. She looked like a petite Barbie doll who'd gone through hell.

They'd have to wait until the drugs left her system to figure out who the heck she was.

Lynne's eyelids half closed as Jax's warmth spread through her. She'd slept for hours, and they'd be home soon. She'd worry about Bret later, and since she had the USB drive and documents from Myriad, maybe she could finally find a cure for Scorpius or at least a way to manage vitamin B.

Tace and Sami shared a dirt bike behind the very full trucks, keeping pace. They'd managed to secure weapons, four generators, fuel, medical supplies, and some food.

Lynne came to wakefulness, noting that Vivienne was still somehow talking. Had the woman babbled the entire trip?

"God, you're pretty," Vivienne whispered, reaching out to rub Raze's chin.

Lynne studied them. Vivienne's light coloring contrasted intriguingly with Raze's darkness as the sun began to rise.

He looked down at Vivienne. "Go to sleep, Vivienne."

She continued to rub his chin. "So pretty. Comanche?"

"Cherokee," he whispered back, gaze on the woman. "My mama's daddy was half."

Vivienne giggled, the sound definitely drugged. "My mama's daddy was a moonshiner."

Raze smiled.

Lynne watched, interested. In the dawn, watching Vivienne, he seemed almost relaxed.

Vivienne snuggled into his chest. "Grandpops called me Vinnie. My whole family did." She yawned. "I miss them."

Raze patted a huge hand down her small back. "I know. Go to sleep."

The woman wiggled even closer. "Do you know where the Bunker is?"

Raze frowned. "The Bunker?"

"Yes. The government facility . . . where hope and the future live." She giggled.

Raze cut Jax a look, and Jax shrugged. "Tell me more."

"Later." She yawned. "What's your last name?"

"Shadow."

"You feel good. Can I keep you?" she mumbled.

Raze sobered. "No, but we can negotiate later."

Vinnie slid into a boneless sleep with a soft sigh.

Jax turned his head just slightly over Lynne's. "I thought she'd never fall asleep. Who knows what they shot into her veins. She seems to like you, Raze."

Raze shot Jax a look, his blue eyes cutting through the morning. "Don't get any ideas."

"Not me. Nope." Jax tucked Lynne closer. "Either of you ever heard of the Bunker?"

Lynne shook her head. "Not a word."

"Me either, but maybe this woman had clearance with the FBI that we can only imagine." Raze stretched out his legs. "Of course, I'm guessing."

"If you say so, and at some point, you're going to tell me how the woman in your arms fits into your plans. Something tells me you knew we'd find her." Jax breathed out.

"I don't have plans." Raze rested his head back and closed his eyes.

Yeah, he did. Lynne nodded slightly against Jax. They had to stick together. She fingered the USB around her neck that she had taken from Bret. Maybe they had a chance now.

Something to worry about for another day.

For now, she snuggled with a man she couldn't believe existed, and she wanted to hold on tight.

Finally, they reached home, and Jax insisted upon carrying her from the truck into the building. The entire community seemed to be waiting for them to arrive, and several people patted her arm or welcomed her back as Jax carried her through the rec room and up to their apartment. Lynne just blinked until he'd locked the door and set her on the bed.

"Shouldn't you get your shoulder treated?" she asked, not protesting as he drew off her clothing and tucked a clean shirt over her head. Her brain was fuzzy, and she needed more sleep.

He smiled and shucked out of his clothes, revealing his hard warrior's body with a fresh bandage over one shoulder. "After Tace bandaged you, he sewed me up in Nevada before we got on the road, so I don't know what else he could do." Jax set her under the covers and climbed in to hold her. "Although after you get some more sleep, you might want to get creative."

She snuggled into his side before levering herself up to look at him. He stared down, bruises marring his deadly face. "You were right. Earlier, when I met you."

His eyebrows lifted. "Right?"

"I, ah, figured I'd find the documents, see if there was a chance, and then be done."

His gaze softened. "And now?"

"Now I want to live. No matter what." She'd found so much more in this man than she'd ever thought to find. "I love you, Jax." No matter what happened, she'd hold him tight as long as she could.

He placed a hand over her glowing blue heart. "All mine, Lynne Harmony. My Blue Heart."

Read on for a preview of *Shadow Falling*,

the second book in Rebecca Zanetti's
Scorpius Syndrome Series,

coming this September!

In individuals, insanity is rare;
but in groups, parties, nations, and epochs, it is the rule.

—Friedrich Nietzsche

The nightmare clawed through Vinnie, ripping and gnashing, until she awoke, her mouth opened in a silent scream.

Thank God. Finally, she'd been quiet this time. They'd moved her quarters three times because her night terrors scared the hell out of normal people. Now she lived in the bottom far corner of a sparsely populated residence in the center of Vanguard territory.

She leaped from the bed, her bare feet slapping cold concrete. Her lungs compressed, and tremors shook her legs. She couldn't breathe. God, she couldn't *breathe*.

Bending over, she planted a hand on her chest.

Air.

She needed air.

Launching into motion, she ran through the dilapidated tenement to the creaky sliding glass door and yanked it open. Rain, cold and drizzly, cascaded inside on a burst of wind. Not noticing the storm or the darkness outside, she pushed through weeds choking torn concrete and stumbled across the muddy earth.

Sharp rocks and pieces of debris cut into her feet, but she

paid no heed. Her feet threw clumps of dirt, and she reached the chain-link fence guarding all seven blocks of Vanguard territory.

Her fingers curled around the slippery metal near her face, and even in her panic, she remembered not to reach up to the barbed wire.

Thunder bellowed above, as what was once the City of Angels gave itself over to the short but devastating rainy season. She held tight and lifted her head, allowing the rain to barrage her.

"You're early tonight." A voice, low and masculine, cut through the storm from the other side of the chain link.

She blinked and stared into the darkness. Several train tracks, abandoned to weeds, stretched in every direction in front of more empty, dark land. "Where are you?" she whispered.

He came into view, silently like any predator, stepping right up to the fence. "You're getting wet, Beauty."

She wiped water from her eyes. "I didn't scream this time." So why was he there?

"I know." Raze Shadow, one of the elite Vanguard lieutenants, had rescued her from hell a week ago while on a mission.

If he hadn't heard her scream this time, was he just patrolling nearby? She shivered. "How is patrol going?"

His eyes, light blue to the point of being odd, lasered through the dark, touching on her toes and wandering up her bare legs, her soaking white T-shirt, to her damp face. Somehow, even in the cold and through the fence, the gaze heated her skin. "Go back inside."

"No." She couldn't. She just couldn't return to the nightmare and that dismal apartment. "I'm fine." Except her left foot hurt. A lot. She lifted her leg and stretched her ankle, squinting to see through the darkness.

Raze tucked an AK-47 over a shoulder, his gaze dropping to her aching foot. His shoulders straightened. "Damn it. Stay there." Long strides took him down the length of the fence until she couldn't see him any longer.

The wind whistled a lonely tune over the barren land, and somewhere in the distance, a lion roared. Probably Marvin. She hadn't seen the beast that shared their territory, but some of the other Vanguard residents had warned her about him. He'd escaped some zoo when the world had surrendered to the Scorpius bacterium, and now he hunted both survivors and Rippers.

Cold blasted through her thin shirt, and she trembled.

"Vivienne?" Raze gave her a warning that he was near.

She turned, and he came into view through the mist. "That was fast."

"Humph." He reached her in two strides, bringing warmth. "It isn't safe out here."

"It isn't safe anywhere," she whispered.

He jerked his head toward the silent building. "Inside."

The cold pricked over her skin, and she nodded, turning. The second her damaged heel touched down, her nerves stung. She sucked in air.

He planted a large hand on her shoulder. "You okay?"

She stiffened. He'd taken great pains not to touch her during her week in Vanguard territory, always remaining distant but polite. "Yes." She gritted her teeth and took another step, trying to balance on her toes.

He exhaled loudly. Then, shaking his head, he lifted her and pivoted toward the building. So easily.

Warmth and male surrounded her in the closest thing she'd had to safety in months. Yet Raze Shadow was nowhere near safe. "What's your real first name?" she babbled, suddenly aware of her thin T-shirt and panties. She should've worn yoga pants to bed.

"Raze." He kept his gaze straight ahead.

No. Raze was short for Razor, which was his nickname from the military because apparently he was a master with a blade. But he didn't owe her his real name, so she didn't press him.

His strides were long, and even holding her, he made no sound. She held herself stiffly, trying not to brush against his hard body. "Why are you babysitting me?" she asked.

"You need babysitting." He carried her through the glass door and into the dingy apartment. "Lantern?"

"Um, on the counter?"

He moved the short distance to the L-shaped area that had once served as a kitchen, somehow seeing in the dark. The fridge was gone, the sink didn't work, and the oven now held extra socks. Once electricity had stopped flowing, kitchens, for the most part, had become useless.

Setting her on the chipped counter, he twisted on a halogen lantern and immediately crouched down, one broad hand wrapping around her ankle. "What the hell, woman?"

She winced. "I panicked."

"No shit." He opened the oven and drew out a pair of socks, having been the person who'd put them there in the first place when he'd helped her to move. Gently, much more gently than a man his size should be able to touch, he wiped grime and blood off her aching arch. "Looks okay—just scraped." He looked up intently. "We're out of antibiotics, and you can't injure yourself like this."

A panic attack didn't wait for reason. "All right."

He slowly shook his head. "You need a roommate."

Not a chance. Often she awoke screaming like a banshee, and she couldn't do that to another person. Even if she could find somebody willing to stay with her. "Okay."

"Stop agreeing with me." His voice remained level, always in perfect control.

"You bet."

He sat back, still on his haunches, a shield over his expression. As usual. "You've been here a week, and nobody has pushed you, but this isn't working."

She swallowed and tried to sit back. "I'll be okay."

"Stop saying okay."

"O—all right."

His eyebrows drew down. "If you talk about it, you'll get rid of the nightmares." He placed both hands over her cold knees, instantly warming her legs.

His touch sent tingles through her skin, and she tried to focus. "I don't want to talk about it." Hell, she didn't even re-member most of her time in captivity. The most dangerous Ripper of them all, who claimed he was the president of the United States, had held her captive and drugged the hell out of her. "I don't remember."

"You remember."

Yeah, but if she shared the agony of that time, she might reveal too much. "Listen. I was held captive and beaten a little bit, but that's all. In fact, although it sucked, it wasn't so bad until he used the drugs from the CIA to try and get me to cooperate." As odd as it sounded, there had been food during her imprisonment, which was more than most people had these days.

"I saw the vials. Those kinds of drugs rarely get the de-sired results, so for him to shoot you up like that was crazy."

"He's a Ripper, which by definition means he's insane." The Rippers were survivors of the Scorpius infection who'd had their brains stripped and now lacked empathy. Typical serial killers ranging from the crazy wild ones to the brilliant deadly ones. Of course, there was nothing typical about a serial killer. "How do you know so much about those kinds of drugs?"

"Training in the military." His sharply cut face didn't give anything away.

Right. She didn't want him probing into her life, so she

should offer him the same courtesy, even though curiosity had always been her cross to bear. "Thank you for rescuing me, by the way."

He shook his head. "I told you to stop thanking me."

She couldn't help it. Bret had planned to kill her, or worse, and her time had definitely run out. "Okay."

Amusement darkened Raze's eyes. "Any idea what he wanted from you so badly?"

She hunched into herself, her gaze dropping to her knees. "No."

Silence ticked around the dismal apartment. She shivered.

"For an ex-FBI shrink, you're a terrible liar." Lazy contemplation leavened Raze's low rumble.

She fought another shiver, this one from something other than fear. A tension, one she barely recognized as sexual, heated the air around her. Her gaze slammed up to his face.

He continued to scrutinize her, seemingly perfectly comfortable in doing so.

Heat rushed through her, rising and filling her cheeks. "Stop staring at me."

"Can't help it. You're something to look at."

Look who was talking. Raze Shadow was six and a half feet of hard-muscled badassery with sharply cut features and the most unique light blue eyes she'd ever seen. Add in the thick dark hair, the weird ability to move without making a sound, and an intensity only the most dangerous of people exhibited? Yeah. She'd stare at him all day if he remained unaware of it. But Raze noticed everything. "Stop looking at me."

He straightened and leaned back against the wall. "There's nowhere else to look."

She shoved off the counter, and the second her feet touched the ground, pain sparked along the arch of her foot. "I appreciate your help tonight."

He grinned, transforming his face from predatory to stunning. "That's a brush off."

Yeah, it was. "I should get some more sleep." Not a chance in hell.

"You're done sleeping." He glanced toward the outside rainstorm. "I have another round of patrol to do—any chance you want to go outer territory and take in some air?"

Her lungs seized. "No." The idea of leaving the safety of the gate stopped her breath. There were Rippers, scavengers, gang bangers, and even Mercenaries out there. The Mercs were a group from northern California who were even more feared than the insane Rippers.

He scowled. "Okay. It'll be dawn in about two hours. Pack your things, and I'll help you move to the main head-quarters."

She bit her lip. While she'd like nothing more than to leave the apartment, she didn't want her nightmares to keep the soldiers awake. "I don't think—"

"You're about to start working for Vanguard, and being at headquarters makes the most sense." Raze rotated and moved, all grace and muscle, toward the slider. "Be ready in a couple of hours." Without making a sound, he slid into the night and closed the door.

Thunder rumbled outside. She hesitated, looking at her meager possessions. It was lonely so far away from other people, and she did start work the next day.

As she reached to gather her socks, her mind flared awake. She knew there weren't any empty apartments at headquarters.

Just where did Raze think she was going to sleep?

Raze nodded to a soldier guarding the rear exit of Van-guard territory and strode into the darkness, appearing to be patrolling. The rain drowned out most of the night sounds, but in the distance, a wolf howled.

Wolves in east central Los Angeles. How crazy had life become?

With 99 percent of United States citizens killed by Scorpius, nature had quickly retaken the earth.

He wiped rain off his cheek and caught her scent. While he'd barely touched her, even now he could smell calla lilies. A soft, sweet, delicate scent from the woman he'd just left behind.

Making quick tracks, he scouted the area to the north of Vanguard, moving between deserted buildings smelling of rot and decay. Most of the Rippers and homeless would be seeking shelter from the storm, but again, since many were nuts, they might attack anyway.

His senses remained on alert as he passed a looted jewelry store, an empty quick loan store, and an abandoned convenience store. Beady green eyes stared out at him from the closest store.

Cat's eyes. A huge black cat sat in the still-intact window, just watching him.

He jerked his gaze away. While he'd fought hand-to-hand with knives an ocean away, while he'd been tortured and nearly killed on one tour, cats freaked him the hell out.

He crossed over rubble and dodged around a several-car pileup in the middle of what was once a busy street. Rust covered the vehicles, and part of a decomposed body remained visible in a Chevy.

The tiniest of scraping sounds came from Luke's Bar on the corner. No light, no movement, but a couple of breaths. He stopped moving and focused all of his senses.

One person only.

Raze reached the heavy metal door and pulled it open, waiting for his eyes to adjust before walking inside.

A lantern ignited.

"You're late," Ash said from behind what was left of the bar. Pieces had been removed, probably for firewood, leaving only a thin strip running end to end, attached with bolts to the floor.

"You're inconvenient," Raze drawled, keeping his expression bored. The door shut behind him and he surveyed the room.

Behind Ash, a cracked mirror decorated the dingy wall, which was lined with empty shelves that had once held liquor. Dirt, blood, and moss covered the floors, while a couple of tables without chairs were broken on the far side of the room. A jukebox, a real one, still sat in the corner.

It was probably too heavy for any of the early looters to take.

Ash shoved back his jacket to reveal a Glock stuck into his waistband. His greasy hair cascaded out of a knit cap, which didn't cover enough of his long, crusty face. Apparently it was difficult to find medicine for impetigo nowadays. "Well?"

Raze kept his arms loose at his sides. "Well what?"

"Where's the woman?"

"Not here," Raze said.

Ash shook his head, his entire rail-thin body moving with the effort. "We made a deal."

"No. *We* don't have a deal," Raze said silkily.

Ash swallowed, his Adam's apple bobbing. "I represent Grey, and you know it."

Raze rubbed his chin. "I have until the end of the week. So get the fuck off my back and stop coming into my territory."

Ash cackled, revealing stained and crooked teeth. "Your territory? You're claiming Vanguard territory as your own now, are you?" He snorted. "You don't have territory, dumbass."

Raze straightened.

Ash breathed out and backed into the counter. "I'm just sayin'. You belong to the Mercenaries, and don't you forget it."

"I don't belong to anybody." The room was rank with the smell of sewage and raw fish. Raze glanced at the window to see the world lightening outside. "I have to go." He turned for the door, keeping Ash in his sights.

"One week, Shadow. That's all you have left."

"I know." Heat circulated through his chest, leaving a piercing pain. Even so, he shot Ash a hard look and waited until the guy paled. "Tell Greyson I'm looking forward to settling up with him."

Ash smiled and flashed his disgusting teeth. "Oh, I will. You have five days to bring Vivienne Wellington here, or you know what happens. Grey wants confirmation you're on track."

Raze breathed in and said the words that would finish off any soul he still had. "I'll have her here in five nights, per our agreement. Midnight." Without another word, he turned and strode into the storm.